PRAISE FOR *HOPSCOTCH*
A Featured Alternate Selection of
Science Fiction Book Club

"*Hopscotch* is a thought-provoking futuristic look at hedonism taken to the ultimate degree. Anderson's execution is flawless in its delivery of gloom and decaying decadence."
—*Romantic Times*

"At its heart, Anderson's story is a classic tale of struggle and redemption. A novel definitely worth your time."—*Tulsa World*

"Ingenious SF fantasy about body-swapping."
—*Kirkus Reviews*

"*Hopscotch* is an eerie story that builds nicely. Anderson is not only writing a mystery here, but a paranoia-laced fantasy that occasionally manages to reach in and pluck the well-guarded strings of the reader's mind. Loss of identity is a very real fear, and Anderson plays it here for all it's worth. Add to this a well-crafted setting that heightens the story's tension, and what you're left with is an excellent psychic crime thriller in the tradition of James H. Schmitz, Katherine MacLean and Alfred Bester."
—*Starlog*

"Anderson has always been a more interesting writer when he is creating his own universes. Some interesting speculation about the consequences of his premise and a nicely paced adventure story."
—*Science Fiction Chronicle*

KEVIN J. ANDERSON

HOPSCOTCH

BANTAM BOOKS

NEW YORK TORONTO LONDON SYDNEY AUCKLAND

HOPSCOTCH
A Bantam Spectra Book

PUBLISHING HISTORY
Bantam Spectra hardcover edition published February 2002
Bantam Spectra mass market edition / May 2003

Published by Bantam Dell
A Division of Random House, Inc.
New York, New York

Some substantially revised portions of this novel have been
published in *Analog* magazine under the titles "Identity Crisis"
and "Club Masquerade."

Library of Congress Catalog Card Number: 2001043264

ISBN 0-553-57640-2

Manufactured in the United States of America
Published simultaneously in Canada

OPM   10 9 8 7 6 5 4 3 2 1

For BRIAN HERBERT

Without his help and friendship in stretching my own creative abilities, I could never have managed such an ambitious project. Working with him has made me a much better writer.

ACKNOWLEDGMENTS

HOPSCOTCH has been a long time in the planning, writing, and editing stages and has benefited from the help and suggestions of numerous editors, including Tom Dupree, Pat LoBrutto, Michael Shohl, Anne Lesley Groell, and Dr. Stanley Schmidt.

Because this story is about so many people and perspectives, I received a great deal of advice from a large and varied pool of test readers. For their help and suggestions, I greatly appreciate the work of Gregory Benford, Neil Peart, Dave Wolverton, Patrick Heffernan, Kate Payne, Michael L. Bowker, Kathy Dyer, Leslie Lauderdale, Sarah Hoyt, Brian Herbert, Stephen Pagel, Erwin Bush, Mark Budz, Marina Fitch, Catherine Sidor, Sarah Jones, Diane Jones, Diane Davis Herdt, and—as always—Rebecca Moesta.

HOPSCOTCH

1

As night fell, the city fractured into a kaleidoscope of lights, like neon sparklers reflecting from rain-washed façades. Unabashedly garish, Club Masquerade hosted a dazzling assembly of humanity—new people, old people, everyone wearing a different body for the evening.

Outside the entrance to the Club, lighted sidewalk panels flashed patterns, numbers inside squares illuminated by each pressing footstep. A gimmick. Split doorways led into tailored environment chambers: a British Empire Safari Club, a discotheque with mirror balls and strobe lights, a rustic Sequoia Room, an Arabian harem with colorful rugs and sweet perfumes, a domed Martian colony chamber with red rock and thermal springs.

The specialized alcoves opened into the main interior of Club Masquerade, a wild environment of lights, music, exotic food, and unusual people. ID patches worked overtime to keep track of who was who, which mind in which body. Sometimes the people had trouble sorting it all out in the morning.

A person could be anyone or anything here, for a limited time—provided the desired body type was available. *Pick a physique, swap with someone, wear it for a while, see if you like it.*

Garth Swan's home-body always looked the same, except when he was on the hunt for new artistic inspiration:

broad shoulders, blond hair, blue eyes. Certainly nothing he'd want to change for the long term. His shirt bore paint stains, charcoal and chalk dust, a smear of still-moving glittergel. To him, the people in Club Masquerade were a catalogue of humanity. Inspiration.

He looked up at the Club's chaotic Hopscotch Board, aglow with *swapportunities,* people wanting to rent a muscular body for a few days of hard labor, old men and women willing to pay for a week's vacation in a young and healthy physique, the usual sex ads searching for a two-night stand, once as a male, once as a female, or a blur of alternations before, during, and after.

At first he didn't recognize Teresa as she dodged across the floor. Today, her build was broad hipped and Rubenesque, her hair rusty auburn, her eyes green-blue. Her clothes were drab, loose fitting, as if they could have been worn by anyone . . . and probably were. She often joined small religious groups or philosophical communes, trying to find someplace to belong. Her latest group didn't seem to value individuality. But Garth certainly did, and he hugged her warmly.

The third friend, Eduard, looked tired from the hell he kept putting himself through, making a fast buck by swapping his body to endure unpleasant experiences—surgeries, colds, dentist appointments—for people who would pay to avoid the misery. He came in late, as usual, but his expression lit up when he found Teresa and Garth.

All three of them had grown up together, fellow orphan "Swans" in the Falling Leaves monastery. Garth assessed him in an instant, using an artist's eye for details. At least Eduard used his hard-won money to buy stylish clothes to fit his dark-haired home-body.

Eduard pounded Garth's broad back, then he took Teresa into a softer, more intimate embrace. He touched a new bruise that seeped through the makeup and freckles on Teresa's rounded cheek. "What's this?"

"Oh, nothing," she said quickly. "And it's not mine, anyway. The last person who had this body got hurt."

Eduard brushed his lips to the bruise. "Better?"

"Always."

They went to a private table Garth had chosen, surrounded by the white noise of conversations. Taking charge, he waved at the cybernetic bartender's image on the tablescreen. "Hey, Bernard. The usual here, please."

A lump of flesh, all that remained of Bernard Rovin's original body, remained inside a windowless control room at the heart of the building, but cybernetic substations kept the bartender's eyes and ears and automatic hands wandering throughout the Club. By now, he was more than familiar with the preferences of his regular customers, and within moments their preferred drinks appeared from dispensers.

"I hate being predictable." Eduard reached over to switch his usual drink with Garth's foamy dark beer instead. "It could be dangerous."

Garth looked dubiously at the slushy blue concoction Eduard usually drank, now that he was stuck with it. Teresa was amused by his discomfiture. "You're always looking for new experiences, aren't you, Garth? Drinking blue cocktail *things* will add to your artistic repertoire."

On the floor of the Club, several dancers moved slowly, carefully, trying to adjust to new heights, new weights, new degrees of muscle control. On one of the floating platforms, a scarecrow-thin man stumbled backward and fell comically on his butt. The short, large-breasted woman next to him moved with awkward, marionette movements as she hurried to help him.

Eduard chuckled. "There should be a law against

letting people dance unless they've had at least an hour to settle into their new bodies."

Garth took another sip of his friend's blue drink, tasted crackling sweetness that burned his tongue. "This is tolerable, once your taste buds go dead."

Teresa turned to the blond artist. "So what do you find inspirational these days?"

Garth's eyes lit up as he talked about his passion in life. "Still trying to understand it all, but there's so *much*. For example, I'm starting to wonder what it would feel like to be pregnant and deliver a baby." He pursed his lips, thinking out loud. "Of course, that would require a long-term swap for at least the last month to get the full experience. And it wouldn't be easy to find a body I'd *want* to live in for that long."

"Especially not a pregnant one," Teresa said.

Eduard rolled his eyes. "Artists! Who can understand them?"

Teresa looked at him with amusement mixed with maternal concern. "This, from a man who gets paid to undergo surgery for other people? Who swaps bodies to sit through someone else's dental appointment?"

He sipped the beer he had taken from Garth, frowned, then traded drinks again. "Hey, I've got to make a living. It beats joining the Bureau, like Daragon."

Teresa brightened at hearing the young man's name. Daragon Swan had grown up with the three of them as wards of the Splinter monks, but he had joined the powerful Bureau of Tracing and Locations, the BTL. "He should be almost finished with his training by now. I should check on him to make sure he's okay."

"I wonder if he spies on us." Eduard flicked his dark eyes from side to side in a comically paranoid furtive glance. "It's what Beetles do."

Teresa rested her chin in her hands. "Oh, I'm sure Daragon thinks of it as keeping an eye on his friends."

"And lucky for us, if we ever get into trouble," Garth said.

The music swirled into a new mix, and the surrounding conversation grew louder. Three effete faux-intelligentsia at a nearby table continued an argument with much gusto and little actual information. A narrow-faced young man waved a pungent purple cigarette back and forth.

"There are other precedents in mental development. Way back at the dawn of time, the human race went through a 'bicameral revolution,' when our minds split into left and right hemispheres." He took a long drag from his purple cigarette with finality and a smug expression. "This is simply another evolutionary step, our consciousnesses becoming detachable from our physical brains. The soul living by itself, interchangeable from physical host to host. I'd say it's a leap forward for the human species."

A second young man drained a flowery-scented drink to fortify himself before he launched into a response. "But it had to start *somewhere*. Think about the first person who could do it. All right, say the first two people—because the ability doesn't matter unless you have someone to swap with."

"And you want to know the biophysics? Does it matter?" The first man sucked delicately on his cigarette. "When you use a COM terminal, do you care about the network electronics? No. You simply tap in, extract the information you need, engage the communication link you want, access your accounts. You don't need a degree in organic matrix management to use the thing. You don't need to understand the dirty details about hopscotching, either."

The second man looked rebuffed. "Is there something wrong with asking questions? Makes sense to me that the whole hopscotch thing was triggered by generations of people uploading and downloading to old-style computer networks and virtual reality environments. *That's* how personalities first became detached from the body. Now we can do it all the time."

The third man had already finished his drink. "Indeed, but the amount of data that needs to be transferred is so enormous, and to be done so quickly—"

The purple cigarette interrupted the argument with a puff of sweet smoke. "Yeah, but at the root level, it all boils down to a form of telepathy. No one's ever accurately clocked the telepathic transfer rate. There's no benchmark."

Eavesdropping on the pointless debate, Garth, Teresa, and Eduard smiled as they shared the same thoughts. They'd heard all the theories a million times before; the Splinter monks often had similar discussions, equally without resolution. None of them knew the true explanation, nor did they care.

Eduard rocked back in his chair, raised his voice so that the posturing faux-intelligentsia could hear him. "Yeah, right—what if it was just from too much *astral projection* without using proper precautions?"

The whip-thin intellectuals looked sourly at him for squelching their continuing argument, then turned to debate matters even more esoteric.

Garth chuckled with Eduard. Teresa put her chin wistfully in her hands. "Oh, it wasn't so long ago when we were just as fascinated. Remember?"

A year earlier, after demonstrating their maturity by proving their ability to hopscotch, the three orphan Swans had finally been released from their sheltered upbringing at the Falling Leaves. Club Masquerade was the first place they had gone after the maternal monk Soft Stone and the other Splinter monks had bid them farewell—not far to walk, but a universe away in actuality.

Drawing strength from each other, Eduard, Garth, and Teresa had approached the mysterious Club, intimidated and anxious. "Let's go," Eduard said without taking a step forward. "I want to see it after all this time."

As children, they had watched this place from the safety of the monastery, which huddled amid the modern city that had grown up around it. Club Masquerade was refreshing, alien, unlike anything they had ever experienced.

The frenetic club was a haze of body-swapping, a confusing blur of shifting identities, a human exchange. A swirl of eager customers flowed in and out, some furtive, others totally open. And the people who went in were not necessarily the same people who emerged again.

Soft Stone had always encouraged her beloved wards to discover new intellectual things, to experiment with their bodies and minds. Splinters were open and relaxed about sex, too, seeing it as a prelude to the far more intimate swapping of physical bodies as soon as the teenagers reached maturity. But the monks offered very little true life experience. It was the Splinters' blind spot.

With a few stipend credits in their pockets and new opportunities before them, the three made their way into the city, as adults. Teresa looked behind her, and the old brick monastery seemed far away. Directly before them, the façade of Club Masquerade fascinated and lured her. Where did all those arches go? Why so many separate entrances? "Which door should we try?" she asked.

Raising his blond head, Garth took a deep breath, steeling himself. "Follow me." He marched across the numbered squares on the sidewalk, making them illuminate under each footstep. "This one."

With Eduard and Teresa following, he stepped onto a floor strewn with dried redwood needles and tiny fir cones. The walls were made of massive knobbed trunks of sequoias with warty bark that oozed sweet-smelling pitch.

Garth stood with his arms outstretched, his head craned upward. High above, in the imaginary upper levels of the conifers, rafts of cool mist clung to the branches. The trees seemed to reach as high as tall skyscrapers, until he realized that the ceiling was the holographic equivalent of a matte painting, projecting an illusion of vast height within a normal-sized room. "Look at this!"

"Oh, smell the air," Teresa said, discarding her expectations of a hedonistic chamber of pleasure. She hadn't imagined this at all.

"Told you it would be amazing." Snooping around, Eduard found a doorway in the side of a massive sequoia trunk. "Let's get to the central room."

At the heart of Club Masquerade, the sunken floor was surrounded by lights, girdled by a neon bar. Seats and floating tables appeared in convenient spots of light and shadow, depending on whether customers wanted privacy or spectacle. Lights and decor, sounds and smells, bombarded them: perfumed steam, colored incense, musical vibrations, and the drone of conversation.

Garth couldn't drink it all in fast enough. "Doesn't this sum up ... everything you imagined the rest of the world would be?"

They climbed to a mid-level table and sat down. Teresa looked at the numerous patrons, overwhelmed by the pressing responsibility of establishing herself from scratch. The monks had secured each of their Swans a low-level job, but for the first time in their lives, Teresa, Eduard, and Garth were independent. Here, even with the comfort of her two fellow orphans, she felt herself to be at the heart of a cyclone, a central calm. She could understand why Daragon had decided to join the rigid fraternity of the Bureau.

"Let's make this our special place. Club Masquerade." She was afraid of losing Garth and Eduard, too. "I want to keep us together. No matter what happens, wherever we go or whatever we decide to do with ourselves, let's promise to meet here on a regular basis. We can do that, don't you think?"

"No problem," Eduard said.

"It's a plan," Garth said, alarmed at the suggestion that they might not always be together, all the time, as in the monastery. "In a changing world, some things never change. Those things become our anchors."

The music continued to throb. They ordered drinks, sampled new concoctions, tasted flavored stim-sticks. For long spaces they just looked at each other across the floating table, until all three of them knew it was time to go.

Then, with the whole world awaiting them, they went out to embark on a great adventure—the rest of their lives. . . .

Now, from a substation in their table, the bartender's remote eye popped up. "Sorry I didn't say a personal hello as soon as you three came in. I got caught multiprocessing a large crowd. Can I get you a second round?"

"Yes, you can, Bernard," Garth said immediately.

He glanced at Eduard's slushy blue drink, now in front of Teresa. "And give us *each* something we've never had before. New experiences. Variety—the spice of life, right?"

When the fresh drinks arrived, Teresa looked at her two best friends in the world. They had been inseparable since they were children, abandoned by their biological parents, taken in and tended by Soft Stone and the other Splinters.

She held up her glass in a toast, not daring to ask the contents of the new cocktail. "To friends," she said.

They all drank.

2

In the Bureau of Tracing and Locations, all training was vital. The BTL instructors had hammered that into Daragon Swan from the day he'd entered their ranks. Since his old life had ended at the Falling Leaves monastery more than a year ago, training filled the void.

Many of the Bureau's recruits washed out in the first few weeks, but the BTL officials had no intention of letting Daragon fail. His freakish recognition ability was too special, his "inner vision" too rare. The coaches reminded him of this often, used it as an excuse to push him harder. He had finally completed the first phase of indoctrination.

Three stone-faced coaches climbed into a hovercar and punched in coordinates. Daragon settled in beside them, small in stature and wiry. He had dark hair and almond eyes that flashed in the light. Now, he squared his shoulders, keeping his face expressionless. He didn't know where the instructors were taking him, and he didn't dare ask.

The emerald-green vehicle raised up onto its selected impedance path, and official COM override codes kicked in as it coasted toward the nearby bayshore.

"Are you ready for this?" one coach asked him, his gruff voice suddenly loud in the white noise.

"I don't know what to expect."

"Be ready anyway."

Daragon clung to his hopes. This was part of

becoming a crucial member of the BTL, a group that appreciated him for his special abilities and skills. The Splinter monks had sympathized with his unusual handicap—unlike virtually everyone else, he was completely unable to hopscotch—but the Bureau didn't belittle him for that. Instead, they saw it as an advantage.

Daragon had the potential to be a great Inspector, perhaps the best, thanks to his quirk, his ability to see identities. He compared it to a blind man having highly sensitive hearing. Craving acceptance, he could not disappoint them.

The BTL used a broad spectrum of methods for locating and tracking people as they moved through a society where physical appearance and identity could be made meaningless by body-swapping. Some of the Bureau Inspectors were slightly telepathic; some were gifted database surfers who had a particular rapport with COM—the pervasive computer/organic matrix—and some were just intuitive detectives. Daragon had to learn everything.

Be ready anyway. Always.

The hovercar left the main traffic patterns behind, cruising high above malls and pedestrian streets. They wove through a complex of warehouses and cranes and launch platforms on sprawling docks that extended like pseudopods into the Pacific. Daragon looked at the scrambled Brownian motion of commerce, bustling workers, small and large craft skating like water striders across the ocean, bullet-boats tugging barges into port.

Far out on the water, towering high enough to be an artificial island, stood a massive offshore drilling rig. It had been abandoned in place, modified into a new sort of building. The platform stood on stilts, a citadel above the waves. Daragon knew the main complex itself was protected under the sea. BTL Headquarters. They headed directly toward it.

The hovercar landed on a metal-plated dock that extended to the edge of the calm water. The emerald doors rose up like an insect shrugging its carapace, and Daragon emerged, standing straight in his dark trainee jumpsuit. The fresh wind struck his face, laden with salt and iodine.

The man who met him on the platform was well muscled, his stomach like a washboard beneath his tight shirt, the tendons in his neck like cords. The man seemed to occupy a much larger physical space than his actual body required. His chestnut hair was short and dark, just beginning to speckle with gray. His eyes were wide-set, an olive-brown. "My name is Mordecai Ob. Perhaps you've heard of me?"

"Certainly, sir!" Ob was the Bureau Chief, a powerful man who kept himself isolated, ambitious but rarely seen except by those in the inner sanctum of the BTL. Why would a person of such importance waste time greeting a mere trainee?

"Walk with me to my offices, Daragon. I'll show you more of how the Bureau really works." Ob shook his hand with a muscular grip. "We expect great things of you, young man."

3

Each weekend, Garth arrived at the artists' bazaar at dawn just to secure himself a decent spot. The pedestrian square was always crowded with other aspiring artists, craftsmen, and vendors.

At first, he had been delighted to discover that the Splinters had arranged for him a beginning-level job as a "painter." Unfortunately, Garth spent hours painting polymer coatings and shifting phase-films on walls inside new offices, without a shred of creativity—not exactly what he'd expected or hoped.

Long ago in the monastery Garth had discovered his heart's calling to be an artist—and now he tried to make the rest of the world see it. Luckily, Soft Stone's years of chores had toughened him to getting up early and working until late. He had his drive and his goal, and no one was going to discourage him from following his dream.

On his days off, he bustled out of his small private quarters, carrying a case of drawing supplies into the stillness of sunrise. Once he had picked his spot at the market, he set up his blanket, burlap seating pads, and working easel. Garth greeted the other craftsmen and merchants as they came into the bazaar, dragging stalls, chairs, cooking equipment.

A portly man sold potent coffee from a thermal chalice. Since Garth was such a regular customer, the caffeine vendor knew him by name now. Garth drank the coffee hot and black from his own large mug. He savored the acrid richness, closing his eyes, breathing in the aroma. Afterward, he felt awake, ambitious, and excited for what the day might bring. *Inspired.*

Garth was amazingly prolific, unable to move his hands as fast as his imagination bombarded him with ideas. Everything about the world was new, a universe of glittering images everywhere he turned. And he wanted to paint them all.

His first attempt, though—when he was only thirteen years old—had been a disaster. The Splinters had never understood his artistic passion. . . .

The Falling Leaves was an ancient building embedded in the modern city like a fossil in limestone. Newer buildings with connecting atriums and cliffs of mirrored windows had grown up around the monastery like younger trees engulfing a deadfall. In simpler times the place had been a brewery.

An exuberant young teenager, Garth had found a hidden spot in the basement of the old monastery, behind thick, long-unused pipes. Inside the shadowy, timeless room, Garth used his imagination to envision chambers crammed with giant beer vats, boilers and fermenting containers, malting bins, roasters, and bottling lines.

Here, Garth could smell the *past,* mystical odors that reminded him of the complex Charles Dickens novels he read to Daragon and another orphan named Pashnak. He had so many ideas, and the paintings in his head were so vivid. Garth decided to keep this spot secret even from Teresa and Eduard. Until he was ready, until his project here was completed.

He found paints and charcoal sticks and surreptitiously carried them into the basement utility closet. To conjure his vision, he sketched outlines on the walls, dipped his brushes into swirls of color. Ignoring the unevenness of the mortar and bricks, he painted a winter scene like a classic Currier and Ives print. Horse-drawn carts pulled up to the brewery's loading dock to receive kegs of Trappist ale brewed by brown-robed monks. Wagons dodged automobiles on cobblestone streets. Portly men in top hats sang Christmas carols under a gas street lamp next to an elevated railway. He made each detail as real as he could, his painting exuberant but unrefined.

He worked on the mural for weeks. At first he attempted only a small idyllic scene, but as he worked, he thought of secondary characters, interesting buildings, thinly disguised renditions of the high-tech skyscrapers he could see from the monastery windows. He kept intending to add finishing touches, to call his painting complete, then he thought of just one more idea, and another.

He became engrossed in bringing to life the panorama he saw in his imagination. He could almost smell the wet snow, the horses, the rich ale pouring into the oak-slatted kegs. . . .

"I cannot believe my eyes!" a firm male voice said, startling Garth so badly that he dropped his paintbrush. "Young man, what have you done?" He turned to see a stern monk named Hickory. "I noticed the light down here, but I never expected to see this! Who gave you permission?"

Garth had never dreamed of asking permission. "I was going to show everyone when I was done."

"Well, you shouldn't have started in the first place." Hickory crossed his arms over his chest. "Don't we give you enough chores to keep you busy? It's easy to see what sort of mischief idle hands can work."

Garth didn't know how to respond. "But . . . *look* at it. This is art."

"When you paint all over a wall you don't own,

without permission, it is called *vandalism*. Come with me to Chocolate's office. We'd better see the administrator right away."

Unfortunately, Chocolate didn't know what to do with him, either. All the "Swan" children in the Falling Leaves were wards of the state, given up by parents who felt no obligation to babies born from bodies not their own, or impregnated during flings, after which the original minds had hopscotched to someone else. The monks received government stipends to teach and raise these young charges, and they took their obligations seriously, considering such children to be entirely new souls, new flames, and therefore something special.

The chubby, soft-spoken administrator seemed flustered, his brow creased with worry. "Oh, why don't we just let him paint scenes on *all* the walls? Maybe then the BTL won't want to take over the monastery, after all."

"Sir!" Hickory said. "We can't encourage this sort of—"

The other monk waved his pudgy hand. "This is really not a very good time, Hickory." He sighed, looking at the papers on his desk. "I suggest we merely have this young man repaint the walls so the room can be usable again."

Garth's knees grew weak at hearing the devastating punishment. "Don't you even want to look at what I've done, sir?"

"I'm sure it's wonderful," Chocolate said, already engrossed in an official-looking document on his desk. "You're a very talented young man, Garth, but you must learn to respect certain boundaries."

Later, the beige paint smelled sour as Garth swathed it on with a thick, inelegant brush. Horse carts vanished under a layer of drab tan. Rosy-cheeked monks continued to gulp foamy brew as he painted right over their faces.

He dipped the heavy brush into the bucket again, swabbed more paint across the rough bricks. Garth wished he'd been able to at least show Eduard, Teresa, and Daragon before erasing his wall. He managed to keep the tears balanced inside his eyelids, not letting them spill down his cheeks.

"That's very good, from what I can still see of it," Soft Stone said. The bald female monk was a mother and a teacher to her wards.

Garth took a moment to compose himself before he faced her. "You should have been here before I covered all the good parts. Now it's all gone."

"Not gone—your mural is still there, behind the paint."

The motionless brush dripped beige droplets on the floor. "But no one can see it. I can't show it to anybody. Isn't that what art is for?"

The old woman nodded her smooth head. "Art is about sharing and communication, yes, but that's not the only thing. There is process as well as product. Did *you* learn from doing this project?"

He swallowed hard. "You told me to learn from everything I do."

"And?"

"And . . . yes, I learned from it, I suppose. I enjoyed doing it, too."

"Then it's not a total loss, little Swan." Soft Stone smiled as she turned to leave. "An artist needs to do more than create pleasant scenes. Use your art as a lens for viewing all facets of life. You can't just imitate what you see, you must first *understand* the thing. This understanding gives your art a life of its own."

He glanced with dismay at his half-defaced mural, and he thought hard about what she had said. With two strokes he covered a street that had taken him hours to paint.

Now, grown-up at last, he had the freedom to pursue his creative vision. Among the aspiring artists, Garth wandered the stalls to glean new ideas, to study techniques. He saw polymerized butterfly wings, clouded crystals carved into prismatic shapes. Some artists worked with fabric, others with string and thread, one with satin spiderwebs. Each medium was a tool to capture life and its possibilities, and he wanted to experiment.

The streets came alive with shoppers and curiosity seekers. A few haughty spectators were sourly critical of everything on display, commenting how they themselves could create far superior art "if only they had the time." Garth had no patience for all their talk; they were irrelevant.

He sat back on his cushion, doodling while he watched the people. With only limited income from his daily job, Garth lived austerely. He couldn't afford high-tech creation and conceptualization gadgets, but he made do with the materials artists had used since the first paintings on cave walls.

A gorgeous woman strutted beside a bronzed, muscular young man, arms linked in an old-fashioned way. The couple anticipated each other's steps, smiling at half-spoken phrases, as if they had been together for decades. Garth wondered if they were an elderly pair vacationing in younger bodies, rich blue bloods who had rented new forms for themselves.

Garth tore off another sheet of sketching paper and rummaged in his box for colored chalk. His hands a blur of motion, he scraped dusty colors across the surface, catching the mood, the shapes. He tried to illustrate two old and comfortable souls in fresh and energetic young bodies, the love they shared, the advantages that wealth and privilege had brought them. Charcoal sticks added shadows and stark definition.

With the forgiving media of chalk and charcoal, he could work quickly, the better to capture his impressions and ideas.

Unlike restless Eduard and constantly searching Teresa, Garth had always known what he wanted to do with his life. He drew anything and everything that caught his eye. His art became a user's manual for his life, a way to sort through and understand and put his own perspective on everything he saw.

Like a ripple on a placid lake, two uniformed Beetles walked through the market, escorting a trim man with dark hair, sunken eyes, and a bushy mustache. The BTL officers deferred to him, so the man was obviously not a prisoner, though his gaunt face and pale skin made him look wrung out. They followed the trim man as he looked at the various trinkets on display.

"Chief Ob, may I remind you that a meeting is scheduled soon back at Bureau Headquarters," one of the uniformed men said.

The tired-looking man rubbed his mustache. "Another few moments, let me finish looking here." He stopped in front of Garth's sketches, appraising them. Garth looked at the Beetles, remembered the problems they had caused at the Falling Leaves monastery, and concentrated on his work.

"Some of these attempts are really quite inept," the man said tactlessly, as if Garth had begged for his opinion. He picked up one of the sketches. "Have you had any training at all?"

The intimidating presence of the BTL officers made him flush, and Garth accepted the insult. "No formal training. I just . . . like to do art."

"Well, you've got more enthusiasm than talent." Then the man's expression softened. "Sometimes, though, sheer persistence may be enough to let you rise above the rest. I always wanted to be an artist myself, but I just didn't have the drive. Somewhere along the line, I lost my inspiration." He seemed distracted for a moment, then turned an intense gaze back toward Garth. "You're a Swan, aren't you? Raised by the Splinter monks?"

Garth was astonished. "How—how did you know that?"

The man just smiled. "I run the Bureau of Tracing and Locations."

Garth thought of Daragon, but couldn't believe this powerful man would recognize the name of a relatively new recruit.

"Sir, we really must get back to the hovercar," the BTL officer persisted.

Chief Ob set the chalk sketch back down. For a moment, Garth hoped the man would buy something, but instead Ob met the artist's eyes. "You need a lot more practice, but keep at it. Don't give up, like I did." He strolled away, the two Beetles trying to hurry him along.

Garth looked at his work, viewing it objectively. Of course he'd had no training, no focus, but he did have a burning desire to create. He could learn.

He plunged into his work with a greater vehemence than ever before.

4

Eduard lay on his narrow bed, cocooned in damp sheets, his pores seeping a feverish sweat from someone else's illness. All alone, he shuddered, pulling up the blanketfilm. He hadn't expected the symptoms to be this bad when he'd sold his services, but he would get through it. He would survive. After all, he had agreed to this.

He had already spent four days in a stranger's body, enduring a miserable round of the flu just so some businessman wouldn't miss his stockholders' meetings. Unglamorous, maybe, but it was one way to make a living without going to work every day.

He squeezed his puffy blue eyes shut, seeing technicolor explosions behind his lids, throbbing in time with the pounding in his head. He clutched the middle-aged potbelly as his intestines knotted up, then swung off the bed and lumbered toward the bathroom.

He could have hurried faster in his own young physique, but this guy had trouble just moving about, and the flu didn't make it any easier. If the man who owned this body had kept himself healthier, he might not have been so susceptible to getting sick in the first place.

The man was a busy executive, with more credits in his account than he could spend. Such an important person couldn't afford to be laid up for days. He had board meetings to attend, fund-raisers to throw, decisions to make. After only one day of the flu, the exec had become desperate.

So he'd hired Eduard, who would be sick *for* him.

For an exorbitant fee, Eduard agreed to inhabit the exec's body until he recovered. In return, the exec lived in the young man's body, doing his business as usual. His wife probably didn't mind him coming home to her in a virile physique, either. . . .

In the exec's ailing body, Eduard staggered into the bathroom and splashed water on his face. The cheeks and skin felt oily, soft from the extra fat padding his jowls. He looked in the mirror and saw a stranger staring back at him.

It was only pain and physical discomfort, after all. With the amount of money he'd get paid for this, Eduard wouldn't have to work a real job for weeks, perhaps even months, if he scrimped. He loved the freedom and independence. He could endure it. No problem.

Eduard's stomach clenched, and he vomited into the sink. Holding himself and shaking to get over the wave of nausea, he splashed more water, rinsed the facilities, then lumbered back to bed, breathing shallowly.

Only a few more days, then he could be back to normal once more. It was just a minor nuisance, hardly worse than a bad cold. He took another full dose of medications, waited for them to take effect.

He slumped onto the sheets, tossing and turning feverishly for hours as this weak body struggled to fight off the illness. Eduard muttered to himself, all alone in the small, stifling room—glad it wasn't his day to meet at Club Masquerade, since he didn't want to see Teresa or Garth like this.

Even after drinking copious electrolyte-enriched fluids, he vomited twice more that night, then eventually fell into a deep sleep. By morning the fever had broken.

He showered twice, trying to overcome the unwashed feeling in this body. He took appropriate medications, rested, recovered as quickly as possible. . . .

The following day he swapped back with the body's original owner. After synching ID patches on their hands, Eduard drew a deep breath, flexed his arms, and looked out the office window.

The exec was glad to have the flu over with, though he did seem a bit reluctant to give Eduard his young body back. Without potent, and illegal, drugs, it was impossible to force an unwilling person to swap, but Eduard wouldn't need to take such drastic measures. He looked at the exec sternly. "Our contract has been consummated, the appropriate waivers signed, and I take it both parties are satisfied?"

The exec had relinquished his hold, and the two men hopscotched. Eduard took a deep breath into his own lungs, glad to be home again. . . .

Grinning, he walked out into the streets, his credit account fat now. He decided to pick up a small bunch of flowers that he would deliver to Teresa in her dwelling. She would like that.

5

Beneath the ocean on the once-abandoned offshore drilling rig, Bureau Chief Mordecai Ob leaned across his desk toward Daragon. Overhead, thick windows looked out on an underwater world of fish and waving kelp. The young man had been assigned to BTL Headquarters for several weeks now, and Ob had taken him under his wing, grooming him.

"From here, we're linked to the mainland through computer and energy conduits," Ob said. "And that's how we do our work. Unobtrusively, if possible." He flexed his thick arms, as if relishing the feel of his own muscles.

"COM infiltrates every aspect of our lives from finances to entertainment to the national infrastructure. Therefore, information about everyone's daily activities can be found somewhere in all of those databases. You need only look for it." Unlike the rest of the undersea facility, Ob's office was plush and warm. An ornamental gas fireplace shed a cheery, natural light.

Daragon stood completely rigid in front of the Chief, impeccably dressed in his new uniform. "COM is a vast place to search, sir."

The other man smiled at Daragon. "Ah, now you begin to see!"

Like a computerized sympathetic nervous system, the computer/organic matrix performed the functions that everyone saw and used but never noticed: turning on streetlights, circulating the air in buildings, monitoring impedance paths through the airways so that traffic flowed smoothly and safely, maintaining stable weather patterns via climate-control systems.

With each mental engram added, COM had grown geometrically in processing power, designing new additions to itself. No one understood the entire network; no complete map had ever existed. The computerized matrix did not spy on people, but the Bureau of Tracing and Locations knew how to use the network to monitor anyone they chose.

Daragon nodded dutifully. "In the past year, sir, I've been taught how to take advantage of COM, but there's so much available data that finding anything in particular is like finding a needle in a world full of haystacks."

Smiling, Ob stood from his desk and led him into a metal-walled corridor. "Yes, and *our* people are those most adept at searching for needles."

The Bureau Chief took him through humid biological reconstruction labs, frigid computer galleries, humming offices, dazzling map rooms, image libraries bursting with information.

Inspectors, guards, tacticians, apprehension specialists, saboteurs, data archaeologists... rank after specialized rank. Some operatives, skilled in evidence analysis, could detect infrared footprints or pick up DNA tracings, compiling physical clues to build a trail for Inspectors to follow. Medical technicians could unravel brain scans, the mental fingerprints of a specific person regardless of the physical body it inhabited.

Finally, his mind numb with everything he was seeing, Daragon turned to Ob. "Can I inquire which section I'll be working for, sir?"

The Chief's olive-brown eyes shone. "With your gift for inner recognition, you are a true wild card. If you can *see* people's personas just by looking at them, without consulting an ID patch, without using special scanning and analysis techniques, you'll perform a function none of these others can, despite all our technology."

Daragon's heart fluttered. When all of Soft Stone's mental training had failed, leaving the boy unable to hopscotch, he had felt worthless, a freak. He didn't know who his parents were, or why he had turned out this way.

But because of his special ability, the BTL had considered him valuable enough to make a deal with the Splinter monks. Daragon alone had saved the monastery from ruin.

A long time ago, the day it had all changed, Daragon remembered looking up into Soft Stone's concerned face, seeing an intensity that frightened him. She was sinewy and bald, with blunt features and a large heart. "Look at me, child. Through my eyes, into my mind. Imagine yourself *here*." She tapped her forehead. "Forget your body. For a person your age, hopscotching should come easily and naturally. I'm willing and ready to swap with you. It can't be completed without mutual consent, but you have that now."

Daragon tried, as he had tried for years. Others described it as a floating sensation, shucking ethereal chains to the body, exchanging yourself with another. Touching foreheads, an exchange of souls. He waited for the drifting sensation, the disconnection. *Nothing*.

"I can see you. I can watch your . . . aura when you swap with someone else," he said, tears brimming in his dark eyes. "But I can't do it myself."

She looked at him abruptly, a different set of thoughts plain on her face. "You can see me? How?"

"It's obvious, your individual persona. I don't know how to describe it." He shrugged. "Can't everybody?"

She held up the back of her hand, showing her personal code number on the tiny swatch of polymer film. "You mean my ID patch?"

"Isn't it just . . . obvious? I never need to see an ID patch."

When Soft Stone touched Daragon's head, her fingers trembled. "I had begun to suspect as much. Wait here, little Swan."

She marched out the door with a swish of sky-blue robes, intent on an experiment. The first monk she found was dour Hickory, in the garden. He sweated in the sun, hacking at the ground with his hoe. He bent over a tomato plant and plucked off a fat green hornworm.

As she approached, Hickory scrutinized the caterpillar, then crushed its head between his fingers. "All things must fertilize the earth." He cast the dead worm onto the ground and rubbed his hand on the front of his work robe.

"Swap with me," Soft Stone said without preamble.

"I hardly think this is the time or the place. Perhaps tonight?"

"I need your body for training purposes." She reached out to take the hoe from him, prepared to let him work in her body. They swapped without synching their ID patches. Hickory seemed nonplussed, but Soft Stone strode off. "I'll be right back."

When she returned to the training room, she smelled of sweat and dirt and warm sunshine. The ache in her male muscles came from exertion rather than age, and Hickory's eyes were sharper than her own.

Daragon looked up at her, still dejected. She spoke in Hickory's gruff voice. "Soft Stone has asked me to continue your training."

"But . . . *you're* Soft Stone." Daragon gave her a puzzled frown. "Are you trying to trick me?"

It was true, then. He *did* have the ability, an incredibly rare skill. There was something fundamental missing in Daragon, but also something *present*. "No, little Swan, I was testing you. Come out to the garden and help Hickory. After we swap back, I'm sure he can find more chores for you to do. I need to talk with Chocolate."

For weeks, the Falling Leaves had simmered with tension and uneasiness, a battle the Splinter monks could never win. The Bureau of Tracing and Locations wanted to acquire the monastery building for their own operations, and the monks had no way of fighting against the government order, no bargaining chip that would buy their continued existence.

But the BTL would be desperate to have what this young man could do. Quite desperate. Soft Stone knew they could use Daragon to save the monastery....

Days later, an anxious Daragon had waited in the Falling Leaves front office. He wished his friend Eduard were here. Eduard was always so cocky, so confident, never bothered.

"Don't worry, child. You'll do fine," Soft Stone said, trying to comfort him. "It is just a test." The lie was plain in her voice. The monastery's corpulent administrator Chocolate paced behind his carved desk.

Footsteps came down the hall, a soft whicker of sandals and robes as counterpoint to the staccato drumbeat of bootheels. A flushed monk led two BTL officers into Chocolate's office, an Inspector and a Sergeant. Both wore neat uniforms; their demeanor suggested confidence and efficiency.

Soft Stone placed her hand on Daragon's shoulder. "Sirs, we have something you may find interesting. Something we believe the Bureau will value highly."

Chocolate bustled forward, grinning with relief. "Yes, he is quite the rarity. While this young man is incapable of swapping bodies, his mental abilities have turned inward. *Quite* the rarity. But he's not a throw-back—he's . . . different."

"That remains to be seen," the Inspector said as the Sergeant withdrew several pieces of scanning equipment. . . .

In the end, after the amazing results of the test, the BTL officers promised to take care of Daragon. He had reached the age of adulthood, but remained young enough to be malleable, to be trained in their ways. The Bureau had a rigorous curriculum already designed for talented people like him.

Soft Stone hugged Daragon, trying to crush away the young man's fear and uncertainty. She mouthed the words, telling him that the Bureau did vital work in society. No other person from the Falling Leaves could hope for such a remarkable opportunity, she said; no one else had ever passed the tests.

Beside him, the Beetles promised similar things. The main difference was that the uniformed men seemed to *believe* what they said.

In the monastery the others gathered in shock at his sudden departure. Young Garth, Teresa, and Eduard stood together in the hall, unable to believe what they were seeing, or understand what Daragon had done.

He pulled away from the grim Beetles standing next to him. "I need to say goodbye to my friends." Daragon came forward to hug Teresa while the officers looked on in disapproval. Garth and Eduard also embraced him, trying to look excited for him.

"Enough," said the BTL commander. "This projects the wrong image."

"Consider it your first lesson in the Bureau," said the Sergeant.

As young Daragon was led away from the protection of the monastery, Soft Stone watched sadly. She had become accustomed to seeing her children leave, one by one, out to a wider life. But the loss of Daragon was quite different. And she herself felt responsible for it.

Bureau Chief Ob beamed at him like a proud father. "In all the years I've been in the Bureau, you're only the second one I've found. There are no more than a few known examples in any one generation." They stood together, deep underwater, surrounded by girders and walls, curved windows that looked out into the sea. Murky sunlight battered its way into the depths. "Having you with us gives the Bureau an extremely valuable tool."

Now that he thought about it, Daragon realized just how important it would be for an Inspector to glance over a crowd and spot the mind he was looking for—in the same way anybody else could look at faces and recognize someone.

"I want you to be my special assistant." Ob patted him on the shoulder. "The world will be under your watchful eye, young Daragon."

6

When she was a girl at the Falling Leaves, Teresa had been enthralled with delving through COM databases, considering the stored thoughts of humanity. But now, in her day-to-day job in front of the COM gateway, the tasks were pure drudgery.

The computer/organic matrix was the circulatory system that ran through society, a worldwide database of monitoring routines, financial accounts, personnel records, statistics, and information libraries. But someone had to sift through all that data, make assessments, offer interpretations.

"Information and knowledge are two different things," Soft Stone had often told her. In the monastery library, the Splinters had imposed a regimen that for every hour spent exploring COM, students must spend another hour contemplating and digesting the new facts they had learned.

Now, though, in her drab work environment in front of a milky-white touch screen, Teresa felt like a tired bee in a hive. A few drooping flowers valiantly tried to cheer her, an arrangement Eduard had given her a week ago. She splayed her hands on the induction-pressure input pads that took impulses from her fingers and turned them into commands. The translucent interface shifted to mother-of-pearl, then opened into a complex data/subject map.

She wished Soft Stone could be there with her, looking over her shoulder. The old monk had been so named because she could be as soft as butter, or hard as granite. "Is your mind ready, little Swan?" she would say. "Ready for more knowledge?"

"I wish you would help me find some answers, instead of more questions." Teresa had always been searching, asking, wondering.

Soft Stone had chuckled. "You're assuming I have answers to give you."

"Can COM give me the answers to why I'm here? What does it all mean? What should I do with my life?"

With its thinking power equivalent to billions of minds, with eyes that could watch over even the smallest sparrow, the computer/organic matrix was seen by the Splinters as a manifestation of God come to Earth—a neural network peopled by the numerous souls who entered and never came back because it was too tempting to stay there. Even Soft Stone looked at it with awe.

"Of course, little Swan. Inside here you can find Heaven."

But there was no Heaven in her daily job. Teresa had spent the past two months working for a survey group as an information sifter who dug through daily records of pedestrian traffic patterns and hovercar movements, trying to ferret out nuances of the way people traveled through the city. An advertising firm needed the information to determine where to best place formscreen billboards and public-service information displays.

Not quite the grand questions that fascinated Teresa . . .

After the day the Beetles had taken Daragon away, Soft Stone withdrew to her quarters and did not emerge. Under the pretext of searching for advice and guidance, Teresa rapped on the old monk's door frame, then drew the curtain aside and entered unbidden. Two candles lit the room, shedding warm light.

Soft Stone was hunched over her cot. "I did not ask to be interrupted."

"I'll meditate with you, then." Teresa hunkered down beside her, waited a few painfully long moments, then finally ventured, "I've been trying to think of what name I should use when I take my own Splinter vows."

Soft Stone's voice held a tone of rebuke. "We fervently hope our trainees will *not* stay with us. Only our failures remain here, those of us who could not fulfill our life's work outside. Your goal is to make this life as kind as possible for as many people as you can. And you can't do that from within these walls."

Teresa couldn't believe what she was hearing. "But you're not a failure."

"I never achieved my potential. I lived outside for years, experimenting, hopscotching. Call it the brashness of youth, the pain of foolish love, but I fled back here, and I've felt like a coward ever since. My only success comes from knowing that the students I teach will go out and do greater deeds than I ever managed. I have failed in so many things."

She looked down at Teresa, her clear blue eyes moist. "I don't want you to take my way out. You are a new soul, a special child. Many important things are in store for you. Find your answers elsewhere, Teresa Swan."

"But where?" she asked. "Where will I find other people who need to know? I want to join a community, be a part of it. I'll never belong the way I do here, with my friends."

"We rarely have that choice, do we?" Hot tears came to Soft Stone's eyes, as if a wound had been reopened. "For Daragon...it is too late. I sacrificed one of my own Swans to the Bureau. Whatever will he do with them?"

Teresa heard the dismay in the woman's voice. "Probably the best he can, don't you think? Daragon always tried very hard."

"They'll make him one of their own." The monk's once clear blue eyes now looked cloudy and old. "He was our ransom, and we . . . *sold* him. I couldn't think of any other way to save the monastery."

Teresa touched the monk's wrist, below her ID patch. "What do you mean?"

"The BTL wanted to oust us so they could have a headquarters on the mainland. Chocolate tried everything, but we were going to be evicted. Eminent domain, a 'greater societal need.' The Splinters had no way to challenge them." She looked Teresa directly in the eye. "Until I discovered what Daragon could do—and how much the BTL was likely to want it. So they made a deal with us. We now have our title, free and clear. Daragon was worth more to them than the Falling Leaves."

One of the candles flickered, as if a ghost had just walked by.

"The Beetles see COM as a sweatshop of souls, rather than a congregation of blessed lives, as we do." Soft Stone shook her head. Gray bristles had begun to poke out of her smooth scalp.

Teresa shifted her position. "I think it would be terrible never to swap with anyone, to experience only your own life and nobody else's. I'm so sorry for Daragon."

"Not just that, little Swan. His soul is anchored, unable to separate from his body. What if that means he is unable to move on in the Wheel of Life? Did I fail him?" Soft Stone's body surrendered to wracking sobs.

Teresa had no answer for her.

Two days later a pale and stoic Soft Stone went to

see Administrator Chocolate. The community of other presences inside COM beckoned to her. She had searched her mind and soul and come to a decision.

"I can hear their whispers behind the glimmering phosphors on the interactive screens." Soft Stone repeated her well-rehearsed words, as if they were a poem. "I can see glimpses of nirvana within the vast thinking sea. I want to be part of it, join those myriad others. I will drink the wine of knowledge, bathe in the milk of unending community."

Behind his desk, Chocolate drummed his pudgy fingers on a desktop. "I cannot refuse your request, though it saddens me deeply."

"We should view this as a time of celebration, Chocolate. You of all people must treat it that way. You must believe in what COM offers to us all."

The administrator remained flustered. "But, is your work here done?"

"It will never be done. But I am done with the doing." She turned to leave the office and said with finality, "I intend to upload myself tomorrow at noon."

The following day they all gathered in the library/database room, Splinter monks as well as their charges of all ages. Some sniffled and looked sad, a few whispered, others blinked with wonder and anticipation. Teresa didn't know what to feel. After the recent loss of Daragon, too many things were changing. Soon, Soft Stone was going to vanish, willingly uploading her soul into the vast computer matrix that was COM.

Since humans could swap from body to body at will, and because COM was organic and multilayered, it was possible through hardware and uplink cables to hopscotch into the network itself. Soft Stone would transfer her consciousness into the labyrinth of data, leaving her body behind, empty and lifeless.

Incense burned, pine needles and cloves—Soft

Stone's favorite mixture. Candles sparkled next to the glowing data terminals, adding a warm light like starshine. Teresa tugged at Garth's arm, pulling him and Eduard forward so they could stand at the front of the crowd. Tears brimmed in her eyes.

Soft Stone emerged from the rear of the library, passing between her favorite paintings and sculptures. A hush fell on the gathered crowd. Barefoot, the lean woman walked with grace and confidence, shoulders squared, chin high. Her sky-blue robes were adorned with brass bangles that tinkled as she moved. Her newly shaved scalp glistened as if she had waxed it.

She walked toward the main interlinks in the center of the library. She reached out to brush the hands of her students in a benediction. The old monk paused in front of Teresa, Garth, and Eduard, and suddenly her expression crumpled. "It's not dying. It is living on a higher level. A much higher level." She reached out to enfold the three friends in a deep hug. "I'll try to watch over you. Remember, COM has eyes everywhere, and I will be part of COM."

She kissed Chocolate on both cheeks, and the beatific smile on the administrator's chubby face flickered for just an instant. Then he backed away, leaving her alone with the computer network.

Soft Stone reached out with callused hands to touch the inputs. All other monitors in the library chamber flared to life. Three-dimensional interactive portals painted an artificial sky with fluffy white clouds on the ceiling of the library. The monk closed her eyes and drew a deep breath.

Living lights swirled like comets along the walls. Chimes sounded in the virtual distance, a resonance that hummed in Teresa's bones. She wondered how much was real, how much miraculous... and how much was staged.

Soft Stone's trembling fingers tapped the edges of the milky screens. Then the scenes changed, crackling images replaced by a different construct. The library was transformed into a great vault, an immense cathedral far larger than the monastery building, with stained-glass windows and a thousand different passages. Her mind could spend eternity in here, wandering among all knowledge, all recorded history.

As Soft Stone's brow wrinkled with concentration, she mentally connected herself to COM and prepared to upload her soul. Surrounded by the illusion, the others in the room held their breath. The behind-the-mind music was like crystal; the light was like gemstones.

Glowing images appeared in the air, luminous beings that swirled like angels come to greet her. She raised her hands, then her eyes. The escort presences engulfed her like a safe cocoon, and a shadow of Soft Stone floated with them, younger and stronger. The spirits vanished into the unexplored stained-glass passageways, and the old monk left her body behind forever.

Then the images faded, and the library came into focus again. Soft Stone's body slumped to the library floor, an empty husk.

Teresa stood in the candlelit room, feeling cold and alone even with her friends Garth and Eduard beside her. Chocolate knelt next to Soft Stone's body, cradling her bald head in his hands.

Garth was awed by the beauty of it. "Someday *I'll* make something that beautiful, something as moving as what we just saw."

Teresa wept, never expecting to see Soft Stone again....

Now, grown-up and on her own, Teresa found her thoughts wandering through the droning monotony of her workday. This wasn't what Soft Stone had wanted Teresa to do with her life, with her philosophical inquisitiveness. She felt lost and discouraged, wasting her time on this pointless job.

Then the data matrices displayed on her screen blurred and went out of focus . . . and Teresa thought she saw an image, the ghost of a human form. A woman's bald head, blunt features, and clear blue eyes stared straight out of the information matrix. At her.

Soft Stone!

Startled, Teresa sat straight, but stopped herself from calling a coworker over. She leaned closer to the barrier of the screen, her heart pounding. Her throat went dry. "Hello?"

From behind the milky wall of the network, the bald woman's image smiled at her—then flickered and vanished, like a fish going back underwater, to be replaced by swirling data again.

Teresa saw nothing, no lingering shadow of the apparition. What did it mean? Clusters of numbers floated before her, shifting patterns that held no significance.

Like this useless job, an irrelevant rearrangement and secondary interpretation of information. It was a waste of her time, a waste of her life and abilities. Soft Stone must be so disappointed in her.

Angry at herself, Teresa dumped the numbers and spent the rest of her workday searching along her own paths, finding the works of great philosophers, studying thought-provoking passages. This was what she wanted to do.

Ignoring the assignment her employers had given her, she found new postulates, random expressions posted by more recent thinkers who considered themselves great sages. Sometimes the concepts were moving and timeless; some postings were mere drivel, typo-filled rantings that the would-be philosophers hadn't even bothered to proofread.

Engrossed in the search for meaning, Teresa occupied herself for hours. It was just like what she had enjoyed so much in the Falling Leaves library. . . .

Unfortunately, her employers did not appreciate her new passion, and Teresa didn't manage to keep that particular job very long.

7

Eduard's first regular job outside of the Falling Leaves had been high up on the outside of the mirrored skyscrapers. Wearing a mag-lock harness that attached him to support struts between windows, he hung far above the pavement. The swirling crowds and hovervehicles far below looked like colored pixels on a grid of the city.

Having fun, Eduard spent his days with a repair kit, zipping up and down one structure after another, sealing windows, patching cracks, strengthening blocks that showed signs of wear. Dangling so high made him feel *alive*, in stark contrast with his safe and calm childhood. For a while, he had felt happy and fulfilled... until his restlessness kicked in again.

His work partner, a lanky and unambitious man named Olaf Pitervald, had big-knuckled hands and scarecrowish arms and legs. His freckled skin flushed easily, and his pale hair was a colorless mass that covered his pink scalp. He had worked this job for years and never planned to change.

By himself, Eduard could cover the side of a skyscraper faster than the two of them could do it together, but Olaf liked to hang beside him in his harness. The lanky man spent more time in conversation than actually doing his job. "We get paid the same, no matter how hard we work."

While Eduard diligently used his polysteel compound

to patch chinks, Olaf would spy through the windows, hoping to catch sight of attractive female bodies. Safely anonymous, he made catcalls, emboldened because he knew the women could never hear his words through the glass. He was single, probably because he'd never found the nerve to date.

Olaf pushed his face close to the glass, where a buxom teal-haired woman sat in a lobby area directing visitors. "How do you like that one, eh?"

Eduard had no idea whether a woman or a man inhabited the receptionist's body. Some corporations simply rented sexy female bodies to act as living artwork in the reception areas; then they hired pleasant and competent employees to swap into those beautiful bodies during the workday. Before important meetings, some executives might even hopscotch with their secretaries, always careful to hide their ID patches, so they could eavesdrop on what their business partners might say before negotiations began. . . .

Suspended in his harness, Olaf loved to leer, letting his imagination run wild. Eduard laughed at his ineffectual work partner. "So save up your credits, rent yourself the body of a stud, and go date one of those women." Olaf balked. He was stingy with his money and preferred imaginary conquests to risking actual failure. With a bemused smile, Eduard went back to work.

One day Olaf had hung in his harness next to Eduard and didn't seem to want to talk, offering only occasional surly comments. Finally, Eduard said, "Either tell me what's wrong or leave me alone."

"Facial surgery. Dental prosthetics. I have to get three teeth replaced." Grasping the harness with the crook of his arm, Olaf jabbed his fingers along his left jawline. "In here. They're going to laser-cut some molars and install organic prosthetics. Too much enamel damage, easier to replace than to fix."

"So?"

Olaf fretted in the harness. "I don't like the idea of somebody cutting up my mouth . . . taking pieces of me out."

To Eduard, minor surgery didn't seem a terribly pleasant prospect, but nothing to be terrified about. "Are you worried about the operation itself? Or is it that you just don't want to be there when it's happening?"

Olaf moaned. "I want it to be all over with, and not have to sit through it and feel what they're doing to me. What if it . . . hurts?"

Eduard looked over at his partner as they both swung high, high above the streets. He began to smile as an idea crystallized in his mind. "Hey, how many spare credits do you have?"

Olaf looked suspicious. "You need a loan, eh? I don't lend money."

"As a *payment*. You pay me, and I'll swap with you. I'll sit through your dental surgery for you. No fear, no pain. You won't feel a thing."

Olaf stuttered, swinging in the harness. "I don't think so. I couldn't ask that of you. . . . Uh, how much would I need to pay?"

"A thousand credits," Eduard said, making up the number.

"What? I can't afford that!"

"Yes you can. Besides, if you swap into my body, you don't need to miss a day of work. I'll do it for you. No problem."

Olaf looked sorely tempted, but torn. Eduard found this amusing and said in a teasing tone, "Hey, maybe you'd rather sit there all alone while they go into your mouth with their lasers, chopping up your teeth, ripping them out. Have you ever smelled burning blood? Smoke drifting from your mouth and into your nose?"

"I can spare you five hundred. That should be enough. It's only going to be a few hours."

"For five hundred, *you* can put up with it for a few hours. Or, for nine hundred, you won't have to feel a thing until it's all over." He flashed a winning smile.

Sweat broke out on Olaf's brow despite the cool breezes. In Olaf's bleary eyes Eduard could see that the other man desperately wanted to make the deal, and Eduard refused to haggle further. Nine hundred credits. Finally Olaf agreed.

The next morning, Eduard swapped with him, spent the afternoon in a stainless-steel polished office with all the high-tech surgery necessities: anesthetics, quiet music, scent-synthesizers that masked medicinal odors, and a competent dental surgeon with robotic assistants. It wasn't so bad.

When it was over, after he'd been paid and they hopscotched back into their home-bodies, Eduard didn't have the heart to tell Olaf that he hadn't felt a thing. The nerve deadeners had worked perfectly, the surgery went exactly as planned, and Olaf still had to endure the miserable throbbing pain as his body healed....

Afterward, Eduard realized the possibilities. He went by himself to Club Masquerade and stared at the complex Swapportunities Board, reading down the want ads, the requests for alternate bodies or partners.

Eduard simply listed himself and his services, and word got around.

8

Daragon had not set foot on the mainland in six months. The Bureau and its concerns had become his life, twenty-four hours a day, with every breath, waking or sleeping. He immersed himself in the databases, studying old cases, absorbed in the nuances of law enforcement.

Once humans had learned how to hopscotch, many new legal definitions and precedents needed to be set. The law stated that the "perpetrator" of a crime was the mind rather than the body. Investigations and prosecutions involved the *person* that had been inside a human vehicle when a felony was committed, backtracking the identity through COM or ID patches or sheer detective work.

It was difficult to track someone who did not wish to be found, but a person's mind left distinctive pathways on a host brain, much as a body itself was marked by its unique retinal pattern—or fingerprints. Unfortunately, such mental identification methods were time-consuming and excruciatingly painful for the suspect body, which more often than not turned out to be innocent.

Bureau Chief Ob had high hopes for Daragon, who could *see* the identities of people. Knowing the person to look for, he could find a guilty party at a glance, no matter which body the suspect wore.

"We've survived for over two centuries now on the

sharpest razor edge human civilization has ever encountered," Ob said during a conversation in his underwater office. "You've lived with the idea of swapping all your life, Daragon, so you don't see what a ticking time bomb it really is. Think of the opportunities for total upheaval, the lack of individualism as we have always known it. Without a ready and reliable means for identification of a 'person,' society would crumble into chaos. The sheer potential for abuse boggles the mind."

"Yes, sir. That is why the BTL is so important." *The expected answer.* "But every person has an implanted ID patch."

Ob tapped his fingertips together. "Useful only if people voluntarily synch after swapping. We each have our identity code, which we are supposed to carry with us, no matter what body we inhabit. After I hopscotch with someone, we are required—by law—to update our patches, so that my new body carries the correct ID. Most people do it without thinking."

Daragon pretended to understand. "I can't imagine a situation where both parties would forget, considering the consequences."

Ob ran his fingertip over the rectangle of polymer film on the back of his hand. "That's why the penalties are so severe for anyone caught with an identity that hasn't been updated. The Bureau is completely justified in cracking down. We dare not allow the public to discover that they *can* get away with fooling us."

"Yes, sir, that would be dangerous."

Ob got up to stare at his gas fireplace. Fish swam overhead. "And the people want it, too, don't you see? They understand the precipice we're on. The human race has managed to keep its balance by *not* allowing this potential to run rampant. Luckily, most people choose not to hopscotch very often. They find it disorienting or uncomfortable. They return to their home-bodies and live their lives in the body nature gave them."

"Still, it seems impossible to control, sir, considering all the potential."

Ob smiled as if Daragon had finally reached some sort of breakthrough. "Absolutely impossible. But that doesn't prevent the Bureau from fostering the impression. Think of art—sometimes subtle strokes accomplish more, have a greater impact, than blatant messages."

The Bureau Chief was like a father to Daragon, who had never known one. Daragon wondered if one day he'd be able to find out the identity of his biological parents. Perhaps he could use the resources of the BTL to do it. . . .

Now, taking a rare break up in the open air at the offshore Headquarters platform, he climbed to the top of the derrick superstructure. Sitting high on the derrick, Daragon breathed the salty air and gazed across to the shoreline. The tall rectangular buildings stood like glittering blocks crowded to the edge of the water, on the verge of tumbling like dominoes into the sea.

He thought of his companions from the Falling Leaves. Daragon hadn't had contact with them in more than a year, but he often took advantage of the Bureau's network to keep an eye on them. He tracked Teresa through her succession of dead-end jobs. Garth ran about trying to become an artist. Then there was Eduard, leasing himself for whatever demeaning activities other people wanted to avoid. . . . He missed them very much.

Once he became a full-fledged Inspector, resplendent in his new uniform, Daragon decided he would show them what he had made of his life.

But not yet. He still had work to do.

As kids, he and Eduard had loved to explore the old brick monastery. Attic room, dusty shadows, the scent of mildewed rafters. With a grunt, Eduard forced the crank on an old half-circle window. Fresh, damp wind gusted through the opening. "Come on, let's slip outside. Soft Stone will never know." He thrust his face into the breeze. "We can hop on the roof, make our way over the eaves to the tube walkway next door."

Eduard was like a big brother to him, someone who had the brashness to attempt the things Daragon secretly wanted to do. His almond eyes flicked back and forth, searching for excuses. "But what if we're caught?"

"Then we'll get sent back here. And if we don't go, we'll be stuck here anyway." Eduard flashed his charming grin. "Friends *do things* together, you know. Besides, I want to get something special for Teresa. Don't you want to help me? For her?"

And with that, Daragon was helpless. "All right, but we need to be careful."

Keeping low, they climbed an access ladder onto a connective walkway, then scampered to the neighboring high-rise. Down at street level, Daragon stared at the towering buildings, a forest of mirrored glass, polished stone, gleaming metal. Walls were colored with finger paintings of chameleon pigment. Elevators like deep-sea diving bells rode on the outsides of skyscrapers.

Grinning, Eduard pointed to a lonely-looking military recruiting station. He nudged Daragon in the ribs. "What do you think, should we join the Defense Forces?"

They had recently watched a heart-wrenching story about brave soldiers during a major mid-twentieth-century conflict. Daragon didn't find the entertainment cycle nearly as engaging as the Dickens novels Garth read aloud to him and another boy, Pashnak. A great general had been mortally wounded during the height of a battle. Knowing the fate of his comrades was at stake, a quiet infantryman (who had been a coward for most of the story) selflessly sacrificed himself by hopscotching with his general, dying in his place so that the military leader could lead the troops to a spectacular victory. Eduard insisted that the twentieth-century wars had occurred long before anyone knew how to swap bodies.

They sat on a sun-warmed flowstone bench to watch the world. Shadows strobed across the sunlight from the row of hovercars humming overhead. Eduard studied people passing through doorways, suspicious shapes slipping quickly from beneath one awning to another. He pointed out a well-dressed man who edged along a building wall.

"Hey, have you ever heard of the Phantoms, people who hopscotch bodies again and again so they can outrun death?" Eduard asked, his eyes full of wonder. "Trading themselves into younger bodies, healthy physiques, doing whatever it takes to stay alive. Imagine, some of the Phantoms are supposed to be five and six hundred years old!"

"People haven't even known how to hopscotch for that long." Daragon wasn't so credulous. For a Phantom to stay alive for centuries, he would have to maintain an extremely low profile, a quiet existence, leaving no trail and attracting no attention. "Besides, the Beetles would know about it, wouldn't they? Nobody has any proof."

Eduard watched the stranger until he passed around a corner and was lost in the crowd. "Well, I believe it." He pointed to a man haggling with a food vendor across the street. "If they found a way to doctor their ID patches, how would you ever know? That man there could be a Phantom." He indicated a woman climbing into a hovercar parked at a charging terminal. "Or *she* could be one. Or that old couple, with their heads down—they could be waiting for their chance to steal young and healthy bodies."

Daragon was more concerned about the people whose bodies they stole, rather than the Phantoms themselves. He shook his head each time. "They've all got ID patches. Besides, can't you just...*see* inside to who they really are?"

Eduard looked at him strangely. "Even the Beetles need scanners and equipment to figure that out."

"I don't."

"Yeah, right." Restless, Eduard got up from the bench. "Well, *I* want to become a Phantom. Like a candle flame passed from wick to wick, never burning out."

Wandering farther, Eduard and Daragon saw the open-air flower market at the same time, a profusion of colors and scents: bouquets of pink and yellow carnations, long-stemmed roses as red as blood, genetically modified exotics in a garish profusion of neon or metallic colors, with selective scents ranging from peppermint to sandalwood. Some blooms had been silica-enhanced so they would never wilt.

Teresa loved flowers.

"But we don't have any money," Daragon whispered. In the monastery, they had no need for credits.

Eduard grinned, good-natured. "We just wait for an opportunity. Maybe somebody will...drop something. Be flexible."

They walked among the flowers, sniffing some, fingering others. A midnight-blue orchid opened from a perfect bud to full bloom, then collapsed back into a bud again, cycling in a single minute.

Suddenly, the COM traffic-control substation across the street exploded, two stories up. The blast tore a hole through the side of the building. Chunks of stone, glass, and hot metal rained down as screaming bystanders scrambled for safety. A restaurant's striped awning caught on fire.

Thinking fast, Eduard snatched a mixed bouquet of color-coded carnations, rainbow-petaled daisies, and talking daffodils. He grinned as if it were a game. "Come on, let's go!"

Daragon gaped at him. "You didn't say we were going to steal anything."

"It's not hurting anybody. Here, I'll let you give half of them to Teresa."

With the disruption of COM, the interleaved sky-lanes of hovercars swirled like a stirred anthill before the backup safety systems kicked in and vehicles automatically landed in rapid succession, filling the crowded streets.

The safety systems lost only one hovercar, a topaz-blue single-passenger model. Directly above the wrecked substation, the vehicle veered from its impedance path, slipped through the protective electronic net, and plummeted into a bistro across the street.

Inside the flaming hulk of the crashed hovercar, Daragon could see a mangled driver trying to free himself. Some people ran toward the scene and some fled, while others remained frozen, watching. "We've got to help. Can't we do something?"

Eduard looked at him in astonishment. "Are you better trained than all those people? Ambulance crews will be here in a minute, and the Beetles, too."

Daragon swallowed hard, still reluctant about breaking the law, but took the flowers from Eduard. With their prized bouquet in hand, the two young men raced back to the monastery....

———

Now behind the heavy desk in his office, Mordecai Ob steepled his fingers like a lobster trap. "Daragon, you must not operate under the misconception that the only reason our BTL exists is to capture criminals. That function often falls under the purview of other Bureaus."

"But sir, I've found a lead on one of our most wanted fugitives. The terrorist behind the bombings that caused such turmoil in COM several years ago." He'd wanted so badly to make Mordecai Ob proud of him.

After thinking about the explosion in the flower market, Daragon had checked on the status of the anti-COM fugitives. When he learned that the leader, a woman named Robertha Chambers, remained at large, Daragon applied his imagination. He followed unlikely leads, vague aliases, until he located her. He covered his exuberance when he brought the news to Ob, but now even his hidden smile began to falter.

"I know you've put a lot of energy into this, Daragon, but we've already captured the rest of her anti-COM band. The last one is due to be uploaded and executed tomorrow. The problem has been eliminated. Robertha Chambers poses no threat."

"But why don't we wrap up the case, sir?" Daragon did not want to reveal his personal connection to the matter. "There's no statute of limitations. We could take Robertha out. Think of what a coup that would be."

Under Ob's olive-brown gaze, Daragon felt that he still had much more to learn. "There are second- and third-order effects of what the Bureau does. Have you considered that perhaps I've known about her all along? Robertha Chambers believes she has a clever disguise, living out in the open where no one will suspect her." He looked hard at the young Inspector. "The simple fact is, the BTL isn't interested in apprehending her."

Daragon sat down in the guest chair. He stared at

the blue-orange flames in Ob's gas fireplace, wrestling with the concept. "I don't understand, sir."

The Chief was a model of patience. "Seems our ringleader has no stomach for a full-fledged revolution. Robertha gathered a band of big talkers and pushed them into violence. She relished the power, enjoyed being in charge. Now that her group is gone and she almost lost her life, Robertha's found a safer way to get her thrills. The BTL considers her effectively impotent where she is."

"But that doesn't mean we shouldn't capture her. She can still hurt people. What if she takes advantage—"

"Daragon, *think,* please." Ob's voice had a sharper edge to it. "With this supposedly dangerous person at large, the BTL can maintain stepped-up surveillance and an obvious presence in places where we have no legitimate reason to be. We can always apprehend Robertha later, if we so desire. But she won't cause us any more problems."

Daragon nodded solemnly. "I hadn't thought of those things, sir." He needed to put the needs of the Bureau above his own wishes.

9

After seeing Soft Stone's image in the COM terminal, Teresa roamed the streets, full of questions. She did not know where to go or how to focus her quest. What did her teacher want her to do? Had the apparition been only her imagination? She knew that wasn't true. The old monk had always encouraged her to seek answers within herself and outside in the world.

Eduard and Garth had never been much interested in philosophy, but Daragon had often listened to Teresa work through her thoughts. Now she went to a BTL subdistrict office and asked how she might go about seeing Daragon, but the attendant gave her only a gruff reply. "We are unable to divulge the whereabouts of any particular officer."

"Oh, but he's a friend of mine. This is a personal matter." She smiled at the attendant, who did not smile back.

"The Bureau frowns on its officers having 'personal matters.'" Teresa insisted on leaving a message, which the attendant grudgingly accepted, though he gave no assurances as to whether it would ever find its way to Daragon.

Teresa wandered from place to place, confident that when the *answer* came, she would see it plainly. "If you want lightning to strike, child, you cannot hide in a cave," Soft Stone had taught her. "You must plant a lot of lightning rods."

As she searched the streets, Teresa didn't even know what she was looking for—until she saw the religious group in the square. They called themselves Sharetakers. The cluster of converts wore colorful clothes to attract attention. They had no actual rented stall—the five volunteers just staked out their territory at an intersection of byways and talked to people who happened to walk by, trying to interest them in the Sharetaker way of life. They tried to sell secondhand possessions to raise money, liquidating worldly goods to scrape up enough credits so they could print more leaflets.

Teresa's chest tightened. Their devotion and passion fascinated her, and she wondered if *this* could be the lightning bolt she had been hoping for. Her own meditations always raised more queries about the nature of existence than they answered. Hard facts on the subject eluded her. "Questions are more important than answers, little Swan," Soft Stone had been fond of saying.

The Splinters had coalesced from believers who no longer knew what to believe. Body-swapping and the all-pervasive computer/organic matrix had changed humankind more than anything in the past several thousand years—yet none of the great religious texts addressed the issue. How could any prophet worth his salt miss something *that* important? Impossible. Doubts had cast many former zealots adrift. Over the course of two centuries, numerous fusion religions had sprung up as people sought new answers....

Teresa found her feet dragging her across the street toward the Sharetakers. The group consisted of two young men and three women, facing outward with their backs to each other. Flashing smiles, they talked and talked, their words overlapping in resonant syllables.

"We offer a sense of community and acceptance. We welcome newcomers with open arms," one woman said, utterly convinced of her message.

"Nobody needs to be alone in this world, if only you join us," said a man. Each spoke a memorized part of the speech, like a rotating information loop.

A second woman looked directly into Teresa's eyes. Though the words could well have been part of the carefully practiced routine, they seemed to be directed specifically at her. "Are *you* searching for something? Are *you* lost? Then come and find us."

Pedestrians bustled around her, ignoring the proselytizers. The message droned past them, just part of the white noise of the city. But Teresa *heard*.

"We believe in mutual sharing, bodies and minds, lives and experiences. What is a home without love? What is a society without cooperation? Only by combining our efforts, by building upon each other's thoughts and sweat, can we rise higher. The Sharetakers are stronger than the sum of our parts."

When the first woman noticed her interest, she signaled her fellow Sharetakers, who turned from their positions to focus on Teresa. They all came forward, accepting her like a hive organism swallowing her in its welcoming embrace.

Since the loss of Soft Stone, since leaving the monastery, Teresa had felt alone and disconnected in the world. She'd kept in touch with Garth and Eduard, meeting them regularly at Club Masquerade, but still she felt adrift.

"Would you like to hear more?" one of the Sharetaker women said.

Teresa couldn't stop herself from nodding. . . .

For an hour, standing among the Sharetakers, she listened to them disseminate their message. When they encountered no other potential converts like herself, the outreach spokesman led her back to their enclave.

Out in front of a nondescript dwelling complex, a square-jawed man greeted the returning missionaries.

With flashing eyes and a shock of bristly reddish hair, he carried a passion about him, a more intense focus than Teresa was accustomed to seeing.

"That's our leader, Rhys," the spokesman said to her, nodding toward the man. "He joined us from a different enclave in another city. We've never seen such all-consuming enthusiasm for our cause. Rhys truly understands what the Sharetakers are all about, how to focus us into a stronger whole."

The redheaded leader's presence captivated Teresa. He welcomed the groups back home, asking each Sharetaker what he or she had seen, how many trinkets they had sold, how many new members they had found.

Teresa took a step closer, glad to see a man whose course seemed so clear to him, whose life had a clear-cut path—all the things she was missing in herself.

Rhys's gaze locked with hers, and she stood like a rabbit afraid of being flushed from the underbrush. It was as if he managed to peel away all of the masks that hid her inner strength from the world. He could look through her, into her mind and heart, and see the hunger and vulnerability in her eyes.

"The Sharetakers are not a free ride for lazy people," Rhys said with a stern edge. "We believe that humans can be complete if they share everything, share their lives, their muscles, their labor. We all work hard so that we can live peacefully together, the way people were meant to exist. One heart, one mind, many bodies. If you join us, you must join us wholeheartedly. Hold back nothing—neither your possessions nor yourself. In return, you will receive all that we have, every person, every body, free for the taking."

Then Rhys smiled, and his expression softened. He reached toward Teresa and grasped her small hands in his, squeezing tightly. He stepped back from the press of people and opened the doors to the building. "Come inside, Teresa, and we'll help you settle in."

The other Sharetakers focused on the newcomer who had caught their leader's attention. Then they all came forward, welcoming her, introducing themselves.

Teresa easily succumbed to their overtures. Her concerns and questions about her own life washed away. She followed the Sharetakers through the doorway into the strange building and a brand-new life. This place was filled with many more mysteries, but perhaps now she might find the answers ... or at least the solace that she sought.

10

Another weekend, Garth went to the artists' bazaar with more artwork and undiminished optimism.

The side of a nearby building carried an up-to-the-minute COM-news screen as a public service. On the broadcast, guards from the Bureau of Incarceration and Executions led a decrepit and shuddering old man to his death. At the bottom of the screen, the BIE logo shone like a red bug.

Garth got the attention of a pottery-artist who molded wet clay, which she would fire into small terra-cotta wind chimes. "What's going on?"

She gestured at the screen with a muddy hand. "One of those idiot anti-COM terrorists from two years ago. The main deputy, I think."

Garth drew a deep breath. "The ones who blew up the substation down by the flower market?"

A beignet chef dusted with white powdered sugar said, "That's almost the last one. The instigator of the whole mess is still at large. Robertha something or other. Now she's hiding under a rock."

Garth closed his eyes. He knew far more than any of these others, but he did not want to admit it, did not like to remember that day.

Soft Stone had stood inside the monastery doorway, blocking their exit. "I'm going to give you three children some credits. Go out and buy flowers so we can brighten up the monastery. I'm sure you can handle that without an escort. In fact, you may want to pay the flower seller a little extra for whatever you purchase today—correct, Eduard?" Her voice was hard, devastating.

"Uh, no problem." Eduard looked deeply embarrassed. Garth and Teresa looked at him, neither of them understanding.

"By rights, this task should fall to Daragon, as well, but he is so far behind in his mental exercises, I've asked him to stay here." The bald woman opened the heavy door, and a flood of daylight poured in. "Be safe," she said, sincere now.

Garth and Eduard each folded one of Teresa's arms in their own, flanking her as they hurried away from the Falling Leaves. When they reached the flower market, they walked among the bouquets, the gaudy stalks, the ferns. Kiosk workers arranged clumps of neon daisies, altered scents and grafted on petals, added ribbons, audio-greeting buttons, or mirrored ornaments.

As soon as they were far enough from the monastery, Eduard told them in excited whispers about sneaking out with Daragon, finding the flower market, escaping from the terrorist explosion. "Look, that's where the hovercar crashed. You can see where the pavement's been wrecked."

Garth stared at the site with appropriate respect. The side of a building had been scarred with black flames and smoke. A blossom of windows had shattered around the midpoint of the blast. A crowd gathered behind barricade tape to watch crews cleaning up the sidewalks. Mag-lock scaffolding hung on the sides of the skyscraper, while workers sliced off shards of mirrored glass.

Eduard lowered his eyes when he saw the vendor from whom he had snatched Teresa's bouquet. "We, uh, better buy from him." The man added two extra stalks of magenta humming gladiolas to round out the purchase. Teresa's arms were filled with a richness of flowers, and she laughed.

Eduard whispered, wearing an impish grin, "Did you hear about the woman who tried to hopscotch with her dog? She was all alone, had the pet for years, and she wanted to give him a chance to be human for a little while."

Garth groaned. "I know where this is going...."

"She ended up nothing more than an empty body. Neighbors found her only because the starving dog kept barking and barking."

Teresa looked at him, astonished. "Do you think it was the slippage disease? She got detached and couldn't find her way back to her body?"

"No, it's because she was stupid enough to try hopscotching with a dog." Eduard laughed at his story; Teresa seemed reluctant to believe him.

Garth looked up at the apartment buildings—and was the first to see the gunmetal-gray BTL chopter cruise into position midway up one skyscraper not far from the flower market. "Look up there. Something's going on."

The ominous craft maneuvered against the mirrored glass. A rubber-lipped transfer tube sealed against the window. Even from far below, Garth could hear cutting sounds, grinding like saw-powered sharks' teeth.

"The Beetles found someone," Eduard said. "Maybe it's the bombers."

Muffled by distance, Garth heard a few faint projectile shots, but he couldn't tell if the weapons fire came from fugitives inside the domicile, or from the Beetles themselves. Suddenly one of the windows adjacent to the besieged apartment shattered, spraying shards to the streets below. Pedestrians took cover under overhangs, kiosks, and tables.

Four people sprang out of the smashed window, all of them wearing olive-green jumpsuits. For a moment, Garth thought they were leaping to their deaths—until he saw that they had secured themselves with snakelike cords anchored inside the room. The four escapees rappelled down, magnetic pulleys humming as they plummeted toward the street below.

Above them, the BTL gunship opened fire with a cloud of stun projectiles, shattering other windows. One of the escaping fugitives slammed against the skyscraper wall, leaving a splash of blood on the mirror glass. Arms and legs hanging limp, he spun down, slowed by the automatic pulley-brakes.

Another window cracked; more gunfire erupted. The fugitives were using lethal armaments, and the Beetles rapidly switched from stun projectiles to seeker bullets.

The other three anti-COM terrorists continued down, bouncing off the sides of the building, picking up speed. They hit the sidewalks with bent legs and snapped off their elastic ropes. Released, the cables spun back upward like angry cobras. Moving with well-practiced confidence, the fugitives tore off their olive jumpsuits, revealing bland street clothes underneath. Dodging weapons fire, they threw the tattered garments into the crowd and quickly blended in.

Pedestrians ran about knocking over flower stands, rushing for shelter inside buildings. As the Beetles came toward them, Garth watched in fascination as the terrorists scattered in a drunkard's-walk of changing directions to keep their moves from being predictable.

One of the three, a redheaded woman, spotted a person in the crowd hiding under one of the vendor stands. The man raised his hand in a signal. The redhead rushed to him and bent down. Beneath the kiosk, the two clasped each other's temples, quickly locking eyes... swapping. Even at a distance, Garth noticed with a shock that neither had ID patches on their hands, only a small squarish scar. Seconds later, the redhead got up and ran in another direction, while the man quietly sauntered into one of the buildings and disappeared.

Garth couldn't believe what he had just seen. "They hopscotched, the two of them! She had a contact in the crowd, and she got away."

Eduard chuckled. "Bait and switch! I bet she makes a clean break."

Another fugitive ran like a bull through the flower stands, knocking over buckets of long-stemmed roses, upending pots of marigolds. Teresa stood alone, still encumbered with the bouquets. The fugitive hissed in her face so forcefully that spittle flecked her cheeks. "Hopscotch with me! Now!"

She looked up at the flushed man. "I...I can't. I'm not old enough."

Beetles ran toward them, shooting into the air and making a fearsome racket. The fugitive let out a snarl of despair and anger, then grabbed Teresa.

Though Garth's mind raced for a way to save her, he couldn't move. He wanted to help, but he froze, completely helpless.

But Eduard didn't stop to think about his own safety. Lowering his shoulder, he plowed into Teresa with enough force to rip her out of the fugitive's grasp. While the man cried out in surprise, Eduard bore Teresa down to the pavement, covering her with his body. The flowers flew around them in a blizzard of color, petals, and scents.

The Beetles targeted the lone fugitive as he whirled, empty-handed, searching for another escape. The enforcers opened fire with a mixture of stun projectiles and deadly bullets. The terrorist flew backward, skidding across the ground. Blood poured from holes in his bland street shirt. Potent stunner-darts poked like bristles from his shoulders, sides, face.

The Beetles marched to him, elbowing people away. They grabbed the dying man's collar, dragged him into a sitting position. "Where's Robertha Chambers?"

"She's not me." The man smiled in triumph with blood-flecked lips.

"*Who* is she? *Where* is she?"

Snapping out of his shock, Garth rushed to help Eduard pull Teresa to her feet, and she clung to him. "She's all right." Eduard cut off further conversation, already moving. "All of us are fine. Let's get out of here!" For now, the Beetles were too intent on their victim to question the crowd, but that wouldn't divert them for long.

The three ducked into an office building, rode a lifter up four levels, and hurried across a promenade. From there, a moving walkway took them to where they could zigzag through a galleria filled with lights and music. Eduard kept glancing over his shoulder. "Walk slowly, casually. Don't draw any attention to yourself. We can't look like we're on the run."

"Why are *we* running?" Teresa asked. "We didn't do anything."

Garth understood immediately. "That man touched you, Teresa. They might think he swapped with you. That's how the redhead escaped."

Teresa looked at her ID patch as if it offered proof. "But I'm still me."

Eduard shook his head, worried about her. "Do you want your mind peeled just so the Beetles can prove your identity? It's what they do, you know." Teresa shuddered.

It was only when they reached the monastery that

Garth realized they had not, after all, brought back the flowers Soft Stone had requested.

Now, in the artists' bazaar, the beignet vendor went back to his pans, dropping globs of dough into hot oil. He shook his head at the COM screen showing the terrorist about to be executed. "Stupid people. As if anybody would really be able to knock out COM. We'd go back to the Dark Ages."

On screen, the decrepit prisoner could barely hold his head upright in the upload chair. Before the scheduled execution, some ailing old man had bought the condemned terrorist's body so he could be healthy and fit again. The swap was now complete. In another chair next to the condemned man, the man's original, healthy physique was now inhabited by the lucky bidder; the restraints automatically loosened.

Garth set his sketch aside and stared at the screen in morbid fascination. Execution attendants finished applying electrodes and upload cables to the now-palsied terrorist. He raised liver-spotted hands to fend them off, but his muscles were too weak.

After stripping away all personality and independent thought, the justice system uploaded a condemned person's mind into COM to add to its engram processing power. The living matrix supposedly grew stronger, more flexible each time. The announcer's description of COM as a "sweatshop of souls" alarmed Garth. If that was the case, what of Soft Stone? What of all the other Splinters who had voluntarily hopscotched into the matrix?

When the on-screen execution countdown ended, the victim trembled, jerked once, then fell slack like an empty suit of clothes. Beside him, in the other restraint chair, the healthy body watched. Now that his role as a propaganda tool had been fulfilled, he was eager to get away and begin his new youthful life.

The artists in the bazaar cheered or made catcalls. Garth blinked and tried to understand.

Without further ceremony, the execution attendants disconnected the empty body and hauled it away. Then the news-screen moved on to another breaking news story, this time about a colorful kite festival being held in the Rocky Mountains.

Deeply moved, Garth looked at the charcoal and chalk dust on his fingers. He always understood the world better if he inhaled it, rolled it around inside, gave himself time to digest it ... then put it forth as artwork.

The daily flutter of activity swirled around him. Merchants and customers went about their business, the execution already forgotten.

11

Wearing his best suit of clothes, Eduard went to the plush upper levels of offices that were inhabited by lawyers of all kinds. He made a cursory check of his appearance, straightened the conservative collar, brushed back his dark hair, and walked into the meeting with a tough expression on his face. When the negotiations started, he had to make sure he got off on the right foot. He'd never had an opportunity this big before, and he relished the prospect.

A crowd of expensive suits waited for him in the boardroom—representatives of the client, family members, and legal counsel. No face bore the slightest glimmer of a friendly expression. All business. No problem.

Eduard wondered if *he* should have contracted a legal advocate of his own, but he preferred to be independent, without relying on supposed "experts." He'd made many swap agreements before, though never with such formality.

Behind the boardroom table hovered several go-fers, lower-echelon employees anxious for any job in a big firm. Their sole purpose was to be on call during long, arduous deliberations. Anytime one of the executives had a full bladder, a go-fer would swap bodies and walk out of the room to relieve him- or herself. No need to put an important meeting on hold to take care of bodily functions.

A cadaverous old woman sat propped at the end of

the long table. She leaned forward, bracing herself on shriveled arms. Her skin hung like loose fabric on her bones, tinted a grayish-green from the bizarre medical treatments she had already endured. Her eyes were sharp and reptilian, her nose pinched. Eduard had never before met a person who seemed so altogether unpleasant.

"I am very happy to meet you, Madame Ruxton." He pumped forced charm into his voice. Her lips compressed like a purse-string drawn tight.

The tallest lawyer stepped up, and others withdrew hardcopy documents from their folders, spreading them out on the table. "You are aware of the risks, Mr. Swan? Madame Ruxton's surgery is very serious, and you are being asked to undergo it for her. Your survival is not guaranteed. We estimate a twenty-five-percent probability that you won't live through the operation."

"I'll survive, no problem. I'm strong, and I'll help the body through it. Madame Ruxton will get her money's worth."

"Nevertheless, we must face reality," another lawyer said. "You have been offered a very large sum. Madame Ruxton has guaranteed that such payment will be made—unless, of course, you don't survive the surgery."

"Come on, she'll make the payment either way." Without being asked, Eduard took a seat opposite the withered old woman. "If I'm going to die in her body, she can still pay the fee. And the amount is triple if I don't survive the operation." He gave them all a harmless grin and shrugged his shoulders. "That decreases the incentive for any sort of medical mishap."

The lawyers looked over at the old woman. She nodded sharply. They hadn't really expected to get away with a death disclaimer anyway. "Of course," one lawyer said, not offended at all. "That's perfectly standard."

"But I get to keep the body, by default," the old woman said. "If you die."

Eduard smiled at her. He had expected that part, too, and he knew this was a battle he couldn't win. "If I'm dead I won't have any more use for it, will I?"

"Quite correct," the woman said.

The go-fers fidgeted, waiting for something to do. One of them, with a hopeful expression on her face, offered more coffee to all the parties.

"Have you chosen heirs or assigns for receiving such money, should you die on the operating table, Mr. Swan?" an attorney asked.

Eduard drew out papers naming both Garth and Teresa as his beneficiaries. He had thought about adding Daragon, but the BTL would take care of him. Eduard was more worried about his other two friends.

"Are you certain you don't want legal representation of your own?" one of Ruxton's lawyers said.

Eduard picked up one copy of the thick contract, leaned back in the chair, and began to skim the paragraphs. "Hey, I can be as suspicious as anyone else." He had been through similar jobs before and was aware of the various ramifications.

Unexpectedly, the old woman made deep retching sounds, as if she had a gravel pit operating inside her lungs. Her family members flocked close by, attending her with the exaggerated concern of soon-to-be-heirs.

Eduard made the bevy of attorneys wait as he read through the entire document, knowing they were being paid by the hour. He flagged certain minor points that he insisted on changing, just for the sake of appearances. "When is your surgery scheduled?"

The lawyers glanced at him, and Madame Ruxton tried to sit up straight, holding her posture with great effort. "Tomorrow." Her salamander eyes glittered. "My body won't last long without it."

Though surprised that they had cut it so close, Eduard gave her his best charming smile. "Don't you worry about a thing. My calendar's open for you. Estimated time to full recovery?"

"Four weeks," one of the lawyers said.

With a flourish of a pen that laid down glittering magnetic ink, he signed the contract. He did not relish the prospect of living in the old woman's body for the operation or the recovery period, but he could do it, and afterward he would have an importance and prestige he'd never had before. It would be the start of many good things to come.

He would have extra credits to give to his friends, since Teresa had recently lost her job, and Garth still hadn't made any money with his artwork. For himself, Eduard didn't need the extra creature comforts he could buy, but he did like to feel the sense of getting away with something.

Smiling warmly, Eduard handed the contracts over while the attorneys swarmed about making copies, certifying documents, and no doubt charging the old crone an exorbitant fee for their ministrations.

After swapping into the aching and withered form, Eduard lay back on the surgery table. Madame Ruxton's body was a collapsing ancient structure held together by cobwebs. The deep agony in his bones spoke of age, and his heartbeat stuttered like the slow drumbeat of a dirge. It was an effort just to endure the heavy weight of sheets around him.

The surgery would repair her deteriorating vascular system, but Madame Ruxton would never feel young and healthy again. Eduard saw her standing there in his home-body, and a calculating expression pinched his familiar face.

For the first time Eduard felt uneasy. He had covered himself with every clause he could imagine, added every legal caveat, but Madame Ruxton was a wily and desperate woman. What if he had forgotten something? What if he had been incredibly naïve?

He ached so badly that he welcomed the anesthetic when the surgeons arrived. His vision blurred. He watched his own physique—Ruxton's, for the time being—through rheumy eyes that no longer saw the world clearly.

Eduard felt the symphony of pain in his sunken chest and lungs, then drifted downward into chemically induced blackness. . . .

12

"**Don't forget**, Daragon, we're not just police." Mordecai Ob raised the COM screen on his desk and punched in a request. "The Bureau of Tracing and Locations finds missing people, uncovers the identity of parents or their children." He printed out the results, handing the hardcopy to Daragon with an expectant smile. "Since you want to do something so badly, let me give you your first official Bureau assignment. You're ready for it."

Daragon flushed with pride as he took the paper and scanned the words.

"You need to track down a lost family member. This woman needs a vital medical treatment, something that can only be cured through parallel DNA-matching therapy. And that can only be done if she finds the home-body of her brother. Unfortunately, he hopscotched out of his original body long ago in a long-term lease, which was transferred to another person, who died outside of the swapped body. Through a record-keeping snafu, the sibling's body then went onto the open market for permanent sale."

Daragon read the particulars, making a special effort not to smile or frown or show any sort of emotion whatsoever. That would have been bad form.

"Thus, the family needs to recover the brother's lost home-body. It's a matter of life and death, and they came to the BTL for help. The brother himself has kept in touch, but he's hopscotched from one body to another as he took job after job. The sister needs the original body to do her any good."

Daragon folded the printout and stuffed it into one of his pockets. "I'll find him for you, sir."

"Don't find the body for *me*," Ob said. "Do it for them."

Daragon ran into dead ends at every turn, no doubt exactly as the Chief had anticipated. But he'd given his word, and he refused to abandon the quest so easily. He would not disappoint the man who had helped him so much.

In windowless chambers filled with bubbling coolants and life-support systems, the Bureau's mutated Data Hunters hung in limbo, living a surreal life with virtual bodies, lost inside the computer/organic matrix. Daragon went into the airlocked chambers and stood inside the dank-smelling room.

As his eyes adjusted, he gazed up at where hairless, stunted bodies hung suspended in harnesses, wired to the vast cosmos of COM. Data Hunters looked like hideous embryos with flaccid arms that had atrophied through lack of use. Their spines were curved, their heads overlarge, their eyes blind, seeing only through neural inputs that linked them into the sea of information.

He waited in silence, not certain of the protocol he was supposed to follow, until finally he said in a loud, firm voice, "I need some help." Bubbles continued to jet into the coolant and recirculation tubes. He saw no motion, no reaction.

One of the embryos drifted in its floating restraints and turned a sightless face toward him. A voice that oozed sarcasm came out of a small speaker on the far side of the room. "Ahh, somebody's come to give my life purpose! What is it you seek? Wait, forgive my lack of social graces...we get no practice in here." The body stirred as if a breeze had wafted through the room. Now, the voice came from a different place, closer to the floating creature. "My name is Jax, and you must introduce yourself properly before you make a request. I'm not just a genie in a bottle who's required to give you three wishes, you know."

Daragon had anticipated Data Hunters to be alien and incomprehensible, not talkative. "My name is Daragon. I need to find someone in order to help a person who requires medical treatment. Can I call your attention to a case file?"

"Ah, a humanitarian gesture. How wonderful!"

He punched in the file, and the hovering Data Hunter scanned it in a millisecond. "Ahh, it'll keep me occupied for a while," Jax said through the speaker. "That's what we're here for, after all. But first, you must promise to meet my payment request."

Not knowing what to say, Daragon smoothed his trainee Inspector uniform. "But you work for the Bureau. We're part of the same team."

Jax's body did not stir, but the voice coming from the speaker had an interesting lilt. "We all have our price. Do you want me to help you or not?"

Daragon sighed. "All right, then. What is your price?"

"I want you to come and talk to me. We don't get much company, and I can find anything else I need through COM. But the network can't provide plain, faulty human companionship."

"If that's all you want, then I agree to your terms."

"Good. Come back in an hour and I'll have the information you need. After you use the information, I want you to come and tell me what you did."

Daragon tracked down the business offices of the person who now owned the brother's original home-body. The current inhabitant was a public relations specialist who dealt with celebrities. His name was Stradley, and he called himself a "hype-meister."

As Daragon waited in Stradley's lobby, he tried to appear properly ominous in his clean BTL uniform. He glanced at the receptionist, who shrugged toward the door where Stradley sat "in consultation" with one of his clients.

Finally, the exuberant hype-meister burst out of his office wearing a grin, and Daragon immediately recognized the missing brother's home-body from the file images. Stradley's false smile transformed into a scowl. "So, what does a Beetle want in my office? You guys certainly don't need *my* help with publicity. Of course, the Bureau could use a bit more favorable coverage."

Daragon didn't rise to the bait. "That's not why I'm here, sir."

Stradley crossed his arms over his chest. The hype-meister wasn't taking good care of his physique. His neck and face seemed slack, a bit jowly, and he had begun to grow a potbelly. The eyes were bloodshot, the movements frenetic, as if he sampled too many stimulants. Daragon hoped the body remained in good enough condition for the necessary medical treatment.

"State your purpose, then. I'm a busy man and I command high hourly rates. I'll start charging if you waste my time." Daragon wondered how the man would ever get a bill through the BTL's bureaucratic accounting systems, but he did not press the matter.

"We've come for your body, sir. Someone needs the loan of it—the sister of its original owner."

The hype-meister narrowed his eyes, trying to figure out Daragon's angle. "Say again? Why on earth is the

BTL messing around with personal problems? Is she your mistress, maybe?"

"She needs DNA-matching therapy. Your body is the only one they can use for the procedure. You have the appropriate genes, and they need to extract some samples."

"Not from my body they won't." Stradley raised his arms. "I've got a burgeoning business here. Check your records—this is *my* body now. I acquired it free and clear, permanent lease, a year and a half ago. And even then, that wasn't from its original owner. This body has been bounced and bounced. Who knows how many other people have lived inside it?"

"Mr. Stradley." Daragon tried again. "The only thing I care about is who *presently* owns the body. That is you. You have the precise genetic match required. Can you find it in your heart to save someone's life?"

"I need this body. I use it every day. I can't find it in my heart to give up what I'm doing here to endure any excruciating medical work. I've heard about this kind of treatment." Stradley made no move to invite him into the office.

Daragon mentally searched through what he had studied. The law remained murky in this area: Stradley was the legitimate current owner of that body, and even former family members couldn't force him to undergo a medical procedure he didn't want to have.

As an idea dawned, Daragon folded his hands in front of him. "Since you bought that body anyway, sir, and you've been in it for a year and a half, perhaps you would consider switching with someone else?"

"I can't afford a new body just at the drop of a hat—that's quite an investment. Besides, I'm working here."

Daragon continued. "Perhaps, sir, I should put you in touch with the family. The parents and the sister may offer enough credits for a replacement body. A better one. That way you can be someone new, and they'll have access to the DNA they need, while you continue your work uninterrupted."

Stradley blew air through his lips. "Might be acceptable. Okay, I could do that—as long as it's a trade *up*."

Daragon nodded brusquely. "I won't take up any more of your time today, sir. I will provide the family with your contact information. I'm sure they'll be able to resolve this matter to your satisfaction."

"No promises," Stradley warned.

As he traveled back to BTL Headquarters, Daragon mulled over the different ways he could have handled the problem, but he could think of no better solution. He had done well, and he knew it. He would tell the Data Hunter Jax all about it, as he had promised.

Then, smiling, he decided to check up on Eduard, Garth, and Teresa. It had been so long since he'd seen them.

13

"While other people call these *apart*ments," Rhys said to Teresa, raising his arms to encompass the Sharetaker enclave, "we name them *together*ments. In our philosophy we all come together and do not move apart."

He flashed her a winning smile, and his words made her feel warm. Teresa had already spent days settling in, working hard to be part of the group. Under Rhys's ambitious leadership, the enclave had grown until it took over much of the building, combining separate domiciles into one interconnected hive.

As a new member, Teresa's daily labor involved ripping out walls and tearing down doors between rooms. The Sharetakers left only a framework of areas where people could sleep or cook or amuse themselves through conversation, games, or lovemaking.

The group insisted that everyone was equal, every body interchangeable; however, they recognized that some physical forms were better suited for certain purposes than others. Teresa hopscotched among the believers, from a tired body to a fresh one, just so she could work extra hours.

Rhys watched the labor and swapped bodies as often as anyone else. He even made a point of spending days inside Teresa's young and fresh female form, while she went about doing the harder tasks, using the muscles of people whose names she didn't even know.

Rhys had taken her as his lover almost immediately, and she had acquiesced, happy to be singled out. Even back in the monastery, the Splinters had been open about sex, seeing it as a rudimentary form of sharing bodies.

The first time, Rhys had embraced her with great intensity, hot and sweaty, breathing hard. His sexual technique, like his personality, was fiery and passionate, almost violent. When he had satisfied himself, he lay back, swapped with Teresa, and wanted to do it again as the opposite sex, but Rhys's male home-body was already spent, and Teresa couldn't perform for him.

She saw her own naked form, flushed from the recent exercise but wanting more. In her own voice, Rhys said, "Go find another one of the Sharetakers, a male, and swap with him. Then you can come back to finish what we started."

Teresa was surprised at how easily she found a Sharetaker willing to do the job. She came back in another male form, but found it difficult to get herself aroused by her own naked body beneath her. But Rhys helped, using her fingers to fondle and knead until the strange male penis bounced erect. His actions bordered on impatience, until they made love again. . . .

Teresa recognized the sketch in the artists' bazaar before Garth recognized her. She had gone out to purchase supplies for the Sharetakers, and enjoyed her day away from the togetherments, out in the sunshine. Wearing the body of a tired, middle-aged woman, she detoured through the marketplace.

With an intent and wistful expression, the blond artist worked on his portrait, drawing the details vividly from his memory. The eyes were perfect, the short brown hair, the narrow chin, facial features showing more beauty than Teresa had ever known she possessed.

"Garth, that's me!" Her heart swelled.

He looked up, not placing her at first. "Teresa?" He lurched to his feet. "Teresa! Oh, how I've missed you!"

They hugged. "I wanted to see you, too, Garth, but I've been so busy with the Sharetakers, my new friends." She told him all about Rhys and how she had been welcomed by the like-minded members of the community.

He asked her to sit across from him while they talked. He stared at her new features, effortlessly reproducing them on a new sheet of sketch paper. Teresa leaned forward to watch, amazed. Somehow, Garth managed to capture the look of the new woman, yet retained a compelling halo that made it intuitively obvious that the portraits showed the same *person*.

"What happened to your home-body, Teresa?"

Her shrug was a bit too quick and dismissive. "It's still at the togetherments. I can have it back whenever I need it."

He lined up the two drawn faces, the lovingly detailed portrait of her original features and the quick study of her current body. "I'll clean this other one up later, mount them side by side." His eyes flashed with a sudden idea. "You have to come see me whenever you change bodies. I can do a whole series of these, portrait after portrait. I'll call it *The Spectrum of Teresa*."

She laughed, then blushed. "Oh, maybe not *every* time I hopscotch, Garth, because I don't know if Rhys would let me out that often." Noticing the time, she squeezed his arm and stood to leave. "But it'll give me an excuse to come and see you."

14

New sights, new sounds, new experiences. Whenever Garth scraped up a few extra credits, he tried an unusual restaurant with brand-new flavors and spices. *Inspiration.*

He'd sold one of his paintings today, a watercolor rendering of clouds drifting over the building tops. He had struck up a conversation with a middle-aged woman—actually an old matron who'd swapped bodies with her fortyish daughter for the day—and the lonely woman had talked with Garth for an hour, chatting about odds and ends in her life while he continued to sketch. Afterward, she'd bought a painting and taken it home with her groceries.

Garth decided to spend his unexpected windfall on a lavish dinner in a tantalizing and exotic Moroccan restaurant. Eduard was still in the hospital, recovering from his voluntary surgery-swap, but Garth wished he could afford to bring Teresa with him, at least. Instead, he had to enjoy the experience alone.

When he passed through the keyhole archway, the smells of mysterious spices wafted toward him, saffron, cumin, preserved lemons, cinnamon, and honey. With an artist's eye, he studied the tile mosaic embedded like a stone rug in the entryway.

A leathery-faced man with short dark hair tucked under a crimson fez greeted him. He wore a billowy brown-and-cream-striped djellaba, the pointed hood dangling between his shoulders. The man bowed and ushered him inside.

Strange, unmelodic music played from automatic synthesizers. The dining room was dim and voluminous, with cloth draped tentlike from the ceiling. Stuffed leather hassocks snuggled against tables barely high enough for Garth to fit his knees under them. A dozen other customers sat engrossed in their meals.

The waiter handed him a menu covered with Arabic scribbles and high prices. Garth couldn't understand a word of it, until he found a touch-spot on the corner, and the letters toggled from Arabic to French, English, German, Japanese, then around again. The waiter returned with a basin and an urn of warm water, which he sprinkled over Garth's hands to cleanse them. Garth wiped his fingers on a plush towel, then he draped it over his lap.

On his small sketchpad, he began to record labyrinthine calligraphy from the walls, stylized verses from the Koran, intricate geometries, marvelous mazes and curlicues. Garth wanted to incorporate them into his work.

The waiter offered Garth freshly baked flat bread, which he dipped into a small bowl of spicy lentil soup. At first he looked around for utensils, but the waiter explained that he must eat with his hands (most definitely not the way Soft Stone had taught him manners!).

Garth chose a sampler of chicken with onions and lemon, lamb with honey and almonds, and a piquant Moroccan stew. The lamb and chicken were delicious, seasoned unlike anything he had tasted before. When he used the bread to scoop out a mouthful of the Moroccan stew, the spices nearly set his mouth on fire. He gasped, his eyes watering as he gulped his water then sucked on a lemon wedge.

Seeing his reaction, the waiter smiled at him. "But does it *taste* good, sir?"

Once the storm in his mouth died down, Garth paid attention to the flavors. "Yes. I am intensely surprised and satisfied with everything."

When he finished his meal, the music from the wall speakers grew louder. Licking lemon and honey from his fingers, Garth leaned against the cushion to observe.

With a surge of sound, a beautiful woman glided through the dangling beads as if she were emerging from a waterfall. She was clad in bangles and artificial silks, her eyes heavy with makeup, her fingers clashing tiny cymbals. She then began to dance with the most lissome, flowing movement he had ever witnessed.

The dancer twirled, her hips oscillating; her mane of dark hair swung wildly, caught up in scarves. She began to remove the scarves one by one, holding them in her hands like peacock feathers. Her eyes sparkled, her scarlet lips parting as she gasped quick energetic breaths.

The belly dancer eased closer to the tables, stretching out her hands, beckoning for volunteers. The other patrons continued their own conversations. Garth's heart jolted. Although his initial reaction was to shy away, he had come here to *experience*. The dancer spun like an exotic ballerina, tapping her heel to her opposite shin, catching the enthusiasm in Garth's eye. She reached out to take his fingers and drew him to his feet. The other customers looked relieved that she had chosen a different victim.

Garth glided onto the floor, fascinated. Her skin was warm to the touch as she put her hands on his hips and demonstrated how to move. He watched her muscles, noted the sweat on her forehead and neck. She lived within the dance, her mind and body focused on whirling, following the music, swept along. He tried to dance the way she did, but his spine just wouldn't bend like that, and his hips didn't have the flexibility.

"Let me hopscotch with you," Garth said, leaning

closer. "I want to feel it as you do. I want to dance like you."

She looked at him skeptically, as if doubting his sincerity. But he needed to *know* what she was like, needed to experience it. In his mind he estimated the cost of his meal, subtracted it from the amount he'd received from selling his painting, then offered her every penny of the remainder. "For fifteen minutes, that's all."

She smiled at him, still surprised. "All right, mister." She arched her eyebrows. "But just because you take my body doesn't mean you'll know how to dance."

She looked at his eyes, reached up to ruffle his blond hair. He touched hers, twining his fingers into the raven locks where only a single green scarf remained. Their eyes met, separated by inches. His thoughts flowed outward, drifted, detached... and suddenly he was behind her eyes, inside her mind.

And her body felt wonderful!

His arms were like violin strings, his legs and hips simmered with energy, skin moist with sweat, hot with strength and balance. He swayed... but he looked down to see the abdomen moving awkwardly, the waist not bowing to the rhythm of the music the way his imagination guided it.

Standing in his own muscular physique, the dancer laughed at Garth. "A lot of it's in your mind, mister. Your mind has to learn to *direct* your body. You can't just swap with me and become an expert belly dancer." Her eyes flashed. "But you have the potential now. The body remembers. It knows how to respond, if *you* know how to tell it what to do."

The other customers watched Garth's blond body dressed in casual clothes now dancing with a slender grace. Most of them quickly figured out what must have occurred, and they looked at the belly dancer, amused at

Garth's attempts to make the same moves in an unaccustomed body.

"Relax, mister." She placed her male hands on Garth's female hips and showed him how to dance. "Forget your inhibitions." This time the body moved more freely. He spun around but only grew dizzy. One of the other customers chuckled, but he didn't care.

The music reached a crescendo. Both of their bodies shook and swirled, and Garth rapidly improved. This female body *did* know what to do. Her reflexes responded the way he pictured them, without the encumbrances of his own untrained musculature.

The fifteen minutes flew by. As he lived inside the dancer's body, there wasn't time to absorb all the astonishing details. Rarely had he seen and done so many memorable things in a single evening.

Filled with enthusiasm, Garth wanted to hurry back to his studio where he could capture everything in his mind. He nearly ran out of the restaurant—until the dancer called after him in his own voice, reminding him that he had to hopscotch back with her, and pay for her and the meal, before he could go home.

15

Nightmares later, Eduard swam back to consciousness. Light fell through his slitted eyelids and into his weary, old-woman's eyes. His brain couldn't think. Cottony clouds in his mind surrounded every word, every memory. His body was now one constant scream of pain, louder than ever before.

How he longed for his own body back.

He managed to focus on the tubes and electronic monitors hooked up to him, then people standing at his bedside. His discomfort ranged from low moans in his arms and muscles, to a shout where the open chest wound had been sutured back together. His heart felt different. Repaired, yes—but battered into submission, not as good as new.

Then he recognized his home-body pacing at the foot of the bed . . . and a dark uniform at the back of the room. One of the Beetles, an Inspector, a man with black hair and almond eyes. Daragon!

Eduard's throat was dry, his vocal cords raspy and uncooperative from the heavy anesthetic as well as the weariness of Ruxton's innumerable years. "What . . . why are you here?" They hadn't seen each other in a long time.

"Just keeping an eye on my friends." Daragon smiled down at him, resplendent in his BTL regalia. "COM found your name on this contract when the records were filed, and I just wanted to make sure nothing...*accidentally* happened during your surgery." He glanced over at the crowd of lawyers, family members.

"Am I...was the surgery successful?" Eduard tried to raise himself up, but his arms felt like wet balsa wood. In his own body, Madame Ruxton stood with shoulders thrown back, arrogant head held high.

Daragon bent closer. "Oh, yes. I spoke to the doctors immediately before they operated on you. We encouraged them to make sure you pulled through." He looked once more at the Ruxton cadre, all of whom regarded him warily in return. "I'm confident your recovery will be a swift one."

"Thank you, Daragon," Eduard rasped through the old woman's wattled throat. "It's good to see you again."

On the day the doctors said Eduard was strong enough to sit in a hoverchair, Daragon returned to push him out of the room. He brought seven impressive-looking BTL officers with him. Forming a grim protective barrier, the Beetles escorted him down the corridors to where Ruxton's lawyers waited.

The old woman's attorneys already had more documents drawn up, but Daragon opened the conversation by saying, "It has been four weeks, as stipulated in his contract. The doctors expect a full and complete recovery. Eduard has done his part."

"I'm afraid my body's not yet entirely recovered," Madame Ruxton said, sitting imperiously in Eduard's form, drinking sweetened tea. In his hoverchair, Eduard wrinkled his nose. Personally, he despised sweetened tea.

One of the lawyers held forth a document. "We have here depositions from the medical professionals who have inspected the body. It still has severe liver problems, as well as the potential for total kidney failure within the next year. The pulmonary system remains at greatly diminished capacity."

Another attorney shuffled papers, found the original contract. "Mr. Swan signed a contract that specifically requires him to remain in Madame Ruxton's former body until *full recovery.*" The man gestured with a clean, manicured hand. "I'm afraid that what we have here is not 'full recovery,' by any stretch of the imagination."

Another smiling attorney looked at Daragon and the other Beetles, pretending not to be intimidated. "Several times we suggested that Eduard obtain his own legal counsel, but he refused."

Eduard felt cold inside, wondering if Ruxton's cronies had managed to outwit him. He had blustered through with arrogance and misguided pride. If the words in the contract did indeed require "full recovery," then he was lost. He had been trapped by his own naïveté. "I guess that was stupid," he muttered.

"Yes, Eduard," Daragon said. "I believe it was." He calmly turned toward the lawyer. "That's not acceptable, obviously beyond the intent of the original contract." The Beetles drew together around him, flanking Eduard in the hoverchair.

Ruxton's lawyers crossed their arms over their chests in unison, as if it were some sort of choreographed act. "We have the resources to tie this up in litigation for years, if necessary. Either way, Madame Ruxton will win."

"And the BTL has the power to impound all of Madame Ruxton's assets in anticipation of our eventual victory. I can cite numerous precedents," Daragon countered, remembering everything Mordecai Ob had taught him. "You'll swap back now."

Eduard didn't have the strength to move or even speak for himself. Daragon nudged the floating life-support chair forward. Madame Ruxton didn't move.

Daragon withdrew a spray vial from a pouch at his belt. "You've heard of Scramble? A drug that breaks down all your barriers and allows someone to swap with you, no matter how much you resist."

"Yes, I know. The BIE uses it for executions."

"Or we use it for situations like this." After a deliberate pause, Daragon smiled at her, still holding the spray vial. "I'm willing to take that action right now. It'll let Eduard rip your soul right out of his body and put it back where it belongs."

Finally Madame Ruxton whirled, staring down at her own weakened body in the hoverchair. Her appearance was completely uncharacteristic of Eduard's usual happy-go-lucky demeanor. "What've you paid them? I can double whatever you offered. What kind of pull do you have with the Bureau?"

Eduard just shrugged his bony shoulders.

She snapped at Daragon and all the other Beetles. "I'll pay you twice what he's paying you. Right now, in cash."

"Twice nothing is still nothing." Daragon's voice was all the more threatening for its bland tone. "And attempted bribery of a BTL officer is an actionable offense. We have a room full of witnesses. Shall I take you into custody now?"

One of the lawyers leaned close to her. "I'm afraid that was very unwise, Madame Ruxton."

"If you swap immediately with Eduard, perhaps we can...forget the entire matter." The other Beetles pressed closer.

Her teeth clenched, her eyes flashing behind Eduard's familiar face, Ruxton sighed with such vehemence that she spat out her breath. "Oh, very well!"

She leaned down to the hoverchair and touched her own temples. Looking up at her with weak eyes, Eduard felt as if she ripped his consciousness free and slammed it back into his own body.

The real Madame Ruxton sulked back into her hoverchair-bound form.

Eduard reeled, disoriented to be young and healthy and energetic again. Each breath seemed like liquid honey in his lungs. His muscles tingled, so alive again.

The attorneys nudged the old woman's life-support chair away as her family members followed, simpering...perhaps even delighted at what had happened, now that their inheritance was one step closer again. The lawyers tried to make excuses as Madame Ruxton railed at them.

Daragon gestured for the other Beetles to leave him with Eduard. Once they were alone, though, Daragon's stony face tightened into a scowl, then a wry half-smile. "That wasn't the brightest thing you've ever done, Eduard."

Eduard did not even try to excuse his mistake; he hung his head with an abashed smile. "I assumed I knew what could happen, but I didn't imagine half of the contingencies. Guess I was clueless."

"You were out of your league. Far beyond anything you ever learned from the Splinters. You're not living in a monastery anymore, and the real world is not like the Falling Leaves."

"I know that. Too well." Eduard sighed, but his healthy body felt so good he could not remain dejected for long. A goofy grin crossed his face. "I'm glad I could count on you." He playfully punched Daragon on the shoulder, unable to contain his relief and his energy. "It's so good to see you again!"

Daragon frowned with an almost motherly concern for his estranged friend. "I may have been gone a year,

Eduard, but I've tried to keep tabs on you and Garth and Teresa. You worry me the most, though—as usual. Impulsive, cocky, reckless. Is this really the way you want to live?"

Eduard drew a deep breath, unable to stop grinning. He traced a finger over the ghost pain in his chest from where the old woman's operation scars had been. "Daragon, you're all nice and cozy with the Bureau, all your needs taken care of. I'm on my own out here—do you know how much Ruxton paid me for that? I can live for a year on those credits!"

"You almost didn't live for a day. Her lawyers had already tried to pay off the doctors, even before your surgery."

Eduard digested that for a moment, experiencing a seesaw of anger, fear, and disgust. "Don't think I'm not grateful. I owe you one." He pursed his lips, thinking. "Yeah, I'll have to be more careful next time."

"Next time? Are you sure you want to do something like this again?" Daragon just shook his head. "Remember when you told me how you wanted to become a Phantom, how you wanted to live forever?"

Eduard smiled with the recollection. "Still sounds good to me."

"Risking your life like that, Eduard, you can forget immortality—you'll never make it to twenty-five!"

Eduard rubbed his chest again, then reached out to hug his friend, but the uniform seemed to be a barrier between them. "Thanks anyway, Daragon. I mean it. Are you going to be able to see us more often now?"

"I'm with the BTL, so you never know when I might be watching." Daragon said a brief, brusque farewell and left to rejoin the other Beetles.

16

When joining the Sharetakers, Teresa was asked to donate all her worldly possessions—which, in her case, were little enough. Happy with her new sensation of total belonging, she presented Rhys with the credits remaining from her Falling Leaves stipend, plus a little of the money Eduard had given her from one of his body-trade jobs.

Each month Rhys leveraged the Sharetakers' assets to purchase larger and larger sections of their building. Under his guidance, the size of their "togetherment" increased. From talking with him in private, Teresa knew the (usually) redheaded man had dreams of eventually commanding the whole building as his fortress. He was very goal-oriented, a good thing for the leader of so many people.

Today Teresa knelt on the floor using a pointed sledgehammer to pound out the separating wallboard. Her arms ached from the constant effort. Rhys would probably ask her to hopscotch into a fresh, rested body so she could finish the job. She didn't mind. It made her happy to feel so useful.

Finally, she broke through into the adjacent two-room condominium newly annexed to the togetherment. After ripping out the walls, the Sharetakers would add firepoles for fun sliding down to other levels and new lifters to take them up through the ceilings. They installed new light tiles to eliminate any concealing shadows. Rhys insisted that there be no private places, because "hiding" ran contrary to the Sharetaker philosophy of openness.

Oddly, the enclave held no COM terminals at all, unlike most dwellings Teresa had ever seen. When she asked him about it, Rhys had glared. "Sharetakers want no interference from a Big Brother network. We create our own universe."

Teresa went through a dizzying succession of bodies. At times it gave her a disjointed feeling to see her familiar body doing tasks that she was not aware of, while she was stuck in a different form on a manual-labor assignment. It was like a shell game with human forms, and she never knew at any given time who was wearing a specific body. She often had to be reminded to synch her ID patch immediately after a swap.

But she had also heard about the dangers of too much hopscotching, the minuscule but not nonexistent danger each time a person detached herself and relocated into a new brain. Finally she asked one of her coworkers, "Aren't you worried about slippage? I mean, with all the hopscotching we do, there's always a chance one of us will get... *lost,* don't you think? I've read COM reports—"

"Rhys says we shouldn't be concerned about it," the coworker said, and that ended the discussion.

More than any other assignment, Teresa enjoyed working in the rooftop gardens, growing fresh food in the high-density agricultural area. She could smell the plants, listen to breezes rustling leaves together. It reminded her of the most peaceful times in the monastery, and she felt content.

Teresa carried heavy bags of chemical fertilizers and mulch; she bent over for hours, straining among bean plants to pluck the camouflaged pods. Her body's shoulders ached, her back hurt. After picking a basket of beans and selecting two perfect zucchinis, she went over to study the ornamental zinnias and asters, grown without genetic modification.

She took a deep breath, sniffing their mingled perfumes. She had been working constantly since dawn, and it was now late afternoon. Her borrowed body was bone weary, her skin was raw from dried salty sweat and sunburn.

After smelling the flowers, Teresa turned around to see Rhys standing there, regarding her. In a low, husky voice he said, "You've been very productive today, Teresa. It's time for your reward. Let's find you another body so that we can make love." His eyes sparkled with an animal intensity.

But Teresa was so tired that she didn't want to do anything but shower and sleep. "Oh, can't you find someone else, Rhys? It's been a long time since I had even an hour to myself."

"I thought you'd be pleased that I've gone out of my way to choose you for sex." He frowned at her, and she could feel his disappointment like a crushing weight. "It's all about *sharing,* Teresa. I don't ask too much, do I? Just get a fresh body. You'll feel better." He turned away, expecting her to follow.

She bit her lip, thinking it wasn't really fair for her to trade out of this exhausted form into someone else. Weighed down by the scorn in his voice, Teresa did as she was told.

Back inside the building, Rhys selected the body that most interested him and commanded Teresa to hopscotch with her. The other woman willingly did as she was told, no questions asked. It seemed important to him that he knew it was *Teresa,* regardless of what body she brought to him.

Teresa swapped without thinking, a completely natural process now, though she remembered how difficult it had been the first time. Following Rhys, knowing something was wrong, Teresa focused on more pleasant memories.

After Soft Stone had uploaded herself into COM, the Splinter monks who took over Teresa's mental instruction were clumsy and unimaginative, repeating rote lessons without engaging her intellect. Garth and Eduard did no better.

Alone, Teresa found the most peace and concentration out in the monastery's garden. She worked there even when she wasn't assigned the duties; dour old Hickory seemed perfectly glad to leave her to it. She stared at the plants, but her mind drifted far away, as if she could let it detach itself and travel elsewhere.

Once she, Garth, and Eduard proved themselves capable of swapping bodies, the Splinter monks would consider them adults, and the three of them would be sent out into the world. Daragon was already gone, as was Garth's friend Pashnak, who had loved to read stories aloud. Of the three remaining companions, Teresa was best at introspection. She knew she could figure out the technique of hopscotching, then she could show Garth and Eduard, since they already had a rapport so close it seemed to border on telepathy.

Working in the monastery garden, Teresa felt the warm sun on her back and tried to imagine what it would be like if she could work in another, stronger body. External appearances wouldn't matter—male or female, old or young, large or small, weak or strong—because it would still be *her* inside, her essence, her spirit.

She parted the velvety leaves and plucked a ripe

tomato, feeling the stem snap free along an invisible but natural line. She focused on the tomato as it came loose—and felt a similar snap in her mind, as if something inside her were also ready to separate. Her vision reeled, and she blinked several times. She picked up the tomato. The stem was broken on top, severed cleanly. Teresa let her mind open, let her thoughts flow and wander . . . and *separate*.

No one else was with her in the garden, so she couldn't test her attempt to hopscotch, but she felt the change, the realization. She *knew* she could swap her mind. Leaving the rest of the tomatoes behind, unpicked, Teresa ran back to find Garth and Eduard. . . .

Taking them by the arms, she led them into the basement to the forgotten storeroom where Garth had once painted his mural. The soft glowplates shone on the brick walls, illuminating ghosts of Garth's painstakingly drawn scene, barely visible behind the beige mask. Here they would be left alone for as many hours as it might take.

"If we all learn this at the same time, then we can leave the monastery together." Her face was happy, her eyes warm with excitement. Teresa gave a sad smile. "I don't want to lose you two, like Daragon." She closed her eyes and reached out with both hands, one touching blond Garth, the other touching dark-haired Eduard.

"This is going to be strange, at first, I think." Her voice was husky with fear and uncertainty. "Here, let me teach you."

Later, Garth stood naked in Eduard's body, staring at himself, at his two friends who appeared the same to him, but different behind their eyes. The three of them had spent their lives leaning on each other; they had learned to depend on their mutual skills. Teresa loved Garth and Eduard wholeheartedly and equally.

And this was so much more. Now they were thrust

together in an entirely different way. They *were* each other.

Garth flexed Eduard's wiry arms, blinked his eyes. "This feels weird, familiar but...not. I'm stronger in some ways, unsteady in others. I—"

Standing inside Teresa's female body, Eduard kept touching his skin, running his palms over his new breasts, tweaking his nipples. "Wait until you try this, Garth. She's got nerve clusters all over her body!" He stroked the patch of hair between his legs, startling himself. "It feels tingly in places that were never sensitive before. And empty in others."

Teresa wore Garth's home-body like a baggy uniform. "It's like I'm in a big suit of armor." She touched her rough face, fondled her new penis, which seemed to have a mind of its own and defied conscious muscle control. "And this—it's like an appendage, but I can't do anything with it."

"Yes you can," Eduard said with a sly grin on her face. "I think you'll figure it out."

A look of consternation filled Garth's face, a puzzled expression that was very much like Teresa. "But it doesn't move like any of my other body parts. I can't control the reactions—oh!" Garth and Eduard both laughed.

"I never thought it'd be this strange," Teresa said, listening to the deeper voice in her head, touching the male muscles, the fine curly hair on her chest. "So many things are the same, fundamentally equal, whether I'm in my own body, or Garth's. But it's different, too."

"Not so different," Eduard said. "It's what you do with the body that matters." He looked at Garth through Teresa's eyes, while Teresa looked down at her own hands, at Garth's hands.

"Then let's...*do* something," Garth said, using Eduard's vocal cords.

They began to explore each other in new ways. Three people, three different bodies. The Splinters had been frank with their sexual explanations. Their young wards, Teresa included, had experimented, more out of curiosity than passion. But never like this.

The boundaries between friendship and sexual love and physical differences blurred, then vanished. Their shadows merged on the walls, becoming indistinguishable. It was a strange and wondrous sacrament, the three of them *being* in their friends' bodies, looking at each other through new eyes.

Eduard made love to Garth, who was in Teresa's home-body, while Teresa herself stood by, wearing the blond-haired male form she had known as Garth all her life. Suddenly, they were inexperienced again, embarrassingly so. But they experimented without shame.

They swapped again. And again.

Teresa coached Garth and Eduard, instructing them in techniques and responses she had learned by exploring her own body. She helped, she touched, she participated.

In a woman's body now, Garth was uncertain, but curious, trying to cope with a radically altered perspective. Making love to a man, he had to be aroused by a man, though he had never thought in such a way before. The mind had to adjust to a new reality, while the body's hormones and natural responses remained the same, assisting.

This was *Eduard*, his friend, his comrade...but when Teresa (in what had been his own body) helped him to touch the ultrasensitive areas on his breasts, his skin, his clitoris—a vastly new sensation—he began to understand what he needed to do. The sensations became overwhelming. The physical body knew what to do, and did it well....

When Eduard was finished, Garth came forward in

Teresa's body, sweating and drained but tingling all over. He gracefully touched what had once been his own buttocks, the backs of his thighs. "Here, Teresa, let me show you something. I know you'll like this. . . ."

The monks had no idea where to find them, and the three had hours to talk with each other, touch each other, swap again and again. They described and demonstrated the way their own bodies worked.

The lovemaking was satisfying, and erotic, and exhausting—but in the end they realized that for such deep friends, the very act of hopscotching into each other's bodies was vastly more intimate than sex. . . .

Now, among the Sharetakers, Rhys made love to her in an open room with others watching. He seemed even more anxious than usual, and Teresa held him and tried to respond.

But it was very different.

17

Garth decided that sitting in a street market with other amateurs and hobbyists would never bring serious attention to his paintings. It was time to make sacrifices for his art, and only a serious investment would kick him up to the next level.

He had sold a few sketches (as had everyone else in the market) when buyers for a new office complex came by in search of inexpensive decorations for a massive number of rooms. Using the money, as well as a generous gift Eduard had given him after surviving Madame Ruxton's surgery, he paid three days' rent for a small place at street level—his own personal "gallery"—then he quit his dead-end job as an industrial painter.

All or nothing.

In a spectacular "coming out" for himself, he would display the paintings and sketches he had done, just like a genuine, dedicated artist. It was the only way to broaden his audience. He had to take a chance.

In preparation, Garth spent four days working furiously in the bazaar. He had drunk great pots of the portly vendor's strongest gourmet coffee just to keep himself awake, to focus his intensity. Some artists watched his verve with a mixture of amazement and jealousy as he produced work after work to fill out his planned exhibition.

Now, inside his makeshift gallery he arranged everything with loving care, from the smallest pieces to the largest rolled film-murals. He posted invitations, sent mailings over COM, and talked to everyone who would listen. They had to come and see.

As the hour for the evening event finally arrived, Garth lit candles, set up light tiles, and burned incense. He put everything into this free exhibition. Even exhausted, Garth remained eager and exuberant about the possibilities. He flung open the door in his rented shop space and waited for the crowds to come.

Garth had promoted his exhibition at Club Masquerade, talking to the cybernetic bartender, Bernard Rovin. But even with elaborate notices for the discriminating patrons of the Club, Garth had no idea what to expect.

Apparently nothing.

Multicolored product advertisements glowed from skyscraper walls. People moved on the streets, some going home after a long workday, others coming out for the night. An endless jeweled necklace of hovercars floated overhead.

Garth glanced at his watch and stood smiling in the entryway. He greeted the passersby. He looked up and down the street, but saw no crowds, no people coming to his show. Not the slightest glimmer of interest. He waited and watched, trying to keep a pleading expression from his face. His art remained on display inside, though no one came to see it.

After an hour, when even Garth's enthusiasm had begun to flag, a woman came inside, smiling shyly. She had drooping shoulders and sad eyes, but he greeted her warmly. "Welcome! I hope you'll see something you'll like."

"I already do, Garth." She came forward and hugged him. "It's me—Teresa. I wouldn't miss this for the world."

"What's this body?" Surprised, he ran his fingers

through her short, mousy-brown hair. "I didn't recognize you."

"Oh, it's just the person I'm wearing today. What does it matter, anyway? We're all human, right?"

"Now I'm going to have to add another portrait to my *Spectrum of Teresa*."

"Take a good look at my face, because I probably won't be wearing it for long." She walked in toward the art on display. "Show me what you've done."

"Is there room for one more?" Garth turned, recognizing Eduard instantly. For once, his friend wasn't wearing a sickly or damaged body, but remained in his own healthy dark-haired form. He clapped Garth on the back.

"Eduard! It's good to see you looking like yourself again," Garth said.

Teresa gave him a warm kiss on the cheek, and Eduard kissed her back on the mouth. He was surprised when she didn't giggle, but drew away instead. Garth wondered what was wrong, what she was hiding.

Enthusiastic just to have his friends there, Garth took them by the arms and led them into the small shop. "Let me show you around the exhibit. It's a new concept, I think. I'm calling it a 'panorama surround' of my impressions. You'll be the first ones to see it." Garth seemed ready to burst with pleasure. "My intention is to capture the real experience of being at the market . . . the gestalt of the bazaar. You have to see it with all your senses, not just your eyes."

On the walls his sketches and watercolors hung askew, a disarray to convey the energy and color of the marketplace. He displayed caricatures of different vendors, interesting personalities he saw every day: the portly man selling coffee, the woman fashioning her clay wind chimes, the beignet maker with his pans of hot oil and a comical dusting of powdered sugar on his nose.

Various customers were preserved, as well: an old

couple wearing young bodies, a frowning critic, young
children playing by food kiosks, curious businessmen
who looked but did not buy.

In the rear of the display, and very understated, he
even depicted a news-screen that showed the execution
of the anti-COM terrorist, though he had been reluctant
and uneasy about including the image. The decrepit old
man hooked up to electrodes, unwillingly having his
mind uploaded ... Garth found the image very powerful
and didn't want it to dominate the show.

Snippets of sound flooded the air, the buzzing chaos
of the market, people laughing, arguing, discussing artwork for sale. Garth had surreptitiously recorded one
interminable haggle at a nearby stand, and it played
now, over and over, never ending. He had also captured
the smells of hot pavement, frying meat, paint, even sun-
warmed canvas awnings.

Eduard startled him by laughing as he turned
around. "Garth, this is amazing. It gives the impression
that you're really there!"

In other alcoves he displayed nostalgic paintings like
the one he had done on the basement wall in the
monastery, Dickensian scenes peopled with characters
from his imagination, a mishmash of historical settings
with anachronistic details he didn't even realize were
wrong. He also displayed the three faces of Teresa he
had drawn, showing her in different bodies but with the
same inner beauty. Now, seeing her again, he would add
another.

"Oh, I love it, Garth," Teresa said. "I'm so proud of
you."

"I'd be happier if there were some other people to
see it."

Over the course of the next three hours, a few other
people trickled in, mostly curiosity seekers, spectators
rather than customers. But he was just glad they had

come at all. They poked around, talked to each other; a
few shook his hand and uttered compliments.

Garth's energy did not flag. With Teresa and Eduard
beside him, he felt as if he could go on for hours. He
showed everyone around, spoke with great delight about
what he had done, pointing out separate items of interest.

At last, near the closing hour, a gaunt young man
came in, the first one who looked as if he had come there
specifically to see what Garth had to offer, rather than a
bored curiosity-seeker. He offered frequent, brief smiles,
so that his lips curved upward with a flickering motion.
His hair was blond with brownish highlights, making it
look prematurely gray.

The stranger came toward Garth and shook his
hand. While other visitors had shown polite interest,
this young man pulled him along, eager to see one thing
and then the next. "Don't you remember me, Garth? I'm
Pashnak Swan."

Garth exclaimed and grabbed the man's hand again,
remembering how he had read to Pashnak and Daragon
from Charles Dickens back at the monastery. "I'm so
glad you could come! How have you been? Did you ever
finish reading *Copperfield*?"

Sitting in a window alcove in the Falling Leaves,
Garth would open his heavy antique tome and read
aloud one deliciously detailed chapter after another. Both
Pashnak and Daragon sat cross-legged on their own floor
cushions, enraptured with the story and with the company. Garth would change his voice to imitate the various characters. Pashnak and Daragon watched him,
savoring Dickens's descriptions, the ironies, the exotic
people. But Pashnak had reached his maturity, learned
how to hopscotch, and left the Splinters before Garth
had finished reading the massive and complex novel.

"No . . . I never got around to it, Garth. It just never
seemed the same." Pashnak smiled, changing the sub-

ject. "I've seen your work in the bazaar, and I'm glad you finally had this opportunity to have it displayed for the general public. Quite a step up."

Garth flushed. "Well, it's not a real gallery, but still better than a blanket in the marketplace, I think."

They talked about some of the sketches, charcoal drawings of people in their artists' stalls, pencil renderings of children flying kites in the parks. Garth's exuberance grew with every breath. Pashnak seemed to understand, seemed to see what Garth intended.

The nostalgic paintings caught Pashnak's attention. "These look like something Charles Dickens might have written about." Garth felt warm inside.

The gaunt young man stopped in front of a detailed study of a smiling young rogue in nineteenth-century clothing; he wore an infectious smile, extending his hand in a gesture of trust, while hiding the other, ready to snatch an unwatched apple from a vendor's cart. The rogue looked vaguely like Eduard. . . .

Garth had worked for many hours on that simple, unframed item—and Pashnak had spotted it right away among all the other art on display. "The Artful Dodger, of course?" Pashnak's eyes were wide and pleading. "I'd love to own it . . . but I was reluctant even to come here. I don't have much money, you see. The Splinters didn't really prepare me for a high-paying job."

Eduard laughed and draped his arm over Teresa's bowed shoulders. "Don't we all know that!"

Desperate to make a sale, Garth very much wanted Pashnak to own the Artful Dodger drawing. He quoted a price that even Pashnak knew was far too low, and not quite as much as the gaunt young man could afford. Pashnak paid him a little more, and once the deal was consummated, the two men pumped each other's hands so hard their lower arms seemed likely to fall off.

Pashnak left the exhibition, cradling the drawing as

if it were his most prized possession in the world. It was the only sale Garth had made all night.

"We can stay to help you clean up, Garth," Teresa offered, as if reluctant to go back to the Sharetakers' enclave.

"Sure, why not?" Eduard said. He had plenty of free time between jobs.

They worked with Garth to sweep the floors and polish the shelves, but he wanted to take the art down himself. Garth had to be out immediately, because he couldn't afford another day's rent.

As they stood at the door and Garth prepared to lock up, they said awkward goodbyes. "Oh, I'm glad we had a chance to talk, the three of us together," Teresa said. "A consolation for not having big crowds."

"That's one way of looking at it," Garth said with a wan smile. Teresa and Eduard went off together down the sidewalk, and he stayed behind in the hollow remains of his exhibition.

Before he closed the doors, though, two other men appeared, startling him. "Daragon!" Garth's instinctive uneasiness at seeing the BTL uniform changed to delight. "Oh, look at you, so professional. I'm glad you could come! You, uh, missed the big crowd."

Daragon smiled knowingly at him. "There were no crowds, Garth—but I did bring my boss, Bureau Chief Ob. He wanted to see your exhibition."

He introduced the well-muscled man beside him, who wore a precisely tailored business suit; his chestnut hair was neatly combed, his olive-brown eyes intense with interest. "You won't remember me, Garth, but I saw your work in the bazaar."

Garth nodded, shaking the Bureau Chief's hand. "I remember. But you were wearing a different body then, weren't you?" He recalled a smaller, dark-haired man with sunken eyes and a bushy mustache.

"Ah, that was my personal trainer's body."

Ob looked troubled for a moment, but Garth didn't notice, saying quickly, "You told me I had the right amount of enthusiasm, but that I needed more practice. You even knew who I was."

"I was curious about Daragon's friends." Ob began to stroll through the artwork on display. "As I said, when I was younger I dreamed of becoming an artist, but I never had the nerve to slog through all the pitfalls. In a way, you've got the balls to do what I couldn't."

Garth hovered beside the Bureau Chief as he bent close to the three aligned portraits of Teresa's various faces. "And what is that?"

"You were willing to make sacrifices for your dream, young man. I never had the heart to suffer through the 'starving artist' uncertainty." Ob's voice sounded somewhat wistful. "I can see a great deal of improvement here, Garth. Hmmm, very interesting. Now you're making me regret my decision."

Daragon interrupted him. "Sir, I think you made the right choice. Look at how much you've done with the Bureau, all the important work."

"Not a valid comparison, Daragon," Ob said. "I'm talking about *heart,* not logic."

Garth led them to some of his other works, feeling oddly inadequate. "I'm not exactly starving...."

"*Yet.*" The Bureau Chief pursed his lips appreciatively at a crystal-sharp pen-and-ink drawing of the coffee vendor surrounded by rough charcoal blurs of customers. "I've had Daragon investigate a bit. I know you quit your job as an industrial painter, and according to COM records as of five minutes ago, you made only one very small sale all night."

Garth flushed. "I'll get by, somehow. I get help from my friends."

Ob placed his hands on Garth's shoulders in a magnanimous gesture. "I think we can do better than that. In my position, as you might guess, I am in possession of considerable wealth—but my BTL duties give me little chance to enjoy it. That seems ... offensively worthless, in a way. I've been thinking that perhaps I can do some small amount of cultural good if I make it possible for an artist to do better work."

Daragon's face glowed with pleasure. Garth looked from the Bureau Chief to the artworks on display. "Are you going to buy one of my paintings?"

"I am going to offer you a personal grant, young man. Call it a stipend, enough to let you pursue your dreams for a year, if you live frugally."

"The Splinters taught us how to be frugal, sir," Daragon said quickly.

Garth didn't know what to say. The Chief of the BTL wanted to give him money so he could keep working on his art? "You want to be my ... patron?" It sounded so old-fashioned.

"I expect you to learn things, expand your horizons, and apply everything to the betterment of your artwork." His olive-brown eyes twinkled. "In my rather large home, I have plenty of wall space to hang your best work, should you ever wish to loan it to me."

Garth felt weak. He wanted to hug Daragon, or Mordecai Ob, but he restrained himself. "This is incredible!"

The Bureau Chief looked smugly pleased with his unexpected generosity. "I just wish someone had done the same for me, back when I was at the fork in my career path." He looked over at the uniformed young Inspector beside him. "Daragon will be watching you for me, Garth. Don't disappoint me."

"Sir, you've just given me all the inspiration I could possibly need."

18

Along with three believers, Teresa took a random assortment of odds and ends to sell, donated items Rhys didn't want to keep (since sentimental objects had no value to the overall community). By liquidating personal items, the Sharetakers could raise cash for the construction materials the enclave needed. Teresa wished she'd had a bit more of her own to sacrifice when she'd joined, but the Splinter monks had provided no luxuries.

She and her companions staked out their usual street corner and spread their wares on blankets and tables. "See these fine necklaces! Beautiful, don't you think?" Teresa lifted one of the prismatic chains to reflect the sunlight. "Good prices here! Grooming kits, collectible dolls, paperweights." She scanned the assortment. "Remote uplinks, personal music libraries, handmade scarves!"

Shoppers, tourists, and businesspeople flowed by, studiously ignoring them.

Teresa raised a pudgy hand to shade her eyes. She wasn't wearing her home-body today—in fact, she hadn't even seen her slender, auburn-haired physique for some time. Now frizzy yellow hair wafted around her eyes, and her plump limbs felt heavy and unresponsive. Since Rhys had sent her out to proselytize, she didn't need strong muscles.

Teresa took her turn speaking to passersby, telling

about their beliefs, about the warm feeling of acceptance and community. As she spoke the words, it felt good to reassure and remind herself. She was proud to be among the Sharetakers. It was the best thing that had ever happened to her. If only other people could open their eyes and their minds, but it was so hard to get the message across. Wasn't anyone else searching for a meaning to life, as she had been? Had they already found their answers, or did they not care about the questions in the first place?

She smiled at a young man who stopped to pick up a portable tattoo imprinter among their wares. He played with it, then shrugged and walked away without once meeting her eyes or asking the cost.

Teresa rubbed her heavy arms. Her swollen feet hurt from standing so long. She appreciated the sacrifice this body's original owner had made, but she hoped she could swap into a healthier body again later, preferably her own.

The day before, when Teresa had asked to get her home-body back, at least for a little while, Rhys was annoyed. "I find this one more attractive today." His sharp eyes cut into her heart. "Don't you want to please me?"

"But it would still be *me* inside—"

"Exactly." He squeezed her shoulder—hard. "It doesn't matter. The body means nothing, Teresa. People are interchangeable. Don't get possessive." He leaned closer, his breath warm on her face. "Aren't you glad I still take you as my lover more often than any other man or woman? I like a little variety—so why can't you wear a different body, if I ask?"

Now, Teresa had no idea who this plump woman had originally been, or who its owner was wearing today. She thought about going to find Garth again, give him another face to draw in his series of portraits. But Rhys probably wouldn't approve of her spending time with her artist friend when there was important Sharetaker work to be done.

Though the commune was a roulette wheel of shifting bodies and interchangeable sex, she had remained Rhys's special partner, as if he owned her. Teresa understood the pressures he faced in the day-to-day operation of their group. The charismatic leader was the glue that held the Sharetakers together, and he did the work in his head, without COM.

"Of course, Rhys."

By the time Teresa and her companions returned to the togetherments, her back and legs were tired and sore—this body was not accustomed to standing in one spot for most of a day. She looked forward to a few hours of rest.

But upon entering the togetherments, she came instead upon a disturbing tableau. Two of the newer members faced Rhys, indignant and defiant, while the redheaded leader stood livid, trying not to listen to them.

"This is a scam!" one female newcomer said. "All you do is exploit people. You take our possessions and make us work the whole day, while you sit back and reap the benefits."

"Your Sharetakers aren't about community and acceptance, Rhys. We share, and you take," the second one growled. "We're leaving before you cause us any more damage."

The first disgruntled believer looked around, calling out. "Don't you see what this guy's doing to you?" She wiped her hands on her pants, as if trying to rid herself of greasy dirt. "Rhys, you're like a tick feeding on an endless supply of blood."

The leader clenched and unclenched his fists. Teresa could see that he was close to the boiling point. Before Rhys could speak, though, Teresa burst out, "How can you say that? We all share here, we all work. When you joined us, you agreed to do the same and—"

"Some people just can't handle it, Teresa," Rhys said, looking in her direction. His voice sounded like rocks rumbling together. "These two came in expecting a free ride, but now we can see *they* don't really belong here."

"Get them out of here!" one of the other Sharetakers said. "We don't need anyone who won't contribute their fair share."

A faint smile flickered on Rhys's face. "They've held back from us since the beginning. I checked on their finances—and these two didn't give everything. They kept a stash in secret COM accounts, hoping we wouldn't catch on."

"That's a lie!" the male newcomer said. "We have nothing left. We believed your promises and platitudes."

Teresa looked at Rhys, growing more and more upset. The Sharetakers based their entire community on trust. She'd given everything she owned, and willingly. It astonished her to think that some of the others might have done less. The gathered believers began to close in on the dissatisfied members.

"And their work has been sloppy, too." Rhys spread his arms. "You've all seen it. Think of the support wall that collapsed, and the broken window."

"We weren't even assigned to those jobs!" the woman said, her voice shrill.

Because the Sharetakers changed bodies so often, Teresa wasn't sure how anyone could tell *who* had worked which jobs at any particular time. But Rhys would know. He stood high and mighty, basking in the support. When the newcomers had tried to spread their discontent, Rhys turned the tide against them.

Humiliated, the two disgruntled members marched off. "You can't take any more from us than you already have, Rhys. We're leaving—and if the rest of you don't see what's going on here, then you'll just have to deal with the consequences for yourselves."

"Get the hell out of here!" someone shouted.

"Quitters!"

"At least we still have our self-esteem," Teresa said. She was angry that these two had unsettled her, had disturbed the peaceful atmosphere of the togetherments.

After the two protesters slid down a pair of firepoles and ran into the streets with nothing but the clothes on their backs, Rhys stood in the center of his flock. Stepping close to his side, Teresa was proud at how the Sharetakers had supported their leader.

Teresa followed him as he stalked off, knowing what he wanted, glad to give him a chance to burn some of his nervous energy. Sometimes his intensity frightened her, but it also captivated her. Rhys always knew the best way to handle a situation.

As he helped her take her clothes off with more impatience than sensuality, he shook his head with a small, superior smile. He studied her large breasts and generous hips, then squeezed her buttocks. "You're so eager to please, Teresa—so pliable. Like a stupid puppy."

"I thought that was what you wanted, Rhys."

They made love quickly, mechanically, and Rhys declined to swap with her afterward and do it again in opposite bodies, claiming he was too keyed up.

When he was finished, he dressed and went back out among the Sharetakers, leaving her to lie there, feeling empty inside. She hoped that he needed her as much as she needed him—but often Teresa felt as if she were getting the lesser end of the deal.

It took her several days to get her home-body back.

In the meantime her form had been passed from one

person to another to another. When she finally did return to her own set of arms and legs, the female flesh and auburn hair into which she had been born, Teresa spent a long time in front of a mirror, just reacquainting herself.

But her arms and chest had been bruised and hurt somewhere along the way, and it no longer felt the same. She was not the same person she once had been.

19

When Daragon went for his weekly meeting with Mordecai Ob, he wore his trim uniform with pride. Newly commissioned Inspector, Grade I. The two men would discuss pending cases and, frequently, Daragon's triumphs in having solved difficult investigations, not just through using his "special" skill, but with intuitive brilliance, cleverness, and hard work.

As he stepped into the ornate underwater office, though, Daragon noticed immediately that his mentor was disturbed and contemplative. Summary stacks, hardcopy memos, and evidence files of investigations-in-progress lay piled around him, covering winking message lights embedded in his desk. Chief Ob sat staring into the gas fireplace, where silent flames forever struggled to consume silica-polymer logs.

"What's wrong, sir? Is there anything I can do to help?"

Ob blinked at him in surprise, then he flashed a warm smile. "Do you now have the talent to read into troubled hearts, as well as spotting identities?"

Daragon stood at attention. "I just try to be perceptive, sir."

"Never mind, it has nothing to do with the Bureau." Ob picked up a printout and scanned it. "Time to get back to work."

"Sir, all aspects of your life concern the Bureau—especially if they impact your ability to function here."

The man's muscular shoulders sagged, but his voice had a hint of bemusement. "That sounds like something *I* would tell my best trainee."

Daragon wondered if the Chief was experiencing more doubts about giving up his dreams to become an artist. He had seemed delighted with the philanthropic opportunity to aid Garth—he even had one of Garth's paintings hanging on his BTL office wall—but occasionally Ob sulked with personal disappointment and regret. "Is it about Garth?" he asked.

"No . . . no, I'm quite happy with your friend and his ambition." Using a control on the desktop, the Chief turned the flames down. "I know it probably sounds like a trivial problem, but I've recently lost access to my personal caretaker, and I need a replacement. Someone to keep my body in shape while I'm too busy with Bureau work." He flexed his arm, gripping the bicep with his other hand. "I find that having my body kept fit sharpens my mind, but I don't have time to do it myself."

Daragon's mind was already working. "What type of person, exactly, are you looking for, sir?"

"I won't entrust my body to just anyone." Ob folded his big hands in front of him. "I need someone honest and reliable to do my workout for me, while I devote my energy to administering the BTL."

Daragon clasped his hands behind his back, standing tall and covering his excitement. This could be a chance to repay the great man for all he had done—and also help Eduard. "I may have just the right person for you, if you'll let me suggest another one of my friends?"

Daragon waited in plain sight in the open-air bistro, scanning the street crowd. His Inspector's uniform seemed to intimidate the customers around him. He pulled up the sleeve of his dark uniform and glanced at his watch. Already twenty minutes late. But then, free-spirited Eduard had never been a punctual sort of person, unless he was meeting a client for a swap.

He had no idea what body Eduard would be wearing when he came, but Daragon would recognize his old friend by his inner presence. He fixed his gaze on an old man hobbling toward the coffee shop. With his fluttering other-sight, he could make out the colorful core he knew to be Eduard, even without checking his ID patch.

Daragon waved to signal him over. Eduard approached with exceedingly cautious steps. His back was hunched, and his skin had a rough and leprous appearance. With a heavy sigh, he slumped into the chair as if someone had severed the puppet strings to his arms and legs.

"Look at you, Eduard." Daragon shook his head in dismay. "What are you doing to yourself?"

Eduard waved a swollen-knuckled hand. "Some old guy had a hot date. Limited term. I'll get my home-body back this evening."

When the waiter came over, Daragon ordered a spiced drink, and Eduard asked for herb tea. "This body can't handle too much caffeine. The digestive system is pretty much shot."

"You can't keep doing this to yourself. How often do you hopscotch? How many times a week?"

"Depends on how many clients I get."

"Aren't you worried about slippage? Too much swapping with too many different people, and you could end up . . . *gone.*"

Eduard shrugged, a marionette movement of his bony shoulders. "I've heard talk about it, but never anything but secondhand rumors. There's no proof, no medical evidence."

"So it can't affect you?"

"Not if I don't let it."

"You're whistling past the graveyard." Daragon leaned forward conspiratorially. "Listen, I've got something much better for you."

Eduard crossed liver-spotted arms over a sunken chest, annoyed at his friend's scolding. "You mean, turn me into some kind of experimental subject for the Beetles?"

Daragon stiffened. "Why do you assume only bad things about the Bureau? If you only knew how much time I spend looking out for you and Garth, and even Teresa, whenever she leaves the Sharetakers' enclave. We watch out for abuses of power and spotlight the dangers inherent in unregulated hopscotching." Even to him, it sounded like rehearsed propaganda. "People are too tempted to sell their bodies, their lives."

"Like me, you mean?"

Eduard gave him a teasing smile, but Daragon responded with a hard look. "You were glad enough for my help with Madame Ruxton's lawyers."

Eduard pursed his wrinkled lips, softening his voice. "Granted. I appreciate that. Sorry if I insulted you." His sagging old face gave a very youthful-looking smile and he tried to salvage the mood. "Hey, this isn't a conversation that friends have. I haven't seen you in months."

Daragon nodded apologetically. "Please let me make you an offer. It's an opportunity I think you'll like."

While Daragon outlined his plan with a rising voice and enthusiasm, Eduard watched his friend skeptically. The waiter came with their drinks, and Eduard picked up his tea with shaking hands and took a quick gulp. "The whole thing sounds...interesting, but I've got some reservations. Remember how your precious Bureau tried to take over the Falling Leaves? They aren't always shining knights on white horses."

Taking this as a veiled criticism, Daragon shifted uncomfortably, very conscious of his own uniform.

"Eduard, wouldn't it be a better job than being sick in someone else's body? Undergoing surgery for a coward?"

Eduard sipped his herb tea, trying not to show how much this crumbling body pained him. "All right, I'll go and meet this Mordecai Ob. If he's done so much for you, and for Garth, he must be a good man. I'll hear what he has to say." He pressed a hand to the small of his back as he stood up. "Doing this crap is getting to be a pain."

They took a hydro-skimmer out to the BTL Headquarters. Back in his home-body again, Eduard looked around in the sunlight on the refurbished oil-drilling platform. The salt wind ruffled his hair. "Nice place. Not much of a tourist attraction, is it?"

"The Bureau rarely allows outside visitors. I had to get special permission for you." Eduard pretended to be impressed, but Daragon wasn't fooled. He just hoped his cocky friend would make a good impression on Mordecai Ob.

Down in the richly decorated office, the Bureau Chief had cleared his desk, turned on the fireplace, and set out an extra seat for Eduard's benefit. Daragon spotted the subtle differences, pleased that his mentor was trying to make a good show.

Ob extended a large hand and took Eduard's in his grip. "Very pleased to meet you, Eduard." He gestured for the guest to sit in the new chair. "Daragon tells me I should hire you as my new personal caretaker, and so far, I have found his advice to be invaluable."

Daragon's heart warmed.

Eduard made himself comfortable in the formal chair. He crossed one leg over his knee, brushed the smooth armrest. "So tell me what this position entails, Mr. Ob. It sounds interesting from the way my friend describes it."

Ob put his elbows on his desk. "I insist on remaining in shape, but I don't have the time or the inclination to put in the necessary effort. Your sole job will be to exercise my body. That's all. Several times a week, we will swap bodies for a few hours and you will go jogging and swimming. You'll do calisthenics, you'll eat healthy food while you're in my body. Meanwhile, I'll do my business in your body and take care of my obligations without wasting time for a workout."

"I can waste time for you," Eduard said with what he hoped was a winning smile. "Anything else?"

"I may need your body in other, rare circumstances. Sometimes, because I am so recognizable as the Bureau Chief, I prefer to go out in public looking a little more anonymous."

"Anonymous, that's me. No problem." Eduard folded his arms over his chest, playing the tough negotiator now. "And the pay will be . . . ?"

"Substantial. I'll also arrange for guest quarters so you can live on my estate, in case I need you at an odd hour."

"That's a tall order," Eduard said, covering his excitement. He couldn't believe the opportunity. It sounded too good to be true.

Impatient, Daragon reproved his friend. "Eduard, you couldn't get a better job than this."

Eduard took a deep breath, clearly pleased with how his own body felt. He gazed across the polished desk, noting Mordecai Ob's muscular physique. "Yeah, I wouldn't mind doing my job in someone else's *healthy* body for a change, instead of just gritting my teeth until it's time to swap back."

"Absolutely," Daragon said, very pleased to be the mediator. "This is a great deal for all concerned."

Eduard and Mordecai Ob shook hands, making the arrangement official.

20

Delighted with what he had done for Eduard, Daragon headed for the BTL computer center. His heels rang on the metal walkways and his heart beat rapidly, but he straightened his back in an effort to dampen his excitement. He couldn't invest too much hope.

Also pleased with his new personal caretaker, Chief Ob had given Daragon an opportunity that was meant to be a reward. An opportunity he couldn't pass up . . .

"Inspector Swan, today I am offering you an assignment," the Chief had said. "Let's call it a graduation present for several months of excellent success."

Daragon suppressed a warm grin. "What kind of assignment, sir?"

"Now it's time to put your knowledge to work, in a practical manner." Ob locked his hands behind the small of his back. "Why don't you tell *me* what kind of assignment—what would you like to do?"

Daragon's brow furrowed. After waiting a beat, Ob leaned back against his desk, relishing the moment. "Come now, is there anything you'd like to know? Any mystery you'd like solved? A particular obsession you've had? I'm giving you the full resources of the Bureau to take on a pet project. Think about it."

The artificial fireplace hissed and crackled with sound effects. Daragon stared at his mentor, mulling over the question, but the answer was immediately clear to him. "I would like to locate my mother or father, sir.

They gave me to the Splinter monks when I was an infant, and I've never known who they were."

Ob let out a quiet laugh. Ostensibly, this project would hone Daragon's BTL skills, but the Bureau Chief did it because he liked his student. He could see the passion in the young man's heart. He waved Daragon toward the door. "Go ahead, then—indulge yourself."

Without taking much time to formulate a plan, Daragon made his way into the isolated rooms where he could pore over scraps of data. But with a question this large and with a trail this old, he knew he couldn't do it alone.

Now, Daragon stood inside the humid chamber, waiting for his eyes to adjust to the dim light the grotesquely stunted Data Hunters preferred. He heard the recirculators, the air-conditioning fans, the bubbles of life-support fluid. "Jax? Jax, are you there?" He looked up at the pale-skinned, wormlike creatures that had once been human but now lived their lives through COM.

One of the blind embryos stirred in its harness. Cables trailed from his eye sockets, connecting the creature's optic nerves directly to the computer/organic matrix. "Ahh, Inspector Daragon Swan! And I'm glad to see that it *is* Inspector now, Grade II even. A promotion due, no doubt, to my brilliant assistance?"

"In part."

"A large part, I suspect." The stunted body swayed in the air, its rubbery limbs useless, but the voice that came from the speaker was animated, jovial, and good-humored. "Oh well, whatever it takes to get you to come in and chat."

"How good are you at finding missing parents?" Daragon asked.

The Data Hunter groaned. "Oh, not *that* tedious

question again! Let me guess—Chief Ob gave you your first independent assignment?"

Daragon flushed. "I take it you've done this kind of search before?"

"And succeeded admirably, I might add. But I'll admit, Inspectors usually do a more thorough job of buttering me up beforehand."

"So I take it, then, that success is practically assured?"

"Not at all," Jax replied indignantly. "You don't understand the complexity of your question. Let's just start with your mother—*who* is it, exactly, that you want me to find? Do you want to locate the biological body that gave birth to you? The womb inside which you gestated, that is—no matter who's living inside the head these days?"

"No, the body won't tell me anything. I want to meet the *person* who made the decision to give me up. I want to talk to the woman—"

"Or man," Jax interjected, "if they swapped sexes. Never can tell."

Daragon sighed. "I just want to have a conversation with the person who decided he or she didn't want to be my parent, whoever chose to let me grow up in the monastery."

"That's clear enough, I suppose." The Data Hunter's body drifted in its harness, turning toward him, though Jax could be watching from any number of optical sensors in the room. "My friend...are you certain you want to know?"

Daragon, the individual, was the result of however many body swaps that had gone on during the pregnancy. He wanted to know the male body, the female body, and whatever two minds had been inside them at the time of conception. No matter what factors had contributed, everything had made him into the person he was today: BTL Inspector, Grade II. Someone a parent might even be proud of.

"Yes, I'm sure I want to know."

"Ahh, very well." Jax swiveled his eye cables toward the COM nexus in the dim chambers. "Now you must tell me one thing, Inspector Daragon—what's the big deal? Why do you care so much?"

"It's personal," he answered, his voice quiet and a bit hoarse. All the questions tumbled together in his mind. What secrets did they hide? Did Daragon have brothers and sisters? Were his parents poor? Did they know why he was an anomaly, unable to swap bodies like everyone else? Who were they? Were they different, like him?

"You realize that this is a discretionary task. You're asking me to bust my figurative derriere to track down this information—don't you owe me an explanation?"

Daragon sighed. "I'll try." He worried that the hardest part would be conveying it to someone else, especially to a half-human creature who had no direct experience with the real world. "Back at the monastery, I had some very close friends. One was named Garth—"

"Of course," Jax said. "And Teresa and Eduard, even someone named Pashnak. All Swans from the Falling Leaves. I keep tabs on anyone I find remotely interesting, and you seemed fond of those three. It gets dull in here, you know. But what does Garth have to do with finding your mother or father?"

"Garth always used to read Charles Dickens books aloud to me and Pashnak. Dickens was an old classic author—"

"I know who he was, Daragon." Jax's voice sounded impatient.

"Of course you would. The tales were about strange people from other times with problems and concerns so different from ours, but still oddly the same. When

Garth read aloud, it was a magical experience, like hearing an old storyteller around a campfire. Very primal, what fiction is all about—not fancy language or convoluted metaphors... just solid, interesting *stories*."

"And...?"

Daragon's brows knitted. "Why the rush? I thought you enjoyed conversation?"

"Only when it has a point."

"Let me tell it in my own way. This is difficult enough." He pursed his lips, considering. "One of the Dickens novels I enjoyed the most was *Oliver Twist*. It brought up the question of whether a simple boy, without parents or any bright spot in the world, might be an unrecognized prince. Oliver didn't know his birthright, thought he was just a poor, unremarkable orphan—and after a series of adventures, he discovered that he was much more than he seemed."

Daragon shuffled his feet in embarrassment as a staticky chuckle reverberated through the speakers. "So you think you might be the heir to some great fortune!"

"I knew you wouldn't understand." Now that he heard someone else say it, the thought seemed ridiculous. "I just want to know."

"Good enough," Jax said brightly. "I can always tell honesty when I hear it. Therefore, I agree to search relentlessly for your parents. But on one condition."

Daragon groaned. "Not again."

"You know we all have our price. Nothing's free."

"What is it this time?"

"I want you to come in here and read *Oliver Twist* out loud to me. Just like you said Garth used to do for you and Pashnak."

"But you can download the whole text anytime you want to. Isn't that more efficient?"

"Downloading isn't the same... experience."

"You're probably right," Daragon said, and agreed to the terms.

Days later, Daragon set out, armed with information and a series of thin active-screen images he had acquired from COM surveillance cameras.

Despite his best efforts, Jax had found no leads to Daragon's father, but he did identify his mother. Daragon's mother. For the first time in his life, he knew what she looked like—at least what she looked like today. She lived in a much younger body now and spent a great deal of time in, of all places, Club Masquerade. Jax had told Daragon he would be able to find her there now. He could meet her face-to-face, if he could maintain his nerve.

As he stood in front of the Club's myriad arched entrances, Daragon took a moment to check his appearance. He had intentionally worn nondescript clothes—a BTL Inspector's uniform would never do, not for this. Before heading out to the streets he had spent long minutes looking at himself in a mirror. With such great expectations, he wanted to make a good impression.

He chose an entrance door and ducked under an arch that led him through a room like an Arabian palace and onto the main floor of Club Masquerade. He scanned his handful of surveillance images again, though he had practically memorized every line in her face. *His mother's face,* though she couldn't possibly bear any physical similarity to him anymore. Maybe with Daragon's special vision he would see something familiar in her soul, a family resemblance.

The Club was a sea of people, lights, and music. He couldn't imagine how he'd ever identify a single person amid such chaos, so many minds and gyrating bodies, swapping at will. But he spotted her almost instantly, as if a telepathic link already existed between them.

She sat alone, waiting, available. Under the changing bath of lights, his mother looked healthy and sexy, flushed with a sheen of glitter and spray-on phero-mones. She nibbled on a stim-stick, legs crossed on a floating stool.

Daragon stood frozen, watching her for a few mo-ments. He could see her aura, her identity, recognizing a flicker in her persona that bore some connection to his own. He could see details in her *self* that were obviously related to him.

This was her, no doubt about it.

With a bored and somewhat impatient expression, she stared at the Hopscotch Board, scanned the people on the floor, looking for no one in particular—but defi-nitely looking for *someone*. Her eyes had a predatory gleam, as if she saw targets painted on every body in the room. She leaned back, tossing ragged ginger hair over her shoulder.

Daragon marched up to her before his resolve could fail. He drew on all the confidence and firm body lan-guage he'd been taught in the BTL. He knew how to confront violent fugitives, but this was far more intimi-dating to him.

As he fell speechless with anticipation, his mother's eyes locked with his. Her mouth tightened, then smiled as she appraised him. "You look like you know what you want." She flashed a hungry smile at him, then sat straighter, close to where he stood nonplussed. "Not a hint of hesitation." She wrapped her arms around his neck, trying to draw him down for a kiss.

"I—I just wanted to find you." Daragon paused a beat, took a deep breath. "You, you're my mother."

Her amused expression melted into a frown. "What did you say?"

"I'm your son, but I've never met you. You gave me up as an infant to the Splinter monks. I was raised at the Falling Leaves—" His words came in a rush.

Understanding came to her face, but no particular pleasure or even interest. "*That* baby? Ah, that was a long time ago."

"I've always wondered about you. I wanted to know who you were, what you were doing. My own mother. I tracked you down."

She was unimpressed. "That was a child that came out of a different body. I wasn't even there at the time. Some people pay good money to experience childbirth firsthand." She ran her fingers over his wrist, still trying to grasp his hand. Suddenly, maliciously, she seemed to become more determined than ever. "It shouldn't matter to the two of us right now."

She slid off the floating stool, more aggressive. She kissed him, quickly and passionately, on the mouth. Daragon pulled away. "Stop! I just wanted to talk to you." He backed toward the dance floor, and she followed.

"Why? Now you've got me intrigued. If you want us to get to know each other, I can think of a lot of better ways. What was your name again?" She drew him close, rubbing her hips against him. "Don't you think this body is sexy? It's new, and I paid good money for it."

"But you're my *mother!*"

"From a certain point of view, I suppose. Kind of kinky, isn't it?" She laughed at him, made him feel silly. "What are you worried about? Incest? That was an old, genetic-based taboo to prevent inbreeding. Nothing to worry about here." Her voice got huskier. "I've never tried anything like this."

Daragon stood firm, remembering what Ob had taught him, remembering that he was a BTL Inspector. He couldn't let this woman dominate the conversation.

This was *his* encounter. He had engineered it, and he could take the lead. "Stop being so immature! You're supposed to be more of an adult than I am."

She laughed at him. The music playing in the background grew louder. People talked and danced, milling about. "Today, someone else has the flesh that gave birth to you, and by now it's old. But you and I can still get it on, just like two virile young people."

"I don't want to have sex with you, Mother. I want to know about you, and about my father."

He could see bright recollections parading behind her retinas. "You might find it surprising, but I do remember the man who was your father—a very special man. We only had a few nights, and I could never find him again. But then, disappearing is what he was good at."

She pulled Daragon closer so she could whisper in his ear. Her words came out with a hot breath that smelled of the spicy stim-stick. "Your father's been alive for over two hundred years, hiding, swapping bodies every so often, staying out of the spotlight. Staying invisible, trying to be immortal." She chuckled. "But I guess he still liked to get laid every once in a while."

Daragon could barely believe what he was hearing. "Are you saying my father was a Phantom?" He remembered Eduard's long-ago obsession to live forever, learning to avoid detection, teaching himself how to pick locks, how to hide.

"You'll never find him. He knows how to vanish, and it's been years. How long *has* it been, anyway? How old are you? In fact…what did you say your name was?"

"I'm Daragon. I'm twenty-two." Bitterness crept into his voice, resentment that his own mother had to ask him such questions. He had looked forward to this moment for such a long time, but his mother was not at all the person he had expected. He had imagined a heartfelt reunion, long conversations, a reconnection. Not this.

She had managed to maneuver him out onto the dance floor and now tried to sweep him along. "I want to stay young as long as I can—your father taught me that. Keep swapping bodies, keep yourself alive, trade up whenever you can. Is anything wrong with that?" She tried to press close to him again, but now Daragon just wanted to be far away from her.

"Well, *I* don't have that option, Mother. I can't hopscotch into any other body—I'm an anomaly. I couldn't swap if my life depended on it."

She looked at him with wide eyes. "I've never heard of such a thing! But everybody—"

"Not me. I just have this, nothing more." He finally pushed her away. "I make do with what you gave me."

"Come on, don't get hung up about it. That was some other body. We can still—"

But Daragon turned and left Club Masquerade, his illusions shattered.

21

Whenever Teresa saw that Rhys was in a surly mood, she did her best to cheer him up. She considered it her duty for the group, and it made her feel warm inside to see the positive effect of her presence on their leader.

Unfortunately, it didn't always work.

Inside the togetherments, Rhys shuffled through hardcopy balance sheets, investment records, and bills. He used a primitive numerical calculator, frowning at each result. Teresa could smell his perspiration in the closeness of the corner where he had gone to think.

She would have suggested that he just use the facilities available in COM for budgeting, bookkeeping, simple information access, but she knew it would anger him. Rhys wanted none of the "spy terminals" in his sight, though Teresa had never heard of the computer/organic matrix actively spying on anyone through an access screen. She felt that sometimes Rhys had unrealistic fears and concerns.

"I will think for *myself*, no matter how many headaches it causes."

Now, she walked up to him slowly, swaying her hips—she was tall and blond today, well tanned, with full lips and long eyelashes. Teresa had made love to him a dozen times in this body, and by now she'd learned what aroused him, how to be flirtatious and seductive. "Can I do anything, Rhys...anything at all, to take

your mind off your troubles?" She made her voice
husky, with a provocative lilt.

He looked back up at her with a dissecting stare,
then a frown. "Why don't you come back in a more interesting body?" He turned back to his paperwork.
"Something I'm not tired of looking at."

Stung, Teresa bit her lip. "Of course, Rhys. I'll try
harder."

Teresa went deep into the togetherments, wanting to
be held and loved. Maybe if she had just married Garth
or Eduard when they'd left the Falling Leaves, they
could have had a stable, normal life. But that hadn't
been what she wanted, and it wasn't really what she
wanted now. She kept trying to convince herself that the
Sharetakers gave her what she needed, but even that was
wearing thin.

She stopped in front of a petite brunette with a body
like a gymnast and convinced her to swap bodies. The
brunette was perfectly happy to become a slender blond,
glad to do something that Teresa said would please
Rhys.

When she returned to where Rhys was working, he
had put away his paperwork and sat waiting for her. As
Teresa stepped into the open chamber, he cracked his
knuckles, appraising her body. "That'll do." He took
her wrist and led her to the thin mattress in the corner.

Although they still hopscotched sexes occasionally,
Rhys preferred his redheaded home-body. Over the past
months he had stopped swapping with Teresa at all during lovemaking. He had developed some kind of aver-
sion to having her on top of him in any form, especially
if she was larger and stronger and masculine. He wanted
to be in control.

Rhys made her switch into so many different body-
types that she made herself dizzy just trying to please
him. Eventually, Teresa realized she had completely lost

track of her original body. When she first discovered this, she was shocked and alarmed. In all the time she'd been with the Sharetakers, she had worn the form of male workers, female lovers for Rhys, male lovers for other Sharetakers whenever Rhys suggested it. She had taught herself not to wonder anymore.

When she tried to track down the person wearing her home-body for that day, Teresa had discovered that it was gone. Entirely gone. One of the quietly disgruntled Sharetaker converts, a woman named Jennika, had left the enclave and never returned. She'd run away in Teresa's body, and nobody knew where she'd gone. Nobody cared.

But some nights she still woke up wondering who she was, what she was supposed to feel like. Teresa would touch herself, even taking a moment to remind herself whether she was male or female, and feel her heart racing. Whenever possible, she would visit Garth and stare at the detailed sketch he had drawn of her original home-body, memorizing everything about it. She tried to remember what it felt like to be *her*...and then she tried to forget. She would have to wear a stranger's body for the rest of her life.

As a girl back in the Falling Leaves, Teresa often lay awake in darkness, surrounded by the peaceful sounds of sleeping companions, quiet snores, the rustle of blankets. Although her eyes were open, she could see only vague forms, nothing clear and definite. Teresa was the only one who stared into the sky and looked at clouds, who pondered the imponderable. "What happens after death? Why are we here? Does what we do *matter?*"

Next to her, Garth had breathed heavily, deep in his dreams, while Eduard tossed and turned on the other side of her, restless as usual. Daragon slept on the opposite side of the room. They had all been brought here as infants, like items donated for a white-elephant sale.

During Garth's recent art exhibition, she had wanted so much to *talk* to him and Eduard, to open her heart...but somehow she couldn't bring herself to share her doubts, not even with her two closest friends. Those thoughts hurt too much to express, even to herself.

Now, in the Sharetakers' togetherment, feeling sore and badly used in the darkness, Teresa lay awake again. She could still smell Rhys's sweat, the sour dampness of their sex, the clamminess of the sheets. He had taken all that Teresa offered...and she had offered him everything.

In the enclave, she could hear sounds of quiet laughter, kissing, breathing. Shared pleasure and sweet nothings, simultaneous moans that became a purr. The noises seemed so different from her lovemaking with Rhys. Rigid but quiet, she listened, trying to pinpoint the difference. What had she done wrong?

Something in her posture must have awakened Rhys. Coming instantly alert, he rolled over to face her and propped himself up on an elbow. Teresa could see his teeth and his eyes in the dimness. Out of the blue, he said, "Do you know where you can get money? The Sharetakers need more to survive."

"Rhys, I already gave you everything I had."

"Well, that was nothing, or damn close." He sounded angry with her, but she knew he was just stressed from the enclave's troubles. "You must know where you can get your hands on more."

Her heart pounded. "Everyone has a different situation, Rhys. We come together because we need the community."

"Sure, sure. But we're not a free ride, either. I don't think you've contributed enough to the group."

Teresa didn't manage to cover her astonished gasp.

"But I work as hard as any other member! I hardly ever sleep."

The leader shook his head. "What about your friend Eduard? He's got plenty of money. Didn't you say he just got a fancy new job? Just ask him again—you don't need to tell him what the credits are for."

"I couldn't do that. Eduard's my friend, and I couldn't possibly deceive him, or take advantage—"

Rhys got up, grabbing his pile of rumpled clothes. "Maybe I'd better leave you alone for the rest of the night so you can think about where your loyalties lie— and who your true friends are."

He stalked away. As she huddled in the dark, alone and afraid, Teresa silently answered the question for herself.

Yes, she knew who her friends were.

22

Eduard perspired heavily in another man's body, but this time it was an exhilarating workout instead of suffering a miserable fever.

He stood under the overhead lights in the exercise room. Two plate-glass window walls looked out onto well-tended gardens and paths; two walls were floor-to-ceiling mirrors in which he could watch his muscles ripple, see how he exerted himself.

Mordecai Ob's strong heart pumped as Eduard exercised, the blood flowing. Warm sweat trickled from his close-cropped chestnut hair. He panted, and fresh air burned in his lungs. According to the clock and his employment contract, he still had another hour of required exercise before his boss would be satisfied with the workout.

Leaving the weight-training equipment with a clank of metal on metal, Eduard gulped half a bottle of electrolyte water and toweled off. He tugged a sweatshirt over his head, plucking at the cloth where it stuck to his damp skin. He already wore running shorts, good shoes. Ob had taken care of everything. Eduard just had to do the time-consuming work.

He waved at the sensor, and one of the windows skated aside. He puffed out two breaths like small gunshots, preparing himself, then set off at a fast jog into the fresh air and morning sunshine....

In the past few weeks, Eduard had settled in at Ob's

expansive estate. The man didn't want to be friends with him, just business associates. In fact, Eduard rarely saw him except to swap in the early morning, then back again, sometimes in a few hours, sometimes not until the evening, whenever the Chief returned.

He had his own separate apartment in a wing of the large mansion, all his meals and needs provided. The Bureau Chief didn't really require much, though he occasionally asked to swap at odd hours, without explaining his mission. *Some shady Beetle stuff*, Eduard supposed. He really didn't care, as long as he got his body back at the end of the day. It was part of the job.

Now, jogging around the estate, Eduard fell into a rhythm along his usual running path, a circuit that encompassed two miles. He ran around hedges, through a quaint shrubbery maze copied from an old English manor house. Some of the stone benches tempted him—rest here!—but he refused to relax. He had his routine. With a sharp grin, he pushed on. This was so easy.

As the running path wound through the extensive rose garden, Eduard waved at Ob's huge Samoan gardener, Tanu. The gardener's upper arms were as wide as most people's thighs; his skin was dusky, as if impregnated with the dirt in which he always worked. Tanu had a mane of charcoal hair like a sword-and-sorcery barbarian's, but Eduard knew the bearlike islander was friendly and good-hearted, somewhat shy. Tanu spent his time alone with his flowers and shrubbery, trellises and hedges. He not only talked to the plants, but seemed to listen to them as well.

As Eduard jogged past, the Samoan raised a hand the size of a boat oar. "I'll come by and talk to you later!" Eduard called. "We can have iced tea."

He glanced over his shoulder, still trying to get a reaction from the Samoan. Not looking where he was going, Eduard stumbled from the path and crashed against one of the rosebushes. A thorn left a long red scratch down his right thigh, but Eduard recovered without missing a beat and lurched back onto the path. He glanced down at the rosebush, but didn't see any obvious damage.

"Sorry!" He brushed his legs, then sprinted onward. Another mile to go.

Eduard brewed a pitcher of iced tea and carried it on a tray with two glasses to the gardener's shed. The ice cubes tinkled, and beads of condensation sparkled, like the sweat Eduard had recently showered off Ob's body.

"Hey, Tanu!" He wandered around to the back of the shed, where he found the big Samoan nestled inside a stand of flame bushes, pruning branches one at a time, as if he knew each one personally. Eduard couldn't imagine how the gardener had worked his bulky form into such a cramped area without trampling the plants. "Come on, let's have some tea. It'll quench your thirst."

Tanu looked down at his bushes, reluctant to move. The gardener's voice was surprisingly rich and gentle coming from such a gigantic chest. "Still lots of plants to work on."

"Plants have taken care of themselves for billions of years, Tanu. They can wait ten minutes while you drink some tea." Eduard set the tray on a bench, poured a tall glass for the gardener, then one for himself.

Tanu downed the iced tea in a single gulp, as if that were the quickest way for him to return to his bushes. Eduard refilled the glass, just so the gardener wouldn't have that excuse. He enjoyed his conversations with Tanu, though the dialogue was mostly one-sided.

He rubbed the red scratch on his leg, which still stung. "How's that rosebush I stepped on?"

Tanu had spent as much time tending the plant as if

it were a seriously injured child in a hospital emergency room. "Fine."

"I'll be more careful from now on. No problem. I've got to pay more attention to where I put my big feet. Mr. Ob's big feet, actually." He flashed a quick grin. "Forgive me?"

Tanu remained expressionless. Finally, after a long moment, he said, "You're not like the other ones."

Eduard raised his eyebrows. "Other ones? You mean Ob's previous body caretakers?"

Tanu nodded, then looked longingly back at his flame bushes.

Eduard couldn't imagine why anyone would give up such a plum job. "Why did they stop working here? What happened to them?"

"They're gone."

Eduard finished his own iced tea. This conversation was harder work than two hours of exercise. "Well, I'm here to stay." He placed the glasses next to the half-empty pitcher. "Thanks for taking the time to chat."

He carried the tray back toward the house. The Samoan watched him go, his dark eyes filled with infinite sadness.

Mordecai Ob returned home at no set schedule, flitting back from BTL Headquarters whenever he felt his day's work was finished. As soon as the Chief arrived at the estate, he would summon Eduard immediately. He wanted his own body back, wanted to spend the evenings as *himself*.

In the foyer Eduard met his employer as Ob set down his documents in a holding area by the door. On him, Eduard's home-body looked weary and drained, his expression covered with a veil of stress. Impatient, the Chief gestured him forward. "Take your body back. I want to feel refreshed again."

After they hopscotched, Ob took a deep breath and smiled, while Eduard experienced disappointment to be in his own form again. The muscles felt lethargic and ragged, without the clean energy that came from a rigorous workout. Ob had left him with a tension headache in the back of his skull.

Tough day at the office, Eduard thought, rubbing his stiff shoulders.

The Bureau Chief stood in the foyer, touching himself, taking a bodily inventory. When he discovered the long scratch on his leg, he glowered. "What have you done?" Ob undid his pants and reached under the fabric to feel the minor wound. "What is this?"

"Just an accident. I scratched it on one of the rosebushes during my morning jog." After having undergone near-fatal open-heart surgery for Madame Ruxton, Eduard couldn't summon much sympathy for the ridiculously minor blemish.

"I don't want to hear about any more accidents, Eduard." Ob's olive-brown eyes blazed.

Eduard's muscles seized up in an unconscious panic reaction. He could see why this man was so successful among the Beetles. "Okay, okay—I'm sorry! It's just a scratch. It'll heal before you know it."

"Eduard, I have entrusted you with my physical being." Ob's voice was low and threatening. "If you can't take better care of my body, I won't need your services any longer."

Eduard struggled to keep his temper and shock in check. "I . . . I'll be more careful from now on."

Ob didn't answer as he strode to his chambers.

23

After receiving Mordecai Ob's first generous stipend as his "patron," Garth wanted to get away from people. And also to be inspired.

Even with the lackluster success of his first private exhibition, he remained undaunted. His head held so many ideas, so many images, that he needed to sort it all out. Soft Stone had taught him to meditate; maybe that would help. He would go somewhere and let his thoughts run unhindered.

Garth did an extensive batch of complimentary art-work for a travel broker in exchange for a deep discount on fares, then used some of Ob's money to travel to the breathtaking Waimea Preserve on the windswept north end of Oahu, a rugged jungle and river capped by a churning seascape.

Within the preserve, he followed a stream through palms and banana trees to volcanic outcroppings over-hung with mosses and epiphytes. Garth stood with crowds on wooden decks to watch the famed cliff divers of Hawaii. The athletes plunged off the blackened rocks, sketching smooth arcs through the air into the foaming gullet of a waterfall.

Marveling at the perfection of their human forms, Garth toyed with the idea of hopscotching with one of them so he could try the dive on his own. But even if he did inhabit such a perfectly trained body, he would never inherit the abilities of the original owner. He might feel improved reflexes, and he might do a creditable job as a diver—or he might get himself killed.

Instead, he went to Waimea Beach, where the air was warm, the breezes stiff, and the sound of the surf like an avalanche. Curling waves battered the shore like blue-white hammers. Surfers carried polymer-lubricated boards and stood atop whitecaps that thundered to shore.

Excited, Garth stripped down to his bathing trunks and ran across the hot sand. The warm water welcomed him as he waded in. The sea, the mother of all life, was like amniotic fluid around his ankles, his knees.

He dove in. The ocean churned around him. Waves rushed one after another to the shore. The surfers went farther out, standing on their boards, laughing with each other. On the sand, families frolicked with their children, using static-wands to build ridiculously high sand castles.

Garth floated out, arms at his sides, kicking and splashing. The current flung him from wave to wave like jetsam after a shipwreck. He lay back, grinning foolishly up at the sky. He licked his lips, and the potent taste of salt startled him.

Everything he experienced filled the catalogue in his mind, and every moment was worth living for the new inspiration he received. When he got out his supplies again, he would somehow convey the powerful waves, using a language of colors and strokes to paint more than what he could see.

A whitecap splashed over his head, and he reveled in playing in the surf. Larger waves rolled in, slapping him down, and he paddled farther out to catch more of them. The foam pummeled him, dunking him under, and he pushed his way back up, laughing and coughing.

Before he could regain his breath, an enormous wave flooded over the top of him, shoving him down.

Garth tried to swim to the surface, flailing his arms. Breaking free, he drew in a mouthful of saltwater and coughed it up just as another wave struck, pulling him farther out. The undertow grabbed at his ankles, sweeping his feet from under him, and ran with him.

Garth didn't know what to do. He bobbed back into the air and sun, thrashing about. He couldn't even see the shore with his burning eyes, didn't know which direction to go. A foamy wave slapped him in the face, blinding him. He went under again.

Garth shouted for help, but his voice was choked and the sea rumbled far too loudly for anyone to hear. He broke the surface, gasping, and swallowed another mouthful. Daylight seemed to have disappeared.

The undertow pulled him down again, deeper this time. All he could see was a blue-green storm that faded to black. . . .

The Emergency Medical Technicians roared onto the beach, their hovercars blasting a whirlwind of sand. Techs ripped equipment from storage compartments and plugged into remote COM links, requesting status and information.

Assisted by three panting surfers using jet-boards, teams dragged Garth's flopping body to shore. When they spilled him onto the wet sand, he still twitched. A crowd had gathered, children staring wide-eyed next to their parents. The techs shouted a rapid-fire rush of commands, questions, and answers. One peeled up his eyelid, then rolled him over, trying to expel water from his lungs.

The medical techs focused their remote uplinks, powerpacks, and diagnostic systems. Brushing caked sand away, they slapped electrodes onto Garth's clammy skin. Automatic analyzers and probes dipped needles into his bloodstream while the techs stood back to let COM do the complicated work.

Garth swam in black velvet, a zero-gravity environment that left him with no worries. He saw no one else, heard no sound, experienced a total absence of sensations. Until he saw a pinprick of light far in the distance.

The spark grew steadily larger, coming toward him until it formed a bright apparition of Soft Stone herself, her bald head shining, her glowing face as blunt featured as he remembered it. But her smile was softer than he had seen in some time, her skin luminous.

"You can't stay here, little Swan." Her voice was quiet, but it filled the blackness around him. "This place isn't for you."

In Garth's befuddled state, the presence of his long-dead teacher seemed perfectly reasonable. "But how do I get out? I don't know where I am, and I don't know the way back."

"Why, use the door," she said. "It's right behind you."

He turned and found himself before a massive wooden door that bristled with ornate carvings. He recognized it as the door from the Falling Leaves.

"Go on," Soft Stone said. "Right out there. That's where you belong."

Not daring to question the monk's orders, Garth grasped the handle. He opened the door.

And opened his eyes.

"There he is," one of the medical techs shouted, looking up from the COM diagnostics.

Sunlight burned into his still-unfocused eyes. He coughed, then retched, then turned his face sideways as a stomachful of lukewarm seawater spewed from his mouth. The techs helped ease him to a sitting position.

Garth's muscles seized up. His knees drew toward his chest, his abdomen spasming.

A black static of unconsciousness fluttered around his field of vision, only to retreat again. He heard the pounding surf like a scolding whisper in his ears. The sunlight was very, very bright, dazzling on the sands.

The other tech, calm and professional, began plucking the electrodes and analyzers, yanking needles out of Garth's flesh. "You're lucky we received the call when we did. We got here immediately and gave you treatment, thanks to COM. You only had about a three-minute window."

"Thank you," Garth croaked. He couldn't think of anything else to say, but that phrase seemed appropriate. He looked around himself, still disoriented, expecting to see Soft Stone herself standing among the people on the beach. If he had almost died, surely she would have come to be there with him....

Perhaps she had indeed been there, in her own way. Soft Stone's image and her words had been vivid in his mind, but it must have been a near-death hallucination, something he had subconsciously wanted to see during the last flickers of his life.

Shaking off the disorientation, Garth huddled on the beach trying to get warm. Despite the bright Hawaiian sunshine, his skin felt icy.

While the first technician hauled the equipment back to the hover rescue vehicle, the other gave Garth a powerful stimulant injection and attached a tiny, temporary cardiomonitor to his chest. "We've got to keep your heartbeat regulated to bring you back to normal."

Garth hung his head in his hands as thoughts reeled around him. He'd traveled to Waimea to see new things, to collect exotic sights and landscapes and details that he could add to his artwork. Instead, he had come face-to-face with his mortality.

He had almost died because of his stupidity, blindly walking into danger just because it had looked interesting. He hadn't intended to put himself at such risk, hadn't meant to be a daredevil—he'd just been foolish. Life was such a transient thing, a thread so thin it could easily be snapped.

As he sat shuddering, it became clear to him how trivial his own quest for inspiration had been. He had to do more than just visit pretty landscapes. He must work harder at understanding *people* if he ever intended to produce art that would have an impact on humanity.

Garth understood now why his art exhibition had been such a failure. The lack of publicity had been only the first weakness; the superficial art itself hadn't drawn in the crowds. He thought back to the works he considered his masterpieces, but now they seemed bland and derivative—images that were captured, yet not tamed. Not interpreted. He'd been showing only *external* things. No depth, no point, no *heart*. He hadn't infused it with a "soul," with any part of himself.

Still shaky, Garth got to his feet, feeling the stimulants coursing through him. His body was alive again, but his mind would never be the same. He looked up and down the beach, saw the people standing around. There were no longer any surfers risking themselves for the fun of it. His ordeal had been a shock to all of them.

Garth brushed glittering sand off his arms and chest, then coughed again. His mouth tasted terrible. He wondered who had sent the alarm to the emergency crews, how the medical techs had known to come so quickly. But the techs were packed up and already leaving, the crowd was dispersing. A few brave souls ventured back into the water, but no one approached him. No one claimed responsibility for saving his life.

Bystanders stared at Garth, and he discovered that he was not embarrassed by this attention, or resentful of it. Instead, he studied the people in return, tried to understand who they were and why they reacted the way they did. Now that he was alive again, truly alive, the world and its people seemed even more interesting to him.

All of a sudden, it seemed so clear to him what he needed to do to capture the essence of *what it meant to be human.* It was not enough just to see everything . . . he had to *be* everything. And the ability to hopscotch gave him an opportunity that artists throughout history hadn't had. Garth decided to embark upon a quest that would change his life and set him on a course of exploration for years to come. He would report to Mordecai Ob, then he would tell his friends.

He didn't really comprehend anything about humanity after all. *But he would learn.*

24

The Sharetakers' money problems did not go away, and Rhys followed Teresa around the togetherments, pressuring her to ask her friends. "Why are you so resistant? If this guy Eduard is interested in your well-being, you should be able to talk him into helping us out. And that artist you keep seeing—Garth?—how many credits does he have?"

"Oh, Rhys, they're not even members of our group." A few workers continued dismantling walls even after dark, converting rooms into open areas. Everything was public, everyone in plain sight. Teresa had no place to hide. "I gave the Sharetakers everything I own. I did whatever you asked, because I want to be part of this enclave. But Eduard and Garth shouldn't be expected—"

When she tried to walk away, looking for something important to do, Rhys grabbed her small bicep so hard that his fingers made painful indentations. "Give me a break, Teresa! You told me Eduard has a plush job, working for some rich man. What could he possibly need all his credits for? The Sharetakers could certainly use the money here. Don't we deserve it?" Rhys frowned at her. "If your friend really cares for you, he would help you out. Help *us* out."

She pulled her thin arm from his grasp, but this body felt so tiny, so easily overpowered. "That's not the way a real friendship works, Rhys."

Certainly some of the other recruits would have better prospects for raising money, but Rhys hounded Teresa in particular. Now, though, being "special" had degenerated into a nightmare.

After so many months of obstinate optimism, Teresa finally began to see the redheaded leader more clearly. Rhys often went out of his way to push her buttons, as if trying to provoke her. His abusive tendencies had been growing more and more apparent, but Teresa was so accommodating, so eager to please, that she often slipped past his wrath—and that made Rhys angrier still.

She kept hoping she could fix him. Perhaps he didn't even know he was doing it, and she could make him see what was happening. "Rhys, all the Sharetakers give what we can . . . but forcing me to pressure other people, that goes against our philosophy. Don't you see?"

His face turned a dark red. "You're talking to *me* about my own philosophy? You think you understand it better? You're just a follower, Teresa, and not even one of the brighter ones—"

As she watched his anger escalate, Teresa tried again, more careful now. "Oh, Rhys, please calm down. I know how much you've done for the group. We know how hard you think, how tough it is to run the enclave." She lowered her already small voice. "All Sharetakers are partners, equals—you don't need to resort to power plays with me, or with any of us."

Inside the open togetherments, the Sharetakers could hear everything she said—and Rhys was acutely aware of the fact. As she tried to be reasonable, Teresa felt many eyes on them, dozens of spectators observing a confrontation. "Rhys, if we need credits, I could bring some work here into the enclave. I've done a few jobs searching COM, and there's always somebody looking to hire those services. We could set up some COM terminals in here, link up to the whole network. Other members have experience, too, don't you think? We could farm out for odd consulting jobs, do outside work. We could get a very good price on a dozen or so filmscreens—"

Instead of being convinced, though, Rhys reacted as if this were the last straw. "No COM terminals!" Teresa flinched. She could feel the heat on his skin. "They spy on everything."

Teresa took a small step away from him. "Rhys, it was just a suggestion. I was only trying to help."

"I'm sick of your useless *trying*. Always trying, never doing." He shoved her away from him, and she stumbled backward, disoriented in her waifish body. He took her fall as an affront. "I didn't push you that hard! Get up."

Rhys jerked her to her feet, yanking her thin arm hard. "Please stop it, Rhys. You're hurting me."

"Don't be such a weakling. Always whining, always finding excuses not to do your share." Teresa honestly didn't know what he was talking about, how he could have imagined such failings in her.

In the adjoining areas of the togetherment, Sharetakers stopped their work. Teresa looked at some of the familiar faces, questioning—but when she turned her gaze, the moment he wasn't the full and complete center of her attention, Rhys slapped her hard across the cheek.

"Look at me, dammit! This is between us, not you and them."

Her skin burned. "Leave me alone, Rhys! I'm doing everything—" She raised her hands, but that provoked him to hit her harder.

"You're doing *nothing*. You yourself are nothing. You're just sponging off the hard work the rest of us are doing."

"That's not true!" Biting back a cry of pain, she pulled, trying to break free. With a wicked grin, Rhys let go of her arm just as she tugged. She sprawled backward, hitting her head against the remnants of the nearest wall.

Two Sharetaker workers scurried away, looking sidelong at Rhys. No one helped her.

"Now look at what you've done!" He stepped closer and kicked her in the hip. Not hard—but he was just warming up. "Not only have you upset me, but you're interrupting the work routine, disturbing other members."

She rolled away, trying to get her footing again.

"What have you been telling them when I'm not here to listen?" His eyes blazed. "Distorting Sharetaker philosophy? We welcomed you into the enclave as one of us, and this is how you repay me? For all the love I've given you?"

"But Rhys, I never said—"

He cuffed her so hard that blood trickled from a cracked lip. No matter what she said, what she did, his reaction darkened, like a tiny pattering of pebbles building to an avalanche. Rhys's words weren't even meant for her: they were intended for the Sharetaker audience around him. He was performing now, putting Teresa in her place.

With a sick feeling that hurt even more than the physical blows, she recalled the previous disenchanted members who had spoken against Rhys—and how they had been ostracized and forcibly evicted. She had never thought it would happen to her.

Trying to get up, Teresa felt a sharp pain in her wrist. Rhys lashed out once more, kicking hard this time. She folded. In the wonderful open environment of the Sharetakers' quarters, she had no doors to lock, no place of safety.

She got to her knees and began to crawl away, but

Rhys hit her in the small of the back with his bunched fist. "You're not welcome here anymore, Teresa!"

Her arms and legs gave out, spilling her flat on the floor. She looked around her for some sort of support. "Help me!"

The Sharetakers backed away. They looked uncertainly at Rhys for instruction, then glowered at her. ". . . never appreciated what we do around here."

". . . always clinging to Rhys . . ."

". . . what did she bring to the group?"

The floor and the archways reeled around her, and Teresa could barely keep her balance. She eventually made it to the half-wall, leaving a blood smear on its freshly painted white surface.

The believers sided with Rhys, their leader, and left her out of their circle. Teresa could see it in their eyes—these people with whom she'd lived, shared, and swapped bodies over and over again. Now they bore the faces of strangers. *Strangers.*

Rhys found one of the small hammers among some tools in a corner. He picked it up and slapped the heavy black head against his palm.

Finally, full-fledged panic overwhelmed her. Teresa lurched away, but through a haze of tears and sweat and blood she couldn't see where she was going. She turned in fear to look at Rhys one more time—just as he tossed the hammer at her. Teresa dodged sideways so that the hammerhead only clipped her collarbone. She heard the dry bamboo *snap* inside herself as the bone broke cleanly.

A surge of adrenaline muffled the nerve-shouts of pain. She looked through a red-black curtain of near-unconsciousness to see Rhys just standing there, watching her. The thrown hammer could have crushed her skull—could have *killed* her—and he had not missed on purpose.

Now he let her go with no more than a smug smile for farewell.

Battered, Teresa fled, forced to take slow lifters and stairs, while her tormentors slid down firepoles to reach the street level and cut her off. Blood tasted salty and metallic in her mouth. Her sides ached with broken-glass pain.

She just wanted to be far away, beyond the reach of the Sharetakers. Teresa would have to take the body she was wearing now, small and waifish and broken. The believers followed her, hurling insults, increasing the pain with their cruel taunts. In a few moments they might even turn into a mob, and she would never get out alive.

Badly injured, both physically and psychologically, Teresa knew of one place she could go, someone with resources who would welcome her and help her, no matter what.

Disoriented, she reeled toward the enclave doorway. She would run to Eduard for help.

25

The estate of Mordecai Ob was mostly dark, except for fairy lights that traced paths through the gardens.

Though his body wasn't tired, Eduard went to bed early. He had to get up before dawn to start exercising for his boss. Some days, the Bureau Chief liked to go to the undersea headquarters at the fringe of morning; other times he preferred to remain at home in his study.

Eduard had to be prepared. It was his job.

But he lay awake, unable to sleep. Breezes whispered against the ornamental vines that clawed their way up the brick walls. Standing like guardians at the corners of the mansion, blue spruces made a gruffer, deeper sound in the wind.

Though Daragon had set him up with a wonderful job, Eduard rarely saw the young Inspector. He wanted to thank Daragon for saving him from the humiliating absurdities he had been willing to endure. Teresa rarely left the Sharetakers, and Garth had gone off to Hawaii.

Eduard missed his friends. He grew restless doing so little, all alone on the estate except for his rare and brief conversations with Tanu the gardener. Garth could have done the exercise duties for Ob, then spent the rest of the day painting. Eduard was surprised the Chief hadn't suggested it, since he was paying Garth anyway. . . .

A sudden, startling signal jarred him out of his sleepless woolgathering. His COM terminal flashed, an incoming communication with high-priority overrides to cut through any other message traffic.

Eduard slid off his bed and activated the receive button before he had time to wonder about the source. It was a brief but desperate message calling for his help. *Teresa needs you.*

He didn't pause to think, didn't ask questions, just sprang into action—as he had done when the anti-COM fugitive had tried to take young Teresa hostage in the flower market. The reasons didn't concern Eduard. Teresa needed him *now*—nothing else mattered.

Within minutes he was dressed and out the door. He wondered how long it would take him to pick the lock to Ob's weapons cabinet and arm himself, but decided not to delay. He borrowed one of Ob's vehicles from the carport, using the Bureau Chief's general access code— no time to ask for permission. Sweating, he raced for the Sharetakers' enclave.

This late in the evening, traffic was light, and COM control slotted Ob's craft into a high-speed lane, cutting off other drivers, rushing him across the city. After docking at ground level outside the enclave building, he leaped from the vehicle and rushed to the entrance. He was ready to batter it down with his fists, if necessary.

Before he could reach the door, a waifish young woman stumbled through the access barrier. Bloodied, she staggered forward, barely able to keep her balance. She gasped with each step, trying to run, but physically unable to do so. One of her wrists hung at an odd angle, broken; raw abrasions marked her face, her eyes bruised and haunted.

Eduard hurried forward, not recognizing her in this body but instinctively suspecting who she was. *"Teresa? Is that you?"*

She flinched as if someone had hit her, then saw him. Her face blossomed into astonishment and relief.

"Eduard!" She nearly collapsed, but he caught her in his arms. "Oh, how did you know to come here?"

"I got your message."

She fell against him, her muscles and bones turning to water. As he held her, she winced with the pain of broken ribs. "Message? Eduard . . . I was trying to get to you. Just now."

People moved in the entrance, shouting after Teresa like peasants bearing torches. Eduard glowered at the Sharetakers, his mind filled with questions, his throat clogged with outrage. "What have you done to her, you bastards?"

When they saw him guarding Teresa, they hesitated. Their expressions showed a collective, unfocused anger, as if most of them didn't even know what had upset them.

A big redheaded man pushed to the front of the crowd, and Eduard recognized him as their leader. Rhys stopped, surprised to see him. "You're Eduard Swan, right? If you'd come sooner, you could have prevented all this. It's your fault." His freckled face changed into a smug, supercilious mask. "Nobody wants you here now."

"Teresa wants me here," he said.

"We take care of our own," Rhys answered.

"Yeah, right. I can see that."

Teresa struggled to pull him toward the vehicle. "Eduard, please! We've got to go." He realized how much this effort cost her. Tears and blood streaked her cheeks and chin, but she held the sobs inside. "Please take me away from these people."

He looked at her huddled against him and cradled the back of her head. "No problem." He tried to soothe her, then locked his gaze with Rhys's. "Damn you— damn you all!"

Arrogant, Rhys gestured for the other Sharetakers to

follow him back inside. If Eduard hadn't been there to stop them, the mob would have pursued Teresa out into the streets and killed her.

Protectively, he half led, half carried her to the hovercar. He moved slowly, helping her to get inside. From the Sharetakers' building, Rhys didn't even bother to watch Teresa leave. To him, she was beneath contempt.

By the time Eduard got her to an emergency medical center, Daragon was already there, intimidating the admittance clerk. "Check your records again, please. She would have been admitted in the last hour."

Even groaning in her pain, Teresa recognized his voice. Eduard called out as he eased her into a chair. "Daragon! We're here."

Looking powerful and confident, Daragon rushed down the hall. His dark hair was mussed, and his Beetle uniform looked as if he had pulled it on quickly. "Is she all right?"

"She will be, now that I've gotten her away from those bastards."

Pulling all the strings of his authority, Daragon bellowed for a doctor. Much faster than Teresa would otherwise have been treated, a medical technician cleaned the worst cuts and contusions, started an IV, splinted her arm, and finally administered heavy analgesics. Both Daragon and Eduard hovered beside her, very concerned.

Even as the painkillers bit through the aches, Teresa lifted her bruised eyes to Daragon. "How...how did you know?"

Eduard leaned closer to Teresa. "He spies on us."

He flushed. "I watch out for you, though without COM terminals the Sharetakers make it very difficult."

The medical technician hummed to herself as she

applied bandages and injected her patient with bone-knitting steroids and cell-division enhancers, then applied polymer struts to hold the broken wrist and collarbone in place. She paid little attention to the conversation. In other circumstances, a doctor might hopscotch with a patient to better assess symptoms and hidden damage, but this one treated only the obvious injuries. And there were plenty of those.

Daragon's voice was grim. "The person who did this to Teresa was Robertha Chambers, a wanted anti-COM terrorist."

"The one from the explosion in the flower market? The fugitives that tried to take Teresa hostage during the shootout?" Eduard still had so much anger inside him he didn't know how to focus it. "Are you saying *Rhys* is Robertha Chambers?"

Daragon nodded. "She went into hiding, traded bodies with a man, took over the leadership of a local Sharetaker enclave. I found her because I was watching out for Teresa, looking into the religious group... but Chief Ob told me there were other priorities."

Eduard looked down at Teresa's battered, beautiful face. "Other priorities? Come on, Daragon—look what they did to her!"

Daragon felt helpless, but he maintained his stern expression. "Robertha had made no illegal move in years, and I could not get permission to act. I didn't think Teresa would be in danger."

"Maybe I'll have a few words with Chief Ob myself—"

Daragon held up a hand. "Rest assured, Eduard. Teresa will be protected now. And the matter has my full attention, regardless of what the Chief says. I have justification now."

But Eduard knew the BTL was hamstrung by the

niceties of law and bureaucracy. "Just don't take too long, or that bastard'll hurt someone else."

The medical technician searched her tray, as if wondering whether to use more drugs or bandages. "There, that's all we can do. Nothing serious, no need for her to stay here. Your body will take care of what's left. You need rest, and time." She looked disapprovingly at the two men, but spoke to Teresa. "Do you have a place to go?"

Eduard spoke quickly. "Yes, she does. She'll be coming home with me, so I can watch over her."

Daragon agreed. If any problems arose, he could smooth them over with Mordecai Ob. "I'll give you an escort."

Already fading from the intense mixture of analgesics and narcotics, Teresa could barely summon the strength to mumble, "Thank you. Both of you."

26

Long after midnight, returning from the medical center, Eduard eased Teresa's half-limp body out of the Bureau Chief's vehicle. He led her one slow step at a time along the pea-gravel path to the rear of the mansion and through his own private door. She sank into his bed like a snowflake melting in warm water. Teresa lay barely awake, retreating inside herself.

Hot with anger, Eduard looked at her bruised and childlike face. Tenderly straightening the sheets, he leaned down to whisper in her ear. "Just rest here and don't worry about anything. You need some peace." He touched her temples. "Hopscotch with me, and I'll take the pain for a while."

Her eyes flickered open, large and wide. She looked so lost. "No, Eduard. You've already rescued me once tonight."

He gave her a brotherly frown. "Hey, remember what I used to do for a living." A few bruises and healing bones couldn't compare with the unending agony of diseased bodies and severe surgeries. "Besides, you don't have the strength left to argue with me."

When he stared deeply into her eyes, touching her head, he felt his consciousness leap across the narrow gulf as they exchanged bodies. Then he blinked to reset his frame of reference.

Eduard lay in the bed, looking up at his own face, noticing the lines of concern written there now that

Teresa could see her ugly injuries from the outside. A whirlpool of pain spun through her body, but he pushed it aside. Through the distant fuzziness of drugs, he sensed each one of her broken ribs, wrist, and collarbone, as well as the cuts and contusions.

It wasn't so bad. He could tolerate it. No problem.

Teresa kissed him on an abraded cheek, and her eyes—Eduard's eyes—filled with tears. She slumped into the sofa. Finally, after hours of keeping herself strong, denying the seriousness of what she'd been through, Teresa began to sob, great wracking convulsions that came out in Eduard's deep voice.

Lying in bed, he wanted to get up, to hold her and comfort her, but in this injured body he was too weak. Teresa wanted to be alone, too. He heard her brokenhearted weeping until she finally fell asleep from sheer mental exhaustion, sprawled across the cushions.

"Eduard, wake up."

He had drifted off near dawn and managed only an hour of sleep in her injured body. Now Teresa stood above him over the bed. He could see his own eyes redrimmed from crying, his cheeks puffy.

"You have to get up," she said. "Swap back with me, so you can do your job."

Eduard tried to sit, felt the wash of pain. Time for more medication. He dosed himself again, waited for the edge of pain to dull all over his body. "Teresa, I don't want to let you come back into this body. It's too—"

"No choice." Her voice was firm. He could see that she had already grown much stronger since last night. "You've helped me so much, but I can't let you get in trouble with your boss. You've got too much at stake, don't you think?"

Eduard knew she was right. He glanced at the clock,

saw that he still had a little time. "All right, but you need to promise me you'll rest—heal yourself."

"Rest sounds like the best thing in the world right now, no matter which body I'm in." They touched, and swapped, and Eduard watched her face fall. She must have forgotten how much her injuries hurt.

Eduard's limbs were stiff from sleeping in an awkward position on the couch. He rubbed his burning eyes. Maybe a hot shower would help. "I've got to get cleaned up." As it was, Ob would scold him for bringing a body that wasn't strong and refreshed.

As Teresa sprawled on the bed, still getting used to the throbbing lethargy from the potent painkillers he had just taken, Eduard hurried to put together a breakfast. He fed her fruit slices in bed, and she savored each bite.

"I'll be back in a few hours, depending on what Mr. Ob needs me to do, then I can take another shift in your body. We'll get through this, together." He smiled at her. "I'm looking forward to nursing you back to health. I've already tried to contact Garth, but he's not coming back from Hawaii for another two days."

The painkillers had already begun to work. Teresa looked at him with heavy eyes. "Oh, thank you, Eduard."

"Hey, it's what friends are supposed to do for each other." He gave her his winning smile. "You're just lucky you sent me that COM message when you did. Otherwise I might have been too late."

Groggy, Teresa raised her eyebrows. "Never got a chance. No COM terminals inside the togetherments." Her voice was raspy, thick with impending sleep.

Perplexed, Eduard went off to find Mordecai Ob and begin another workday.

While jogging, Eduard had time to let his mind wander. His anger built into a bonfire as he thought about Rhys and Robertha Chambers. He had experienced Teresa's physical pain, though he could never feel the mental anguish she was still enduring.

As he ran along in Ob's physically fit body, he pushed himself harder, jogged faster. Cool morning air cut into his lungs, and perspiration soaked his exercise suit. As he thought more and more about the redhead striking Teresa, kicking her, throwing a hammer at her, he ran twice his usual distance. Ob would probably complain about sore muscles that evening, but Eduard didn't care. Right now he'd rather be sitting beside Teresa, tending her, trying to make everything better.

But he didn't know how he could fix the damage that had been done.

As he finished his second circuit of the grounds, at the limits of his stamina, he came across the massive gardener. The Samoan wrestled with a new ornamental tree, trying to heave it upright so he could lash on a support. His arm muscles bulged, but he managed to prop the strut before he exhausted himself. Tanu straightened the bindings and touched some of the bent branches, fixing every detail like a fussy mother tugging the collar of her son's shirt.

Panting, Eduard stopped short, wiping sweat from Ob's forehead. Tanu gave a quick wave before turning back to the tree. Making up his mind, Eduard caught his breath and strode over to the gardener. "Tanu, I need to ask you something."

The Samoan turned to him, his expression open and uncertain. "I have work to do."

Unable to think of a better alternative, Eduard said, "I want to swap into your body. Just for a little while. I...I have a job to do."

Tanu shook his big, black-maned head. "Lots of people offer for my body, but I don't like to hopscotch."

Eduard realized that the Samoan's physique would have been desirable to many people. He sat on one of the stone benches and folded his hands in his lap. "Tanu, I wouldn't ask if I didn't have to. This is important—at least let me tell you about it."

The Samoan stood like a statue next to his tree as Eduard explained Teresa's desperate situation, what had happened to her. His expression became grave and deeply saddened. "I'll think about it."

Eduard got up again, feeling the stiffness of overexerted muscles. Sweat had dried on his arms and the back of his neck. "Let me finish my exercises. I've got to do a few laps in the pool. I'll shower and change, and then I'll come back."

As Eduard jogged off, Tanu trudged toward the rear of the main house, looking through the windows of Eduard's private rooms. Inside, he saw Teresa's battered form asleep on the bed. With his large, dark eyes, he stared at her for a long time.

Later, wearing the Samoan body, Eduard felt as if his mind were in the driver's seat of a massive piece of construction machinery. With rolling steps, plowing through the air as he moved, he returned to the togetherments. He shoved through the building doors without knocking.

The Sharetaker recruits kept busy with menial tasks. One woman stroked a spraybrush over a dried blood smear where Teresa had held herself upright the night before.

Inside the open-structured quarters, Eduard stalked past curious cult members without saying a word. The Sharetakers stared at him, intrigued. They were used to an endlessly changing succession of bodies and identities, but a form as impressive as the Samoan's was unforgettable.

One lantern-jawed man stepped in front of him. "Welcome! I can answer questions, if you'd like. Have you come to join our group?"

Eduard glowered at him, remembering this man as one of the people who had hurled insults at Teresa. "I want to see Rhys."

The lantern-jawed man flicked a glance over his shoulder through skeletal arches and halls. "I . . . I think he's busy."

"No problem. I'll find him myself."

Inside an area strewn with rugs and pillows, he found Rhys busily having sex with another Sharetaker. Eduard clenched his fists at his sides. Rhys had wasted no time in choosing his next victim.

Grunting, sweating, the two thrashed about, oblivious to anyone who might have been watching. Sharetakers were accustomed to being out in the open. The woman rode on top, her head flung back, blond hair tickling her shoulder blades, her mouth open in ecstasy.

"Which one of you is Rhys?" Eduard demanded, satisfied to see them twitch with surprise.

The woman slid off the redheaded man. Her eyes were hard and narrow. Without answering, she reached down to look at her man's face, touching him. After they swapped, the redheaded man sat up, annoyed at the interruption. "I'm Rhys. What the hell do you want?"

"I'm a friend of Teresa's." Eduard balled both fists. Each one looked the size of the abusive man's head. "Maybe you remember her?"

Rhys shoved the woman away as he scrambled to his feet. Naked, she fled toward the other Sharetakers. "So? What the hell do you want?"

In Tanu's body, Eduard outweighed Rhys by about

two hundred pounds and stood a foot taller. "What I want is to beat the shit out of you ... just like you did to Teresa."

Rhys swallowed and backed against an exterior wall. "You're outnumbered here. The Sharetakers are a group. We stick together." He put up his fists in a pathetic attempt to defend himself.

"Just like you all stood by Teresa?"

Two of the other Sharetakers clenched their fists and took a step forward, but Eduard whirled on them. He knew it had been foolhardy to come here alone, even in Tanu's massive body. Normally he would have been more calculating ... but this was for a *friend*. For Teresa. With one look at the fury on his face, the would-be defenders hesitated, and all their resistance scattered.

The redheaded man, still naked and sweaty from sex, made a break for it, trying to slip past his attacker. Eduard stuck out one of his muscular arms like a boat oar that tumbled Rhys backward. He then picked the man up by the throat and slammed him against the wall.

Rhys flailed, kicking out with his bare feet. Eduard punched him in the stomach with more force than he knew he possessed. Rhys coughed an explosive breath, then dropped to the floor. He rolled over, got to his knees, and vomited.

"Personally, I've never had any desire to pick on people smaller than myself," Eduard said in a low voice, "but you've made me reconsider."

Rhys tried to crawl away, scuttling on his hands and knees. Eduard kicked him square on the buttocks, which made Rhys skid across the floor on his face and chest.

"Stop! Help me!" Several Sharetakers hurried forward, looking at their leader, but the large angry Samoan held them at bay.

"They won't help you any more than they helped Teresa." Eduard watched as they scuttled off like ro-

dents. "They're no good for anything but watching."
He hauled Rhys back to his feet, and the leader's legs
turned to water.

"What do you want?" His eyes were wide and desperate. "I'll give you—"

"You can't give Teresa her innocence back." Eduard
hauled off and punched him in the face. "Rhys." Blood
sprayed from the leader's smashed nose and split lip.
Not fully aware of his new strength, Eduard held up the
redhead and struck again, feeling teeth break and bone
crack.

He shook his hand, then punched a third time.
"*Rhys*. I want to keep saying your name out loud so that
I'll always connect that name with the sound of my fist
slamming into your body." Then Eduard hit him with
the other weapon he had. "Or should I say *Robertha?*"

Wailing, spitting blood and broken teeth, the redhead collapsed to the floor, shocked to hear the old
name. "Did you get tired of sabotage and terrorism?
The Beetles know where you are." Eduard let go of the
redhead's body as if he had soiled his hands.

"Why did you pick Teresa? Did she give too much?
Did you choose the most inoffensive person in your enclave? She is so caring and loving and . . . unsuspecting.
A ripe target for someone like you." He grabbed Rhys's
red hair, pulling his head up. "Or do you just like picking on women?"

"You don't understand anything about women."
Rhys/Robertha touched blood on his lips, looked at his
finger as if the color frightened him. His words were
slurred through a battered mouth. "Not everyone gets
the sheltered, naïve life your precious Teresa had."

Eduard couldn't believe the man wanted to have this
conversation, now, in his condition. "Teresa has more
love to give than you'll see in your entire life."

He couldn't even articulate how vile he found this

person, but he glowered, knowing the Samoan's wide face and flared nostrils looked intimidating. He took another massive step forward and watched as the leader wet himself, pulling up knees and trying to shrink into a ball of garbage. Eduard let him crawl toward the main room, watching how he moved as if on a carpet of broken glass, how he left a pattern of blood and urine like a slug's trail on the floor. He followed, one step behind him.

Finding reserves of energy somewhere, using adrenaline to push back the pain of his injuries, Rhys snatched a small sledgehammer near the wall and swung the wicked club toward Eduard's knees.

He saw the blow coming and jumped out of the way. Tanu's body was large and lumbering, but his muscles were strong, and he skipped just out of the arc of the swing.

The momentum of Rhys's unconnected blow made the redheaded man fall sideways. Moving quickly, Eduard stomped hard on the hand that had grasped the hammer. With Tanu's more than four hundred pounds, his heel shattered all the bones in Rhys's hand and wrist.

The redhead screamed.

Eduard yanked the heavy hammer from the man's grip. Rhys's wrist now had the flexibility of a licorice whip.

Seeing a bloodred haze, Eduard raised the hammer. He thought of how Rhys had broken Teresa's collarbone with a similar tool, how he had kicked her, cracked her ribs, snapped her wrist. His muscles tensed.

Rhys looked up at him with the wide eyes of a sheep in a slaughterhouse. One blow to the head with the pointed end of the sledge—

"You're not worth the effort. Not in the least." Instead, Eduard threw the heavy tool across the room, where it left a gouge in the fresh wallboard. He had already won his victory. The great cult leader had been laid bare before his followers, naked in his impotence— and none of the other Sharetakers had bothered to help him. How could the group ever be the same? "If your life was so bad, Robertha, you should have learned to be more compassionate." Eduard turned his back. "Not how to be a better bully."

With bloody fists and the crunch of bone still ringing in his ears, he went back to Teresa, satisfied at last.

27

As usual, Garth arrived first at Club Masquerade, newly returned from Hawaii and still shaken from his near-death experience. He had already made an appointment to see his patron, Mordecai Ob, the following day, to describe some of the new plans he'd made, the new inspiration he had found.

Explosively eager to talk to somebody while he waited for Teresa and Eduard, he told the Club's cybernetic bartender how he had nearly drowned, and how he had found a new quest to experience everybody and everything.

"Aren't you being overly ambitious, Garth?" Bernard Rovin's face asked from the tablescreen.

"It's doable." He wandered over to stare at the Hopscotch Board, which made him dizzy with its possibilities. So many choices! The complex listing of swapportunities and "experiences wanted" gave him a broad starting point for everything he had to do.

Not long afterward, Eduard came in, leading a bruised and fragile-looking young woman. Garth ran over to greet the two of them, astonished. "Eduard! Teresa? What happened?"

The injured woman raised a cautioning hand as Garth leaned forward to give her a welcoming hug. "*I'm* Eduard."

Eduard's home-body spoke up. "And I'm Teresa, for now. We're taking turns in his body while I heal. We're splitting the pain between us. It's really kind of Eduard, don't you think?"

Without a moment's hesitation, Garth reached out to the hurt woman's form. "Here, swap with me. You can rest inside my body, if you need to."

In a normal situation, Eduard might have brushed aside the offer, but he knew Garth's gesture came from the heart, and he did not hesitate. They touched temples...and Garth suddenly felt every injury Teresa had endured, the contusions, the snapped bones, the bruises. Even with the pain-blocking medication that fuzzed the details, it was all he could do to lift his mending wrist to synch ID patches.

In the fragile, injured body Garth stumbled over to the nearest table. "All right, Teresa, but if I'm sharing the pain with you—and Eduard—you'd better tell me what happened."

Comfortable in the artist's blond physique, Eduard helped to settle the aching form onto a levitating stool. Teresa propped sharp elbows on the table. Eduard had to do most of the talking, his voice cold, and Garth could see the anger and hurt reflected on Teresa's face. Every time she heard Rhys's name mentioned, she flinched as if at the sound of a distant gunshot.

Garth remembered the BTL raid on the anti-COM terrorists, how he had frozen in panic when young Teresa needed to be rescued. Eduard had saved her that time as well, without thinking, throwing himself into the line of fire to protect her. "Sorry I wasn't here when you needed me," Garth said. *Again.*

The bartender's scarred and image-processed face popped up on their tablescreen. "Sounds like you three could use a good drink."

Eduard, in Garth's home-body, sat up, indignant. "Bernard, this was a private conversation."

Rovin's image smiled placatingly. "Part of my job is to listen to the customers' problems."

Eduard marched up to the main bar, behind which the bartender's organic remnants hid. Garth winced in his chair and mumbled to Teresa, "I don't know why he thinks he's going to have a better conversation down there than right here from the screen."

"Neither do I," Rovin's image said from the table.

Eduard leaned over the bar to get as close as he could to the sealed door of the control room. Behind there, what remained of the man sat implanted in a mobile life-support system. "All right, Bernard, quid pro quo. Let's hear *your* story. How did you get to be this multiplexed, cybernetic hodgepodge?"

Rovin chuckled from one of the screens in the bar surface. "All right, my friend—it's a deal. But you head on back to your table, so I can tell you all at the same time . . . and we can have some measure of privacy."

When Eduard returned, his small lilt of a smile suggested that his indignation had mostly been an act. Rovin's image paused as his other "parts" continued to cater to various customers. As soon as he had the multiprocessing sorted out, he began to tell his tale.

"When I was younger, I used to come in here as a customer, wild in the body-swapping scene. Hopscotching from body to body, having a grand old time. Wasn't worried about slippage in the least. Never thought anything bad could happen to me.

"Then, a few years ago I was in the wrong place at the wrong time, flying too close to a terrorist bombing near the flower market. My hovercar crashed in a truly spectacular wreck—or so they tell me. I was unconscious at the time. Some people called me a lucky survivor."

"It was spectacular, all right," Eduard said with a gasp. "A topaz-blue hovercar? I used the distraction to steal a bouquet for Teresa. Daragon felt guilty about it for a month."

"Well, I'm glad somebody benefited from my accident."

Rovin's duplicate images on other tablescreens continued talking with customers, taking their orders, making parallel chitchat. His cybernetic arms and hands worked busily mixing drinks.

"The crash left me a mangled lump. I'd spent all my credits on fast living, and I didn't have any resources left to lease myself a new body...not that I was likely to find anyone willing to swap with me at any price."

Eduard brooded, squeezing his fists tighter. "Score another victim for Robertha Chambers, or Rhys. If it's any consolation, Bernard—" He told Rovin how he had pummeled the renegade terrorist into a bloody lump, since the BTL didn't seem to care about finding her. "Sometimes you can't wait for the law. Not when somebody's hurting you."

As he sat at the table, Garth felt the bruises in Teresa's slender body, the knitting bones, the deep soreness. He couldn't imagine the flaming agony Rovin had endured. "So what did you do after the accident, Bernard?"

"Well, I'd known the owner of Club Masquerade, and he made me a proposal, not that I had any choice at that point. I came here to be *installed*—literally—as the Club's permanent bartender, linked up to these prosthetics. With multiple arms and eyes, and a lot of concentration, I could watch over the entire Club and all its different rooms, all by myself. Not only did that save the salaries of numerous employees, it also added one more gimmick to this place. You wouldn't believe how many people come here just to watch me work."

"Don't you feel exploited?" Teresa asked.

"Exploited? I'm fully recovered, healed inside and

out, and content with the fact. Where else would I get an opportunity like this?"

"Do you ever leave here?" Garth asked. "Ever go outside to see what you're missing?"

"I'm not missing anything. I've had plenty of experiences already. Here, I can observe a thousand lives from the safety of my own." Rovin's image smiled. "I delight in watching other people—like you three."

Teresa sat stiffly in Eduard's body, frowning. "I'd rather have watched a few things, instead of experiencing them myself."

"We'll help you, Teresa." Garth focused on her again. "Any way we can."

She reached over to touch the bruised, waifish body. It would have to be her home-body from now on, since she had lost her original form and had no idea where to look for it. "Oh, I know. And thank you. But sometimes I need to do things for myself."

She and Garth and Eduard swapped and swapped again until they were in their own forms once more. Garth felt a pang watching her wince, faced again with her slow-healing pain. Teresa was strong inside, but she wouldn't hesitate to ask for assistance, if she genuinely needed it. Not from them.

Eduard stood. "Come on, Teresa. Let's get you back to my place so you can rest."

"I'm tired of being a burden, even on you, Eduard. The sooner I'm on my feet again—and *independent*—the happier I'll be."

Garth didn't know what to do. Seeing Teresa's loss of innocence and good cheer made him want to cry. He had felt her deep bodily ache, but could not so easily feel her heart's anguish, the dark shame of what had befallen her.

But he *needed* to feel it somehow, for the good of his artwork.

Arms linked, the three friends prepared to leave. For just a moment, in a pause between fixing drinks and making conversation, the cybernetic bartender lifted every one of his mechanical arms around the Club to wave goodbye.

28

The very idea of life and all its unexplored terrain unfolded before him like a treasure map. Garth needed to understand so many obvious things he had never thought about before. Sitting alone in a retro coffee shop and drinking strong espresso, he figured that the best thing would be to compile a list of experiences he wanted to acquire. A formal plan for his artistic growth.

The List.

A month earlier, using a frugal amount of the credits Mordecai Ob had given him, Garth had purchased an inexpensive used datapad from a group of Sharetakers selling odds and ends on the street corner. He had gone to visit Teresa, and at the time he'd been hoping to help her, but now he felt guilty about it. The abusive group didn't deserve his support in any way.

He sat under the coffee shop's green awning, sipping from a tiny porcelain cup. He let his thoughts wander, mulling over new ideas, the breadth of what he needed to learn. Possibilities and possibilities.

Through hopscotching, Garth could actually *be* different people, from the ugly to the sublime. It was an opportunity the great classical artists had never had. His art had to speak to each man and woman, to all of humanity. Therefore, he must experience every facet of the human condition from the point of view of each individual, not just as an outside observer.

Nursing his espresso, Garth recorded ideas on the datapad. The magnitude of the task gave him a headache, but he scribed so quickly, adding new ideas, that his fingers were a blur. It was both exciting and overwhelming.

He would slog through his List one item at a time. He had to comprehend being a man, being a woman. Was there any difference inside, in the heart and the soul, or just societal training from childhood in his home-body? If he could swap genders at will, was he still somehow fundamentally *male,* or did all the differences ride on the chromosomes and hormone cocktails of the cells?

He had to know what it was to be old and frail, and to be young and athletic. He needed to be exhausted to the core from a lifetime of hard work . . . and filled with manic unreleased energy, never able to sleep.

He would be muscular and he would be obese. As a woman, he could be flat chested or well endowed. He would be short, and tall; he could wear different colors of skin. He wanted to be pregnant and give birth to a child. In one deformed body he'd be looked upon with disgust; in another, he'd be stunningly beautiful, stimulating the glands of every person who looked at him. And he would do it both from the male side and from the female side.

Garth had to experience everything.

He finished his tiny cup, the caffeine singing through his system, but he felt more energized than even the espresso could account for. He scanned the List and knew he had written barely half of the things that would occur to him. But he could keep adding ideas even as he removed completed ones.

He had a mission now. Life itself would be his fulltime job.

After the new painting was hung in a well-lit hallway in Mordecai Ob's house, the only thing that looked out of place was the Bureau Chief himself. Garth just couldn't get used to seeing the man wearing Eduard's body.

Without speaking to the blond artist, Ob appraised the eerie painting of glitter-oils that gradually flowed across preprogrammed paths. Garth had re-created the tumbling breakers from Waimea Beach, but replaced the frothing wavetops with a scatter of stars that spilled into a black universe, showering upon a vague luminous representation of a human form, a soul.

"It's very compelling, Garth." Ob at last turned to look at him with a very un-Eduard-like expression. "Hypnotic, but disturbing. I'm glad you're not painting flowers or puppy dogs."

Garth had told him about his trip to Hawaii, about his near-death experience. Then he told his patron about the List. "It's like a quest, Mr. Ob. A specific catalogue of things I want to do and experience."

"Such enthusiasm! I truly envy you your ambition and your inspiration. I just wish I could capture some of that for myself. Does this mean you'll be wanting additional money?"

Garth felt embarrassed. The thought hadn't even occurred to him. "No, sir. I just wanted to tell you what I intended to do. I thought you should know."

The Bureau Chief gave him a patronizing smile. "Of course. I'll transfer more credits into your account within the hour." His shoulders sagged, as if Eduard had gotten too little sleep in his own body. He began to lead Garth down the hall toward the exit.

Garth hesitated, looked at his friend's familiar features. "Would it be possible for me to visit Eduard while I'm here? Just to say hello."

The other man frowned, then slowly shook his head.

"I'd rather you didn't, Garth. Eduard will be exercising my body for another hour, and I don't want to distract him."

Disappointed, Garth agreed. "All right, maybe next time. I'll bring you another work soon."

No longer spending his weekends among the aspiring artists, Garth returned to the bazaar as an *observer*. Now, as he walked among the stalls and rugs, he gazed upon the marketplace with new eyes. He studied faces and illustration techniques, including sculptures made of colored plasmas, gravity-defying paintings fashioned from 3-D gels, aroma symphonies.

Excited, he took notes, seeing things he had never *seen* before. Some vendors gave him strange looks, suspicious of his questions and scrutiny. One woman even asked if he was working undercover for the Beetles or some other investigatory agency.

With an artist's eye, he jotted down details, questions to ask someday. He noted how the vendors were attentive to well-dressed customers in healthy bodies, while a swarthy, hirsute man had to clamor to get the attention of the person behind a chocolate stand.

The incident piqued Garth's curiosity, and he wondered if this short hairy man had a stunning wife at home, or someone just as lumpish. Perhaps the man was a convict finishing a probationary term in a brutish form, and would not receive his own physique back until his sentence was up.

Over the past century of hopscotching, equality had come with particular force . . . but only in certain areas. Skin color and gender didn't matter much, men and women, blacks and whites, Hispanics, Asians—anyone could be anyone, by choice. On the other hand, different manifestations of discrimination crept in with a vengeance, creating a clear-cut and striking physical class system. Anyone wealthy or powerful enough could lease a young and attractive physique, while poor and downtrodden people were forced to trade away their bodies to make enough money to survive.

Garth wondered how much real variation there was at the ultimate core of a human being. If he could answer that question, he could make the most profound statement any artist had ever produced.

He remembered the amateurish mural he had painted in the basement of the Falling Leaves, how his one small idea had grown to encompass new details, new characters and scenes. Now Garth was attempting a vastly larger task: a mural of all humanity.

The next step would be to figure out how to *implement* that plan.

Club Masquerade provided the most opportunities all in one place. The majority of people didn't hopscotch indiscriminately, too shy or too afraid, viewing the process as more personal than sexual intercourse. But many Club patrons already wanted temporary new bodies, wanted different experiences. Garth saw them as resources for his work.

One heady evening, he picked up an attractive ginger-haired woman for a one-night/two-body stand— no strings attached, no expectations, just hedonistic fun. They danced, and touched... then swapped, and danced and touched again. Later, during the hours in her bed, the woman pleasured herself in her own body, and then in Garth's.

The woman played strange mood music and insisted on keeping the bedroom air temperature uncommonly cold. They were forced to keep themselves warm through body heat, which she happily provided.

Garth had been a woman before, and he'd had sex in Teresa's original body, but this time he paid complete attention to how everything *felt,* how everything *fit.* As he touched his soft female skin, her moist openings, Garth wished he had placed his electronic pad within reach. He needed to document his impressions before they faded from memory. In a woman's body, the nerve endings were different, distributed in new patterns. Various movements produced alternate responses.

He wanted to jot down his observations as a man, then as a woman, comparing the differences in intensity and sensation during orgasm in each gender. But the ginger-haired woman kept him too busy with her own agenda. She seemed very familiar with the workings of both types of bodies, but had no particular interest in contributing to the world of art.

When Garth continued to ask questions, the woman was at first delighted but eventually put off. Clearly, she'd never done such internal self-analysis. Before long, Garth knew the answers and the subtleties better than she did herself.

The ginger-haired woman gave him an insincere invitation to look her up again. After he left, Garth realized that of all the questions, he'd forgotten to ask her name....

29

Flowers, surrounded by beautiful flowers. Glad for her new job, Teresa went on her rounds through office buildings in search of customers for whatever bouquets hadn't been presold.

During her weeks of recovery, Tanu the gardener had contacted a friend and secured Teresa a job from the cavernous central greenhouse hangars. Fully healed now, she found peace in her baskets of colorful blossoms, accompanied by their delicate perfumes, the gentle pastels.

Something that would let her forget the dark times with Rhys.

Since Teresa had little else she could give back to them, she always kept extra blossoms to send to both Eduard and Garth as a special thank-you. The Beetles wouldn't let her send flowers to Daragon. She was starting her life fresh once again, a cleaner beginning than when she had departed from the Falling Leaves. This time she swore it would be different.

At first, Teresa had thought about returning to the monastery as a place to contemplate, despite Soft Stone's admonition to the contrary. She wanted to be safe again, protected behind the walls. But she eventually realized that she had made her own mistakes, and she would make her own solutions. Teresa was determined not to disappoint her mentor.

While she occupied herself selling flowers, Teresa

went back to considering the Big Questions that had fascinated her for so many years. She had been fooled into thinking the Sharetakers offered the answers she needed; instead, they had simply taken everything from her. From now on, she had to find the revelations on her own.

Eduard had invited her to stay with him at Ob's mansion for as long as she needed. He even offered to marry her, if that was what she wished. Teresa held him long and hard, feeling his unconditional devotion to her—as always—but she wanted to be by herself, to prove that she could live on her own, without depending on other people. As with Garth, their friendship was deeper than romantic love or sex, and *that* was what she needed most from Eduard.

She made other promises, too. After such a dizzying flow with the Sharetakers, Teresa resigned herself to remain inside this waifish body that was not really her own. She couldn't just toss it aside for another, as the Sharetakers had done. From now on, this slight, large-eyed female would house her identity.

Teresa pushed through the revolving door into an office building, where she arranged roses and carnations in boardrooms and reception areas, brightening the enclosed spaces. Enough bouquets remained in her basket for one more building, then she would return to the central greenhouse hangar for another load. But she was in no hurry and had no real schedule to keep. She did not feel the urge to grab an even larger piece of business than the previous day.

Outside, Teresa walked across the plaza and stopped by a stylized modern-art fountain made of gray and tan stone. Crude flint mirrors protruded at odd angles, distorting reflections. Balancing the flower basket on her lap, she sat on the fountain rim, leaning back on her outspread arms. The COM weather programmers had selected a cool, clear day with a bite of salt breeze from the nearby bay. She took an inventory of her remaining bouquets, inspecting each bloom, plucking wilted petals to keep the flowers looking fresh. Childlike, she tossed petals into the fountain.

"Good thing our fingers and hands don't fall off like that when we get old," said a man who shuffled up to her. "It would mess up the entire physical system." Teresa was startled by his appearance, but not frightened. The thin stranger had ice-blue eyes, yellow-gray hair, and an unevenly cut beard. His brow was furrowed, as if frequently creased with deep thought.

"I...I don't have any spare credits to give you, if you're panhandling."

"Panhandling? No, I have all I really need." His skin pallor and his scrawny physique belied the statement.

"What about your clothes?" Teresa could see he lived on the streets, probably alone. His shirt and pants were out of date, dirty, tattered.

"These?" The man plucked dismissively at his faded sleeves. "Outer coverings. Only a shell. I keep my *body* in good condition. That's what I was born with. Everything else is just...adornment."

She watched the flower petals on the water, thinking again of the Sharetakers and her lost dreams, how so many things had already drifted away from her. "Some people might say hopscotching is like casting off petals from a flower. Discarding an old body once it's fulfilled its purpose."

The man frowned in sudden distaste. "Who's to say what the body's purpose is and when it's been fulfilled?"

He sat beside her on the edge of the fountain, and she felt sorry for him, decided she could help. "Well, it looks as if you could use a solid meal if you're so concerned about your body, don't you think?"

"Okay, I admit malnutrition is sometimes a problem." The ragged man dipped his hand in the fountain and self-consciously rubbed water to rinse his arm. "Gotta watch for any cuts to make sure they don't get infected. I exercise to keep my body functioning smoothly." He squeezed his bicep with mock seriousness.

Teresa looked down at her waifish body. The flowers in her lap smelled sweet and warm. "I have a friend who maintains his boss's body, exercising for hours each day."

The stranger laughed, a braying chuckle so loud it caused other pedestrians to look at him. "Exercising for somebody else? You think that would help anyone understand how a body works?"

His ice-blue eyes became suddenly intense, and he blinked repeatedly. He reached out to take Teresa's hand and thrust her own palm in front of her face. "Once you know the details, you can't help but worship the complexity. This delicate and intricate machine is far superior to any mechanism human beings have managed to devise. Okay, just look at your fingerprints, at the blood vessels beneath the skin. See your pores." He bent two of her fingers down. "See the way the tendons move in your wrist. Magnificent, isn't it?"

"Oh—I never really thought about it before."

"No one should take the human machine for granted. No one should ignore it or treat it badly, discard it like a bad card in a hand of poker." He let out a shuddering sigh. "And all this hopscotching, one person to another to another! You shouldn't change bodies like you change a set of clothes."

Teresa looked at him, thinking of the special times she had swapped with Garth and Eduard, and how often she had hopped from member to member in the Sharetaker enclave. "You have a very odd way of thinking, sir," she said.

"Please call me Arthur."

"All right. You have a very odd way of thinking, Arthur."

"Okay, but it's my own philosophy, and I'm proud of it."

Smiling curiously, Teresa stood up. "I've got more flowers to deliver."

He shook her hand again, then gazed into her large eyes. "I'll be around. I hope I recognize you again."

Since she didn't plan to do any hopscotching in the near future, Teresa knew that wouldn't be a problem. "You will."

For the rest of that day, Teresa pondered her conversation with the shabby old man. Everybody hopscotched—it was only natural to switch bodies if you needed to, though some people were frightened by the occasional stories about slippage. When Daragon had proven unable to swap, the Splinters had considered it a tragic flaw.

Now Arthur's ideas intrigued her. From that point on, she sought out the old man as she went on her delivery rounds. He wasn't hard to find: he sat on benches in the sunlight or in secluded spots in the shade, reading through an ancient book he carried.

When she sat next to him, sharing her meager lunch, he paid her back by letting her look at his precious book. "Found it in a dump behind a museum." Arthur showed her the cover, then some of the text and the illustrations. Obviously, he revered the volume as if it were a religious artifact. "It's a facsimile of the original Gray's Anatomy, annotated with medical commentary and updated drawings."

As he flipped from page to page, Teresa stared at meticulous drawings: the circulatory system, musculature, tendons, glands, bones, the central nervous system. Arthur became so absorbed in the book that he seemed not to notice her. He ran his fingertips over a diagram of the heart's chambers, and his voice held a quiet awe. "Okay, I've read this book from front to back at least six times, and I still don't understand how my body works."

"Arthur, if you're interested in this stuff, why don't you just get a data uplink from COM? The latest medical studies, detailed electron microscope holographs, even interactive—"

Arthur slammed the book shut and tapped hard on the cover. "I'm not interested in sheer quantity of information, but in the best *quality* information. I want the right reference, rather than every single reference. And this one has stood the test of time." He regarded her with his eyebrows cocked. "Look."

As Teresa listened to him, the old man showed her his hands, his fingers, the veins beneath the skin, the calluses built up from a life of hard work. He pushed his fingers so close to her face that she had to squint before she could focus on the whorls and lines of his fingerprints.

Teresa had never before thought about the minutiae, the clockwork mechanisms of her human form. "I don't have my original body anymore. I haven't even seen it for a year. It . . . got lost somewhere along the way."

Arthur pursed his lips. "I'm sorry to hear that. You've lost an opportunity to . . . to get to know yourself, as it were."

Strangely enough, Teresa got the sneaking suspicion that this ragged man understood more about reality than she did. And she had promised Soft Stone she would never stop looking.

"I like talking with you, Arthur," she said.

"Likewise," he said.

30

The man was so incredibly obese he could barely walk. His girth was enormous, his garments made from acres of cloth. He took each plodding step with care and intense concentration, like a captain guiding an oil tanker through treacherous reefs. He overheated easily, sweating from the simple effort of moving his own mass across the street.

As soon as Garth spotted him, he knew that this must be one of the first targets on his List. With no inhibition whatsoever, he jogged up to the puffing man who stood on the street corner. "Excuse me! This is...this is amazing." Garth took a deep breath. "Sir, I'd like to swap with you, live in your body for an hour or so. Would that be possible?"

The man looked at him with suspicion. "What do you want?"

"I want to hopscotch into your body. If I paid you...uh, fifty credits, would that be enough?" Garth blinked at him like an optimistic puppy. "I don't have a lot of money to spare."

Looking at the artist's healthy body, the obese man reacted to the offer with astonishment, then with even greater suspicion. Breathlessly, his words tumbling together, Garth explained his creative quest to experience different aspects of being human. The man cautiously agreed, still suspecting some kind of practical joke. "No paperwork? Nothing?"

He quickly transferred the credits directly from Garth's card onto his own. His massive ham-hands touched Garth's face, thick fingers resting against his temples. They switched, then synched ID patches to legally complete the identity transfer.

Dizzy and overwhelmed, Garth stood motionless, needing the time to settle into the enormous new body with its heavy burden of flesh. He flexed his pudgy fingers. This physique seemed so clumsy, so unwieldy—like an overloaded truck rather than a sporty hovercar. When he inhaled, his lungs didn't seem to have enough capacity.

"This is amazing," Garth said. "I've never felt anything like this before." The spaces around him seemed closer, smaller. Fascinating. His agility was affected, but not his reflexes. The body itself adapted to balancing the weight.

The other man, delighted with the resilience of Garth's slender and healthy body, seemed to burst with energy. He laughed out loud.

And then bolted.

Garth couldn't believe what he was seeing. Inside Garth's body, the stranger ran harder, crossing the street, ducking under low-flying hovercars, through a disorganized farmer's market full of fruits and vegetables. Garth realized with a start that they hadn't arranged a meeting point. "Wait!"

The man sped away with Garth's blond, muscular physique, moving nimbly as he dashed down the street. He didn't know the man's name; worse, he didn't know how to find him ever again.

Puffing and lumbering, Garth tried to pursue the body-snatcher, but his overburdened leg muscles wouldn't cooperate. Simple movement seemed to require an effort equivalent to that needed for construction machinery, and within moments he was exhausted.

His face flushed with the effort, Garth staggered to a halt on the next corner. Winded, he tried to get the attention of other pedestrians, but he could not raise his voice.

Meanwhile, the man wearing Garth's body fled through a skyscraper doorway and disappeared into a crowded building.

The body-snatcher sprinted up the escalator stairs. His muscles felt electrified, his body so responsive, his footsteps light, as if he were running in reduced gravity. He pushed his way across the slide tube, deeper into the building complex . . . trying to get away. And succeeding.

He couldn't believe the stupid innocence of the artist, but couldn't let an opportunity like this go to waste. After a lifetime of hormonal imbalances, of enduring extreme obesity, he had never imagined that such a ridiculous chance would simply be thrust into his arms. After a clean transfer, he retained his identity. The patsy had no idea who he was, or how to track him down. The obese man would never go back to his clumsy, worthless form.

On a higher level, he reached a glass-walled mezzanine that contained a suite of clothes stores. From this vantage he looked down into the street and saw, far below, his lumbering body, unmistakable in the crowd. The guy was hopelessly lost. What a fool!

He could barely restrain himself. He touched his new body with delight. It had been so easy, so fun. He hadn't paused to think about what he was doing. He had just run. Now he dashed up a staircase, bounding two steps at a time—and he didn't even get short of breath!

A moment later he ran into a stern-eyed man wearing a dark Beetle uniform. Weapons drawn, the BTL Inspector stood directly in his way, blocking his escape.

"I don't take kindly to people who hurt my friends," Daragon said.

Daragon led the prisoner to where Garth stood hopeless, helpless, and confused on the street. Barely able to move in his overexerted body, Garth just hung his head, enduring Daragon's disappointment and fury.

"If I hadn't already been here, Garth—if I hadn't been watching you, because Chief Ob wanted to protect his investment—" He raised his voice, letting anger cut like a knife. "You didn't even know his *name?* Didn't check his ID? Didn't set up an irrevocable exchange clause? No contract whatsoever? That was stupid! Every formal hopscotch must have a time limit assigned and provide an avenue for resolving disputes."

Still wearing the enormously overweight body, Garth cringed, as if trying to shrink to a much smaller size. His chins jiggled. "It was only going to be for a few minutes."

"Even an artist has to take simple precautions, Garth—whether the swap is for five minutes or five months. Don't leave yourself so vulnerable. You're in the real world now, not inside the monastery walls."

"I never realized that what I was doing could be so . . . dangerous. I thought I could trust people." Garth wished he didn't have to feel so ashamed for making that assumption.

"You should know better, Garth—especially after what happened to both Eduard and Teresa." He shook his head, as if disgusted.

Summoned by Daragon, BTL reinforcements arrived in insectile hovercars. The terrified body-snatcher babbled excuses that no one wanted to hear. Daragon gestured with his weapon, supervising while Garth and the fat man hopscotched back into their own bodies.

Once returned to his obese home-body, the stranger wept and stammered more explanations, more pleas. After BTL apprehension specialists took the man away, Garth tried to explain what he'd been doing, why he needed to share the experiences and perspectives of other people, but Daragon was unimpressed. Since he could never hopscotch at all, he didn't know what to make of Garth's quest to "be" everybody and everything.

Daragon sighed and took his friend's arm. "You'll have to be careful if you plan to hopscotch so often. I can draw up a standard, simple contract template for you." They stopped by a tree. Seeing the BTL Inspector's uniform, another pedestrian quickly left a nearby bench and went on his own way.

"That would be great." Garth sat on the bench as if all the strength had gone out of him. Daragon remained standing, pacing back and forth in front of him.

"You didn't think this through, Garth. What do you know about this stranger you just swapped with? What if he had used that disguise to commit a terrible crime, and *you* were positively identified? Without legal proof of a swap, you might find yourself convicted."

Garth shuddered suddenly, uncontrollably, as he recalled the COM-upload execution he had witnessed in the open-air bazaar. Daragon saw the extreme reaction and felt ashamed. "Okay, I wouldn't let that happen to you. The Bureau has techniques for picking up residual brain imprints. I was just trying to spook you into being more careful."

"I'm spooked, all right, and I...appreciate it." Garth's smile was forced, but the gratitude in his eyes was real. "First you saved Eduard, and now me. Thank you, Daragon."

As Daragon climbed aboard a BTL transport and streaked away, Garth remained seated on the bench. He had a lot of thinking to do. He had learned something about human nature he hadn't even intended to.

From now on, he needed to take precautions, especially in wildly unequal exchanges, such as with the obese man. This insight into human nature—and the realization of his own naïveté—enriched Garth even as it saddened him. How could such a miserable person *not* be tempted to run off?

As he hurried back to his makeshift studio, he promised himself he would establish rules for working his way through the List. In fact, he needed to find an assistant, someone who could watch over him and attend to the business details of daily life, while handling the stipend Ob gave him.

When he got home, however, Garth's first priority was to rush to his datapad. He powered it up and opened new files. For the next two hours, he diligently recorded all his impressions of being in such an enormous body: the sensations, the emotions, other people's reactions to him.

Then, feeling triumphant, he crossed off the first item on his List.

31

Morning in the mansion, time to exercise again. Another day at work.

The sheets retracted, and Eduard crawled out. His muscles were unusually sore, and even his bones felt somehow bruised. "I should take better care of my own body," he said out loud, looking at the walls. Unfortunately, after spending so much time conditioning Ob's well-tuned physique, he was daunted by the prospect of exercising his own body.

Worse, his mouth tasted awful, as if Mordecai Ob had eaten cold squid and garlic before swapping back with him. He rinsed with a strong mouthwash, but the foul flavor lingered. On mornings like this, Eduard gladly traded bodies with the Bureau Chief.

Out in the conservatory, Ob wore a thick bathrobe and sat on a white wrought-iron chair eating his breakfast. Eduard reported for duty in an Ever-Pressed suit, just in case Ob needed to go into BTL Headquarters. "Have you eaten yet, Eduard? I'm going to need the energy for a long day."

"Sorry." Eduard bent over to the fruit plate and wolfed down some pineapple and bananas.

"Enough." The Chief gestured, and the two men hopscotched so they could go about their business. Ob bustled out of the conservatory without saying goodbye, apparently in a hurry to get to work locked in his secluded home office.

Eduard sat back down in the white garden chair, wishing he could relax and enjoy the remaining breakfast on the plate, but Ob had already eaten his fill, and this body was no longer hungry. He went into the gym to change from Ob's bathrobe into exercise clothing.

On his morning run, he paused for a few minutes to talk with Tanu. Ever since he'd borrowed the huge Samoan's body to use against Rhys, Eduard had tried to draw out the quiet and introspective gardener. From simple snippets of conversation, he discovered that the big man had many deep thoughts. Tanu spent much time in quiet contemplation as he worked among his silent flowers and trees.

Eduard circled and came to a stop, jogging in place to stay warmed up. "You've worked on the estate for a long time, haven't you?" He panted as he tried to catch his breath.

"Years," the gardener said, his typical extensive conversation.

"So . . . you must see a lot of things going on around here."

The Samoan just looked at him with sad, dark eyes, then found the Japanese maple beside him intensely interesting. He plucked one of the small leaves off a branch, but refused to speak what was on his mind.

With a sigh, Eduard knew he had overstayed his welcome. He jogged in place for a few more moments to build up energy, then ran off again.

After what the Sharetakers had done to Teresa, Daragon took pleasure in his subtle, inexorable revenge. He had known about the fugitive Robertha Chambers, and *Rhys,* but the Sharetakers had removed all COM terminals from their enclave, refused to use the computer network, and had therefore effectively blinded the Beetles. So much could have been prevented. . . .

The Data Hunter Jax would have taken a particular delight in assisting him, but Daragon drew satisfaction from his staged humiliation of Rhys/Robertha. He would not, could not, go against Mordecai Ob's explicit orders—but the resources of the BTL gave him plenty of alternatives.

Eduard had already done a marvelous, though brutal, job of exacting revenge on the Sharetaker leader. But that simply wasn't good enough. Not for Daragon. And not for Teresa . . .

During his routine meetings with the Bureau Chief, he was often bemused to see Eduard's familiar features sitting behind the massive desk. Though the younger body was compact and wiry, Ob behaved with the same confidence, took the same dominating stance as when he wore his own form. His forceful personality did not change with his physical appearance.

Daragon said, "So, I take it everything is satisfactory with Eduard, sir?"

"He's adequate, though occasionally careless." Ob had smiled behind the younger man's dark eyes. "I think we've got it all worked out, though. I depend on swapping with him to keep myself in peak physical condition."

"I am glad to know that, sir. There have been times when I doubted you saw any benefits in the swapping process."

Ob had laughed at the suggestion. "I have never been fool enough to speak out against hopscotching! There isn't a single married couple that hasn't tried it, at least behind bedroom doors, experimenting with each other's bodies."

He brushed his fingers down Eduard's chest. "Some people go to work in another body, just like your friend here. But not everyone needs to make a game out of it. When simple moral common sense doesn't work, we try to scare people out of swapping too much. Take slippage, for instance. You realize, of course, that the disease isn't real?" Ob raised his eyebrows in a very non-Eduard expression.

The information took Daragon aback. "Slippage doesn't exist?"

"Just a well-intentioned fiction that we put into propaganda stories released regularly to COM newsnets. The sinister threat of having your mind detached and floating through space adds just a touch of uncertainty. We can't prevent body-swapping, but we can certainly make it seem more risky."

Daragon remained standing at attention, for once relieved that he was different, unable to hopscotch at will. "I...understand, sir."

Today, though, the Bureau Chief had decided to work from home, and Daragon quietly embarked on his plan against the Sharetakers. One by one, he selected members of the enclave, people who had refused to help Teresa, who had watched Rhys's abuse and ignored it. He dug through their pasts, found reasons to discredit or embarrass them. Body and property leases were mysteriously canceled or annulled; some members were arrested for fraud. Severe fines were levied for the most obscure or minor infractions.

The Sharetakers didn't know what had hit them. They desperately tried to sell expensive items to recoup credits. With a smile, Daragon input a string of commands that marked those goods as stolen property, thus rendering them ripe for confiscation. Because of his secret identity, Rhys didn't dare file an official complaint.

Someday, he would tell Teresa what he had done. But for now, Daragon kept it as his secret.

Furtive in his mansion, Mordecai Ob locked himself in his study. There would be time to go to BTL Headquarters later. For now . . . *inspiration*.

Hibiscus shrubs covered the window glass of his study, obscuring his view with a tangled green curtain. All the privacy he required. He couldn't let anyone see what he was doing. *Not this*.

So far, Daragon had restored some exhilaration to the Bureau Chief's work, and watching Garth Swan's passion had reminded him of his early days, before he'd lost the courage and stamina to follow his dream. Ob had been so young and enthusiastic once, so full of creative energy, so driven.

But those days were long gone, swallowed in cynicism and boredom. He had more money than he knew how to spend. He ran the Bureau of Tracing and Locations, doing a great service by finding fugitives and reuniting families. A man in his position might well dabble in politics, but Ob had no interest in such things. Secondary agendas created more problems than advantages.

However, as with so many celebrities who had everything they could possibly want, ennui had set in. He had forgotten his drive to be an artist, and he had lost his interest in the Bureau. Mordecai Ob looked for ways to enjoy life again, challenges to face . . . or at least some sort of creative stimulus.

He had fallen into the trap of Rush-X.

The potent, illegal drug was distilled from an extract of shellfish found off the Yucatán coast. The precipitate dried to a glistening powder, like crushed pearls, which was then suspended in a glycerin solution, meant to be delivered under the tongue. As part of their job, ruthless BTL investigators had tracked down a major manufacturer of the drug, and the confiscated samples had come to Ob as evidence.

Rush-X gradually caused a body to disintegrate, scrapping the neurons and causing a condition akin to multiple sclerosis. Despite its known hazards, people paid enormous amounts of money and risked their own health just for the thrills the drug provided: increased energy, euphoria, unbelievable creative inspiration.

Back then, Mordecai Ob hadn't understood why.

Feeling adrift at a time when he had so much of the drug available to him, *entrusted* to him, Ob—against his better judgment in a moment of intense boredom and indecision—picked up a glasgel capsule of Rush-X. He had never stopped regretting his unrealistic dream of becoming an artist. One dose couldn't cause significant harm, or so he'd hoped. The drug inventory had already been documented, and all the samples were to be incinerated. No one would question him.

Before he could change his mind, Ob had placed a tiny capsule of the pearly liquid under his tongue. He broke the quick-dissolving shell and let the drug penetrate the soft sublingual tissues. At first it tasted awful, fishy and spicy, like sushi mixed with cleaning fluid.

Then the effect hit.

The experience was amazing. Though he had been bored and depressed, Ob's mind suddenly opened. He was energized, exhilarated. Everything around him looked colorful, vibrant, *inspired!* In only a few seconds, the Bureau Chief rediscovered a passion for life.

Later, with his BTL connections, he was able to get his hands on Rush-X seizures often enough to supply his habit. The contraband drug was destroyed weekly, and Chief Ob could "inspect" the batches scheduled for destruction. He could experience this rush of energy anytime he wanted, anytime he needed particular stamina, or passion for his work.

But the threat raised itself with a particular horror. Ob had seen dying Rush-X addicts and vowed never to let that happen to his own body, no matter how badly he wanted chemically induced thrills. Then he'd remembered his personal caretaker, and the solution had come to him. . . .

That had been years ago, and still the glamour and drama of Rush-X had not grown old. It made him remember the way he had felt on his best days as a young artist, trying to draw everything, to capture his vision of the world. No challenge seemed too great.

Now, inside Eduard Swan's borrowed body, Mordecai Ob leaned back in a padded chair. The office door was locked. He cracked a capsule of pearlescent frozen fire with his teeth, then tucked it under his tongue. He rode the racehorse of energy that burned destructive flames through Eduard's flesh. As the euphoria hit, a smile froze on his face.

Ob wouldn't be able to keep his secret forever. But he could last longer than Eduard would. . . .

32

The fountain became Teresa's regular place to meet with Arthur, but it was just a starting point. From there, she and the interesting old man would walk along the streets, through the parks, into the shops. Arthur talked and talked, and Teresa listened to his musings. She had never met such a complex and unpredictable person, who had thought through deep questions that few other people bothered to consider.

He led her down mysterious alleys packed with out-of-the-way boutiques that sold exotic herbs or hypnotic trinkets from ancient cultures. In front of a ramshackle storefront under a sign written in Chinese characters, Arthur rummaged in a basket propped askew on a doorstep. From inside, they could smell the spicy scent of drying knots of genetically engineered ginseng.

"I'm delighted you're interested in my oddball ideas, Teresa." Arthur withdrew a carved lump of fossil ivory and looked sidelong at her. Teresa watched him with intent eyes, more captivated by the old man than by the exotic paraphernalia. "No one's really listened for a long time. Everyone either ignores me or scorns me. I can't tell you how often people have said I was crazy."

"Oh, you just look at things in a different way, see the world in a different light." Teresa looked at the carved ivory in his hand. "Do you like that? I'll buy it for you."

He set it back in the basket. "You don't have to buy me anything."

"Then how about lunch? You look like you haven't had a decent meal."

"Okay, but don't make it expensive."

"I can't *afford* anything expensive, Arthur." She took him by the scrawny arm and led him to an automated cafeteria. Inside, customers shuffled down the line, looking at picture menus and touch-selecting items. Aroma diffusers provided whiffs of what the food smelled like.

Teresa used image software to arrange the food on her plate and distribute the condiments to suit her tastes. Arthur contented himself with vegetable stir fry and a double portion of brown rice. When the plates appeared at the end of the tray line, the food didn't look much like the glorified pictures, but Teresa was hungry, and Arthur seemed in heaven as he went to work on his meal.

As they ate, Teresa said, "Just listening to you, Arthur, makes things clearer for me. I really appreciate your taking the time to explain human physiology. But... your own body, I can tell it's not too healthy. Are you okay?"

"Nothing serious." Arthur studied his plate instead of her eyes. He toyed with his chopsticks. After weeks of talking to him, she had noticed his frequent cough, his shaking hands.

"Would you like to experience being young again? Spend some time feeling healthy?" Teresa brushed her fingertips along the back of her other hand. "This body isn't perfect, but it's very nice. I would... I'd be honored if you would hopscotch with me."

Arthur almost choked on a mouthful of diced vegetables.

Nervously, Teresa tried to fathom his shocked expression. "Oh, what did I do wrong? I just want to thank you in some way. If . . . if it makes you uncomfort-able to be female, I could come back in a male body. Would that make you feel more at home?"

He squeezed her hand in his own callused grip. "Teresa, you've got to work with what you've *got,* not just jump to the next body whenever a problem comes along. Changing to a different body doesn't change you into a different person."

"But . . . don't you like to hopscotch? Did you have a bad experience once?" She felt giddy, her cheeks hot and flushed. She *needed* to give him something.

"Never done it. Never had the desire to."

He went back to his lunch as Teresa stared at him in astonishment, remembering Daragon's inability. "You've never hopscotched?"

"Not once." With the lines of weariness and pa-tience apparent around his eyes, he took her hand, trac-ing the lines of blood vessels, feeling the pattern of muscles beneath the skin. "Listen. Each individual is a marvel of construction. Every portion of this body, every cell, every nerve fiber, is part of an incredibly intri-cate pattern imprinted on each strand of DNA. It makes even COM look like a child's toy."

Teresa frowned, trying to understand.

Arthur continued. "And I believe the soul is an inti-mate part of the body, part of the overall pattern, de-signed as a perfect match for the complex machine. How could I just swap my soul into someone else's shape, a physique that was never tailor-made to hold it?"

Though she felt rejected, Teresa still experienced the swelling debt inside, could think only of how she had managed to please Rhys during the good times. "Oh, Arthur, I've got to thank you in some way. If you don't want to swap . . . then why don't you let me make love to you? Let me share my body in a different way?" An automated cart rolled by and, unnoticed, snatched their dirty plates.

The old man looked at her in astonishment, then he chuckled to himself and smiled wistfully at her. "Teresa, I am flattered—and sorely tempted. But the fact that you're *listening* to me already means more than anything else you could ever do."

Disappointed, she forced herself to smile at him so he wouldn't see her hurt feelings. Then she got an idea, and her smile became real. "Arthur, come with me. I want to show you something. I think you'll enjoy it."

Garth's small apartment was much too crowded to serve as both living quarters and a functional studio, so he had relegated his sleeping area to a small corner and used the rest of the space for his art.

When Teresa brought Arthur to his door, Garth welcomed them with delight and made room. "Teresa! Please come inside—" He almost tripped over a stack of boxes filled with a clutter of supplies. "Or maybe we should go out somewhere? Who is your friend?" His open expression showed no judgment or disappointment at the old man's shabby appearance.

She hugged the broad-shouldered artist. "This is Arthur, someone I like to talk with. I wanted to bring him here so he could look at your sketches and paintings."

Garth shook Arthur's hand. "Especially your portrait spectrum, I'll bet."

Teresa flushed, which made her look even more waifish. "I think he'd find it interesting. He's only known me in this body."

The artist did his best to show them around. "Forgive the mess, but I'm starting to pack. Thanks to Mr. Ob, I have enough credits to move into a larger place, where I can have a room to sleep *and* a room to work. I'm also looking to hire an assistant to help me keep track of all the details."

Teresa chuckled. "No excuses, Garth. It's always looked this cluttered."

Curious, Arthur poked through the piles of sketches, the paintings leaned against the walls. "I like that you use your eyes to see things around you, and pay attention to what other people never notice."

"Ah, but lately I'm trying to see with more than just my eyes. I'm starting to experience all the facets of humanity." With a sparkling expression, Garth described his List, so enthusiastic with the possibilities that he didn't even see the disturbed look on Arthur's face.

Teresa took the old man by the arm and led him through the obstacle course on the floor to a sequence of faces Garth had hung on the wall. She felt a lump in her throat to see that he had given her portrait spectrum prominence in the precious space he had available.

Arthur looked at the faces, an arrangement of people that seemed to have nothing in common with each other, male and female, beautiful and plain, beginning with the long-lost home-body Teresa had worn in the Falling Leaves, through many of the permutations Rhys had forced her to wear among the Sharetakers, finally to her large-eyed and waifish look.

Arthur studied them, looked into the eyes, the expressions. "They're all you, aren't they, Teresa?"

"Yes, they're all me ... but still *me*. Garth found a way to capture that." The artist smiled at her.

Arthur stared for a long time. "What I see is a lost soul."

"Maybe," Teresa said, then in a much smaller voice, "but I'm not sure that has anything to do with which body I was in."

Arthur didn't seem convinced.

33

With his extensive List in hand, Garth advertised for an assistant who could help him manage the massive undertaking. He needed someone to be his lawyer and administrator, and *mother,* if necessary. After his near-disaster with the obese body-snatcher, Garth didn't dare attempt this alone. He had a big, creative heart, but not much of a business head.

From the COM terminal in his small studio, Garth exchanged messages with a few halfhearted hopefuls who showed minimal interest in his quest and no real background in art. Since he couldn't pay much, even with Mordecai Ob's stipend, his ad attracted little attention.

Finally, he did receive a message from someone who seemed sincerely glad for the opportunity to work with an aspiring artist, Garth in particular. The letter sounded interesting and mysterious, and the applicant said he preferred to make his case in person, if Garth would give him the chance. Intrigued, Garth arranged to meet him in a nearby espresso bar. The applicant readily agreed, claiming to be a connoisseur of fine coffees. *Another good sign.*

As he sat at a metal-mesh patio table, Garth sipped from a wide cup of foamy, cinnamon-dusted cappuccino. When a gaunt, fidgety man came up to him, exactly on time, Garth blinked in surprise. "Pashnak!"

The gaunt man flushed as Garth sprang to his feet so

quickly that the metal chair screeched backward on the patio stones. "I still have your sketch of the Artful Dodger," Pashnak said, embarrassed. "I even took the time to frame it, though it cost me a week's pay."

Surprised and delighted, Garth didn't know what else to say. Taking a deep breath, Pashnak looked up to meet his blue gaze. "I'd really love to work for you. I've been cleaning fountains for the past six months, can't get a better job. And I decided that if I'm not going to be paid well, I may as well put in my best work for something I believe in. And ever since the Falling Leaves, I've believed in you."

Garth grinned, embarrassed at the man's intensity of emotion. "My career is still nothing to brag about, even with Mr. Ob's support."

"But it will be." Pashnak ordered his own cappuccino and looked at the artist with an admiration that Garth felt sure he didn't deserve. "Especially if I help you. I know I can make a difference."

Garth decided on the spot to hire the man.

While they talked, he hauled out his datapad, leaning across the table so his new assistant could see. He keyed up a file to display a long, scrolling table. "This is my List. These are all the things I need to do with myself."

Pashnak read down the column, his eyes growing wide. "We've got a lot of work ahead of us."

Inside Garth's new, larger studio apartment, they waited for the old crone to arrive. Pashnak had already screened her personal file in the COM database, checked out everything about her. She seemed to be exactly what she claimed: a tired old woman who had lived a harsh life. She had no idea why an artist would call her to his studio.

Before the old woman knocked on the door, Pashnak came out of the kitchen carrying two mugs of gourmet coffee. He had brewed it fresh and strong from a machine Garth had just purchased.

"You don't need to do that for me," Garth said.

"I wouldn't trust anyone else to brew my coffee...or yours." Good coffee was as much his passion as were the works of Charles Dickens. Sometimes Garth and Pashnak spent so many hours talking about their common interests that Garth wondered if he would ever get any painting done.

Without a second thought, Pashnak checked details, kept track of activities, planned ahead for simple daily routines. The high-strung young man was shy and uncertain of himself, but he clearly loved being a part of Garth's work. Pashnak would never have had the nerve to push *himself* forward to meet the public, to put his creativity on display the way Garth did. He feared failure—but feared *Garth's* failure even more, and wanted to do everything to prevent that from happening.

In short, Pashnak was a superb assistant.

Pashnak sat with his steaming cup and looked at his watch. The assistant couldn't remain still for long, intimidated by silence and relaxation. "Okay, we've got to discuss some details before she arrives."

"Sure. I know what I need to feel and need to encounter. When I'm in the old woman's body I want to go down to the market, talk to some people, see how they react to me in an aged and poor-looking body. Plus, I want to mark how my arms feel, how my muscles are—"

"I don't mean those things." Pashnak sipped his coffee and stood up to pace the room. "We need to protect you from legal problems. Using the sample contract Daragon gave you, I've already drawn up terms and conditions for the old woman, and I can't see any loopholes. We'll use the document as our boilerplate from now on."

Garth read the terms. They all looked fine to him.

"In addition, from this point on, I insist that you register each hopscotch. We've got to make it a public record, so that if anything goes wrong, there's no question about your real identity, when and where the exchange took place, et cetera. ID patches notwithstanding."

"Good thinking."

"Just doing my job." He was owlish and detail-oriented, meticulous to the point of being anal retentive—just the type of counterpart Garth needed.

Finally the old woman arrived, baffled at what Garth could possibly want with her. "This better not be a joke." Her voice was brittle, but her eyes were bright and strong, daring them to take advantage of her. The light struck her face, highlighting her wrinkled skin, the bent posture, the gray hair. *Marvelous.*

Pashnak escorted her to the sofa, pouring her a cup of coffee, as well. As the assistant laid out the terms and explanations, Garth studied her externally, noting how she chose to dress, how she held herself. In his mind's eye, he imagined her as a younger woman, finding echoes of the beauty she exhibited in youth. Though much had changed for this old person, he could see the younger years buried in her face, in her body.

Pashnak established a set time period for Garth to inhabit the old woman's body, then recorded the contract in COM. "Don't try to do anything illegal while you're in my client's home-body."

She chuckled. "It's like Cinderella having to be back by midnight before the spell wears off." She smiled with wrinkled lips. "But I do think I'll have time for a good spicy meal and a long and refreshing walk."

"You do that." Garth squeezed her shoulder. "Enjoy yourself."

Before Pashnak could think of other pressing concerns, Garth hopscotched into the old woman's body. She laughed with delight, a deep and gratifying sound instead of a scratchy and suspicious cackle. Pashnak watched nervously as she departed from the studio in the young and energetic form.

Garth, though, was captivated by his new/old body. He flexed his arthritic hands, walking slowly about. His feet seemed distant and wooden, his worn-out joints and fragile bones ached. "This is just what I needed."

With Pashnak nervously in attendance, Garth set out to experience being *old*. Picking up the electronic datapad, the assistant followed him around the studio, then finally—slowly—down the stairs and into the streets. Garth had places to go, plans to make, prejudices to test.

"Stay with me, Pashnak—but don't get in the way. I have to get the pure impressions. My eyesight isn't very strong."

"I should be recording your comments, Garth. Tell me what to jot down. I can keep notes to help you chronicle the sensations you're feeling."

Garth looked at him through age-bleared eyes. "Notes are fine, but I need to capture it *here* first." He rapped a gnarled fist against the center of his chest. "In my heart. That's the only place it'll do me any good anyway."

34

Outside the window, the gardener's trowel chopped, chopped, *chopped.* Each blow pounded like thunder through Eduard's splitting skull, as if he had the mother of all hangovers.

He tossed and turned on the bed, feeling every one of his aching muscles. Even the afternoon sunlight hurt his eyes, piercing his pupils like tiny spears. Mordecai Ob had returned at midday demanding to switch back to his own form, and now Eduard felt so bad he had no choice but to take a nap to sleep off whatever Ob had done to his body.

Tanu worked in the flowerbed under his window. Just weeding. He might as well have been using a jackhammer.

Groaning, Eduard stared at the ceiling for several minutes before he could finally stand up, fighting the wave of nausea. His ears rang, and beads of sweat broke out on his forehead. No, it couldn't just be a hangover. He must be sick, afflicted with some kind of drawn-out flu. The illness seemed to have been coming on for weeks now.

He had already run a viral and bacteriological scan on himself to see if he was getting sick, but he had found no infections of any kind. And this didn't have the same *feel* as the severe illnesses he had endured earlier in his career. Of course, nothing approached that level of misery.

Lately, Ob often seemed annoyed or dismissive when he saw Eduard. He had to tread lightly. He didn't want to lose his job, not for himself and not for Daragon's sake. His friend had done this for him, put his own reputation on the line with his boss. Eduard bit back his complaints. He could imagine plenty of worse things.

He remembered the days of selling his body, enduring all kinds of agony just for a few credits. By comparison with Madame Ruxton, this wasn't so bad. He would get through it, too. He just wanted to know what the problem was; then he could put it out of his mind. No problem.

Eduard staggered over to the window and shifted the polarized curtain film. Below, Tanu worked shirtless in a petunia bed. The gardener bent over, sweat trickling like oil down his bronzed back. He dug up old flowers, making room for the new flats of hyper-phlox stacked on the lawn near the walkway.

Sensing Eduard's scrutiny, Tanu looked up, blinking in the afternoon sunshine. Eduard stared through the window, seeing his ghost reflection and noting the surprise on the gardener's face, as well. His own eyes were sunken and shadowed with pain, his cheeks gaunt. He tried to find a glimmer of humor. "Hey, I didn't know working with flowers could be so loud."

Tanu looked at him, then hung his head. He set down the trowel and gathered an armful of uprooted petunias, looking like a large child embracing a Christmas tree.

Eduard leaned out the window, but the smell of the fresh air and dirt made him queasy. As if fleeing, the Samoan gardener trudged away toward a mulch-processing enclosure.

"Hey, Tanu!" The desperate sound in Eduard's voice must have struck a chord, because the gardener slowly turned. "What happened to Ob's other physical trainers? Why did they quit this job?"

The Samoan shook his head. The rustling petunias quivered in his arms.

"At least tell me who the last one was. What was his name?"

"Sandor, his name was Sandor Perun. But he never took the time to talk to me like you do." Intent on his gardening, Tanu refused to give further details.

At least now Eduard had a name to track down, a place to start. Maybe he could talk to this Sandor Perun. He took several potent painkillers left over from Teresa's recovery, stood under a gushing hot shower, and finally felt refreshed enough to tackle his questions at a COM terminal while the Chief was away at BTL Headquarters.

On the interactive filmscreen he searched through a jungle of data, trying to track down Mordecai Ob's previous body-caretakers. Any information about BTL business was naturally restricted, but the workings of a private estate should be subject to the same COM-accessibility requirements as any other piece of public information.

Sandor Perun. Eduard found a subset of data behind several pseudonyms and translucent filenames, but he could find no record of Perun's current status, where he lived. Next, backtracking through the man's name, he bumped into the relevant fields of employment at Ob's estate, searching for hiring histories.

He uncovered previous employment listings—his own file, first, and then Sandor Perun, a thin man with a bushy dark mustache. But there had also been two others: Janine Kuritz, and before her, Benjamin Padwa.

At that point, their files grew thin. Eduard's brow furrowed with suspicion and concern. When he tried to uncover details about the former employees, he found no further record. No information at all. COM had no listings of what they had done after leaving service here.

Trying numerous tactics, Eduard hacked away, approaching the names from the rear, using any peripheral connection...with little success. Even their medical records had been entirely cleansed.

He supposed a person could live on the fringes of society, avoid using the computer/organic matrix—just like the immortal Phantoms he had once wanted to emulate—though that seemed highly unlikely. Where were they?

Didn't it make more sense that the head of the Bureau of Tracing and Locations could also make people *disappear?*

He didn't know how long it would be until Ob returned home. Uneasy, his fingers stabbing at the keys like knives, Eduard erased his search.

Suddenly everything about this too-good-to-be-true job, everything about this estate, seemed like a trap. He dared not trust anyone but himself until he found some answers. Not even Daragon.

35

Months passed in a heady waterfall of artistic experiences. Garth journeyed through the spectrum of human life, from power to weakness, glamour to pain. He checked off each item on the List, like an explorer planting a flag.

Garth became a weight lifter, then a gymnast. He spent a day being blind, and then deaf. He lived half-paralyzed by a stroke, his mind trapped within the prison of an uncooperative body. He experienced perceptions through the brain of a schizophrenic as if it were a cracked mirror. He jogged for three miles in the body of a runner and never tired.

Faithful Pashnak stood on the sidelines, making the opportunities possible, drawing secondhand joy from seeing the artist's accomplishments. He sent regular reports and summaries to Mordecai Ob, who continued to marvel at Garth's ambition.

It was a collection of snapshots, not a deep understanding. The brevity of his visits prevented Garth from experiencing the full differences, but he didn't have time to spend months or years on each one. The List was too long, too daunting.

Perhaps the most important thing he learned was that these people did not consider their lives to be defined entirely by physical shortcomings, or even by extraordinary skills or abilities. Though he chose each body to match a particular criterion on his List, Garth found that the candidates considered any disability or enhancement only one aspect of their individuality. As a transient visitor, though, he found it hard to concentrate on anything else.

Throughout the journey, Garth gathered ingredients, storing details to use in his art and enriching himself as a person. Yet he had barely begun to make headway. The tapestry of humanity held so many different threads. The more experiences he completed, the more he thought of. The List grew longer and longer.

Pashnak bustled about, setting up appointments, seeking out contacts, negotiating terms—and, of course, brewing coffee. He had no aggressive tendencies of his own, but when acting on Garth's behalf, Pashnak became a veritable bulldog. He *knew* in his heart that Garth would be a great artist.

Garth spent hours locked in his new studio to make that dream come true. He dabbled with form and raw materials as well as artistic substance. He would not be satisfied until he developed something wholly new. He had no desire to imitate classical works. Instead, he assessed the tools available to him, then started from his own heart.

When Garth finally emerged from the studio after dark, Pashnak had a light meal ready for him. The artist's clothes smelled of paints and solvents, his fingers ached from twisting raw materials, hooking up electrical connections, focusing holo-lasers. Pashnak asked, "So, have you finally created your masterpiece? Is this it?"

Ravenous, Garth dug through the bubbly cheese shell of his baked onion soup, slurping and talking at the same time, barely tasting his food. "You know the original meaning of the word *masterpiece*? Traditionally, a journeyman had to complete a single outstanding work to earn the title of master craftsman. That work was his 'master piece.' But a real master went on to produce many more remarkable works. His 'masterpiece' was just the first one."

Pashnak hadn't touched his food. "You'll be a master, no doubt about it."

Garth's eyes twinkled. "What I've got in there is an extension of something I've done before, but truly groundbreaking. I finally figured out how to do it right. After I'm done, I just might step up from being a journeyman to a master." He looked down at his spoon, finally tasting his dinner. "Good soup."

In the grip of his ambitious project, Garth worked obsessively to drag out the memories and sensations he had compiled during months of hopscotching.

Though the artist had never prevented him from looking at a work in progress, Pashnak displayed a superstitious fear of going inside the studio. "It's enough of an honor just to know I'll be the first to see it . . . when you're ready."

He hovered outside the studio with fresh coffee, wishing Garth would get some sleep. When the artist finally emerged, surprised to find his diligent assistant waiting there, Pashnak pleaded with him. "Don't burn out on this first big project. You need a break. Why don't you take time off, just a little? Get some rest, a long night of sleep—"

Garth downed half a cup of coffee in a big gulp and shook his head, looking longingly through the doorway. "Not now. I can't risk losing my inspiration—it won't let go of me." He sighed, grinning like an idiot. "If only you could sleep for me, then I wouldn't have to interrupt my work." His voice trailed off.

Pashnak blinked in surprise. "Why not? If that's what you need me to do."

So the assistant hopscotched into Garth's exhausted

body. Pashnak practically collapsed onto a sofa as the weariness overwhelmed him.

Then, alone in the quiet studio, Garth worked far into the night. . . .

He swapped back as soon as his home-body was sufficiently rested. Pashnak then dropped off to sleep once more in his own body, which was itself exhausted. "I can work nonstop like this for days," Garth said, elated.

Pashnak's gaunt body did not have the innate artistic ability Garth was accustomed to, but he still had the vision and drive. He could do prep work, broad-strokes development, and save the fine detail for his skilled hands.

"Plenty of people would love to get paid just to sleep," Garth said to him jokingly, then added in a more serious tone, "You're a good assistant, Pashnak. I couldn't do it without you."

Beaming, Pashnak shuffled back to bed after they had swapped yet again. "Just don't forget that your mind needs sleep just as much as your body does."

"Not now."

Inside the studio, using every artistic resource from high-tech holograms and reflected chromatographs to stubby lumps of charcoal, Garth brought forth the art of *experience*, using emotions as his canvas.

When people went to see an exhibition they generally applied only one, perhaps two, of their senses. They listened to a symphony with their ears, or scrutinized a painting with their eyes. But Garth attempted to paint with multiple stimuli that evoked emotions, using the full palette of the senses to forge a tactile and experiential weapon that would strike the heart of any viewer.

And he was almost finished.

Garth built upon what he had attempted during his first art show, when he'd tried to create the full sensory impression of being at the artists' bazaar. Now he had to be even more ambitious.

His new work was incredibly vast in scope. He explored a single human emotion in all its facets, conveying it through every mode: music, colors, holo-images, paintings, smells, neural stimulation, even videoclips and sound recordings. He used mud and stones and bricks; he used magnetic fields and pheromones, static inducers and ultralow frequency thrummers. He wove a complete fabric that showed how different people with different backgrounds and problems experienced the same emotion.

He called the piece FRUSTRATION.

Working for days without a mental break, Garth portrayed the obese man attempting to move in a lumbering form, seeing every physical obstacle as a challenge. Gravity conspired to fill every day with difficulties. He showed the old woman with a body frail and in pain, knowing that her life was near its end, wishing she had done more. He included the blind man and his desperate dreams to see, the stroke-paralyzed woman shouting inside her mind to express simple thoughts, the deaf man trapped in a world of smothering silence, the retarded man frustrated by trying to understand so much of the world around him, the ups and downs of the schizophrenic....

Garth added snippets of his own inability to convey the images that screamed inside his head, and the despair it caused him. He composed a scene of his younger self painting over a mural in the monastery basement.

All together, the experience packed a profound emotional punch. FRUSTRATION. When he finished, his imagination and creativity worn ragged, Garth sat in the middle of the studio and wept.

Every human was familiar with frustration in its

many forms, but this work laid it out, raw and powerful. He found common ground in all walks of life and forced his audience to see the similarities with everyone else. Any person could experience the same emotion through different eyes, and see how they were all the same. All *human*.

When he finally showed it to Pashnak, the wide-eyed assistant stepped inside the studio as if approaching a minefield. He could tell the gaunt young man feared he wouldn't like it and knew he would have to tell Garth the truth.

But Pashnak remained in awe for half an hour until he finally staggered back out, face tracked with tears. His mouth worked without uttering words, then he hugged Garth. "I can't thank you enough for that."

He composed himself and got down to business. "Now our real work starts. This piece is something that must be seen by as many people as possible. Your message and your art *must* be witnessed."

Garth sighed, excited but weary, as if he had suddenly realized the major effort that lay ahead. Then he brightened. "I think it's time to call Mr. Ob."

The Bureau Chief responded to the request to visit the artist's studio, polite but cool, and could not find a spot in his schedule for two days. Garth waited in an agony of impatience, riding a pendulum between optimism and dismay. He tinkered with the exhibit, tweaking images, rearranging sounds and impressions, making so many minor adjustments back and forth that the end result was indistinguishable from where it had started.

When Ob finally arrived, escorted in a BTL hovercar and flanked by two unfamiliar Beetles, he seemed distracted and impatient. At least he came in his own body, not in Eduard's borrowed one.

Pashnak met the Chief at the studio door. "We wanted you to see the work objectively, without Garth breathing down your neck. I think it speaks for itself." Squaring his shoulders, Mordecai Ob went alone into the exhibit while the Beetles remained outside as sentinels, as if nervous Pashnak might pose some sort of threat.

Garth waited around the corner in a coffee shop so he wouldn't be around during this audition, but he stayed close by, wondering, worrying. Steeling himself for disappointment, he returned ten minutes later, just as the Bureau Chief emerged. The vulnerable and amazed expression on Ob's face told him all he needed to know.

"Garth! You have created something...truly... *moving.*" He chose his words slowly, as if none of them were adequate, then his conversation came out in a rush. "Other artistic types have done this sort of thing before. Writers researching a character, a painter getting into the feel of a type of worker. But this is so much more...broad-based. Garth, you're like a sponge soaking up everything, and then squeezing it all back out onto your audience."

Ob's olive-brown eyes twinkled. "I see I have made a good investment. If I had ever been able to create something so powerful, I never would have joined the Bureau!" The two uniformed officers looked at their Chief in alarm, but Ob kept talking in a commanding tone, assuming a businesslike posture. "On the other hand, I would not then have the resources or the connections to make sure FRUSTRATION gets the right kind of debut. Let me take care of the next step."

Working behind the scenes, Mordecai Ob instructed Pashnak to contact a professional publicist, a self-proclaimed "hype-meister" named Stradley. "He has already been instructed to take your call."

At first, the busy publicist fended off numerous pleas and pitches for his time . . . but finally agreed to come to the studio and take a look. "Now, I don't normally have much love for the BTL, but Chief Ob was quite insistent," Stradley told Pashnak, moving through the doorway. He was a mass of frenetic energy and easily channeled excitement. "All right. Let's see this FRUS-TRATION thing."

Pashnak grinned provocatively. "You won't be disappointed." Pursing his lips, skeptical already, the hypemeister stepped inside the studio.

Stradley wasn't disappointed. Not at all.

He emerged from the room so shaken that Pashnak could see cracks in his façade of cynicism and bluster. "That's . . . that's—" Being at a loss for words seemed a very strange sensation to him.

Garth tried to control his smile. "Does that mean it's good?"

Stradley looked at him as if he'd asked a particularly stupid question. He took a breath, then launched into his immediate thoughts on how he could promote Garth's work.

"All right. This sort of 'panorama experience' art is a combination of low tech and cutting edge, wrapped into a sublime whole that affects every part of the audience. Much, much greater than the sum of its parts." Stradley's eyes narrowed wolfishly. "Bring Garth down to my offices—today, if possible. We've got to get started."

Stradley did no part of any job with less than full energy. Later, sitting at his desk in his offices, the hypemeister talked with his hands and eyes as much as with his mouth. After a few moments of brainstorming, the barrier of the desk was unable to contain him. Stradley stood up to pace the room, circling Garth and Pashnak, who sat awed in their free-form chairs.

"First, we'll send listings with a thousand different provocative key words all through COM. After my years in the business, I've got a rapport with that old computer matrix. I know how to get postings, how to get ads, how to get attention for my clients where other people can't seem to hack their way into a simple classified ad." He grinned, showing plenty of teeth. "And I have special coding that'll allow our message to get past those signal-to-noise filters people use in their personal services."

Garth was unable to get in a word edgewise as Stradley rattled possibilities into the open air. Microphones implanted in the walls recorded everything and organized it with note-taking software. "First, we have to set up a major coming-out exhibition in exactly the right place—not too gaudy, not too exclusive. We need a location that's widely accessible but still important. Mr. Ob has already given me a budget." Stradley stared out the half-closed door to his office, then scanned his calendar, then glanced at the tropical wall images. "And we have to pick the proper date, of course. Timing is everything."

He went to the door, shouted for his receptionist to get them something to drink, but when she returned a moment later carrying a tray, he scolded her for interrupting their important meeting. He had already launched into a new train of thought.

Though words poured from the publicity specialist like water thundering down a waterfall, Garth didn't sense any depth. "But you're not saying anything about the art *itself*. How do we make sure we get it in front of the right people?"

Stradley came to a complete stop and fixed him with a surprisingly severe gaze. "Who are you to select the *right* people, Garth? I'm not going to pick and choose who might understand or enjoy this work, and you shouldn't, either. Don't get all snooty. We put FRUSTRA-TION in front of as many people as we can, and let them sort it out. That's what I'm best at."

Stradley continued without even taking a breath. "Listen, Garth, your exhibit is not safe, but it is profound. You've learned some things about humanity, and portrayed your insights in a compelling way. You provide a punch of reality to people who are probably too afraid to experience it themselves—and that's exactly how I plan to promote you!"

He circled his desk one more time and came back to stand in front of the free-form chairs. Snatching one of the untouched drinks from the tray, Stradley gulped it down. He wiped his mouth with the back of his hand and looked at the two men, as if challenging them. "Are you guys ready to work? We've got a lot to do if you want to be ready for the big debut of FRUSTRATION."

They both gave a resounding yes. Garth felt as if he had just plunged into white-water rapids in a kayak, but he was delighted, too. He was having the time of his life.

36

Arthur poked delicately at the remaining Madonna lilies in Teresa's basket. Their scent had been changed to a bright spearmint, like an air freshener. "Okay, bend closer so you can see the details. Lots of things to notice."

Teresa scooted over to the ragged man on the cool fountain rim. Arthur nudged open the soft white flower. "Look at how everything fits. The petals surround the anthers and the stigma, where the slightest brush of a bee's foot will distribute the pollen grains." He touched the anthers and came away with a smear of yellow dust. "A grain of pollen travels down the pollen tube and fertilizes the seeds inside this receptacle." He turned the lily over so she could see the green sepals embracing the petals. "This part becomes the seed pod."

He handed her the flower. Teresa cupped it in her hands.

"Now look at the cut end of the stem, see the tiny straws. Each one is a fluid vessel to carry nutrients from the roots, like plumbing and electrical conduits in a skyscraper, or the circulatory system in your own body."

Day after day, she came to the old man, usually when she finished her flower-delivery rounds. Arthur didn't want anything from her, didn't have an agenda. He just enjoyed the conversation and attention, and Teresa learned everything she could. "Oh, Arthur, you've made the world so much more complicated."

"I hope that's a good thing." His smile warmed her heart.

She clasped his bony wrist. "It's more interesting that way. I'm ashamed at how I never noticed what was right there in front of me." She hesitated, never having asked about his past. "How do you know so much? Were you some sort of doctor or surgeon...before?"

Arthur gave a high and hoarse laugh, which degenerated into an alarming spate of coughing. When he had recovered, he looked at Teresa with amusement. He gestured to the tall buildings that ringed the plaza. "No, no—I used to work in those skyscrapers. I was just a plumbing engineer."

Another day, Arthur took her inside one of the buildings, showed her the ancient keycode for a maintenance entrance. "These are areas the general public doesn't see, but that's where you'll find the most fascinating things, the systems that keep everything running."

They slipped along dimly lit passages between walls, access shafts, and hatchways. They ducked under a thick black pipe and followed as it ran along syncrete blocks before turning left and plunging through an opening in a wall.

"I didn't even know these places existed," Teresa said, breathless.

"Nobody understands the whole picture," Arthur said. He tapped a water pipe with his fingernail, making a dull sound. "The city, this building, even your own body—the closer you look, the more complex it becomes. Like fractals. You never get to the bottom of it all."

The echoing passageways were lit by harsh glow tiles not designed for the comfort of human eyes. The air smelled dank in the untraveled tunnels. Creatures stirred in the shadows, spiders and crickets and mice.

"I used to map and maintain the water systems inside this building, all seventy-eight stories of it." Arthur moved with a spring in his step she had not seen before. He seemed to forget his aches and pains, his poor health. "It's good to revisit my old stomping grounds, especially with an eager pupil at my side."

He rattled off statistics relating to the building, pointing out minute details she would never have noticed. He explained the intricate conduits, power connections, and overflow systems.

"I had a lot of time to myself down here. A lot of time to think. When I understood how this building worked, I realized how much it reminded me of the human body—structural supports like bones, plumbing like a circulatory system, electrical conduits like nerves, thermostats and optical sensors and alarm systems like our senses." The old man lowered his voice. "But even the greatest networks inside the mightiest skyscrapers can't truly compare to the elegant complexity of the human body."

Arthur held up his gnarled right hand. "I finally got it through my head that the fluid-flow pathways in my little finger, designed by the pressures of evolution or by God Himself, far surpass any system that centuries of human engineering has managed to construct. We're just ... amateurs at this."

He led her up a narrow metal staircase that paralleled an elevator shaft. Teresa listened to his labored breathing as he clomped higher and higher. With a humming rattle, an enclosed elevator car whisked past them and a counterweight shuttled upward in an opposite shaft.

Arthur rested on the steps. "When I found that discarded copy of *Gray's Anatomy,* it seemed like a sign. I abandoned my work and took to living as best I could on my own limited resources. I needed more time to study."

Teresa held herself back, trying not to push him faster than he wanted to go, but Arthur climbed level after level, driven from within. "You must have made up your mind before then never to hopscotch."

Arthur finally paused at a landing. "It'll take me a century just to understand *this* hunk of flesh. Why should I make the problem more difficult by stepping inside someone else's guts and muscles?" He inspected his scrawny bicep with renewed interest.

"But aren't you curious about other people? Their perspectives, their sensations?" Teresa had been in so many different physiques, so many men and women— strong and weak, beautiful and average. She had noticed a host of differences, but also an underlying *sameness*.

"Okay, I could be healthier, more energetic—but at whose expense? Every body has a given life span, like a warranty, and if I take good care of mine, maybe I can extend its service lifetime." He shrugged. "Regardless, I'm satisfied with the body I was given at birth. No regrets."

Later, Teresa helped him back out into the sunlight, away from the skyscraper's maintenance corridors. Arthur looked bone weary, his feet dragging and his shoulders slumped. The fresh air seemed to do him no good. He urged her to be off, to complete more deliveries for the day. "Go. I don't want you to get in trouble on my account."

Teresa hugged him gently, afraid she might break his old body. "I'm worried about you, Arthur. You need to rest."

He waved her off. "Okay, I'll take a nap. Don't worry—I'll be fine."

She left him at the fountain, hurrying to pick up another load of bouquets for the afternoon deliveries. The old man was too tired to watch her go.

37

Still achy and dizzy, glad to be away from Mordecai Ob's mansion, Eduard made his way to Garth's big exhibition. He felt worse each day, and his mouth always tasted awful. But even if he'd been on his deathbed, Eduard would have found some way to make it to his friend's opening. He wouldn't have missed it even if he had to steal a body to get there.

FRUSTRATION. Now that was a familiar concept.

Accompanied by an immaculately uniformed Inspector Daragon Swan, the Bureau Chief had left his estate earlier for the show. Ob clearly wanted to keep a master/servant distance between himself and his body-caretaker, though, and suggested that Eduard find his own way. *No problem.*

He followed the huge signs and a swirl of people. Animated shooting stars and insistent arrows in the sidewalks guided pedestrians to the show. Ahead, under floating spotlights, Eduard saw the gallery building surrounded by a web of intersecting lasers that diffracted and sparkled through a dance of water-fans. Arches and cyber-Greek columns braced an ornate doorway through which people filed.

How much had all this cost? He couldn't believe the extravagant support Ob had invested here. The aloof Bureau Chief must have plenty of confidence in Garth.

Invitations were checked, celebrities welcomed by name. Holding his VIP pass in hand, Eduard worked his way through the crowd. A redheaded woman in a voluminous pink dress jostled his arm, and he winced at the surprising ripples of pain. Taking a deep breath, he blocked his aches and pushed forward. He had lived through far greater pain in his life, and he would damned well put on a good show for Garth's big night.

Inside, the floor's synthetic semiprecious stones were polished to a luster that Egyptian pharaohs had only dreamed of. Attendees in the outer foyer sipped from fluted glasses of champagne or nibbled hors d'oeuvres. Rich patrons had rented fine bodies for the evening, some dressed so gaudily they appeared to be on exhibit themselves.

Bureau Chief Mordecai Ob wore an exquisite tuxedo, standing beside Garth, who looked greatly out of his depth. Ob beamed with pride, as if taking credit for the exhibition—which he could, in a way, since it had been his patronage, his important connections and possibly even bribe money that had generated the intense buzz necessary to launch Garth into stardom.

From the cavernous lobby, a line of spectators worked its way toward the main exhibit room. A doorway on the other side of the showroom let out a stream of wavering people who had completed their circuit of the FRUSTRATION exhibit. Most were visibly moved, their expressions stony or fallen, some openly weeping.

Seeing this, Eduard felt honored and filled with joy for his friend, though Garth hadn't seen him yet. He took a deep breath, finding strength inside. Chin up, he entered the mass of well-dressed people, searching for Teresa in the crowd.

"You should have seen Garth's first show," Pashnak said to Stradley, his voice strong and pleased. "I think I was the only person who bought anything. Total disaster."

The hype-meister beamed at the turnout in the exhibition hall. "Well, he didn't have me to help him out last time. It's not enough for an artist just to do good work. Someone has to convince the masses that it's good. Someone has to sell it—otherwise nobody sees it."

Pashnak nodded. "This is *great* work, Mr. Stradley, and you did a remarkable job bringing people in here to experience it. Once word gets around about FRUSTRATION, Garth will never have publicity problems again."

Stradley shrugged. "Never underestimate the short attention span of the consumer base, especially in the artistic community." He snagged a glass of champagne. "I hate this stuff, but it's tradition." He took a gulp, grimaced at the fizz, then finished off the bubbly drink. "This is my favorite part of a star's career, the first big break. You can never re-create that adrenaline rush, though they try. Heaven knows they try. It's pathetic to watch later on."

From a tray, he plucked a cracker spread with salmon mousse, continuing to talk while he crunched. "Even with Chief Ob's assistance, I have to admit I'm amazed at how easy it was to get publicity for Garth— the right *kind* of publicity, too. I was able to make perfect connections. My e-nouncements popped to the top of the stack, and media attention magically appeared. I wish all my hype worked like that. If I was superstitious, I'd say COM *wanted* to help this kid."

Pashnak surveyed the crowd, maintaining a professional smile. "Garth deserves it, Stradley. You don't know how long he's worked for this."

"And I don't care, either. For every Garth Swan who makes it, a thousand others work just as hard with just as much talent...and remain wanna-bes for the rest of their miserable lives." He flashed another professional smile—Stradley was good at that. "Me, I enjoy the *challenge,* the battle to create a new star. For Garth, it was almost too simple!"

"I'm not complaining." Pashnak continued to survey the crowd, greeting people he was supposed to recognize—famous socialites, politicians—but who could ever be sure which body was which? "My God, that's Teresa!" he said under his breath and left the hypemeister to graze the hors d'oeuvres by himself.

Blinded by adrenaline and praise, Garth extricated himself from Mordecai Ob. Seeing Eduard, he fought through the press of people, dodging autograph hunters and paparazzi who worked with triangulating cameras to catch the artist in full holo. He embraced Eduard in an exuberant bear hug, so excited that he didn't even notice his friend's pained reaction. "You believe all of this? Is it real, or am I just hallucinating? At the moment, I'm so frazzled that Pashnak had to tie my shoes for me."

Around them, camera crews caught the entire encounter. Eduard patted the big blond man on the back. "It's real enough, Garth. You'll be able to see it again and again on all the newsnets if you do a topic search. No problem." He made a comical face for one of the imagers.

Pashnak hurried up to them, leading Teresa. Laughing, Garth warmly hugged her. "You know, I'm getting used to you in this body. Big eyed and innocent looking. It suits you after all."

"Good, because this is where I'm going to stay." She looked with concern at Eduard's haggard appearance, but before she could say anything, Garth gestured toward the inner exhibition room.

"Have you two been through yet? Come, let me take you to the front of the line. I want you to see what I've been trying to do for so many years. Maybe this'll convince you that I wasn't crazy all along."

Teresa chuckled. "Oh, Garth, we've all been crazy in our lives, don't you think?"

"You can say that again," Eduard said.

As soon as Garth had escorted them into the inner chamber, Pashnak and the reporters dragged the artist away again. "Sorry, Garth. Mr. Ob insists." With a wave, the blond artist vanished back into the swirl of people.

Now Teresa stood next to Eduard, lowering her voice. "You look terrible." She ran a loving hand along his face, like a concerned mother. "I can see shadows all around you."

"I'll be all right, Teresa."

She huffed. "You'd never let *me* get away with an answer like that."

He walked ahead into the experience room, seeking refuge in the darkness. "I've already run my own scans but couldn't find any disease, any virus. No known toxins, poisons." Eduard shrugged, then scowled at the sharp pain in his shoulder. "Still, I think...my boss might be doing something in my body."

She looked across the faces in the crowd, seeing where Garth was shaking the hand of a statuesque woman in a dazzling formal dress. The Bureau Chief smiled beside him, as if basking in the artist's glow. "Mr. Ob seems like such a generous person. Look at how much he's helped Garth."

"Tell that to his other three trainers—if you can find them. Everyone who's had this job before me has disappeared."

Alarmed, she took his arm. Her unfortunate experiences with Rhys had taught her not to trust people as much as she wanted to. "Oh, Eduard—maybe you need to leave that job? Have you talked to Daragon?"

He responded with a sharp laugh. "Daragon thinks Mordecai Ob is God, and after tonight Garth would probably agree. No, this is something I need to take care of myself, and I'd rather not just walk away from this job."

She grabbed his hand before they could disappear into the dim exhibit. Behind them, people pushed forward, urging them on. "Eduard, you've never been good at asking for help. Promise you'll come to me if there's ever anything I can do for you. I owe you enough already, don't you think?"

Eduard placed a gentle finger on her lips to stop further protests. He noticed with alarm that his hand was trembling. "You don't owe me anything." He kissed her gently on the forehead. "Teresa, I promise. I'm not hiding anything from you—I just don't know the answer myself yet."

He took her hand and drew her farther into the exhibit. "This is Garth's night. Let's be happy for him."

Outside the gallery, keeping away from the bright lights, Daragon watched it all, enjoying Garth's success. Tonight, Mr. Ob was with him, separate from the Bureau, probably imagining a different life for himself, how it might have been if he'd been a successful artist instead of the BTL Chief.

Daragon strode along the edge of the crowd as if his job were to maintain order at the show. People gave way, letting him move unhindered around the perimeter of the exhibition building, past the water-fans and lasers. Before the opening, accompanying Chief Ob, Daragon had seen the exhibit in a special showing with Garth, Stradley, Pashnak, and several VIPs. Nothing in the auditorium, though, could give him more pleasure than to see the attention his friend had finally received.

As he watched the ebb and flow of people, he noticed how many of the guests departed looking contemplative, uncertain, disturbed. Some chuckled nervously, some remained silent, hurrying to their hoverlimos. A few smiled wistfully, shaking their heads. Yes, Garth's work had touched them, all right.

"Congratulations, my friend," he said quietly.

Then he saw Eduard and Teresa standing near one of the exits, deep in conversation, both excited and moved. Noticing him, Teresa rushed forward to take his hand. "Oh, Daragon, come inside with us! Garth would be so happy to see you."

"He came with Mr. Ob," Eduard pointed out.

"I've already talked with him and seen the show. It's better if I keep a low profile out here." Daragon felt very self-conscious in his uniform. "I know how intimidating my presence can be."

Teresa let out a sparkling laugh. "You don't intimidate us."

"I doubt the people who came to see Garth's art would feel the same way. I don't want to cast any shadow, not on this night of all nights." He looked toward the doors. "But I had to be here."

From behind his shadowed eyes, Eduard forced a smile. "Just to keep an eye on your friends? Watching over us?"

"To make sure nothing goes wrong. As always."

As quickly as he could, Daragon found an excuse to go. He walked away from the lights and music, leaving his friends behind.

38

Swapportunities!

It was a cute word displayed on the big flickering board in Club Masquerade. The postings always changed, shifted in a fountain of possibilities, needs, and desires. Prime material for his List.

Hands clasped behind his back in a Napoleonic stance, Garth stood before the Hopscotch Board and read listing after listing. People placed their requests here, some valid for that hour or day only; more unusual requests remained unanswered for months—including some of his own.

Many of the postings were sexual invitations for instant flings and afternoon diversions. Hopefuls posted bounties for stolen bodies, rent requests for better physiques. A desperate few offered their own bodies for sale.

Garth came here on his search, forever on the lookout. Sometimes he thought he would never finish his quest...though that might actually be a good thing. Life and learning should never be finished. After the huge success of the recent FRUSTRATION exhibit, Garth already wondered what to do next. Stradley insisted that the second success was even more important than the first.

Munching on a cinnamon stim-stick, he settled in at a small table to watch the people, to take notes on his datapad. Dance music continued in the background, droning with primal rhythms. Though the Club was relatively quiet on a slow afternoon, pleasure-seekers did their best to re-create the chaos and color of peak business hours. From here, he could also keep an eye on the Hopscotch Board, in case anything new came up.

On the tablescreen, the cybernetic bartender's smiling face appeared. "Ah, Garth, at it again, I see."

"Always need new inspiration, Bernard."

Down at the main bar, Rovin's arms buzzed about, each set making a different cocktail for a different customer. Though his mind was multiprocessing dozens of orders and hundreds of minor business details, Rovin seemed attentive to Garth alone. "I've read reviews of your art show. Sounds like you made quite a splash. An overnight success!"

Garth smiled wryly down at the image. "An overnight success after years of working in total obscurity."

"You weren't wasting your time. You were learning your craft."

Garth's lambic beer appeared, and he took a refreshing sip. "All that time I spent studying people and places really paid off. Last week I lived two days as a dwarf, and it really changes your perspective. Nothing's at the right height—not door controls, not COM terminals, not the transport systems. Quite a challenge just to climb up onto a barstool."

"Easy to fall off, though," Rovin said with a grin. "So, are you finished with your List?"

"Not by a long shot. I haven't even had a baby yet. I could spend a lifetime just living other lives."

The music changed on the dance floor. Hovering platforms shuffled in the air, bringing groups closer together and allowing members to hop from one disk to another.

"No matter how much swapping you manage, Garth, you could never experience as many things as I do every day." At the bar, mechanical arms continued to mix and deliver drinks. Screens glowed at countless tables, where Rovin engaged in numerous conversations, independent of what he was saying to Garth.

"What do you mean, Bernard? I've always felt sorry for *you*, trapped in here, never able to go outside and see the world. Unable to...go see my art exhibit, for instance."

"I've already seen the world, Garth. I had a lot of fun in my younger days, but I got swatted down with a terrorist bomb and a hovercar crash. In here, I'm safe and in control of it all. Through my different substations, I have everything I want. I can watch my customers, hear each conversation, participate in a thousand things at once. How can a single pair of arms and legs match that?"

Garth pulled out his datapad and scanned the items on his List. "Thanks for giving me another item for my List, Bernard. Would you be willing to hopscotch with me today? Or should we wait awhile?"

The screen flickered for a moment, and Garth watched the bartender's expression shift. "Whoa, I didn't mean it as an invitation."

"Why not? You're right. You've got a kind of life I've never experienced before. Besides, you know what I'm after, why I'm doing this. How about...say, an hour? That'll give me a good impression of what you're all about, and you'll have a chance to do a few things. Minimal risk, for either of us."

Rovin paused, decidedly uncomfortable. "But I've got the Club to run, Garth. I'd have to stay right beside you. Some of this gets very complicated. I'll need to monitor what you're doing, help you out every second—"

"No you won't," Garth said, already starting toward the closed door to the central control chamber. "*You* are going to go for a walk."

Though it was his job to seek hopscotch opportunities for the artist, Pashnak fought his inner anxiety. He hated putting himself in front of strangers, making odd requests and negotiations. However, he was willing to do it for Garth.

By now his employer had absorbed the easy things on his List, and Pashnak had to go far afield. In the lull after the frantic activity of the FRUSTRATION debut, he went out to scout candidates. At least the money derived from licensing the successful exhibition had given him sufficient funds to make decent offers on Garth's behalf.

Some things, though, made Pashnak feel very much out of his depth.

Wearing a forced smile, he stood in front of a work crew of convicted criminals. The unfettered labor gang was composed of hirsute, muscular bodies, squat and ugly forms like the museum paintings of Neanderthals.

As punishment for certain crimes, guilty parties were forced to hopscotch into undesirable bodies, enduring sentences in lumpy, unpleasant forms. The only way a felon could have his or her own physique back was to hope for parole. Rarely were the criminals desperate enough to flee in their stunted bodies. Ugliness itself was often sufficient deterrent.

Such a tradition created a misshapen "criminal class," a caste system within legal boundaries. The original owners of these hideous forms often made good lives for themselves as they swapped into the varying bodies of criminals awaiting the ends of their sentences. It was like a vacation.

The crew boss clearly thought Pashnak was mad to make such a ridiculous request. Pashnak paced back and forth under the hot sun, looking at the crooked teeth and matted hair of the labor gang. Their musky perspiration smelled of animals, though their eyes held the fire of people who had once lived successful lives, but were now trapped in hideous shells.

"These are your best candidates?" Pashnak asked the boss.

The man was blocky and strong, with broad shoulders. "This lot has plenty at stake—enough that you can probably trust them to make your trade." The boss obviously remained skeptical. "Still sounds like a fool's errand to me."

"Regular people always have trouble understanding artists." Pashnak turned his attention to the hairy, misshapen men on the labor gang. "You'll get a day's reprieve from your sentence, while my employer does your labor for you. He wants to sweat like you sweat. He wants to feel the eyes of the public loathing him, the way you experience it every day."

"And every night," another ugly male snapped. "I'm testing the limits of my husband's devotion to me."

Pashnak felt a lump in his stomach. What marriage could withstand that?

"Well, your mate won't get any benefit out of Garth's body. You'll still have to remain under tight security, in prison instead of out here on the labor gang. But you get a normal body again, healthy and strong and attractive—and a day to relax instead of work." Pashnak looked at the repulsive band and raised his head high, trying to appear tough—or at least confident. "You know the terms, and the restrictions, and the pay. One day, that's all. Any takers?"

The crew boss rolled his eyes, but Pashnak had far more volunteers than Garth could ever use.

———

Like a thief entering a forbidden temple, Garth slipped past the busy mechanical arms to the isolated central control chamber where Bernard Rovin lived. The metal doors unsealed, and Garth ducked inside. The barricade automatically closed before any curious customers could peer inside. This was a private matter between him and the bartender.

Garth stood in a womblike chamber surrounded by videoscreens, microphone pickups, and display monitors. In the middle of it all sat the ruined lump of the bystander who had almost died in a hovercraft crash years earlier. The real Rovin was little more than a scarred head and part of a spinal column implanted in a network of pseudo-body parts that extended to all corners of Club Masquerade.

"You sure you want to do this?" Rovin asked, his voice uncertain.

Garth stared, more intrigued now than he had ever been. "Without a doubt." He came close enough to touch the living flesh of Rovin's head.

"I haven't done this in a long time." The bartender's real lips moved now, his skin pale. If he'd had a body to move, he probably would have fidgeted.

"Hopscotching isn't the sort of thing you forget how to do." Garth touched the waxy, scarred skin. Rovin flinched.

They swapped.

Garth suddenly felt as if he were falling. He tried to catch himself with a thousand flailing hands. A dizzying snowstorm of images poured into his optic nerves, as if he were now looking through a fly's compound eye.

"Focus! Garth, focus!" a man called in a very familiar voice.

Garth funneled his attention and noticed his blond-haired form standing in the control chamber. He centered on that image alone, and found himself looking at Bernard Rovin, now occupying his home-body.

"Some things you do forget after all." Rovin stared down at Garth's broad hands, wiggling his fingers experimentally. Then he snapped his head up to look at where Garth now rested in the middle of his own sensations.

"Okay, I've tried to prep plenty of things here for you. Don't mess it up for me. I've set the secondary systems on autopilot. Your hypothalamus automatically regulates things like lights and temperature, the plumbing, the doors. The music selections are based on random patterns, so don't worry about monitoring them."

Garth's attention splintered into fragments, full of innumerable sensations pouring in from different directions. He wanted to explore and think and see everything from the bartender's perspective. Despite the distractions, though, he also heard and understood everything Rovin said.

"I take it you don't need any instructions on how to use *my* body?" Garth asked. Simply finding his vocal cords posed a small challenge.

"Not like that!" Rovin slapped his forehead. "You just broadcast to all the screens in the Club." He hurried to adjust several controls. "There, that'll help you select where to direct your conversations. Remember, you're wired to do many different things at once." Using Garth's nimble hands, he fiddled with the monitors. He paused, sick and uncertain, sweating profusely. "Maybe this was a bad idea. We should just swap back."

"Not a chance, Bernard. Now get out of here, and come back in an hour."

Dubiously, Rovin left the central chamber. Wearing Garth's body, he wandered around inside the Club, touching things, studying tiny details that were out of range of his optical sensors. He picked up small objects, holding them in front of his face, smelling and feeling.

With his new optical sensors, Garth watched him move about, inspecting his beloved Club from a new perspective. As Rovin brushed his fingers against the smooth surface of an empty chair, Garth used his new equipment to eavesdrop on a nearby conversation.

"Look, it's that artist again. The FRUSTRATION guy." A ginger-haired woman shook her head, bemused. "You gotta expect odd behavior from him."

Rovin showed no sign of ever intending to leave the Club. He seemed intimidated, preferred staying close to home. He moved meticulously, each step a conscious effort, as if afraid he might damage himself in some way.

Finally, as Rovin passed an empty table, Garth used his new skills to illuminate the screen. His voice rang out, scolding. "Bernard, you've got places to go. You can see this old place anytime. Do I have to call security to remove you by force?"

"All right, all right." Rovin reluctantly headed for the nearest labyrinthine exit. "I'll be back soon. Don't worry."

Garth switched from one camera to another to another. Rovin chose to use the passage through the *Titanic* chamber, modeled to look like a large stateroom on the ancient ocean liner. Finally, he went out into the streets.

Now Garth had Club Masquerade to himself.

Though only moments had passed, he noted that customers were already clamoring for drinks, talking to screens and expecting answers. He had work to do here!

Like a sentient centipede, Garth flexed his mechanical arms, then he tapped into the bartending database so he could program the requested drinks. So many variations! With a distracted corner of his mind, he discovered the actual contents of the slushy blue drink Eduard always requested; he wasn't sure his friend would actually want to know the recipe.

At first, Garth panicked, but he worked through it, feeling his extensions one at a time and figuring them out. Through this disjointed body, he experienced the cybernetic bartender's extensions and connections. Inside the Club he was omnipresent, a hundred places at once. He could listen to overlapping conversations, take care of simultaneous requests for drinks—he could do it all.

He *was* Club Masquerade, a biomechanical Wizard of Oz running a circus of tables and drinks, lights and music, conversations and secrets. He laughed, his chuckle ringing out simultaneously from all the substations in the bar.

He maintained a conversation with twelve different groups of people at once. He found it confusing, but delightful and exhilarating. The customers didn't seem to notice any change, more interested in hearing themselves talk than in his responses.

So this was how Bernard Rovin experienced each day. The man's body had been crippled, destroyed except for the control center in his brain. But these new and complex sensations made up for the difference.

Garth learned how to multiprocess, how to trust his body's enhancements. Mechanical arms delivered drinks without spilling a drop; credit recorders deducted appropriate amounts from customer accounts; music played and changed and kept the dancers happy. Acquaintances engaged in banal chitchat that required very little effort for Garth to uphold his end of the conversation.

Using external cameras under the arched entrances, he spied on his own body as Rovin wandered around outside in the fresh air. The bartender stretched his legs, smelled the leaves on trees, stared up at the sun gleaming off polished windows of the skyscrapers. But he didn't venture far. Rovin kept looking toward the sparkling Club, then checking the time.

Well before the hour was up, Rovin hurried back, slipping past the surrounding rooms into the main bar. He practically ran to the central control chamber and pounded on the sealed door. "Okay, come on, Garth. Come on!"

"Are you bored out there already?" Garth asked, using parts of his mind to carry on four other conversations in various rooms, tables, and alcoves. "I was just starting to get the hang of this."

Rovin's bright eyes carried an edge of fear. "I was afraid you might refuse to hopscotch back if you spent too much time as me."

Garth considered the absurdity of the comment. The bartender was a wreck of flesh, only fractionally human, trapped inside a single building for all of his life ... and he was afraid that *Garth* wouldn't give him his body back? The insight took him aback. Clearly, everyone had their own standards, their own needs—and Rovin had fashioned a life that satisfied him.

"Don't worry about that. I've learned what I need to," Garth said. "It's ... strange, but oddly compelling. Let's get back into our own shoes."

Once restored, Rovin took a deep breath, his disembodied head barely moving in its harness. His eyes took on a glassy look as he scanned the Club through remote eyes, as if afraid Garth had conspired to burn it down or let barbarians trash the place.

His scarred head smiled at Garth, using his own eyes and mouth. The screens flickered, the views changed, and all of Club Masquerade seemed alive around them. Rovin took a few moments to settle into himself, to pick up his mechanical arms, to listen in on the conversations from tables around the bar. He cleaned a spilled drink and altered the tempo of the music to time it better with the throbbing lights.

"Thanks for the experience, Bernard," Garth said. "Now I need to jot down some notes."

The metal door to the control chamber unsealed itself. Offhandedly, the bartender chased Garth away, his voice somewhat embarrassed. "Go on, get out of here. I've got work to do."

39

She saved the last rose for Arthur, a beautiful cream-white bud. She thought about plucking the thorns from the stem, but Arthur would never have liked that. He wanted the whole object, the good parts together with the bad, the way nature had intended.

After tucking the flower at the bottom of her basket, she completed her delivery rounds through buildings, lobbies, and open-air markets. When she reached their usual fountain, however, she did not find the old man watching the water dance over the geometric shapes and flint mirrors.

Teresa sat holding the creamy rose, waiting for him. She had arranged a special surprise for Arthur. Garth had given her passes to see his FRUSTRATION exhibit, and that afternoon she would take Arthur through the wonderful maze of experiential art. The old man had helped Teresa to understand so much about her inner workings, and she wanted to share back with him.

She couldn't help smiling in anticipation. Her eyes flicked from person to person as she stared at passing businessmen, shoppers, young couples. She paced the square, peering down side streets and alleys. Expectant, she waited the better part of an hour. Arthur had never missed an appointment before. With growing alarm, she knew that it would not have slipped his mind.

Feeling a tug of urgency, Teresa didn't know where to look. The old man had no home that she knew of. He simply stayed wherever he liked. But she knew he'd been sick the last time they were together.

She went first to the automated cafeteria where they had planned to eat, hoping that Arthur had just confused their plans. When she saw no sign of him there, she moved to other places where the two of them had talked, shops and stores they sometimes visited. Teresa hurried down side streets, went to parks and other fountains, looked under trees and playground equipment.

But Arthur wasn't there.

Finally, she remembered Arthur's delight when he'd taken her through the maintenance corridors of the skyscraper where he had once worked. He had seemed so alive and excited that day.

Dodging pedestrians, Teresa ran until she found the maintenance access door Arthur had used. When she reached the rear of the building by the heating systems and air ducts, she let herself in with the simple code she'd seen him use.

She wandered the passages, following water and electrical conduits, squeezing into the tiny spaces between walls. She couldn't remember the exact route Arthur had taken when he'd showed her this place, but she was determined to look everywhere if she needed to.

"Arthur!" The sound echoed among the pipes. Rodents and insects stirred in the shadows, but she heard no answer, only her own voice thundering in the confined space. Its loudness frightened her. She hurried onward.

Suddenly she saw a pale object at the bottom of a steep stairwell. She rushed forward to see the heavy book, *Gray's Anatomy* with its cover open, facedown on the syncrete floor. Arthur must have dropped the book from above . . . but this was his most prized possession. He would never have just abandoned it.

"Arthur!" she called. "Oh, Arthur, are you up there?"

She thought she heard a sound and raced up the stairs, grabbing the metal rails. Her legs worked like pistons as she pumped up one floor after another, paralleling the elevator shaft.

She found the old man collapsed on the fourth landing, huddled in a corner and unable to get up. He gazed at her with dull eyes and tried to sit straighter. "Teresa, you found me. I must have led you . . . on quite a chase." She knelt next to him, grasping his bony shoulders. Arthur was clearly dying. "Didn't mean to be so difficult," he gasped.

"You always told me I should welcome challenges," Teresa said. "Here, let me help. I need to get you to a medical center."

He just smiled up at her. The skin on his face looked like a leather wrapping, slowly sagging. "I'm not sure that'll do any good. We're probably too late." He forced a brief chuckle that degenerated into a wheezing cough. "You know how often I've told you about the complexity of the human body. Okay, the problem with a system so complicated is that too many little unexpected things can go wrong."

Frantic, Teresa hauled the old man to his feet. Though she was not very muscular, she found the strength to lift him. "I've got to get you out of here. You can't die yet."

He leaned on her and coughed again. "I'm afraid I don't have much choice in the matter."

Teresa refused to give up. Slipping an arm around his waist, she wrapped one of his bony arms around her shoulder. "Let's get you down these stairs."

Arthur struggled to assist her, but he was helpless. "That's too much trouble, Teresa. My only real request is for you to get me outside again." His cracked lips curved upward. "I'd rather die surrounded by sunshine than walls and shadows."

She struggled to haul him down one narrow metal step at a time. Her waifish body was small and weak. At any moment she feared she might drop him, letting the frail man tumble downstairs with a crack and a snap of bones. Teresa wished she had somehow managed to keep her home-body, that she had not let the Sharetakers blur her mind as she swapped from person to person. As someone else, maybe she could have helped Arthur more now.

Regrets. It was much too late for such regrets.

Halfway down the stairs, Arthur gasped and Teresa felt him slump into unconsciousness. Limp, he was actually easier to carry, since the stuttering movements of his trembling limbs hadn't helped her much anyway. She just prayed that he hadn't already died.

Finally she wrestled the old man to a maintenance exit. She popped open the metal door on the mezzanine level and dragged Arthur outside. She slumped with him onto the concrete and loose pebbles of a hovercraft loading dock that overlooked the square.

The fresh air seemed to revive the old man. He took a deep breath and shook his head. Yellow-gray hair lay around his skull like dirty straw. Teresa propped him up, resting his bony shoulders against her chest. She hugged him. "Arthur, please fight. Please stay alive."

"My, but you're demanding," he said weakly, then coughed again. She saw blood on his lips. The whites of his eyes had hemorrhaged, turning a deep crimson. His whole body shuddered.

As Teresa held him, she knew he was slipping away. Leaving her. She would be alone and adrift again. She swallowed hard and decided to try one last time. "Oh, Arthur, please hopscotch with me. You don't need to die."

He shook his head and groaned.

"I mean it, Arthur. This is my only way to thank you."

He shook his head, blinked his watering eyes.

"Look, if we swap, I don't plan to give up and die," Teresa continued. "I'm sure I can survive long enough in your body to reach help. You're totally worn out. You must have been fighting this for years. But I'm strong. I can take care of your body just long enough to reach the medical center. It's your last chance."

"No," Arthur said, his voice hoarse and husky.

"I can *save* you! But only if you let me."

She needed Arthur to stay alive, to keep teaching her, even if it meant he had to give up his stubborn principles and switch bodies. Even if she couldn't survive in his fading body, Teresa decided that his life was worth more than hers, because he *understood* so much more about it.

But as he stared at the bright blue sky, Arthur seemed disappointed that she would even suggest such a thing. "Haven't you heard a word I've said?"

Teresa held him. He clung to his principles to the end, and she felt ashamed that she had tried to convince him otherwise. Arthur gazed into the sun, then his eyes stopped blinking. The bright light reflected from his face, and he died.

She stared at his face, looked at the air around him, hoping she could somehow watch the soul leave his body, much as she had witnessed during Soft Stone's upload into COM so long ago.

But she saw nothing, no spirit, no angels, no wondrous passage. Arthur was gone, his old body empty. A lifeless husk.

She held his lifeless form on the landing, silently sobbing.

40

After they swapped for another morning routine, Mordecai Ob frowned as he settled into Eduard's home-body. With an expression of distaste, he flexed the sore, weakening muscles. "Eduard, you feel like crap. If you can't maintain yourself better, I'm going to have to get a new caretaker."

"Sorry, sir. I'd hoped it would get better by now. Is it possible that something you're—"

"It's your problem, Eduard, not mine," Ob said with a scowl. "It's hard for me to do my own work when I'm in a body that feels this bad."

"If you'd like, sir, I can swap back." Eduard watched the man closely for his reaction. *Maybe I should just keep your precious body for myself and run off. Leave you stranded in mine, whatever it is you're doing to it.* "Should I make an appointment for a deep-level medical scan to identify what's the matter?"

"No, no." The Bureau Chief shooed him out of the study. "You've got a long workout to do, and I have an important teleconference meeting that requires absolute privacy here. Don't disturb me."

Eduard departed, trying to hide the flare of suspicious anger in his eyes. Ob sealed the door to his sanctum and switched off the lights. Sunshine filtered through the leafy screen of hibiscus vines that covered the window. The world seemed dim and dreary again, especially after he'd seen Garth's triumphant success, and he needed more inspiration.

Using borrowed trembling hands, Ob popped open the bottom desk drawer to reveal a case of glasgel capsules. Eduard had been his addiction receptacle for months now, but the young body-caretaker was nearing the end of his usefulness. Ob didn't dare let him consult a competent medical professional, since a deep-level scan would detect the residue of the illegal drug, and then there would be too many questions.

Ob had reconfigured the capsules himself, increasing the dosage. Eduard's body had grown so accustomed to Rush-X that he needed more and more of the drug to achieve the full effect. Eduard had lasted longer than his three predecessors, but the body had reached its limits—a larger amount would be quite dangerous, even for someone who had already tolerated so much Rush-X.

Once again Ob shuddered at what might have happened had he used the drug in his own body, instead of surrogates like Eduard. Since there was a chance he might still get caught, he had already used the resources of his Bureau authority to set up Eduard to take a fall. He had even planted several capsules of Rush-X and related paraphernalia in the caretaker's quarters, which Ob would conveniently "find," if necessary.

Now, he withdrew the fragile capsule and held it in his fingers, anticipating how the dissolvable glasgel would break and the vibrant fluid dribble under his tongue. He raised it to his lips.

The videoscreen on his desk rang, demanding his attention. The priority tone was so loud and sharp that Eduard's jittery fingers nearly crushed the capsule. Regaining his composure, Ob hid the Rush-X from view and activated the receive-call button. His mouth was very dry.

Inspector Daragon's image stared back at him,

attentive and expectant. "Sir," he said without waiting for a response, "you and I had our regular caseload meeting scheduled for this morning. I'm out at Bureau Headquarters, but I understand you're working at home today? Would a teleconference discussion suit you instead?"

Ob controlled his surprise, taking special care to keep the capsules hidden. He had been so focused on the morning's drug fix that he'd forgotten entirely. "I apologize for not being there as promised, Daragon. I've been very busy and needed to handle several urgent matters at once."

"I understand, sir. I can be as concise as possible." His voice was calm, his demeanor indisputably professional. Ob wondered what he had done to engender such loyalty in the young Inspector. Daragon Swan was probably the best of the lot, the finest achievement the BTL could hope for.

It shamed him to realize how far from the mark he himself had fallen.

Daragon summarized his cases, updating him on the Bureau's progress in numerous fugitive hunts and investigations. Ob pretended to listen, fighting to keep a mask of interest on his face while the back of his mind clamored for the drug. He felt the slick capsule in his sweaty fingers.

Would Daragon never finish? Why did he take on so many cases, and why did he have so damned much progress to report?

Finally Daragon summed up, then hesitated. Impatient, Ob blurted, "Is there something else, Inspector?"

"Sir, you're not looking at all healthy. Eduard's body seems to be experiencing some sort of illness. Perhaps he should see a specialist?"

Ob stiffened. "I am sorry to inform you, Inspector, that your friend isn't working out very well." He raised a hand, palm up, to cut off any excuses. "He exercises well and does his job, but unfortunately he just doesn't take care of his home-body with the same dedication, and I have to deal with this discomfort during my work-day." He looked somberly at the screen. "I've given him every possible chance, but I believe he has problems that neither of us suspects."

Daragon frowned. "I understand, sir. Still, I'm very concerned about Eduard's health—"

"Well, I'm afraid I can't put up with it anymore. I have already advertised for his replacement. I should have a new personal caretaker in a few days. I do hope Eduard recovers from his personal problems, but I've simply got too many vital Bureau duties to allow this kind of distraction to go on any longer."

Daragon swallowed his reaction, torn between wanting to please Ob and wanting to protect his friend. He nodded crisply. "I had counted on him to do better than this. I hope you aren't upset with me for bringing Eduard to your attention."

Ob couldn't have asked for a better outcome or re-action. "It was nothing you could have predicted, Daragon. Your friend Garth has been an exceptional find, exactly what I hoped. But with Eduard, well... sometimes people just let you down." He reached for the screen controls. "Now, if you'll excuse me. I have important matters before me."

"Yes, sir." Daragon dutifully signed off.

Ob opened his mouth and slipped in the glasgel. His jaws cracked down—releasing the blessed flood of liq-uid creativity, exuberance, and sense of wonder, to soar through his system.

While he jogged, Eduard wished the exhilarating feeling would never stop. Ob's muscles were so strong, so well conditioned. The way his own body should have felt. *What is he doing to me?*

Teresa had suggested that he simply walk away from what was obviously a worsening situation. But he had been stubborn, trying to uncover what was going on. Soon, he wouldn't have any choice.

The night before, Eduard had stumbled out of his apartment and fallen to his knees in the cool air as the wind rustled the tall blue spruces. He coughed and dry-heaved on the walkway. As he huddled on his hands and knees in the darkness, he'd looked over to the gardener's brightly lit cottage, quiet and peaceful. Eduard considered going to talk to Tanu, but he simply felt too bad. He couldn't present himself like this.

Now, though, wearing Ob's home-body, he was reminded of the way a healthy human being should feel. He ran along the extended jogging course, past his second wind, beyond the "wall" where he ceased to concentrate on what his muscles were doing.

The Samoan gardener stepped in front of him and gestured for him to stop. Eduard barely snapped out of his trance in time. He stumbled to a halt. The look of concern on Tanu's face shocked him.

"Eduard," he began, then seemed at a loss for words. "This has gone on too long. I must . . . must show you something."

Astonished, Eduard sucked in a quick mouthful of air. "What changed your mind?"

"I saw you last night, how sick you were." He swallowed hard, and his huge neck seemed barely able to contain his Adam's apple. "This isn't right. It's not what you agreed to do. I watched the others, and I did nothing. But not this time. In a few days, you'll be gone, and Mr. Ob will have a new caretaker . . . and he'll do this all over again." His brown eyes were large and sad.

"A new caretaker?" A jab of fear ran down Eduard's spine. "But I've done everything that bastard—"

"You have done more than you know. You are my friend, Eduard. I don't want to see you go. I don't want to see you die." Tanu gestured for Eduard to accompany him. They crept along the side wing of the house, staying out of view of the windows and moved to Ob's private offices.

The brick walls were overgrown with thick hibiscus, and the heady perfume was nauseating in its sweetness. Tanu put a finger to his lips as they approached the main window in Ob's study. The Samoan hung his shaggymaned head in sorrow and disappointment.

Heart pounding, Eduard crept up to the window and parted the leaves.

Inside the private office, behind a locked door, the Bureau Chief sat at his desk, complacent about security precautions. In Eduard's body, he leaned back with his eyes glazed and milky. His hands were spread out, tapping fine tremors on the desktop. A thin line of spittle ran down his chin.

In an open case on the desk, Eduard saw individual capsules of a milky substance. He remembered the terrible squid-and-cleaning-fluid taste in his mouth. "You son of a bitch."

The pieces dropped into place. Rage seethed deep inside him, and he wanted to smash through the window to grab the man by the collar. All along, the Bureau Chief had known full well what was wrong with Eduard, why he felt so awful. And he'd blamed Eduard anyway.

Ob had been riding his addiction, risking nothing for himself. Sandor and Janine and Benjamin—the previous trainers. Eduard was next in line, to be completely used up. Ob would then find a new caretaker, his next victim—a fresh body to addict and destroy. And Eduard

Swan would probably vanish, just like the others, erased by the capabilities of the BTL.

He drew back from the study window, his face red. Eduard had been the perfect patsy. Trembling, he stepped away from the vine-covered glass, before he could betray his presence.

Tanu frowned. "There's still time for you to get away. Run, now."

But Eduard couldn't think of fleeing in Mordecai Ob's body. The Bureau Chief with all the resources of the BTL would stop at nothing to get his own form back before Eduard could talk.

Instead, his thoughts grew vengeful, his outrage greater than when he had gone to avenge Teresa at the Sharetakers' enclave. Ob's deeds were worse, more malicious, even than Rhys's.

Disturbed, Tanu shook his shaggy head, as if he could tell what Eduard was thinking. "I won't swap with you this time. You can't use my body to kill."

Eduard brooded in silence. This was more personal. This required something more . . . appropriate. "I'll take care of this problem myself," he said, his voice a grim icicle. "In my own way."

No problem.

41

At last Garth was expecting a baby, with all the bodily changes and hormonal roller coasters that pregnancy entailed. A new and interesting experience, one of the best yet.

Pashnak didn't know how long he, himself, could last.

Some pregnant women rented out their bodies to infertile females who wanted the experience of childbirth, to doctors doing research, even to curious men, like Garth. There were plenty of female candidates to choose from, but Garth had been selective, and the women themselves were choosy, adding numerous restrictions to the contract about the eventual disposition of the baby and about the care the "inhabitant" would give to the pregnant body.

Pashnak had arranged for Garth to interview numerous women because he needed to find a body he could tolerate for at least four weeks. Someday, when he had time, the artist thought about going through the whole experience, from start to finish. For now, though, he was most curious about the last month of chemical buildups and changes, as well as the actual birth itself. He figured he could learn a lot from it.

He settled on a short brunette with soft curly hair that fell in waves to her shoulders. She was retaining water, her aching joints were swollen. Because of the substantial cushioning weight her body had acquired, her lower back hurt chronically. Garth waddled around the room, taking note of all this as he tested out his new body.

Standing in his broad-shouldered physique, she laughed at the artist's sense of wonder. "You've got it easy, buster—you missed two straight months of nausea and morning sickness. Interrupted sleep, weird food cravings, Braxton-Hicks contractions, swollen feet and hands. All you get are labor pains, hemorrhoids, backaches, and having to pee all the time."

"You make it sound so delightful."

"It's what you're paying for, buster." They arranged a regular meeting schedule so the mother could keep up with the progressing pregnancy. "The baby's going to be a girl, by the way."

At first, the experiences added interesting new insights to his understanding of people. However, after living in this woman's cumbersome body for one week and then another, he began to feel the emotional differences. Hormonal imbalances caused him to fly into a rage or wallow in despair. He did obsessive things that seemed absolutely necessary at the time—arranging and rearranging his art supplies, demanding a particular color of mug for his coffee—though when the moment was past, he realized his actions made no sense. It was very confusing, this motherhood.

Sometimes Garth sat with his artwork, hopeless, unable to regain a shred of inspiration. In such moments, he sobbed uncontrollably, and nothing—not even Pashnak's concern—could snap him out of it.

Pashnak did his best to tolerate his master's changing moods. He exhibited superhuman patience, holding Garth's hand when he needed it, helping him take a seat when his swollen body became too unwieldy to control, feeding the artist whatever bizarre menu items he requested. Garth often had heartburn or complained of being full without having eaten very much. Pashnak insisted that he take vitamin supplements, at the very least.

Mornings, Garth fretted about being fat. In the afternoons he worried about being ugly. But there were magical, transcendent times too, when the joy of carrying the life growing inside made him just sit alone on the sofa, cradling his enormous abdomen, sensing the baby's heartbeat...and he would begin to cry all over again. "I'm not worthy. This is too *special*. I don't deserve this."

Pashnak trotted around the apartment and studio, working out schedules and rearranging meetings and obligations. During Garth's stay in a pregnant body, all other List items had to be postponed. When the hypemeister Stradley dumped interview seekers at him, Pashnak judged whether or not the artist was able to handle incisive questions or media attention at the time.

Shouting, Garth made demands as, encumbered by his girth, he was unable to do simple tasks for himself. Despite his frustration with an already eccentric artist who didn't know how to deal with storms of unusual hormones, Pashnak convinced himself he could last a couple more weeks, until things got back to normal again. He hoped.

"I want coffee," Garth said as he worked hard to develop a second exhibit for his portfolio of experiential artwork. "Bring me some coffee, and make it strong! I need to be awake." Pashnak had been slipping him decaffeinated coffee in his daily mug. So far, the pregnant artist hadn't noticed the difference.

Humming to himself, Garth stood among the old-fashioned paintings, watercolors, grainy videoclips. He had begun to assemble laser-bursts, sensory cracklers, and holograms to create the desired "experiential" effect. None of the pieces satisfied him, and he had refused to let Mordecai Ob view it. After the success of his FRUSTRATION exhibit, at least he no longer needed the Bureau Chief's patronage and funding so desperately.

Frowning, Garth pressed one hand against his lower back. Sweat sprinkled his brow, and he rubbed it with his free hand, darting his fingers into soft dark curls. Sometimes he had trouble breathing with the added weight, and he could not sleep comfortably, which only added to his general distress and tension.

Now, just inside the studio, Pashnak hesitated, smelling the fresh coffee, smiling at the endearing sight of the pregnant artist's back. Even in the Falling Leaves, Garth had taken everything at face value and assumed that other people had warm, giving personalities, just like he did.

Because his grand goal was so lofty, so far out of his reach, Garth had only a blurry notion of how to get there anymore, though it had once seemed so clear. Pashnak took on the responsibility of breaking down this massive undertaking into manageable steps and then helping the artist focus on each task.

Finally noticing the coffee's aroma, Garth scowled at his assistant. "Don't sneak up on me like that. I was concentrating on my work. You could have made me mess up."

"Sorry, Garth." It was a typical comment these days. Pashnak knew the artist meant nothing by his outburst.

Garth slurped his coffee, let out a contented sigh. "Just what I needed." Then he set the cup down and went back to tweaking the sketches he'd been trying to arrange, drawing lines and charcoal connective designs.

His creative work had gone more slowly since he'd hopscotched into the pregnant woman's body, now that his swollen fingers were much less precise. But Pashnak could see that this display already had an added depth, a spark, a greater richness than Garth's smash debut of FRUSTRATION.

His new work was brighter and more optimistic, called simply JOY. In it Garth displayed the various forms of human happiness. The images and senses ranged from the simple childish wonder of a young boy feeling a raindrop on his skin, to the triumph of a belly dancer flawlessly performing a difficult dance move, to the sweeping arc of a cliff diver plunging along a Hawaiian waterfall. Garth also added a moving portrait that showed the contentment of an elderly grandfather surrounded by his children and grandchildren.

On good days, Garth included his pregnancy as well, aware of the baby maturing inside him, a second heartbeat close to his own.

Deep in concentration, sketching thick charcoal lines on a broad pad, Garth winced and clutched his abdomen. The spasm caused him to scrawl an unexpected zigzag across his drawing.

Pashnak barely restrained himself from dropping the coffeepot on the floor. "What is it, Garth?"

"Another labor pain, I think. Just a contraction." Then he looked down in dismay at his ruined drawing in progress, saw no simple way to salvage it. In a rage, he tore the sketch to shreds, scattering the papers in the air. "I'll never get this done! I'm so clumsy, and I can't finish what's in my mind."

"You're doing fine, Garth. This new work is already very powerful and very moving."

"Don't patronize me! You're paid to say that."

Pashnak held his temper in check, telling himself again that it was hormones, that the artist couldn't help himself. "I've never lied *to* you or *for* you, Garth, and I'm not going to start now." He knew Garth anticipated that the experience of giving birth would be the magnificent center of his new masterpiece.

Exhausted and cranky, Garth sipped more of his decaffeinated coffee and appeared to be on the verge of apologizing, but he checked himself. "I'm tired, Pashnak. I need to rest for a while."

Pashnak opened the door, knowing just what to do to cheer up the artist. "Why don't you sit on the sofa? I'll read to you." They had already finished *David Copperfield, A Tale of Two Cities,* and *Oliver Twist.*

Garth smiled, and Pashnak felt warm inside. He helped Garth lie back on the sofa with a series of groans and winces and sighs, until the artist finally adjusted his awkward body into a comfortable position. Pashnak then spread an instasilk coverlet over his legs and bulging belly. He returned from the bookcase carrying a thin, leatherbound volume, another of Dickens's best. "I'll continue with *The Old Curiosity Shop.*" Garth propped himself up, pushing his curly hair behind him so that he could look at his assistant.

This story was Dickens's most melodramatic, a shameless example of untying the purse strings of his readers' emotions, but Garth seemed to be in that mood these days, and he loved to have Pashnak read to him. He closed his eyes, leaned against the pillow, and listened to the rich language and humorous descriptions, and envisioned the vivid characters.

"You know the sad part's coming," Pashnak warned.

Garth sniffed and nodded. "I've read it before." Even forewarned, he wept as Pashnak read the tragedy of little Nell. "I hate being so...so maudlin," he said and wiped his nose on his sleeve.

Pashnak patted him on the shoulder. Garth reached up, needy and clinging, pulling the assistant down as he cried on his shoulder. "Thank you for everything you've done, Pashnak. I know I've been...terrible."

"It's part of my job to put up with you." He softened his words with a smile.

Garth wouldn't let him go. "You're so good to me. I don't know what I do to deserve your loyalty. I'm sorry for my moods."

Pashnak squeezed him one more time, then extricated himself. "I love you, too, Garth."

Then Pashnak hauled out his electronic day planner and scanned the calendar, wondering just how much longer it would be until the baby came ... until he could have his Garth back again.

42

The cream-colored rose had faded. Teresa held the limp flower in her palm. She plucked one petal and tossed it into the fountain water, then another, then another, watching the white bits of blossom drift away.

Teresa felt shaken and alone. She had spent her childhood and now her adult life with a hunger to *understand,* mixed with a dread that she would never quite succeed. She spent hours just listening to the fountain spray, as if she could hear Arthur's whispering voice buried in its trickles and gurgles and spurts, telling her more secrets about life . . . and about death.

By the time she had exposed the flower's inner parts, her grief was overwhelming, and she tossed the rest of the rose into the fountain. She walked away, through oblivious crowds past Club Masquerade, through a financial district with skyscrapers and mass-transit tubes humming overhead. She kept her gaze in front of her, sometimes focused on the far distance, other times just on the sidewalk ahead.

She still held the passes to Garth's FRUSTRATION exhibit. She had meant to take Arthur there, to show him the facets of humanity as seen through the eyes of an artist. Now the old man would never see it. Walking numbly, Teresa made her way to the exhibition hall anyway. If nothing else, she would wander through the images and be reminded of other times, other friends.

Exhausted, she stopped in front of the hall and

watched an active-matrix billboard shift to display a new ad proclaiming that the sensational artist Garth was nearly finished with his new masterpiece, JOY, and the debut would be scheduled soon.

Teresa's face broke into a grin, proud of her friend's success. She envied Garth his passionate drive. He'd always known exactly what he needed to do. With all the items left on his List, he was searching, too, just like Teresa—though at least Garth's search had a clear goal.

She handed over her pass and entered the exhibit again, experiencing FRUSTRATION anew. It meant something different to her this time. Teresa would rather have seen the artist's interpretation of JOY.

She also envied Eduard his ability to live for the day, satisfied with whatever life brought his way, wherever he was. He reveled in every success, always so generous to his friends. If he failed, he just flashed his cocky smile and tried harder next time.

Even Daragon had a successful career with the BTL. He was justly proud of his Inspector's uniform and his duties. He was no longer searching. He was right where he wanted to be.

Only Teresa remained lost. She wanted an anchor for her life, but so far every anchor had been tethered by flimsy rope. She had flitted for years from place to place, body to body, hoping for some brilliant revelation. She tasted different philosophies, searching for one that was right for her. She hadn't found it yet.

As she wandered through the FRUSTRATION holograms, the photographs, the paintings, the sounds, Teresa thought again of all the times Arthur had patiently taught her about the intricate wonderland of her body. Within her original cells, her DNA coded every subtle aspect of her being. Arthur had believed the soul to be part of that complexity, connected with the workings of the marvelous human machine.

Teresa needed a goal, some kind of target to inspire her and give her drive. She wanted to race toward a finish line, a point at which she could claim success.

On the first spectacular night, with all the crowds and paparazzi, she had not noticed a side gallery, where Garth displayed some of his other art that didn't fit in with the overall gestalt of FRUSTRATION. Now, though, she smiled to see the detailed Artful Dodger sketch Pashnak had bought during her friend's first unpopular exhibition, other sketches of life in the artists' market— and then, covering one entire board, she saw his cherished "portrait spectrum" of the many faces of Teresa.

She looked at the sequence of faces, barely recognizing some of them, recalling how easily she had once danced from one form to another to another. What had she been thinking? At the far left of the board, her eyes caught on the lovingly detailed drawing of her original home-body, the face she had grown up with, the features inextricably associated with Teresa Swan. *Gone forever now.*

Arthur had called her a "lost soul," just looking at these paintings. She wondered if losing touch with her original body had made any difference, if by bouncing from body to body she had somehow lost something in the translation, unwittingly set herself even more adrift.

Maybe that was the problem! She had felt cast loose ever since she'd left the Falling Leaves, particularly after she'd joined the Sharetakers and gotten lost in a merry-go-round of body-swapping. Perhaps her soul had lived too long apart from its original home. Perhaps that was why she felt so lost.

Teresa was a wandering spirit in a body that was not hers, one in which she did not belong. After learning how to hopscotch, a person could move from body to body, but if Teresa never returned home, she might be diluting her own soul. Maybe it would all change again and she could feel grounded, if she could only go . . . *home.*

Leaving the FRUSTRATION exhibit, galvanized, Teresa decided on her new quest—a search that would mean more to her than anything she had ever done before. She needed to find her home-body, the place where she truly belonged. Perhaps then she could reestablish a connection and erase this feeling of loss.

Teresa hadn't seen her body since those terrible days with Rhys. She had *misplaced* herself among the Sharetakers. A member of the enclave, a woman named Jennika, had fled in Teresa's body. Now, she needed to "find herself"—literally. She wanted to feel whole again.

But she had no idea where to start looking.

43

When Mordecai Ob swapped into Eduard's strung-out and sore body, it was all the young man could do to keep himself from cursing the man to his face. *I know what you're doing to me, you bastard!*

The Bureau Chief scowled at his caretaker's body in disgust. "Eduard, I simply can't tolerate this any longer."

With great difficulty, Eduard held his anger in check. He drew a deep breath, feeling refreshed and vibrant. *This* body moved the way it was supposed to: without pain. "I'm sorry, sir."

He looked through a stranger's eyes at his familiar form, seeing the weariness and jitters, sallow skin, sunken eyes. How dare Ob complain, when his own addiction had caused the debilitation?

Ob growled, "I have to go away on important Bureau business for a few hours. Just go do my morning run and meet me here before lunch so we can swap back." He held up Eduard's jittery hands. "This is simply unacceptable."

Eduard clenched and unclenched Ob's strong fists, debating whether or not he should accuse him. Before he could speak, though, Ob made an annoyed gesture, dismissing him. "That will be *all*."

Eduard stalked off, but Ob paid no further attention to him as he prepared to leave. The Bureau Chief had never treated him as more than a servant who exercised his muscles and maintained his body. A disposable human being.

Eduard didn't even bother with his regular exercise rounds. On the way back to his apartment, he took a petty pleasure in stumbling sideways, brushing against a rose hedge and scratching himself along the legs and arms. *My, my, wouldn't that upset Master Ob?*

After the Bureau Chief had departed from the mansion, Eduard dashed barefoot through the corridors until he reached the locked private study. The hall windows glared at him like malevolent eyes, and the rooms were filled with shadows, even during the daytime.

But there were no alarms. The feared BTL Chief was strangely lax with security in his own sanctum. A simple dead bolt locked the door, and with a few minor tools and a tiny magnetic device, Eduard was able to let himself in.

When he'd been younger, it had been a game to imitate the Phantoms, playing at how to change his identity, how to slip through locks in order to snatch a meal here and there. These skills were his resources now.

The study door creaked open like the gateway to a haunted house. It wasn't that Ob had neglected the hinges; no doubt, he'd retained the squeak as insurance against any stealthy approach.

Neatly stacked on a corner of the desk were papers, pictures, and a portfolio of someone named Candace Chu, who was scheduled to report for work as Ob's new personal caretaker in three days. His own job. "What the hell?" Ob had continued to swap with him every day, complaining about his caretaker's aches and pains, all the while advertising for a new patsy. Eduard stared at the face in the image, read the interview notice. Identical job description, identical pay; starting date "in the near future."

A red haze filled his vision, anger strong enough to

clear his mind and start working on a plan. Once he got away from here and Ob stopped poisoning his body, Eduard wondered if he could recuperate, or if the damage was already too deep, his muscles and nerves shredded beyond repair.

A quick search revealed one locked desk drawer; Eduard fiddled with the cheap metal tongue, popping it down to find a closed box that wasn't even well hidden. Inside the black case, nestled in folds of velvet, were four capsules of a whitish pearlescent fluid. A single dose? Skin crawling, Eduard held one glasgel up to the light. He knew what this drug did to a human body, to *his* body.

He fumbled with the folds of soft cloth, removed all four capsules, and pocketed them. Eduard returned the empty box to the drawer and reset the lock, leaving the office exactly as he had found it. Not a skilled job, but Ob would suspect nothing. *Yet.* He wouldn't have to fool the Bureau Chief for long. The man would be back soon enough.

Before he dimmed the lights, Eduard glanced a final time at the file image of Candace Chu. An optimistic young woman, convinced she had landed a dream job. He remembered that feeling. He smiled wryly at her oval face, with its bright eyes and anticipatory smile. "You'll thank me for this, if you ever learn the truth."

Then he closed the office door behind him and returned to his own rooms, trying to decide what to do. He wondered if he should contact Daragon, reveal everything to him—but he knew how much Daragon revered Ob. The Bureau Chief would never meekly confess what he had been doing. After all, his three previous personal caretakers had simply vanished from COM. Mordecai Ob was not a man who played by the rules.

Therefore, neither would Eduard.

The boundary between friendship and duty was a blurred line for Daragon.

He sat at the undersea Headquarters, not seeing his caseload summaries. By now he had become a prominent Inspector, and he didn't want to do anything that might jeopardize his future with the BTL. With his ability to *see* the identity of a fugitive, he had received accolades and commendations, but Daragon's most coveted reward was just to continue doing his job and doing it well. And to have Bureau Chief Ob proud of him.

On the other hand, Eduard had let him down. Daragon felt as if he himself were to blame, since he had urged Ob to consider his friend for the caretaker job. He had thought Eduard would be perfect for the position, but obviously he'd been wrong. Daragon couldn't imagine why the young man would slack off under such ideal circumstances. What more could he want?

It deeply bothered him that his friend had turned out to be such a poor employee, so irresponsible. But he should have known—Eduard had always been impulsive, like when he'd stolen the flowers for Teresa. Happy-go-lucky, without a care for the consequences, Eduard never thought twice about breaking the law. Rules had not meant much to him, even when he was young.

Daragon left the computer room and marched down the corridors to the BTL transport depot. Maybe if he talked to Eduard, they could work out some compromise to salvage the situation, though he suspected it was already too late.

In the hovercar pool he used his ID patch to sign out a vehicle. He had to do this on his own, without telling Mordecai Ob. Daragon would take this one last chance for his friend.

Setting his jaw, he flew away from the ocean platform, setting a course for the Bureau Chief's estate.

Meek and subservient, Eduard came to meet his employer as soon as he returned, tracking him down in his
office, before he could discover the missing Rush-X. He
lowered his eyes and stood ready to hopscotch, determined that Ob would not realize what Eduard had discovered. Not yet.

This would be the last time. *The last time.* First,
though, Ob would get a taste of his own crimes. A suit-
able threat, a humiliating revenge—though, as with
Madame Ruxton, Eduard had a fluttering sensation that
perhaps he was again out of his depth.

Would Ob really just let him go, let him walk away
from the mansion with his drug-wracked body? Since
Eduard was friends with Inspector Daragon, could Ob
risk making him simply disappear, like the other caretakers? Or did the Chief believe he had Daragon so completely indoctrinated that he could do anything with
impunity? Eduard felt cold inside.

Ob would make up stories, distort the truth, probably plant evidence—who would believe Eduard's word
over the testimony of the powerful and benevolent Bureau Chief?

Eduard could imagine Daragon's response if he
claimed the young Inspector's mentor was a deceitful,
manipulative bastard who used other humans as recep-
tacles for his own pleasure, regularly ingesting illegal
drugs and enjoying addictions at the expense of unwit-
ting host bodies. That the Chief was in all likelihood a
murderer himself, disposing of strung-out caretakers before they could reveal his secret . . .

No one would believe it. Not even Daragon. No one
else would ever exact justice for himself or for Sandor

Perun, Janine Kuritz, and Benjamin Padwa. Unless Eduard did it himself, as he had done with Rhys and the Sharetakers . . .

Already, he had deftly slipped the four pearlescent capsules one at a time into his mouth, tucking them on either side of his tongue. He would have to keep his head down. Luckily, Ob wasn't much of a conversationalist.

Time to give the man a taste of his own medicine . . .

Now, at Ob's private office, Eduard strode forward, breathing through his nose, keeping his lips clamped shut, his gaze averted. Completely on guard. He just wanted to swap back and get out of this abuser's body.

From behind his desk, the sickly-looking form of Eduard stood up. "We have business to discuss, about your performance on my behalf."

Eduard grunted noncommittally and came closer. He could feel the fragile glasgel starting to dissolve in his mouth. He couldn't swallow, couldn't move. He didn't even know how fast the drug would act, or how large a dose this body could stand.

Ob came around the desk toward him. "I'm afraid I will have no choice but to terminate your employment. Swap with me, and be done with it."

Why was the man talking *now?* Why didn't he swap first and then continue with his lecture? Ob stopped, looking with extreme annoyance at the rosebush scratches on the well-muscled arm and the side of his leg. "You've done it again! This is inexcusable."

Eduard reached forward and grabbed Ob's temples even as he bit down, shattering all four capsules in his mouth.

The instant before they swapped, he felt a cold, awful-tasting fire surge into the sensitive tissues in his gums, under his tongue, and through the roof of his mouth. Ob had been doing the same thing to Eduard's body all along. *See how you like it.* He felt a lightning storm begin to surge through his mind, through his nerves—

Then his mind was displaced, flicked across the gulf...and Eduard found himself in his own aching body again. Back home.

The look of wide-eyed horror on Ob's face was comical. He swallowed convulsively, then opened his mouth to spit out the fragments of already dissolving glasgel.

Eduard leaned forward, ferocious now. "How do you like the taste, Master Ob? I know what you've been doing to me, but this time it's your own body being damaged. Four capsules should be just about enough to make my point. Enjoy the sensation."

Ob grabbed at his throat, blinking his eyes, but already his vision glazed. "Four? Rush-X...four!" He staggered forward, stretching out his hands. "Swap back!"

Eduard easily sidestepped the disoriented man, steeling himself against pity. "I don't think so. You deserve some pain for what you've put me through." Eyes blazing, he leaned forward like an avenging angel. "And all your other caretakers, too?"

Eduard had never been so glad to be back in his own body, despite its flaws, despite its weaknesses and its degenerating condition. It was *his* body.

Ob slumped to the carpeted floor, his fingers clenched in a clawlike grasp. Then his face grew slack and subsided into an idiot grin as drool poured from one side of his mouth. The Bureau Chief's crotch darkened as he lost bladder control.

With a flash of remorse Eduard wondered if he should call a medical team. During the addiction, his body had developed a tolerance, but Ob's perfectly tended body was clean. It had acquired no resistance. Eduard didn't know how bad the Rush-X overdose would be. He took a tentative step toward the COM screen, then looked back at his employer.

His indecision dissolved into disbelief as he watched Mordecai Ob die.

Shock washed all thoughts of justified vengeance from his mind. He'd imagined a suitably nasty poetic justice against the man who had addicted his body to Rush-X, and he'd acted impulsively. Paralysis overtook him as he realized what he had done. Eduard had never meant to *murder* him.

He would explain that it was an accident, that he had acted out of self-defense. Surely, based on what had happened to the previous caretakers, Ob had intended to make him "disappear" after terminating his employment. Eduard knew it in his bones.

But who would believe him? Even if Tanu the gardener spoke up for him, he still had no proof. He had taken the last of the hidden Rush-X capsules, removing even that evidence.

Ob's loyal Beetles—including Daragon—would never rest until they captured him. Eduard had killed the vastly powerful leader of the Bureau of Tracing and Locations. In all likelihood, they would never let him make his accusations and besmirch the revered memory of the BTL Chief, patron of the arts. Eduard remembered how the BTL apprehension specialists had gunned down the anti-COM terrorists in the flower market....

Frantic, he looked around, trying to decide what to do. He had to get away.

Just then he heard footsteps in the hall. An identity chime rang through the intercom system as an officer entered the foyer after being recognized by the security systems. "Mr. Ob, it's Daragon, here for our weekly briefing." His boots clomped on the floor, approaching the office. "And I'd also like to see Eduard, if that's all right?"

For a frozen moment, he thought about surrendering to Daragon, his former friend—who was now totally devoted to the BTL. Especially to Mordecai Ob. Eduard would never convince Daragon that his mentor had been a malignant parasite. As the unsuspecting Inspector came down the corridor, Eduard knew he was trapped.

Leaving the still-twitching corpse on the floor, he picked up the desk chair and hurled it through the window masked by hibiscus shrubs. The hole was just large enough for Eduard to get through. He would have to move fast.

Hearing the glass break, Daragon ran down the hall. "Mr. Ob!"

As Eduard climbed to the windowsill and pushed himself through the vines, Daragon burst into the room. Eduard looked over his shoulder, his eyes fearful, frozen for a moment.

Their eyes met. "I'm sorry, Daragon." Then he dropped to the ground outside.

Daragon noticed the Chief sprawled on the floor. "My God!" He fell to his knees, touched the man's cheeks, grabbed his shoulders. He saw the drool and smelled the drugs, felt the oily slick perspiration covering the man's already cooling skin. He felt for a pulse but found none.

"Eduard! What have you done?" He ran to the broken window.

Eduard sprinted across the estate grounds toward the gated exit.

Daragon crawled through the smashed window, ripping his neat uniform. He jerked tangled branches away from his face, scrambled clear, and dropped to the ground.

Hearing the shouts, the huge Samoan gardener hurried toward the outside of the office. Tanu stood there, blocking Daragon's way. "What's happened?"

Daragon looked after Eduard. "Not now!"

But Tanu grabbed his arm, clumsily stalling the Inspector. "Tell me! I need to know."

Daragon yanked himself free. The big gardener moved as if to block him again, but the Inspector ducked under his massive arm. "Damn you, Eduard!"

His former friend dashed through the gate and out into the streets. Eduard ran and ran for his life. . . .

44

Eager to see her friends, Teresa came early to Club Masquerade, arriving even before Garth for a change. She sat in a comfortable floating chair, listening to her turmoil of thoughts. The pain of losing Arthur and his *ideas* was still fresh, but she determined to turn it into something positive.

She bought a wintergreen-flavored stim-stick and kept an eye on the various entrances. Music throbbed like a jogger's heartbeat in the background.

The last time they'd met here in the Club, she had told Eduard and Garth about the wonderful things the old man had taught her, but now she needed more from them. Maybe the two men wouldn't understand her quest to find her original body, but at least they would listen.

An enormously pregnant woman with curly brown hair waddled in. She scanned the faces until her eyes lit upon Teresa's waifish form. The pregnant woman waved at her, then huffed up a small set of stairs to the raised table where Teresa sat.

"My back hurts." He pulled one of the chairs out much farther from the table than he actually needed to and struggled to maneuver his body. Slowly, carefully, he sat down. "I asked for this, so I can't complain. But the . . . unwieldiness is affecting my ability to work."

"Garth, you look absolutely radiant," she said with

a smile. "Tell me, what does it feel like? Having a baby inside you, another life growing."

"For one thing, it's triggered my nesting instincts. I worry about things I never thought of before—and spend as much time cleaning the house as I do creating my art. I don't know how much of it is biochemical and how much is mental." He cradled his belly and ran an eye over her delicate form. "You should try it sometime. Or would you rather just swap with me for an hour? As long as you don't tell anybody. I've got a very strict contract with the conception-mother."

Teresa shook her head quickly. "No...I'm done with fast hopscotching, until I can find my own body again."

He regarded her with curiosity, but respected her choice. When Bernard Rovin's face appeared on the table filmscreen, Garth ordered a carbonated juice drink, forsaking his usual beer. He placed a hand on his abdomen as a flicker of pain traveled across his face.

Teresa leaned forward in alarm. "Oh, you're not going to have the baby here, are you?"

"Don't be melodramatic. It could be just gas." Garth laughed. "These irregular contractions are coming more frequently, though. I'm due in only a few days." His juice drink arrived from the dispenser, and he took a long sip.

"You going to name the baby after me, Garth?" the bartender asked from the screen, image grinning.

"It's a girl, Bernard. Besides, that's out of my hands. Within a day after delivery I swap back with the conception-mother."

"It sounds like she's getting the better end of the deal, don't you think?" Teresa said.

Rovin's face changed on the screen, this time speaking with a sharp tone. "Your friend Eduard's coming through. He's in a hurry, and he doesn't look at all good."

Teresa stood up, scanning the various entrances. She saw the haggard young man dash from the Arabian Nights room into the main bar. His face was drawn, his brow and hair misted with sweat, his dark eyes wide and frightened.

She waved. "Oh, Eduard! Over here!"

He flinched at the sound of his name above the pulsing music, then made eye contact with Teresa. Garth raised his hand in greeting, struggled briefly, then abandoned the effort to get up.

Eduard hunched down and averted his face as he moved through the crowd, but his furtive efforts only attracted more attention. Teresa met him halfway to the table, draped her arm across his shoulder. His clothes were drenched with sweat and smelled rank. Ravenous, he plucked one of Teresa's wintergreen stim-sticks from a tray. "Can I have this? I really need it."

He crunched down the stick, and Garth pushed his remaining half-glass of juice toward his friend. "Here, drink this, too. We'll order another round, and some food. Did you hear that, Bernard?"

"Got it," said the screen.

"Eduard, what is it? What's happened?" Teresa asked.

He gulped Garth's juice, then looked with hunted eyes first at Teresa, then at Garth. "I'm on the run, and I'm desperate. I need help. And money." He sucked in a deep breath. He looked down at his ID patch with dismay. "I don't dare use COM. The Beetles would trace any transaction, locate me anytime I try to log in."

Garth and Teresa shifted their chairs closer, like covered wagons circling. Their new positions would keep anyone from spotting Eduard from the door.

"What happened, Eduard?" Garth said.

"You know you can tell us anything." Teresa's voice overlapped Garth's.

Eduard looked at his hands, which clenched into gnarled fists. His hands trembled with inner quakings. "I was too damned impulsive." Then he frowned more deeply. "The bastard deserved it, but I never meant for *this* to happen."

"Who?" Garth persisted.

"Ob—I . . . I think I killed him." As they sat stunned, he explained what the Bureau Chief had been doing to him, addicting him to Rush-X, destroying his body as he had done to his previous three body-caretakers.

Garth looked as if he couldn't believe it, nor could he *dis*believe anything Eduard said. He gasped as another labor spasm hit him, but he was just as astonished to think of what Mordecai Ob had been doing to his friend, even while he was acting as a patron for Garth's struggling artistic career.

Teresa kept her voice low, remembering that she had talked with Eduard about this at the FRUSTRATION debut. "Why didn't you come to us sooner? Either one of us would have helped you out—"

"I knew you two would be here. Maybe I'll be safe for a few minutes, maybe not. It could be my last chance to see you both. From now on, the Beetles will be watching everyone, *especially* you two, and I don't want to put you in danger."

"Turn yourself in," Garth said, surprised to find tears pouring down his cheeks. "You can't just run."

Eduard's haggard face turned hard. "Don't be ridiculous! I killed the head of the BTL, and then I ran. I couldn't look more guilty if I tried. Ob wasn't stupid, and look how he made everybody love him—you included, Garth. He wouldn't have left any clues, and his previous caretakers have all disappeared. Since he was going to get rid of me, he probably even left evidence to set me up."

"But what about Daragon?" Teresa suggested. "Why can't you just explain what really happened? Talk to him—"

Eduard hung his head. "After . . . it happened, before I knew what to do, Daragon saw me. He's probably called in BTL reinforcements by now." He looked around, haunted. "By now, he believes I betrayed him in the worst possible way. He'll never let me tarnish the image of his great mentor. None of the fanatical Beetles would. I'll be 'accidentally' killed during my arrest."

Teresa said in a firm voice, "Then we've got to do something for you—right now."

With swollen fingers, Garth grabbed his hand. "If you've got the BTL after you, and you can't use COM, what are you going to do? How are you going to get out of this?"

"Good question," Eduard said. "Any ideas?"

Garth dug into the purse slung over his shoulder and hauled out his account card. He transferred a large balance onto a blank voucher. "Unmarked credits, same as cash, so don't lose them. You can spend them without leaving a trail. Use them to go far, and be safe. Get away from the city."

Eduard's eyes widened at the amount. "Is this some of Ob's money?"

"He cut off my stipend as soon as my first exhibition was successful. And another gallery paid me in advance for the rights to showcase my next work . . . if I ever get it finished, that is."

"I can't repay you." Eduard's red-rimmed eyes glistened, and he squeezed Garth's shoulder with a shaky hand. "I can't even thank you enough. Not for something like this."

"Don't be ridiculous, I can spare it." Garth's throat

thickened with emotion, and the hormone storm in his pregnant body intensified the response. "You helped me out when I needed it. When I was struggling to be an artist, I survived because of your generosity whenever you got a big payoff. Now it's my turn. And don't you dare argue."

Teresa fixed her large eyes on Eduard, and he saw something in her expression. "I don't have any money for you, Eduard, but let me do something else. I'm offering you my body . . . literally. Swap with me, and run. Get away, use me as a disguise. It'll throw them for a little while."

Eduard flinched. "Teresa, you can't! The Beetles have my ID, my fingerprints, my blood type, my COM accounts."

She jabbed a finger toward his chest. "They're looking for this home-body. For *you*. You saved me from Rhys and before that you rescued me from that fugitive in the flower market. Don't argue now." Arthur had not let her repay him before he died, and she *needed* to do this for Eduard.

"Teresa, you don't want this mess." Eduard held up a shaking hand. "My body might already be irreparably damaged, thanks to what Ob did to me. Even best-case, you'll probably go through a horrendous withdrawal."

But she would not be swayed. "Oh, this isn't even my original body, Eduard. This body or that—it doesn't matter to me, if it's not the right one. But it may mean the difference between life and death for you. I'll take care of yours, make it healthy again, if I can." She grasped his hand with an iron grip. "Hopscotch now, Eduard. I insist." He tried to back away, but she forced herself upon him. "You don't have any other options. And you know you'd do it for me if our roles were reversed."

They touched. Swapped.

After synching their ID patches, Teresa stared at herself across the table. She felt his strung-out body, the aches, the drug-induced damage to his nerves and reflexes. She reached for her tart drink, hoping it would burn the awful drug aftertaste from her mouth.

As he looked at her from behind what had been her wide eyes, Eduard's expression changed to guilt and dismay. But Teresa, seeing him inside the waifish body she'd worn for so long, didn't even feel a sense of loss. She only hoped her friend could get away.

Knowing this might be the last time she ever saw him, she embraced Eduard gently, wetting his bony shoulder with her tears. She knew how fragile this slight female form was. Rhys had already broken it once.

Garth also hugged Eduard, pulling him against his swollen belly. "You stay well, Eduard. Stay alive."

"That's what I intend to do," he answered. "And no matter where I am, no matter how far down I fall, I will always remember that I have friends like you."

Saying goodbye for what might well be forever, Eduard fled in his new identity across the crowded dance floor and ducked through one of the Club's random exit arches.

45

On the windswept platform out at sea, BTL investigators and apprehension specialists gathered for their orders. Down in womblike chambers, teams of Data Hunters scoured COM for any trace of Eduard. Every person in the Bureau knew how important this manhunt was.

Chief Mordecai Ob had been assassinated, and the killer was on the loose.

The killer was my friend! Daragon thought.

Choppy water foamed against the derrick's broad steel supports. The cold sky hung slate-gray around them. Daragon stepped into the salty breeze and inspected the assembled troops. Though he hated it, this responsibility had fallen to him.

A thorough search had uncovered Rush-X paraphernalia cleverly hidden in Eduard's quarters. An autopsy verified that Rush-X had killed Ob, though the Chief's body showed no evidence of previous exposure to the drug. Daragon recalled the many times Ob had mentioned Eduard's deteriorating physical condition; now, in hindsight, the signs of addiction should have been obvious.

The answer was painfully clear, and Daragon had no trouble thinking the worst of him. Eduard had always made excuses, taken shortcuts, looked for fast answers and avoided blame. It would have been just like him to seek the thrills of Rush-X, disdaining the damage it was doing to his body—after all, he had put himself through far worse plenty of times.

When Eduard took the drug in Ob's healthy body, though, it had been unable to tolerate the exposure. The coward had somehow tricked the Chief into swapping with him at the last moment. Daragon's thoughts returned to the unforgettable sight of his mentor lying on the floor, his mind already destroyed by the overdose... and Eduard fleeing out the broken window.

Why would you do this, Eduard? And how can I see it through? How could he defend his one-time friend?

"Attention!" Daragon shouted into the wind. The BTL specialists snapped into formation. He scanned the rows of trackers, enforcers, and interrogators assigned to the elite teams. "You all know the crime that's been committed, and the fugitive must be brought to justice. We know the identity of the perpetrator, but we do not know his current location. He has been on the run since yesterday." He stared at the stony, attentive faces. "But we are the Bureau of Tracing and Locations, and we will find him."

Gruff acknowledgments and brisk nods—no wild cheering. These people were too professional for such theatrics.

"The suspect is smart and he is desperate. We have no reason to believe he has remained in his home-body, so we must look elsewhere, as well."

COM transaction spotters, evidence techs, and Data Hunters like Jax would scour the ocean of available information for any indication of Eduard's body, any access of his credit accounts, use of mass-transportation systems for local or especially long-distance travel. Blockers and surveillance systems would spot him if he tried to go to another country. If nothing else, the BTL would keep him bottled within the city limits.

Daragon could not do less than his utmost. Love and

hatred had become a blur in him. From now on, his friendship with Eduard no longer existed. He had once admired the young man, even wanted to be like him, but Eduard had burned every bridge that joined them, permanently separating them.

Daragon watched the teams disperse to Bureau hovercars parked in the holding area. He stood waiting as the vehicles shot off toward the skyline, following COM-specified search patterns. With his special skill to *see* a person's true identity, Daragon's own eyes were the greatest weapon in such a manhunt. He needed only to glimpse the real Eduard, no matter what body he wore.

Daragon would search the city, person by person if necessary, monitoring a thousand COM surveillance screens, until he spotted his former friend. He would catch Eduard, sooner or later.

No problem.

Trying to predict what the fugitive would do, Daragon immediately went to see Garth, hoping the artist could offer some insight into where Eduard might have fled. He doubted, though, that Garth would volunteer anything that might result in his friend's arrest.

He rang insistently outside the elaborate studio, growing suspicious at the silence, until finally a harried-looking Pashnak threw open the door seal. His hair was tousled, his skin flushed, but he was too flustered to pay much attention to the visitor. "We don't have time for this, Daragon. Garth's in the medical center." He turned to grab a duffel, which he had carefully packed weeks earlier. "I just rushed him to the hospital an hour ago."

"The hospital! What? Oh—the baby! Is it due?"

Pashnak hustled out the door, carrying the duffel. "They say there's no need to rush but . . . come on, you can take me there in your official vehicle! I presume with Bureau authorization you can get us traffic overrides?"

Once they were at the medical center, Garth had sent Pashnak racing back home to pick up a batch of unnecessary items. The doctors insisted everything was normal, but Pashnak seemed to operate better in a panic. Garth was even more concerned, refusing to heed the calming advice of the surgical professionals.

All the muscles in his abdomen squeezed like an angry fist. The skin on his distended stomach hardened like the rind of a melon. The contraction built as a wave, more and more intense, like a leg cramp that involved his entire body, instead of a sharp squeeze as he had expected. He barely had time to catch his breath before the next one hit.

Then warm salty water gushed out of him in a completely involuntary stream. It felt like gallons and gallons, making an outrageous mess that didn't seem to bother the medical center personnel at all. "Is this it?" he gasped, just as another contraction hit.

"Nah, this is just the beginning," said the head midwife, a lean woman with thick, dark eyebrows.

Garth had gotten accustomed to the active baby inside him, the secondary life attached to his own. Totally out of his control, he felt the infant girl moving, twisting, turning. She would kick out, pressing one tiny foot against his ribs like an archer trying to string a bow. The strangest part had been a jarring rhythm when the unborn baby battled a bout of hiccoughs.

Now, during the actual labor and the delivery, the avalanche of experiences came much too fast for Garth to do more than ride them. How foolish he had been to expect that he'd be able to take notes!

When Pashnak returned with Daragon in tow, rushing to the calm lights and music of the delivery crèche, the attendants would let only Pashnak in. He hovered about like a proud but nervous father.

"Hey, you," the lead midwife said to him, "make her more comfortable by massaging her back and legs."

"It's a *him,*" Pashnak corrected.

"Sorry, but any person giving birth in my ward is a *female,* as far as I'm concerned."

Pashnak dutifully rubbed Garth's legs and swollen ankles through another wave of labor pains. "It's like an out-of-body experience," Garth gasped, trying to put his feelings into words. "It's happening to *me,* inside of me, but I have no control over what's going on here. Like someone else is running the show."

Then he could form no more words as his whole body felt ready to explode, full of extreme pressure everywhere. His tissues stretched far beyond the limits of anything he had ever imagined. The pain made his focus fade into a red blur. "Maybe I need painkillers after all, a lot of them. I don't know how much—"

"Garth, we agreed this would be natural childbirth, so you could get the full range of—" Pashnak dodged as Garth reached up in a sincere attempt to strangle him. From a distance, the assistant continued to urge him to concentrate on breathing and think of his artwork. Finally, Garth relented as the contractions gave him a brief respite. Very brief.

After an eternity he transitioned into hard labor, and at last the contractions seemed to have a purpose, slamming him with an irresistible urge to push. He felt so full inside as the baby positioned herself, then began to move down the birth canal.

Sweat ran off him in rivulets. Pashnak wiped Garth's face and neck with a cool, damp cloth, keeping up a stream of encouragement like a cheerleader and blithely ignoring any callous insults Garth spat out. When the baby's head finally emerged, then the shoulders with even greater pain, the rest came easily, and the slick body slid out. The attendants placed the newborn, still connected by the umbilical cord, onto Garth's semideflated stomach.

As he reached out with trembling fingers to touch the stirring infant, Garth forgot about the pain and struggle he had just endured, all the dramatic changes his body had wrestled with. Now that he was done, none of it mattered. He had a newborn daughter in front of him, a new life that had been *part of him*.

"You may think it's over," the head midwife said, "but it's not."

Next, giving birth to the placenta also cost him quite a bit of effort, but that part was much less satisfying.

Afterward, he was more exhausted than he'd ever been in his life. But the birth experience had filled his body with endorphins, released a new hormone in his brain that gave him an emotional rush unequaled in his other experiences. He wanted to feed his baby, get to know her, protect her from the world—he would die for her, if need be. Tears of wonder trickled unheeded from the corners of his eyes. How could he have lived so long without ever realizing that such deep and instinctive emotion *existed*?

He had no idea how he was ever going to convey these feelings in his artwork. The sum of them went beyond JOY.

Back in his room, Garth settled against crisp pillows, cuddling his baby. This would have been a good time to sort out his thoughts and assimilate the whole experience, but he was too numb to think.

After a light tap on the door, the real mother—still wearing Garth's body—came in to see her child. "Thanks for doing all the work. So, was it worth it?"

"Priceless." Garth smiled, his expression typically radiant. His eyes had a distant expression, still partly in shock.

By the time Pashnak and Daragon were finally allowed to enter, Garth lay slumped on the sheets, his skin pale, his eyes shadowed with exhaustion. Curly brown hair spread out in a tangled mat on the pillow.

Daragon found it an odd scene, not one he'd ever expected to witness. He recognized Garth's persona in the female body on the bed, while the familiar blond-haired male—inhabited by the conception-mother—sat in a chair close to the bedside, cooing over the rail at the wrapped bundle.

Garth perked up at seeing his two new visitors. "Daragon! I haven't seen you in so long. Not since the night of my FRUSTRATION exhibit." He reached out a hand. "My new showing of JOY opens in two weeks, as soon as I add the birth experience. No excuses. I want you there." He lifted a finger to point sternly.

"Joy." Daragon could only frown. "There's not much joy in my life at the moment, Garth. I've got too much...too much on my mind." He hesitated. "You've seen Eduard, haven't you?"

Garth glanced sharply at Pashnak and handed the baby to her mother. "Leave us alone for a few minutes, you two. Please." The assistant looked concerned, but the mother was delighted for the opportunity to hold her infant. They left the room.

Daragon bent closer to the bedside. "You've got to help me find him, Garth. Eduard must be held accountable for what he's done."

"Do you even know what he's done? Exactly?"

Daragon stood stiffly, as if his uniform were a shield. "He murdered a man who was my boss, and my friend."

"Eduard's your friend, too."

"Not after this."

"Daragon—your boss, your *friend*—was destroying Eduard. Mordecai Ob addicted Eduard's body to Rush-X. It was killing him. Ob intended to use him up, and then hire another personal caretaker."

Daragon saw black static around the fringes of his vision. "That's ridiculous. Mr. Ob died from an overdose of Rush-X—an overdose Eduard gave to him. I saw him fleeing the scene, and we found incriminating evidence in Eduard's own quarters."

Garth glared at him with accusing eyes. "A good investigator keeps his mind open to all possibilities."

"You're talking about the Chief of the Bureau of Tracing and Locations! I can't let friendship twist an interpretation of a crime scene into something absurd." In disgust, Daragon turned away. "Eduard ran from me that day. If he doesn't turn himself in, he'll be tried anyway, in absentia—and there's no way I can defend him or help him."

He had given Eduard too many second chances. Ob had already been forced to hire a replacement for him. Perhaps Eduard had learned he was going to be dumped and couldn't abide being kicked out.

"You're wrong about him, Daragon." Garth sat up in the plush, overly comfortable maternity bed, his expression intense. "You're making a big mistake. Eduard would never do the things you're thinking."

Daragon shook his head and turned to leave the hospital room. "Garth, no matter what excuses he might make, no matter how much he means to you, Eduard *did* murder Mordecai Ob. If there was a problem, why didn't he trust me? If I don't bring him to justice, somebody else will."

His mind in turmoil, Daragon departed from the medical center, summoned his BTL hovercar, and cruised low over the streets, watching the pedestrians below. He stared at the crowds, remembering when he and young Eduard had gone out in secret, fantasizing about hidden immortals who lived in the shadows of society. "Is that a Phantom?" Eduard would ask. "Is *that* a Phantom?"

This time, though, Daragon would be able to answer the question. He searched the unfamiliar faces for a flicker of the persona he knew so well. "Is that Eduard?" he thought. "Is *that* Eduard?"

Daragon vowed to keep looking until he found him.

46

Even with a clearly defined goal for the first time in her life, Teresa still felt lost. Where to find her original female form, her home-body that she hadn't seen in over a year? It seemed an impossible task even before she started. Without Garth's sketch in his portrait spectrum, Teresa wasn't sure she even remembered what she had looked like.

Logging onto COM, she used all the skills Soft Stone had taught her in the monastery library, but she found no trace of the woman named Jennika who had fled the enclave wearing Teresa's home-body. She wondered if "Jennika" had even been the young woman's real name.

As a start to her search, she knew she had to retrace her steps, go back to where her original body had disappeared. But asking the necessary questions meant returning to the Sharetakers. Teresa swallowed hard. It would be the most difficult thing she'd ever done.

With gray clouds blanketing the sky, she stood in Eduard's aching and wasted form. She tried to put aside the discomfort, her reluctant need for more Rush-X, the awful taste in her mouth. For two days she'd been trying to rest, to eat nourishing food, doing what she could to restore her vitality.

Eduard's body was weak and sore, maybe irreparably damaged. Even the fresh air smelled sour in her nostrils, and the constant headache wore her down. During the worst pain of withdrawal, though, she did not regret her choice for Eduard. He was still out there, somewhere. Alive, she hoped.

Now, her stomach in knots, Teresa stood outside the enclave from which she had fled, where Eduard had rescued her. The familiar building looked rundown. Inside, the open area now looked cluttered and unfinished. The Sharetakers had once owned most of the building, but many of the levels had been repossessed and rebuilt. She wondered what had happened here.

Where once she had worked joyously among a bustling crowd of fellow believers, now they all looked uneasy, stressed. Only a few Sharetakers remained, victims of disappointment and confusion. People moved with their heads down, carrying boxes, distraught.

Upon seeing her enter, unrecognizable in Eduard's haggard body, two of the members ran out of the room, as if to fetch someone. "Maybe he wants to join," suggested one woman, her voice doubtful.

Some doors were sealed, marked with new ownership tags. Construction workers moved about, measuring, marking, pounding. Support struts stood in the open rooms where the Sharetakers had knocked down walls to make their togetherments. Now the communal areas were being subdivided, new walls framed, individual living spaces mapped out once again.

She stepped uncertainly into the dusty open area, at a loss. "I . . . I'm trying to find someone. A person who used to be a member here. Her name was Jennika. Does anybody remember her?"

None of the remaining Sharetakers seemed to care. "Too late. She's probably gone."

"If she got out of here, then she's definitely in a better place. The Sharetakers are bankrupt," said a frowning older man. "I lost everything. We all did. We're closing down."

Teresa held on to a plaswood brace. She vaguely

recognized this man's weathered face, had no idea who lived in his body now. Names on ID patches meant nothing to her, and she knew they never kept any records. Steeling her nerves, she asked with dread, "Where's Rhys?"

The middle-aged man sagged. "Who knows?" Then, bitterly, as if he too had been betrayed, "Who cares?"

A woman stopped, setting down a box full of miscellaneous items. "He ran away, actually. The Beetles kept sniffing around here, and one night Rhys just disappeared. He abandoned us, after all his talk about trusting and sharing, his compassion, his promises." Her weathered face grew ruddy. "We trusted him."

Teresa tried to hide her instinctive relief. "It sounds like just the kind of thing Rhys would do."

The weary man snapped back to the situation at hand. "Sorry, can't talk anymore. We've got work to do. Our group has been evicted from the building. No more togetherments, and we have to be out by today. I've still got some packing to do." He sighed. "Well, not much to pack, really."

Teresa realized that it would do no good to keep asking. Jennika was just a name in an unremembered body; her loss had been of no consequence to the Sharetakers, especially not now, when everything was gone.

She looked around, trying to recapture a single warm memory of this place where she had spent so much time, where she had once felt loved and at home. But she only felt as empty as the repossessed rooms.

Walking away from the enclave, Teresa tried to think of where else to search. She had not even returned home in a day. Restlessness kept her moving, searching. As always.

Now, though, she hadn't gone more than a block before she heard shouts and running feet. Weapons sensors activated with a crackling *zzippp*.

"Eduard Swan! Freeze!"

A swarm of dark-uniformed Beetles converged from side streets, drawing heavy weapons. Overhead, with a loud whirring sound, an armored chopter cruised low. Long barrels of laser-tracking munitions protruded from the hull plates, all zeroing in on a target. On *her*. She was in Eduard's body.

Teresa stood motionless. "I'm not Eduard." Her hoarse voice was drowned out by the chaos of apprehension activities. She made no threatening move, no twitches or gestures. They wouldn't bother to use stun projectiles this time.

The remaining Sharetakers who had slogged outside with packages and crates dropped their possessions and scrambled back inside, perhaps thinking that this was a raid on their enclave.

"I am not Eduard!" She held up her hand, turning the ID patch for all to see, but no one came close enough to read the code.

Orders were bellowed from loudspeakers. BTL troops surrounded her, but they maintained a substantial distance, as if her body might be wired with explosives. Teresa stood in the middle of it all, very slowly turning to show that she was no threat to anyone.

The apprehension commander came forward without lowering his weapon. He glared at her through a face-protective shield. "Prepare to be taken into custody. Be advised that we will show no tolerance for resistance."

"My name is Teresa." She quietly repeated it, like a mantra. "Run an ID scan, and we'll clear this up." At any instant she expected the weapons to fire, the first shot taken by an enforcer who imagined a threatening motion, or even sneezed at the wrong moment.

The heavily armed chopter cast a shadow over the prisoner. Another BTL hovercar streaked down the street, coasting to ground level with a blast of exhaust. The door swung up on glide pistons, and an Inspector leaped out.

Teresa saw him, and her heart swelled. "Daragon!" The name came out in Eduard's familiar voice.

Daragon marched forward, face grim. He snapped at the other Beetles. "Lower your weapons! I want no shooting." He pushed two of the armed hunters aside. "Absolutely none."

"But, sir—" the apprehension commander said.

"If you believe one unarmed man can break through your entire cordon, Sergeant, then the Bureau needs to train its troops better."

"We haven't ascertained yet that he's unarmed—"

"Of course he's unarmed. I know Eduard—" Then his face paled as he got his first real glance at her. "Teresa!"

She tentatively lowered her arms. "That's what I've been trying to tell them."

Daragon slapped the apprehension commander's weapon away. "Back off! This isn't Eduard—he's already hopscotched into a new body. We knew this would probably happen." He stared long and hard at her. "I just didn't think the red herring would be you."

"Eduard has done the same for me, whenever I needed it. *Whenever.*"

The Beetles grumbled at each other, disgusted. Daragon ordered them to fall into ranks. "This person is in my custody for now, until we get the matter straightened out." He took Teresa's arm, walking boldly through the encircling ring of troops, getting her away from all the weapons. The uniformed men parted with a rattle of boots and firearms.

Daragon looked into her eyes with disappointment

and saw only Eduard there. "How could you help him like this? Where did he go? Tell me. You must tell me—it's your duty."

"To let you kill my friend?" Teresa yanked her arm away. "How can you side with a monster like Ob? He addicted Eduard's body to illegal drugs—oh, just look at me!" She plucked at her shirt, touched Eduard's scarecrow chest.

Daragon shook his head. "So you believe that crazy story, too? I knew Chief Ob as well as I knew Eduard."

"Have you tried to check his story at all? Did you find Ob's other caretakers?"

"I have teams working on it. All three are still missing."

Teresa's body trembled, aching from Rush-X withdrawal. "Doesn't that make you at all suspicious?"

"Chief Ob dismissed his caretakers because they were unreliable. I didn't really expect to find them working comfortable jobs."

"So, all four were dismissed for being unreliable? A coincidence, don't you think? And what about the gardener? He saw it all. He was the one who warned Eduard."

"He didn't have proof of anything. But *even if it were true,* that changes nothing in the eyes of the law. If a hungry man steals from a store, he is still a thief. If a disgruntled employee kills an abusive employer, he is still a murderer. Eduard murdered a man, a powerful man, and he fled."

"It was an accident," Teresa said, setting her jaw stubbornly. "Deep down inside you know Eduard isn't a killer."

Exasperated, Daragon forced himself not to shout, not at Teresa. "I could arrest you for aiding and abetting a wanted murderer. How can I protect you from this? Do you know how much I've already done for you and

Garth—and, yes, dammit, Eduard, too! Why didn't he *trust* me?"

"You aren't exactly giving him the benefit of the doubt right now, either. This is Eduard we're talking about!"

A cascade of emotions flowed across his face, and he tried a different approach. "Teresa, aside from Soft Stone, I was the only one who ever listened to you talk about the mysteries of life. When Eduard was sneaking out of the monastery, and when Garth was painting the walls of the basement, *I* was the one who sat next to you. I listened to you."

Her expression remained torn. She had once cared deeply for him, but the Bureau had turned him into a stranger. "Oh, Daragon, you only came to listen to me back then because you wanted to be my friend. You didn't care about those questions any more than Garth or Eduard did."

Daragon nodded slowly as if she were his confessor. "No, but you three had a different, closer bond. I wanted to be friends like—"

She shook her head, frowning at him. "Friendship like that was only possible because we would have done anything for each other. Anything. You tried to be close to me, but you always kept a piece of yourself hidden. And now that uniform has made the wall even thicker. Until you realize that, and as long as you keep trying to kill Eduard, we'll have nothing to talk about."

Teresa shook her head, feeling the stiffness in her neck, the pounding in her skull. "Eduard's probably swapped out of my old body by now anyway. I honestly don't know where he might be."

Daragon's voice lost all compassion. "Are you telling me the truth now, Teresa?"

"I would never lie to you." She turned back to him, her face rigid. "I thought you knew that."

"But you wouldn't do anything to harm Eduard, either, would you?"

Teresa didn't even hesitate before answering. "Of course not."

Frustrated and hurt, Daragon didn't press the issue. He knew the other Beetles would be disappointed, even outraged, but he couldn't ask her more. He longed for the closeness they had shared in the past.

But before he could say anything, she walked away in Eduard's drug-ravaged body, leaving the Beetles behind. She didn't even glance back at him. The priorities of the Bureau meant nothing to her.

47

On the run for his life, with limited resources and limited possibilities, Eduard used every scrap of his abilities to stay one step ahead of his pursuers.

And worst of all, Daragon knew him very well. Years ago in the monastery, Eduard had shared his dreams of becoming a Phantom, of disappearing into the cracks of the city to live as an invisible immortal. He had shown young Daragon how to slip out of the Falling Leaves, to elude pursuit, to dart in and out of crowds....

Now all that would come back to haunt him. Daragon knew Eduard's tricks—so, he'd have to come up with new ones.

On foot, he drifted along the streets. All routes out of the city would be blocked by now, or at least closely watched—and Eduard didn't want to do anything stupid.

Once Daragon found Teresa, he would need only a glance with his eerie talent to see that a switch had been made, and he would begin pursuing a different body. Her large-eyed, narrow-featured face would be transferred throughout COM. Everyone would be looking for him in this form.

So Eduard had to become someone else, and fast, much as it saddened him to leave Teresa's waifish body behind. He had defended and tenderly nursed this battered physique back to health. But he had no choice.

He stopped in front of his reflection in a mirrorglass window, propped one hand on his narrow hip, and inspected Teresa's body. She was small-boned, her hair a mop of mousy brown hair framing delicate features and a finely structured face. The breasts were small, barely noticeable, her hips narrow. After Rhys's abuse, Teresa had not felt inclined to look attractive to anyone.

But Eduard could see the potential there, especially in her big, dark eyes. His own intensity burned behind them now, making the gaze bright and flirtatious instead of haunted and withdrawn. This woman's body could be sexy—if she wanted it to be. Attitude was half the battle. He lifted his chin high and stepped along with a saucy confidence in his walk.

He used some of Garth's unmarked credits to buy a set of impractical, scanty clothes and a nonprescription pheromone spray. Prismatic makeup to highlight the eyes, blush around the cheekbones, some mousse for the hair, a splash of color, a hint of costume jewelry.

An oil-slick wraparound tube top drew more attention to the exposed skin above and below than to the small breasts themselves. The bare midriff was flat and strong. A temporary sunburst tattoo surrounded the navel, with enticing flames that dipped into mystery below the waistband of a glistening short skirt.

He laid a trail of sparkle powder along the backs of both smooth calves, feathering and widening out as the line rose up the backs of his thighs to disappear tantalizingly beneath the high hem of the scarlet skirt. It would draw the eye, fire the imagination.

Finished, Eduard headed toward the lifters. He saw eyes turn, tentative smiles, eyebrows rise appraisingly. Because of Teresa's withdrawn shyness, most people wouldn't have noticed her before (which was in itself a blessing), but now he needed to set a hook. He was confident enough in the animal magnetism that he could have seduced any of those looking at him. Given time.

But he was in a hurry, and Eduard knew where to find a sure thing.

The buildings towered high above him, taller than he remembered. It had been a long time since he'd spent his days dangling in a mag-lock harness. Years ago, fresh from the Splinters, he'd worked the windows of these skyscrapers.

He took the lifter to floor 26. There, outside the broad windows, he spotted the autoscaffolding that held a maintenance specialist. As Eduard had suspected, even after all this time, his former coworker Olaf Pitervald hadn't changed jobs, hadn't been promoted to anything better. He remained stuck in his unambitious rut, right where Eduard could find him.

Knowing that Olaf spent more time gawking through windows than paying attention to his job, Eduard caught his eye, making the lanky man reel, as if he might fall backward off the autoscaffolding. Eduard strolled forward, swaying his hips as he kept his eyes on the window. His smooth thighs flashed beneath the skimpy skirt.

Dangling on the autoscaffold, Olaf blinked in disbelief. Watching Eduard approach in his sexy body, the gangly man looked as if he might panic and zip upward a few levels. Eduard paused and flashed a sensuous smile, then strutted forward again. Olaf froze, and stared.

Eduard stepped right up to the windowpane, pressed Teresa's body against the smooth surface as if he desperately wanted to get closer. He touched his lips against the glass in a big, moist kiss. "I've always wanted to do it on the roof of a skyscraper. . . ." Eduard raised his delicate eyebrows. "Think you could help me out?"

"On—on the rooftop?" Olaf grabbed his mag-lock harness to keep his balance. "Hey, I've got access!"

Eduard blew Olaf another kiss and pointed upward. "Meet me up there. I'll take the lifter, but you'll have to open the main door." Olaf swallowed visibly and nodded. The autoscaffolding hummed, carrying him up and out of reach.

Slightly queasy at what he was doing, Eduard took a fast lifter to the top level and made his way to the locked access door in the maintenance shaft. Normally, no one would come up this high except under special circumstances. Eduard checked his skimpy clothes, shivered, then used another light mist of pheromone spray. It felt oily on his skin, like old sweat. He hoped Olaf hadn't lost his nerve.

He didn't consider Olaf the least bit attractive, or even interesting. But he had endured dental surgery for this man—he doubted sex with him could be much worse.

Eduard heard a fumbling on the other side of the lock. Lights blinked green on the panel, and the rooftop door opened, spilling sunshine into the stairwell.

"You're here!" Olaf said in disbelief. "You're really here."

Eduard climbed the remaining steps. "I'd rather be . . . out there. Alone with you. Don't *you* get a thrill out of having sex with perfect strangers?" He smiled, trying to make his body relax, to feel some sort of arousal. "I've always wanted to do it up here, so high, under the open sky."

Olaf gulped. He closed the door behind him, and the keypad automatically locked it. Then he followed the petite woman's body as Eduard walked across the open rooftop.

Eduard stripped off the oil-slick tube top, but held it coyly in front of him, covering his small breasts. He concentrated on his crotch, trying to feel a need there, trying to get wet, to be aroused. He felt no anticipation, though . . . only determination.

"Just one condition." Eduard delicately licked his lips with the tip of his tongue. "I want the . . . full experience. We have to do it twice, once in each body. Get undressed."

Olaf was only too eager to agree. He fumbled with his work coveralls, trying to undo the fastenings. His hands shook. Eduard felt guilty for using the gangly man so blatantly, but despite the inconvenience, this would probably be the high point of Olaf's life.

He let the oil-slick top fall from his hands and gave Olaf time to gawk at the small, perfect breasts. Cool breezes chilled Eduard's skin, made his nipples harden. "If I'm distracting you, Olaf, I can find a more private place to undress."

Olaf swallowed hard again, and went back to undressing. "No, no—that's just fine. Hey, how did you know my name?"

Instead of answering, Eduard wasted no time stripping off Teresa's sexy new skirt and dropping the panties. He twirled around naked, pretending to revel in the open air. He found a smooth, sunny spot on the concrete rooftop and lay back, beckoning Olaf.

Sex with this nervous, middle-aged window maintainer was demeaning, but no worse than all the other things he had done in his life. In the end, he found he could tolerate it better if he closed his eyes. No problem. Olaf couldn't contain himself and was quick enough to finish—embarrassingly quick. At least Eduard managed to avoid much kissing during the ordeal.

He slid out from under Olaf, who was panting and grinning. "Now for part two of the bargain." Eduard reached toward him. The gangly man leaned back, looking frightened—but the two of them swapped before

Olaf could think of any excuses. They synched the ID patches; if he stole Olaf's identity outright, he would be too easy to trace.

With different eyes, Eduard looked down at the naked woman, seeing her petite form, the smooth skin he had learned to know so well, both when it was his own flesh and when it was Teresa's. As he looked through the eyes of a man again, Eduard saw only a reflection of *Teresa* lying flushed from the hurried sex.

Olaf seemed withdrawn and frightened behind Teresa's big eyes. Eduard guessed the window maintainer had never before experienced intercourse as a female, outside of his fantasies. "Don't worry," he said consolingly. "I'll make it easy for you."

Eduard strutted around in Olaf's lanky body, stretching, feeling the muscles. "Let me get accustomed to this, so I can perform better." He glanced at the waifish body sitting naked on the rooftop. "You'll see how easy it is." He strolled around the perimeter of the building, peering over the edge to the streets far below.

"Okay, I . . . I think I'm ready now," Olaf said, shivering in the tiny female form. "But it's getting cold up here."

Eduard reached the spot where he had dropped his sexy new clothes. He picked up the scarlet skirt and oil-slick tube top, removed the last of the unmarked credits Garth had given him—then tossed the garments over the edge, where breezes yanked at them and carried the clothes away.

"Hey!" Olaf scrambled to his bare feet, disoriented in her small body. "Those are your clothes."

Eduard quickly grabbed Olaf's coveralls. "No—they're yours now." He fumbled in the pocket for the access card and ran toward the locked rooftop door.

"What are you doing?" Olaf said in complete disbelief, his voice a pale reflection of Teresa's. Eduard hated that he needed to do this. It wasn't fair. But then, life wasn't fair—especially not lately.

He swiped the keycard, unlocked the access door, and tugged it open, dragging Olaf's clothes along with him. He would get dressed in the stairwell, after the door was safely locked behind him.

Olaf stumbled after him in Teresa's petite body, but Eduard pulled the access door shut before he could reach it. In the dim stairwell the reader panel blinked green, then red, automatically slamming dead bolts into place. The hapless maintenance man now found himself stranded on the roof, without clothes, in a strange woman's body. Muffled pounding came through the door.

After he climbed into the worn coveralls, Eduard pocketed the keycard, but then decided he had no use for it. Instead, he set it on the top stair, where someone would find it. Olaf shouldn't have to pay a fine for losing that, at least.

Eduard finished dressing. His clumsy fingers had difficulty with the seam-sealing tape, but at last he felt comfortable in his new identity. He could easily fake being a building maintenance man. After all, he'd been one.

As he trotted down the stairs, already tired, he realized how out of shape Olaf was—especially in comparison to Mordecai Ob's physique. Even as the victim of a scam, Olaf had gotten the better end of the deal. He'd probably be too embarrassed to report it anytime soon. Eduard certainly hoped so.

Meanwhile, Eduard had what he needed: a new, unrecognizable face and form. Now he could run.

48

Lights flashed, media spotlights dazzled the audience ... but this time the attention wasn't for Garth.

Pashnak accompanied him to see the debut of Juanita Cole, an innovative new creator whose work had been billed as "the most intriguing, most breathtaking to hit the art world in decades." Garth heard this with a bemused smile, because the same hyperbole had been used to describe *him* not long ago. Joy and several other "panorama experience" art exhibitions had been raging successes for Garth. In only a year, Stradley had made him a star.

Now, the hype-meister had presented them with two VIP invitations, encouraging Garth to see Juanita's astonishing accomplishments (not surprisingly, she was another one of Stradley's "projects"). It was always good to study the work of another groundbreaking artist.

"Juanita's doing innovative things with aerogel sculpture," Pashnak said as they wove their way through the well-dressed crowds. Tuxedoed security guards scrutinized each special invitation. "I could quote you some of Juanita's preliminary reviews, if you want more background."

"I've seen the reviews." Garth studied the trappings of the exhibition: the laser rainbows and media scancopters, familiar from his own FRUSTRATION show, followed by Joy. Back then, he'd been swept up in the excitement, but this spectacle made him feel oddly un-comfortable. Perhaps a twinge of jealousy? "Maybe we shouldn't have come on opening night. We'll be lost in the noise, and we won't get a chance to have a good look. Let's come back in a week, when there's more el-bow room."

Pashnak grabbed his arm. "It's not the same as opening night. Besides, you should get out more, keep in contact with your audience, understand what they want. How else can you connect with them?"

Garth gave a reluctant sigh. "Even when you're pes-tering me, you're right." He remembered how he had wandered among the innovative craftsmen at the open-air bazaar, searching for inspiration, studying tech-niques. Now that he was a success on his own, was he afraid to see what miracles another hot new talent could produce?

He had increased his audience with each subsequent offering: FRUSTRATION, then JOY, then TRIUMPH. Thanks to the springboard Mordecai Ob had given him—despite what the dead Bureau Chief had done to Eduard—Garth was a bona fide sensation, a feeling both new and refreshing after so much obscurity.

Still, as Pashnak led him into Juanita Cole's splashy debut, he felt the uneasiness return. Right now, he would rather have been visiting the baby—Emily—again, though that was impossible. Even after months, some part of him still responded to the psychological bond he had formed with the baby girl during preg-nancy and childbirth. Sometimes, when his longing got bad enough, Garth wanted to hold Emily, touch her, but the mother seemed uncomfortable with his continued interest. She had fulfilled their contract, she said, and he'd gotten his birth experience. She asked him not to come again.

With no other place to direct his emotions, Garth

had incorporated those feelings into a new project. Maybe he'd send the curly-haired mother a free pass.

Passing through the sparkling door arch, they were welcomed by professional greeters. Some of the smiling attendees even knew Garth's name, and Pashnak automatically made the appropriate acknowledgments for him.

Garth walked through Juanita's wilderness of art. The hall had been made into a labyrinth of eerie, alien sculptures, free-form moldings of translucent aerogels, ultralightweight foams that were little more than solidified air. Juanita had concocted impossible geometries, overbalanced and distorted forms that gravity would never have allowed. The phantom material flexed and contracted with temperature variations, pulsing like something organic and alive.

"It's a fairyland," Pashnak said.

"Or a nightmare." But Garth's face held a flickering fascination.

In the surreal multicolored forest, spangles of fiberoptics bristled through the aerogels. Mood lights shifted spectrum from red to blue; some of the sculptures were photoreactive, emitting time-delayed photons in different colors.

They walked through the twisted, flexible forms and colors, ducking low and squeezing between. Spectators chattered excitedly among themselves. On their faces Garth saw childlike delight.

Sensing his mood, Pashnak said, "This is totally different from your panorama experiences, Garth. You've got nothing to worry about."

He looked up at the ceiling, where aerogel clouds hung like frozen smoke. "Of course not. Who said I was worried?" His denial rang hollow, though. He had never been able to hide his feelings from his perceptive assistant.

Working feverishly and never slowing down, Garth had achieved more fame than he had ever dreamed. Stradley had set him up for exhibition after exhibition. Everything ran like clockwork.

In quiet moments of taking pleasure in his accomplishments, Garth usually turned his thoughts to Eduard and his plight. Pondering his friend's downfall and continuing ordeal, Garth was exploring darker territory in his next work—Loss, a counterpoint to TRIUMPH. In Loss, he examined broken dreams, failed attempts at finding happiness, the cruel emptiness after death, discord, or circumstance. He wove in subtle emotional threads, from profound grief to simple bittersweet regret, a mother's separation from her child. Life went out of control sometimes and crashed into a wall. Like Eduard had.

Garth had not heard from his friend since the final night in Club Masquerade. Eduard was still on the run, still a fugitive, while Daragon and the BTL continued to pursue him. Garth wanted to help, but didn't know how. So he had created his new masterpiece in honor of Eduard...though he doubted his friend would ever see it. He intended to make Loss his best work ever.

Stradley had openly expressed skepticism about the work in progress, though. "Garth, you did your brash debut with FRUSTRATION. That's okay. It was an 'angry young man' piece—not pleasant but profoundly moving. Everybody's entitled to one of those. The critics loved it, you got plenty of attention, and you made your audience. But nobody wants to pay credits for a show that'll depress them. Loss? Who the hell wants to see that?"

"I need to do it. It's the piece that...that wants to come out next."

Rolling his eyes, Stradley had muttered about crazy artists with no business sense. "All right, but I advise you that it won't be good for your career. Something called Loss will be tough for me to push in a big way. You understand that?"

"I understand. But I have to do it." His work would speak for itself.

In the wake of his successes, Garth had watched many people imitating his "panorama experience" technique. He had broken new ground, and now others trampled the same path, making it wider. Garth had been a pioneer, and a successful one at that . . . which placed him one step away from being passé in the fickle world of critics.

Tonight, though, he found a new pioneer blazing a new trail. Juanita Cole's remarkable aerogel work dazzled him. These bizarre sculptures evoked primal reactions, a flowing feminine sensuousness, a powerful male rigidity. Her creations appealed to more than just his eyes and mind; they appealed to his instincts, as well. Young and angry, brash in her own way, she would make her mark, too.

Garth stopped to contemplate a swirling mass of blue-green aerogel, a foaming circular funnel called *Descent into the Maelstrom* that seemed to draw him into its center. Fiberoptics cascaded in a descending ellipse, and his stomach twisted. He was forcefully reminded of the ocean in Hawaii, the clutching water and the undertow, the sensation of drowning. . . .

Dizzy, he reached out for Pashnak. Once he regained his balance, he touched the sculpture's outer edge, pressed down on the ethereal material.

"Please do not touch, sir." A strident, automatic voice buzzed close to his ear as protective systems activated. "If you persist, security will be notified."

Garth stepped away, embarrassed.

On their way back to the studio, Pashnak marveled at what Juanita had created. Garth, though, found it difficult to concentrate, and his reactions disturbed him. He wished it didn't bother him that Juanita Cole had begun to garner the same kind of attention he himself used to get. It seemed petty. *I should be happy for her. I really should.* But the paparazzi already considered him old news. Would the fickle public soon stop enjoying his exhibitions, quickly tiring of the "same old thing"?

Pashnak looked at him with compassionate eyes. Attuned to Garth's thoughts and moods, the assistant understood what had triggered his funk. "Don't worry, Garth. You aren't one to rely on your past triumphs. Complacency leads to stagnation, after all. You have to keep pushing the envelope to redefine the boundaries. It's part of who you are."

"If you say so," Garth said as they approached the door to the studio.

"Yes, I do say so. And you'd better listen to me," Pashnak said. "I'll make you some coffee. Then you'll feel better."

Garth slumped down on the sofa and thought about Juanita Cole. Before going to the exhibition he had checked on her background, learning who she was, where she'd come from. He imagined her to be a person filled with enthusiasm and drive, someone who had recovered from remarkable adversity, used her inner agony for artistic inspiration. She intrigued him.

Instead of an anguished upbringing, though, Juanita actually knew her parents, had even grown up with her mother. They lived a comfortable, uninteresting, middle-class existence. She hadn't endured any tragedies, any hardships. She'd lived a bland, quiet, normal life.

He couldn't figure out where Juanita got the power to put into her work. In order to achieve such pathos, wasn't an artist required to experience flaming emotions, highs and lows, the proverbial agony and ecstasy? Like he had endured with each item on his List?

Somehow, though, Juanita Cole had found the flame within herself.

Pashnak brought him a steaming cup of coffee. Garth took a sip and burned his tongue. The assistant hovered for a moment, before realizing that Garth wanted to be left alone. He touched the artist's shoulder compassionately, then quietly departed to his rooms.

Alone, Garth contemplated in silence. He needed to regain his inspiration.

Inspiration.

Setting the coffee aside, Garth picked up his datapad and switched it on. Scrolling through the files, he scanned to see if there was anything worthwhile left on his List.

49

Eduard had managed to survive for months—that was something, at least. But with each passing day, the prospect of safety became slimmer and slimmer. He found himself at the ragged limits of what he could do.

This wasn't the way he had imagined life as a Phantom would be.

In the dead of night, Eduard crept out of a dark doorway from the access tunnels where he'd been lurking. In this quiet and cluttered section of the city, the streets were narrow, the shadows deep, tinged only by reflected lights on the popular boulevards.

With COM monitoring all travel, he couldn't leave the city. Even so, the sprawling metropolis contained a million hiding places, but now he was hungry. Hungry enough to venture out again.

Eduard listened, holding his breath. He glanced both ways, took another step into the open, exposed now but ready to dash back into hiding. Nothing... only the night and the distant sounds of traffic.

The Beetles would never drop the case. Daragon would die before he ceased his search. Eduard had been fleeing, hopscotching from one person to another, scamming, running. He had thought it would get easier, but guilt made each swap as distasteful as the first. He had hated Mordecai Ob for using people, and now with each snatched body Eduard was himself doing a similar thing to escape prosecution. But fear kept him on the run.

Eduard didn't know where he was anymore, or even what he looked like. Before long he'd traded Olaf's mediocre physique plus some of his precious unmarked credits to a dumpy-looking woman. No questions asked.

Because of his dire straits, Eduard had been unable to check her health beforehand. He should have been suspicious when she'd agreed so readily to take Olaf's uninteresting body, without requiring a medical scan. Only after he'd run off, with no way to trace her again, did Eduard realize that something was terribly wrong. The dumpy woman suffered from a degenerative muscular condition, and Eduard was stuck with it until he could trick someone else into swapping.

From there, he'd hopscotched into a swarthy, ugly parolee who'd been sentenced to live in a brutish Quasimodo body for a year. The parolee willingly accepted the overweight woman's body, degenerative condition or not, though he would suffer a stiff fine at the end of his term. Still, he could at least go about his business without being bombarded by scornful expressions and glares and insults, and he'd get his original form back at the end of his sentence anyway.

After a while Eduard traded the muscular parolee for a rail-thin underground worker, a weakling often tormented by fellow employees in the subsurface tunnels. To the worker, the parolee's ugliness didn't matter—only the sheer brawn did. Down in the dirty tunnels, no one could see what he looked like anyway....

Eduard took one crisis at a time. He did not worry about slippage, the ever-present chance that he might lose himself in a swap. That was the least of his concerns. He was forced to hopscotch for keeps, in a hurry and without a record of the transaction, without any legal contract or medical scans. Therefore, he had to keep

swapping into less desirable bodies as his resources ran
out. He always got the worse end of the deal—older,
uglier, more decrepit.

He'd done his best to cover his tracks. With all of his
precautions, everything he had done—backtracking,
hopscotching, hiding—he should have slipped through
the Beetles' net, but they maintained a tight, nearly invisible cordon at all routes out of the city. Thanks to
public COM reports, Eduard knew that Daragon remained hot on his trail. Each time he hopscotched, he
left a vital clue or loose thread.

After Olaf had gotten himself rescued from his embarrassing rooftop predicament, he'd reported the body
theft to the Bureau of Tracing and Locations. Before
long, Olaf had gladly traded back to his original lanky
form, offering Teresa's waifish body to the delighted
woman who had suffered from the degenerative disease.
Not long afterward, the parolee had sought medical
treatment for his new dumpy female body, which had
then placed *that* transfer on record.

Thus, Daragon followed Eduard step by step.

Now, Eduard stood in the dark streets, shivering in
his rail-thin form. He had few clothes, few resources
left. He began to walk toward the boulevard, to see
what food he could find or scam.

The business district beyond the darkened fringe
glistened with holographic advertisements. Eduard
could be anonymous among the shops and restaurants
and mingling groups of people. The boulevard seemed a
long way to walk, beyond a greenway and darkened
park. He didn't have many unmarked credits left, but he
needed a decent meal. . . .

As he crept toward the central business district,
Eduard looked up to see a shadow eclipsing the faded
starlight: a surveillance chopter, completely black except
for the white BTL logo on the side.

A blaze of lights pounded around him. Eduard knew better than to ask questions or concoct explanations. He bolted back into the shadowy alleys where the buildings pressed close together. Debris was piled around the collapsed entrances.

With warbling alarms, BTL hovercars streaked into position. In the buildings around him, lights winked on, then went dark as people opaqued their windows, barricaded their doors.

And Eduard ran.

He raced for the nearest doorway with his head bent low, lungs already burning, heart pounding. This rail-thin body was weak and tired, never meant for such sudden turmoil.

Over the thunder of booted feet across street stones, loudspeakers bellowed his name. "Eduard Swan, we know you're down there. Surrender yourself immediately."

The voice changed as another person picked up the transmitter. "Eduard—it's Daragon. I'm here. I won't let anyone kill you. Stop and give yourself up. This is foolish."

Eduard didn't answer. That would take too much breath. He ducked into the sagging doorway and plunged down a metal staircase into tunnels beneath the old buildings. He had lived here for weeks and knew his way around better than any of the Beetles did—he hoped.

But his pursuers had computer-guided maps and infrared detectors that could sense the residual heat of his every footstep. Eduard didn't have the energy to outsmart them. He just had to get away.

Inside the tunnels, homeless refugees scrambled out of his way, faces he had seen but not spoken to in the shadows. Everyone down here was hiding from something, and though he wished he could have done something to help them all, Eduard had no time or resources to solve anyone else's problems.

He heard a door crash open far behind and above him. Armored feet pounded down the stairs. Lights blazed into the murky darkness, making everyone shield their eyes. Two brief bursts of gunfire rang out, but Eduard didn't slow for a second.

He found a ladder up to an access hatch. He scrambled up, hand over hand, gripping the cold rungs. His hands and legs shuddered from exhaustion, stretched taut. He climbed into the night, letting the hatch slam behind him. He cursed the noise, which would surely give away his position.

He bypassed the densest alleys and rundown buildings and found himself on the periphery of a large sprawling park that bordered the business district. He fled, leaving footprints on the damp grass. Firefly lights hung from cables strung from tree to tree, enough illumination to deter criminals but not so much that it ruined the serenity of the park. Insects swirled around the globes.

Eduard kept to the shadows, but he didn't know how much farther he could go. He passed a nighttime jogger and a couple cuddling on a bench, but he kept running. They had seen him and would report his position. The Beetles couldn't be far behind.

Ahead he saw an old man sitting on a park bench with a sack cradled in his lap. He reached in with a gnarled hand and tossed phosphorescent crumbs like lightning bugs into the air. Dark shapes swooped around—trained bats that gulped the bread crumbs out of the air. The old man dipped into the bag again and tossed another glittering handful. The dive-bombing bats snatched the morsels before they could fall to the ground.

Eduard skidded to a halt, panting. The old man

looked at him with a pleasant smile, unperturbed by his urgency. "Good evening."

"Please," Eduard gasped. "I know this is a crazy request, but would you swap with me? Take this body. Keep it. It's younger than yours and healthy enough. Good trade."

The old man raised a set of thin eyebrows, and Eduard backed off. He had to keep running if this man wouldn't agree. "I have nothing to offer you. No money. No reason to convince you. It's just that I'm desperate, and I need to get away. This could confuse them for hours."

The old man rolled up the sack, though the phosphorescent bread crumbs continued to shine through the paper bag like a Japanese lantern. "That body of yours might have a few more miles left on it than mine does. You sure you want to do this?"

Eduard paused, one foot raised, ready to run again. "Yes! Completely sure!" He touched the old man's temples, looked into his tired eyes and felt the rushing and drowning sensation as their personalities switched. He stood up from the bench, orienting himself to the new physique.

He could feel arthritis and sore muscles, but that didn't concern him. This body felt no worse than the other one had, not stressed to its limits by terror and exhaustion. He turned, anxious to get away.

"Wait," the old man said, sitting down in Eduard's rail-thin former body, suddenly trying to catch his breath. "Hand me my bugcrumbs, please." He took the glowing bag while Eduard tottered off. "Hey, we didn't synch our ID patches."

Eduard froze for a terrified instant of indecision, then heard the Beetles coming. The old man didn't seem bothered. "Never mind, I'll be here. Just circle around and come back later."

Eduard bolted, ducking low to slip into the hedge shadows. He heard shouts behind him in the park. Spotlights from cruising shapes in the sky skewered anyone moving in the park. Eduard pushed through the thick boughs until he reached an open street and lights and other pedestrians. He tried not to look as if he were running. It would take a while for them to figure it out.

He heard gunshots and shouts, then Daragon's booming voice. Eduard hoped the old man would be all right as he vanished into the swirl of the street.

Rushing forward, his breath short and sharp, Daragon raced to accompany the squad. Though the apprehension specialists had been armed only with stun pellets, he wanted to be there when they captured Eduard. Overhead, surveillance choppers blasted lights down, set off their sirens. They had found him! BTL shock troops swarmed into the park, converging near a pond.

Hearing shouts, Daragon ran faster. "Eduard!" he called, without a loudspeaker this time. "Don't let this go on—give up now!"

Anxious, the Beetles charged toward the park bench where a rail-thin man sat alone, looking surprised and confused. He tossed a handful of sparkling crumbs into the air.

"Look out!" one of the officers shouted, and opened fire.

A cloud of stun pellets rained all around the man. The ensuing spatter of shots threw him backward over the bench. A spray of phosphorescent morsels flew into the air. The weapons fire continued, as if each BTL pursuer wanted to put a dozen darts into the fugitive.

Daragon shouted in dismay. He dropped to his knees beside the body they had pegged as Eduard. The man had become a pincushion, peppered with a hundred times the lethal number of stun pellets.

"Look at the ID patch," one trooper said, grabbing the victim's spasming hand. "It's Eduard, all right."

Daragon stared at the contorted face, his wide eyes, his quivering lips. He looked and *looked,* but saw the wrong persona.

"This isn't him. You shot the wrong man, idiots! *This isn't Eduard!*" He cradled the dying bystander, who surrendered a few last gasps, but managed no words.

Daragon continued to gaze deep into the old man's soul as it faded into darkness. Then he looked up and stared at the night shadows and the silent, sprawling park all around them, but Eduard was already gone.

Sickened and terrified, Eduard realized what had happened behind him. He hadn't intended for the old man to come to any harm, hadn't believed the Beetles would be so bloodthirsty. They should have talked with the old man, perhaps detained him briefly, and then learned their mistake. They weren't supposed to use deadly force! Hadn't they been charged with *apprehending* him, not just slaughtering anyone who stood in their way?

Daragon had promised him safety—even as they opened fire. So much for any lingering hopes of trusting his former friend. All bets were off.

Eduard slunk away into the night. Now, he didn't even have his ID patch anymore, but he could use the old man's COM access to get more money, until Daragon picked up the trail again. It wouldn't take him long.

The next day Eduard traded down again into another body and escaped. One more time.

50

After seeing Juanita Cole's debut exhibition, Garth felt another extremely talented artist breathing down his neck. It reminded him that he wouldn't be on top forever, jolted him with a sudden drive. He didn't want to lose a valuable moment. "Pashnak! It's time to reclaim some lost glory. Enough sitting around."

The assistant loved to see the renewed enthusiasm after Garth's recent malaise. The artist had rushed through Loss, put it into the exhibition hall that had contracted for his next work, then plunged into a new project. Garth bustled out of the studio, his hands scrubbed and wet.

"Set up a meeting with Stradley—he needs to start earning his commissions again." Though still a commercial success, Loss had drawn smaller crowds than the previous three works, and it had turned the artist's attention to composing a biting commentary on another side of human nature, APATHY. "He's been resting on our laurels for too damned long."

Pashnak contacted the hype-meister's offices, requesting a conference. When his image sprang into focus, Stradley spoke without even taking a breath. "Is Garth finished with it yet? Please tell me that's what you're calling about. We've got people already waiting."

"He's working like a maniac, Mr. Stradley. He asked me to set up an appointment with you. He wants to discuss some of the promotional efforts."

Stradley frowned. "I hate it when creative types worry about business matters." He glanced off to the side of the screen, already distracted by another emergency, another opportunity. "All right, send him around this afternoon. Three o'clock."

"He'll appreciate this, Mr. Stradley."

"Well, I'd appreciate it more if he spent his time working on his exhibition instead of talking with me. I'm the one who's supposed to be doing the talking."

Ideas bubbled in Garth's head as he waited in the lobby while the hype-meister finished last-minute arrangements for another client. The receptionist gave him a fizzy orange drink without being asked.

Stradley finally gestured for him to enter. Garth plopped into the self-form chair in front of the desk. Message lights blinked; handwritten notes lay draped on image cubes or tacked to the wall next to gaudy tropical images. Three COM filmscreens blazed at the same time, chewing through different subject-searches.

Garth rubbed his hands together. "After Loss, I think we need to figure out a different strategy to make more waves when the new work comes out—"

"Garth, I should warn you I've got a busy afternoon." Stradley looked pointedly at the chaos of ongoing plans scattered about his office. "You should remember too that Mr. Ob is no longer footing the bill for my services, nor is he able to apply BTL pressure on me."

"Excuse me?" He stiffened. "I know Mr. Ob's patronage might have helped me get attention at first, but my exhibitions have been successful enough to line a lot of pockets. After all the commissions I've given you, I'd think you could spare a few minutes to talk about my career, my comeback."

"Comeback? I didn't know you ever left the limelight. Sure, the Loss numbers dipped a bit, but so what? You're on solid enough ground."

"But I want to keep building, not take a step backward. We're going to have to continue pushing the envelope."

The hype-meister sighed, as if perfectly familiar with the way this conversation was going to go. "Look, Garth, you're not the only client I have, and you're not the only client who makes me money. Right now, I just landed a hot follow-up contract for Juanita Cole that's going to require most of my resources. I don't have a whole lot of extra energy at this time."

Garth reeled as if a bomb had just dropped on him. Folding his hands across his desk, shoving notes aside, Stradley explained in an oh-so-sincere voice, "I know what you're thinking, what you're feeling. I've seen a lot of careers."

"Including mine."

"Including yours. Every client is a challenge, every prospect a conquest to be made. But once the conquest is over, I've got to move on to take the next hill, develop a new property, make a new star."

Garth frowned at him. "So, since my works are already sought after, you're no longer interested in hyping me?"

Stradley forcibly kept his hands folded in front of him so he wouldn't fidget or sort through unwanted messages. "It's already done, the battle won. I don't want to sit around and milk past accomplishments. What's the challenge? That isn't what I do."

The receptionist popped her head through the doorway, signaling Stradley, but he waved her off. Garth wondered if the interruption had been staged. *Give me ten minutes, then tell me I've got an important call....*

"What more do you want, Garth? You're already on top of the world."

"But I'm not *done.*" He thumped the heel of his palm on the free-form chair to keep it from making him too comfortable. "We've already got the public's attention, and we have to punch them in the gut harder than ever before!"

"And how are you going to make yourself interesting? Forgive the joke, my friend, but do you really expect the consumer base to be interested in a work called APATHY?" Stradley looked at him as if he were incredibly dense. "You're *famous,* Garth—get that through your head! Your work will never be ignored. Critics and viewers will come without being dragged. Publicity runs on autopilot for you. Juanita Cole is the one who needs my help right now. She's the skyrocket."

Garth clenched his teeth, tasting sour orange from the fizzy drink he had finished while waiting. "So you just put my career on a shelf while you chase after another star."

Stradley shook his head, and for the first time Garth saw real emotion behind the publicist's eyes. "Why do you think you need my services at all anymore, Garth? I'm helping someone else get to the level you're already at. I was there for you when you needed it, and now Juanita needs it a lot more than you do. She's my challenge and my passion—and in a few years, no doubt, I'll be having this same discussion with her, too." He sighed and mumbled to himself, "Artists! They never learn."

Feeling lost and disappointed, Garth stood, ready to leave. Stradley pawed through his gathered messages. "Look, Garth—Juanita's coming for a meeting in just a few minutes. I'd like you to meet her. You've seen her show, right? It would be a good idea for you two to talk. She's experienced your work, too, and was very impressed by it."

Confusion buzzed around Garth. He backed toward the door. "No . . . no, sorry. Not interested."

Stradley crossed his arms. "What are you afraid of?"

"Afraid? No, that's not it. I've got to get back to work."

Stradley flicked his head back and forth as he scanned all three of his COM screens. "We're pushing the deadline on your new show, and it's got to be finished on time. Even if it is APATHY. Don't lose the brownie points you've earned from the past exhibitions."

Garth departed from the hype-meister's offices. Juanita Cole was due to arrive at any moment, and he left in a hurry so he wouldn't risk meeting her.

51

Being so close to capture, for so long, made Eduard feel even more alive. Every moment passed with heightened awareness, deeper suspicion, faster reflexes... and frazzled nerves. He had to pay attention to *everything*.

But the stranger who reached out for him from the dim alley was a real master at stealth. The man touched his arm, and Eduard leaped aside, ready to whirl and fight, if necessary.

"Whoa, I'm not one of *them!*" the man snapped in a whisper. "Don't make a scene. Someone will notice."

Eduard had learned the danger of drawing attention to himself. He froze. "What do you want?"

"Been watching you, rabbit. Come on, I want to save you—and protect myself." The man had an average body, plain clothes, unremarkable features, and very, very bright eyes. "You're good, but not good enough."

Grasping Eduard's elbow, the stranger led him toward the alley's private dimness. "You've got the potential to be one of *us*. Potential. But they're huntin' hard, and you could make it come crashing down. Can't let that happen. Gotta teach you what you've gotten yourself into, otherwise you muck it up."

Eduard had acquired the narrow-eyed, skeptical gaze of a combat-weary jungle soldier, attuned to peripheral vision, senses heightened for anything out of the ordinary. He followed, but kept his distance. "You have no idea who I am. If you knew, you'd call the Beetles without a second thought."

"Well, that's my other option, if you prove to be too dumb to be trained." The stranger waited as a cluster of laughing athletes walked past on the nearby street, jostling each other. "You're Eduard, right? One of them Swans from the Splinter monastery?" He flashed his bright, bright eyes. "Must be crazy even to talk to a rabbit as hot as you. This manhunt has made my life a living hell, but I may as well show you what you're doing wrong. Live longer, both of us."

Eduard found it hard to restrain himself. "I haven't done too badly alone."

"One mistake can screw up everything. Just like your little mistake with Chief Ob. Or was that something you did on purpose?"

Eduard stared at him in disbelief. The man found this greatly amusing, and he laughed without making a sound. "I don't have any particular love for the BTL— especially not Mordecai Ob, so in a way you've done me quite a favor." He glanced around, found a relatively clean spot in a recessed doorway, and squatted against the wall. "Do you know what I am?"

Eduard refused to lower his guard. "A crazy old man?"

Angry, the stranger jabbed a finger at Eduard. "I'm a *Phantom*. The only one you're ever likely to see."

Eduard caught his breath. "A real Phantom? How old are you?"

"Spent the last two centuries outrunnin' death. By my reckoning, I'm two hundred and thirty-seven years old. Does that count as a real Phantom?" The man spread his hands wide. "I call myself Artemis, though it's probably high time to change that name again. Guess it'll do for the moment."

"And what do you know of Bureau Chief Ob?"

"I know that *Inspector* Ob almost caught me twenty years back. Closest I've ever come to having my balls clipped. I stole the body of some starving young artist, didn't know who she was, but Ob took it as a personal insult, came after me like an express train. Took me months to muddy the trail enough to shake him. For decades I've been hiding while Ob climbed the Bureau ladder." He grinned. "But which one of us is still standing, eh?"

"Twenty years ago? And you think the Beetles are still after you?" Eduard couldn't believe it. "Does the word *paranoia* mean anything to you?"

Artemis glowered at him. "I know how to spot 'em, even with all their tricks. Here, let me show you one little thing that'll make you a believer. A true believer." He scuttled off down the alley without looking over his shoulder, confident that Eduard would follow. He did.

Artemis ducked into a small street, where they went through the side entrance of a clothing shop. From there, the man took a lifter to the third level and across to an open food court.

"Go to those benches near the window and look outside onto the streets. Don't worry—the glass is mirrorized. I already checked. The only thing they can see is a reflection."

"Who? Who can see?"

"Just look, rabbit!"

Feeling a sudden chill, Eduard peered through the broad window. Hovercars passed in interleaved lanes, people walked below, businesses went about their daily activities. Cloud shadows dappled the buildings. He saw nothing out of the ordinary.

"Pretty good, isn't it?" Artemis leaned close to his ear. His breath smelled of onions. "Look at that man on the corner, handin' out sandwich tokens." He tapped the glass. "Does he really fit? And that woman holdin' blue balloons? Gotta know the crowd, see the patterns, understand how it all works, so you can pick out sharks ripplin' through the currents."

Artemis continued to point out unsettling details—a furtive man here, a too-casual person there. Eduard saw nothing compelling about any individual example, and he began to suspect the Phantom's overactive imagination.

Until he spotted *Daragon.*

He was wearing a sport jacket, muted plaid shirt, casual pants—but his facial features, his dark hair and almond eyes, remained the same. Daragon had disguised himself as a solitary businessman on lunch break, trying to be unobtrusive. Eduard gasped and drew back from the window.

Artemis patted his shoulder paternally. "Now do you see it? I saved you from a setup, a stakeout. You owe me, rabbit."

Eduard walked unsteadily back into the food court. He wanted to get away, but he didn't dare go out into the streets. He had swapped bodies since the last time the Beetles had almost caught him, and he had lost his own identity on his ID patch—but Daragon had his uncanny ability to see someone's real persona. The Inspector needed only to get a glimpse of him. . . .

"Whoa, careful, careful," the Phantom whispered, catching up to him in the food court. The smells of hot oil and condiments cluttered the air. "Don't call attention to yourself."

Eduard skewered him with a stare. "How did you know?"

"Survival." Artemis laughed. "You don't stay on the run for so many decades without being able to spot somethin' like that."

They glided through the ever-shifting crowd, making no waves. A woman in a gray suit set down two wrapped sandwiches on an empty table, then headed toward a napkin dispenser. Without hesitation, Artemis casually snatched the sandwiches and walked with Eduard toward the lift tube.

"Come on, I know a safe place." He held up the sandwiches. "Let's have lunch, and we can talk some more."

One of the places where Artemis liked to stay was a forgotten back room in a former hotel. During the chaos of remodeling operations years ago (which Artemis claimed to remember), he had slipped in at night to wallseal a door here, disguise an opening there, and create a private chamber for himself.

The room was dim and stuffy with an unpleasant chemical odor, but Artemis assured him it was safe. A tiny, low-energy glowplate burned in the corner, not enough to make the room bright. The scattered darkness made the place seem hushed and secretive.

The Phantom flopped down on a narrow cot with well-worn fabric and a frayed blanket. He unwrapped the two sandwiches, peered under the bread, and chose the one he liked best. He handed the other to Eduard.

Eduard gobbled the food. He found it difficult to let down his guard, but he enjoyed the stolen lunch more than any food in recent memory. While he ate, he studied the other man huddled over his sandwich. Even here, Artemis still flicked his eyes from side to side.

"I used to idolize immortals like you," Eduard said around a mouthful of mortadella and provolone sandwich. He picked out a pepperoncini. "I'd study the crowds, always wondering if I'd ever see a real Phantom."

"You'd never know it, even if you did." Artemis brushed a hand across his lips. "There's no way to tell."

"I fantasized about what it would be like to outrun death."

Artemis grinned, his mouth full of food. "It's exciting."

Eduard glanced around the dim room, recalling how the Phantom had sneaked to this claustrophobic hiding place, how he had stolen an inexpensive sandwich. "I always thought a Phantom would accumulate a lot of wealth over so much time. I expected you to be living with a bit more . . . extravagance."

Artemis finished his lunch and wadded the paper, tossing it into the corner where other old wrappers made a disarrayed pile. "Wealth means too much attention. To be a Phantom, you gotta learn to be invisible and to value other things—such as personal safety and anonymity." He stretched out on the cot with an exaggerated yawn. "Sorry I don't have another cot, but you can curl up there on the floor. Get yourself a good night's sleep, a safe one. No worries."

Eduard found a clean spot against the wall. He had slept in worse places. On the run, he'd grown accustomed to napping anywhere he could hide for a few hours. Artemis hit a switch, and the glowplate's weak illumination faded.

"Stick with me, rabbit, and you'll learn everythin' you need to know."

Eduard settled back to sleep, but for a long time he was unable to feel safe, despite the other man's reassurances. Artemis snored, content with his place, but Eduard's disappointment deepened.

The Phantom might know how to *survive*, but he had forgotten how to *live*.

52

In the ranks of the Bureau, political scramblers fought to divide the pieces of Mordecai Ob's empire. In the past several years, after his meteoric rise up the chain of command, Daragon could have been one of the contenders himself, the Chief's heir apparent, his golden boy. But he would not give up the search for Eduard or delegate it to anyone else.

Back inside Headquarters, he sat in the Chief's office, which had remained unclaimed in the turmoil surrounding Ob's death. The newly appointed Acting Bureau Chief preferred his own offices on the mainland, and no one contested Daragon's right to be there. As he worked at the expansive desk in silence, looking at the cold fireplace, the place struck him as very uncomfortable. Too quiet, too empty... too haunted. It was difficult to concentrate.

But this workspace was just a spot for him to pile papers and collate the hints and threads that might eventually lead him to Eduard.

Daragon spent his days pounding the streets, continuing the relentless search. He joined tracking teams at random, then he went out for hours alone, walking the nights, studying the ocean of people and looking *inside* for one familiar identity, one recognizable persona....

Daragon ran his hands through his dark hair, staring at the discolored fiberceramic logs in the fireplace.

Weariness descended upon him like a lead blanket. This manhunt had gone on for so long already.

Against his better judgment, he had poked into the wild stories Garth and Teresa had told about Ob's alleged addiction to Rush-X. True, the Bureau Chief's previous trainers had been dismissed under curious circumstances, and through some sort of COM glitch could no longer be found. True, Ob *could* have used his authority to divert confiscated shipments of the illegal drug for his own use.

If Daragon hadn't known his mentor so well, he might have considered these possibilities, but he had no intention of tarnishing the memory of his martyred Chief. No one else in the Bureau was interested, either. It was an open-and-shut case, and Eduard had already been convicted in absentia. The sentence was set. If they ever caught him, the Bureau of Incarceration and Executions would terminate him.

Daragon brooded in front of the artificial fireplace, oblivious to the flickering shadows of fish overhead. He had once loved Eduard and now felt betrayed, more disappointed than he'd ever been. His friend had ruined everything, had even turned Garth and Teresa against him. Daragon was trapped, and only the Bureau could give him the strength and support he needed.

The private message signal on his COM screen startled him, and Daragon turned back toward Ob's desk, feeling a sudden wariness and perplexity. Very few people knew his direct code here.

He was utterly shocked to watch Eduard's familiar face appear in front of him. He grasped the edge of the desk until his knuckles turned white.

"Oh, Daragon, I need to see you," Teresa said. "It's very important."

With no place else to turn, all of her other search options careening to dead ends, Teresa had finally decided to contact the Bureau of Tracing and Locations. With his much-vaunted BTL resources, Daragon could help her in a way no one else could.

"Teresa...I didn't think you would ever speak to me again." His formal composure seemed ready to crack.

"Can I meet with you in person, and in private?" She swallowed hard, trying to remain businesslike, but she found it difficult not to let her emotions seep through.

His face filled with boyish delight, and he jumped at the chance. "Stay right where you are—I'll have escorts there in a few minutes." He reached forward to terminate the transmission, then paused. "It'll be good to see you, Teresa. You look...a lot better."

After months, her body had grown gradually stronger. The awful Rush-X taste in her mouth had begun to fade...or maybe she'd just gotten used to it. During the first weeks, she had wondered if she would die from withdrawal. She woke up shivering, nauseated, dizzy. The body knew what it needed, but Teresa could not, *would not* get it. Each second stretched out, taut as a piano wire.

With surprising speed an official BTL hovercar dropped from the skylanes to land on the sidewalk. Pedestrians scattered out of the way as the door hissed open on pneumatic lifts, and a dark-clad officer gestured her inside. Shoppers and businessmen stared as she ducked her head and climbed into the back of the vehicle. From the pilot's compartment, the BTL officer looked back at her with suspicion, remembering Eduard's face from scores of emergency bulletins.

The dark vehicle shot through commuter traffic patterns in an override lane. She should have been nervous, should have been terrified, but she had already reached the point of desperation. She had to trust Daragon now.

COM authorized a crow's-flight path out of the city and low across the green-blue waves to the superstructure of Bureau Headquarters. The hovercar dropped precisely onto a painted target circle, and Daragon strode forward to meet her as she climbed out. Rigid and waiting, he remained silent for a long moment, as if the breezes had snatched his words away, then his lips formed a sad smile. He took her in a stiff embrace, which she returned. "Come on, we'll talk inside. I've got an office, of sorts."

Daragon led her down yellow-lit halls and past aquarium windows. Bureau workers marched through database rooms while evidence technicians hunched over lab analysis equipment. Two junior Inspectors sat at a bare table in an empty room, comparing notes.

Inside Ob's plush office, Teresa primly took one of the fine leather chairs, across from the broad desk where Daragon stationed himself. Looking at her, he shuddered with déjà vu, recalling when he'd first brought Eduard here to audition as the Bureau Chief's personal caretaker. That had been the biggest mistake of his life. Daragon wished he had just let Eduard scrape by with his miserable body-selling practice. But he'd tried to do Eduard a favor, as a friend.

In the uneasy silence, he saw *inside* to the woman he had cared for so deeply. "Teresa, if you've come here to request clemency for Eduard, I can't do it. You know I have to track him down, even if it means ... sacrificing our friendship."

"Do you really think Eduard's a threat to anybody, even on the run?" Teresa shook her head. "No, I don't want to talk about that. I need to request your help in something else. I want to enlist the Bureau to find someone—to find *me*. I need to track down my home-body. It's...lost."

Daragon was taken aback. "Right now our resources are mobilized on a manhunt. I'm not sure I can justify the time for a project like that."

She wouldn't let him off so easily. "You always told me the Bureau did good and important work, more than just tracking down criminals. You were so proud of how the BTL helped to locate family members and find missing people." She leaned forward in the chair. "Now I need you to help find *me*—the original me." She looked intently at him, using every coin she had. "The one who held you and talked with you in the night."

"Teresa...I can't—" He still refused to meet her eyes.

"Is it because I look like Eduard now?" She waited a beat. "This is important to me, Daragon."

He looked at her, wishing he could see the real Teresa again, the woman he had touched and loved in a wistful younger way. This might partially heal the breach between them, though he realized nothing would make her forgive him. She had always been more devoted to Eduard. "All right. Give me whatever information you have, any leads I can use. I'll keep my eyes open."

It might be as easy as running a simple COM trace, but he doubted he'd get an answer with so little effort. It could take a long time. Teresa would continue her quest, wandering the city, talking to people, retracing her footsteps.

In the meantime, Daragon had his own quarry to catch.

53

Having thrown in his lot with a Phantom, Eduard accompanied Artemis to the carefully hidden and well-provisioned bolt-holes he'd established throughout the metropolis. A Phantom always kept a wide range of hiding places.

"You'll need plenty of alternatives if you want to live forever, rabbit. Gotta be willin' to drop everything and run. Nothing matters as much as staying alive. No possessions, no home, no friends. Stay mobile and quiet."

They climbed a metal staircase outside a rib-walled automated distribution facility. The buildings were occupied primarily by COM robotic systems that did the tedious, repetitive work of inventory and shipping.

"One of my favorite hideouts." Artemis punched numbers on a recessed keypad. "In a week or two, I'll give you the code number. If I think you're worth keepin' around." He flashed a humorless grin. "If not, I'll just let 'em catch you."

Eduard followed, not surprised that the man still didn't trust him. Artemis had intercepted Eduard in some weird gratitude for killing Ob, supposedly to keep him from exposing other Phantoms. But at times, he realized that Artemis must have been lonely, too.

Closing the door behind them, Artemis used another code on an internal readerpad, paused until he heard a high-pitched buzz, then strode inside. "Safe now. I've added my own infiltrator to the security systems."

Inside the cavernous building, conveyors and articulated arms stacked and sorted crates of materials, components, and consumer items. Machine-readable inventory codes marked the boxes with gibberish. Subdued lights dangled above like garish fireflies, and the ventilation system was set cold to protect the electronics and the mechanical devices. This place wasn't made to be inhabited—which was exactly why Artemis enjoyed living here.

They crossed a catwalk to a false wall where the Phantom had constructed an apartment for himself. He showed Eduard how to release the bottom latch so they could pull themselves up into the hiding place. Artemis had cobbled together furnishings, a stove, and food-prep equipment; entertainment disks lay piled around, mostly out-of-date classics.

Eduard was reminded of the small attic room in the Falling Leaves where he and Daragon had hidden when they were kids. *Daragon.*

The Phantom always remained on the alert for anyone watching him, hunting him. "What are you so afraid of all the time?" Eduard asked. "I'm the one who's on the run."

Artemis flashed him a toothy grin. "Rabbit, you don't live two centuries on the fringe without bein' forced to break the law plenty often. It's safe to say I've done enough to get me uploaded to COM. More than you, I'll bet."

Artemis seemed glad to have a confidant to whom he could tell tall tales. He told Eduard how he'd once impersonated a BTL Inspector during a stakeout for him, how he had avoided pursuit at a crowded fair by forcing a swap with a scheduled speaker and giving an impromptu lecture about politics in a changing world of hopscotches. He bragged about how he had left several wives and husbands, how he had fathered at least three children, all unknown to him now.

Eduard lounged on the threadbare sofa while the Phantom heated soup. He closed his eyes and drew a long breath, relieved to find a bit of peace. As he listened to Artemis recount decades' worth of adventures, he didn't know how much to believe. The other man had lived a long enough life to have experienced such perils—and he also had plenty of solitude in which to concoct preposterous stories.

Using their warehouse as a base of operations, they changed clothes frequently, wearing different guises every time they went out onto the streets. Artemis taught him to become invisible, and Eduard learned how to walk between people, avoid glances, and become inconsequential in the eyes of the masses. Like a lesson from a text—*How to Be a Phantom.*

They frequented crowded shops and storefronts, mingling with groups of no fewer than three. Artemis pointed out a few undercover Beetles dressed as common workers. Though Eduard didn't know for sure, he feared they were searching for him; similarly, Artemis believed *he* was their target.

"So we'll both have to be careful," Eduard said.

"Whoa, not to worry. We're smarter than they are. The Beetles have a few tricks, but they're always the same ones. Once you know the routine, you can spot 'em, easy."

Today they planned to spend unmarked credits stolen from a battered vending machine. Artemis reached over to touch Eduard's scrawny arm. "You've been in this body for ages, rabbit, and it's not worth much. I suggest you pick somebody new. Not good to keep the same appearance for too long."

Eduard tried to remember all the shapes he'd worn during his long run, then he thought of Teresa, who had been stuck with his strung-out, drug-addicted homebody. "Right. But I don't have any money. No resources. Nothing I can offer someone to swap with me."

Artemis gave him a scornful look. "Don't worry about it. That sort of thing is never a problem for a Phantom."

Sitting at a central table, nestled among other diners in a crowded cafeteria, Artemis told Eduard about his many loves, the women and the men, depending on what gender he'd worn at the time, not that it mattered all that much. "Sure, I grew close to some of them, for a time, but in the end I always moved on."

"So you dumped them. People you loved?"

Artemis shrugged. "It got old and boring. Nothin' ever lasts. Anyway, their lives are too short—normal lives, I mean."

Eduard covered his disturbed expression by wiping his mouth with a napkin. "If you're immortal, what does a normal human life span matter? Why *not* just stay with someone who loves you? There's always time."

"Time for them, or time for me? I've got other things to do." He didn't say what, though.

Eduard finished his meal in silence. This Phantom had stepped on other human beings right and left, just like Ob had. As he watched Artemis in his daily life, he wondered how much the man had *accomplished* in all those years. Without achievements, wasn't life empty—regardless of how long it was? "Did you ever stop to think that the people you've used might have been trying to do something worthwhile with their lives?"

Artemis just laughed with his silent clucking. "Whoa, don't be an idiot. Normal people are there to be used. What else d'you think they're for?"

Back at the warehouse bolt-hole, the two of them sat far into the night. Troubled, Eduard didn't speak much, but Artemis noticed no difference in his mood. He had uncorked an old bottle of brandy that had achieved an exquisite mellow taste by virtue of sitting around for decades.

"Everything gets better if you wait long enough." Artemis swigged from his glass. "Let's have some music." He selected a clamorous neosymphony, but before he could switch on the sonic enhancers, he froze, cocking his ear. "What's that?"

On the threadbare sofa, Eduard listened. He heard more than the methodical noises from machines going about their business. It sounded like someone moving around in the warehouse levels.

Artemis went to the false wall and slid aside the peephole cover. He placed an infrared filter over the glass and stared down into the dim warehouse. Suddenly overhead lights flicked on, dazzling him. Artemis drew back frantically, blinking. "I think we're caught."

Eduard pulled away the peephole filter, squinting to accustom his eyes to the garish light. "No—just listen. The Beetles would have brought a whole team. That's just one person, and he's not even trying to be quiet."

He and Artemis peered into the automated sections until they saw an inspec-tech moving from engine housing to inventory station down one of the robotic lines. He had an average build, brown hair, a neatly trimmed mustache. The inspec-tech punched notes into an electronic pad, adjusting the machinery.

"Whoa, never seen another human in here before." Artemis's words were barely more than breaths touching Eduard's ear.

"I suppose someone has to do maintenance from time to time."

Artemis grabbed his arm and grinned, flashing his teeth. "Can't pass up an opportunity like this, rabbit!"

Like an eel, he glided out of the trapdoor, blended into the shadows, and padded barefoot along a catwalk. From his pocket, Artemis withdrew a small spray nozzle connected to a tiny vial. Signaling Eduard, he held it up and waggled his eyebrows.

Artemis slithered down a thin-runged ladder, hugging the walls. The inspec-tech showed no concern that someone else might be in the place. He hummed to himself, fine-tuning magnetic conveyor belts, logging maintenance routines.

Eduard reached the metal ladder but hesitated, watching as the Phantom stalked the unsuspecting technician, a wolf in human form. Artemis crept along the hard floor on the row of machinery opposite the inspec-tech. He waited there in a crouch.

As the technician walked past a gap in the machinery, Artemis sprang out with a banshee yell. The hapless technician stumbled back, and Artemis dosed him in the face with his spray nozzle. When the drug mist struck, the technician reeled, turning in a slow pirouette until he finally sank to his knees. He shook his head groggily as if someone had whacked his skull with a thick board. Droplets glistened on his mustache.

Artemis gestured frantically. "Come on down now, rabbit. It's safe, but we gotta hurry. Need your help." He set the spray-mister aside and took out a stun-pellet pistol.

Eduard stumbled down the ladder and trotted to where Artemis knelt by the disoriented man. "What did you do to him?"

"Ever seen Scramble work? It's the drug the BIE gives to convicts who have to swap into a crappy body before they're executed. Breaks down all your defenses, scrambles your thought patterns, makes it impossible to resist if someone wants to hopscotch with you."

Artemis squatted over his victim like a vulture. "Soon as I swap with him, you stun my old body." He slapped the pistol into Eduard's palm. "Once he and I switch, *I'm* gonna be the disoriented one. You'll have to act fast. After I hopscotch into this drugged-up body, I'll be just as vulnerable." He touched the inspec-tech's face. "Ready?"

Eduard could almost see the transference of mind and personality. Artemis stood reeling and perplexed, unable to function in his new drugged body, the technician's body. Conversely, his familiar, average body sank down. Just as the inspec-tech grew aware of being inside a stranger, Eduard shot him with two short *hiss-thumps* of stun pellets. The tech crumpled to the floor. . . .

Later, after Artemis had recovered, he wiped a sleeve across his new mustache. "That drug really smells bad." He looked over at Eduard, preening. He touched his upper lip. "I've been behind that other face for four years now. Thought it was time for a change."

Uneasy, Eduard gave a faint shake of his head. He had done horrible things himself—beating up Rhys, killing Mordecai Ob—but those men had deserved it. This tech, though . . . he could see only totally selfish reasons for it.

Artemis synched his ID patch to switch over his identity code and erase any obvious trace of himself in his former body. "Puts an end to our nice hideout here, though. Good bolt-hole, but we gotta clean it up, erase all evidence."

He dug in the pockets worn by his former body. The stunned technician didn't resist, arms and legs flopping. Artemis withdrew another chemical vial and slapped it into the spray nozzle. "Quick poison. It'll leave no traces." He pointed the dispenser at the unconscious man's eyes.

"Wait! There's no need to kill him."

"Whoa, of course there is. I got his body. Once he comes back to himself, he'll report it. Then BTL comes looking. Can't have that."

Eduard thought of how he had unwittingly caused the death of the old man feeding bats in the park. "No. This isn't necessary. We're leaving anyway. Nobody'll find us. Change your appearance, leave the ID patches unsynched."

"You're an idiot, rabbit. There's nothin' complicated about immortality. You just have to take it."

Eduard glared hard at Artemis. "Since I need a new body anyway, let me take that one. Use that Scramble again, and he'll be left with this scrawny physique of mine. There's absolutely no connection to you. No problem. Nothing you need to worry about."

Artemis stood up, miffed. "I can always find something to worry about. You think he has no proof of what he used to look like?"

"Sure, if anybody can find you again and match the appearance. Do they still put pictures in post offices? Are you being ridiculous?"

Artemis looked embarrassed. "Do what you want. And damn you to hell if they catch us because of it."

When Eduard woke from the residual effects of the stun pellet inside Artemis's former body, he looked over to see the inspec-tech on the warehouse floor, now unconscious and inside the body Eduard had worn until recently. Not the most efficient way to do a three-way swap, he thought, shaking off the fading paralysis.

He hated to leave the poor tech in this weakling form, but the man was alive, and that was better than what Artemis had wanted. Eduard joined Artemis, looking around. "So what do we do? How do we clean up?"

The Phantom ran back to his secret bolt-hole and rifled through the cupboards, grabbing a few irreplaceable items and stuffing them into a pack. "Take anythin' you can carry." He tossed a few entertainment loops at Eduard, reconsidered, grabbed one back, and threw it on the floor. "Tired of that one."

When they had stuffed their packs, Artemis withdrew two gleaming silver balls from a small drawer. He depressed a red button on the top of each and tossed them to the ground. The balls sprouted whirling, grinding spines, like manic sea urchins. The little mobile jaws began to roll about the tiny room, chewing everything into mulch.

"They'll keep working for five hours. By that time there'll be nothin' left but ribbons." Artemis dropped through the trapdoor. "You'll want to get out of their way, rabbit."

The two shredders crawled across the hidden room, picking up speed as they bounced against walls, ricocheting, taking new paths of destruction to chew away the surface and destroy the stolen furniture, obliterating every bit of evidence.

"Why not just use fire?" Eduard asked. "Seems a lot easier."

"Because the automatic sensors would go off immediately, stupid. The authorities would be here in minutes. Don't you know anything?"

Fleeing the automated warehouse, the two men slipped into the night and walked at a brisk pace away from the warehouse district. Artemis seemed particularly happy, even while destroying one of his favorite homes. "Just remember, rabbit, everything's disposable."

Eduard easily kept pace with the Phantom. His new body felt stronger, more energetic. But the very idea of what they had done made him sick at heart.

54

The studio had always felt like a womb, a warm and inviting place filled with inspiration and possibilities. Now Garth struggled with his materials, but nothing seemed right. Nothing seemed *alive*.

He stood in the middle of his half-completed project. APATHY. Though Garth felt he had a better technical mastery and sophistication than he'd ever shown before, after the lukewarm success of LOSS the critics were saying he had fallen into a rut. He could not figure out what else to add to APATHY, how to make it more exciting. He just didn't care—which, he supposed, was the point.

Juanita Cole's shooting-star success had surprised and disoriented him—not because of her amazing work, but because of what it showed him about himself. At first, she had seemed a threat to him and his position, but Garth eventually realized he was really angry at his own career misconceptions. The success and the accolades had become addictive, and he could see why Mordecai Ob had wanted so much to be a part of it. Now, he didn't want to see it trickle through his fingertips.

He stood in front of a glowing filmscreen, scrutinizing flat images of Juanita's new works, which Pashnak had surreptitiously clipped for him. PR holos showed a tattooed young woman in her studio, smiling as she immersed her hands in vibrant aerogel foams. He watched sound clips, heard her talk about the ideas bursting out of her, as if the world might not offer her enough time to accomplish everything she wanted to do.

Garth remembered exactly how that had felt, but he didn't know how to recapture that enthusiasm. He blanked the studio COM screen, turning back to his work in progress.

At Club Masquerade, Garth often wandered through the outer experience rooms, the imaginative decor of the Arabian Nights room, the Mars colony room, the safari room, the *Titanic* room. Standing under the towering faux sequoia trees, Garth recalled the first time he had entered Club Masquerade with Eduard and Teresa. The three of them had come through this very room, lost and amazed. They had been so young then. . . .

Standing in front of the swapportunities board, Garth realized it had been a long time since he had found a single item that managed to catch his attention. He would scan the flurry of hopscotch requests and let out a long, slow sigh. Even the most bizarre appeals had a monstrous sameness about them.

At one time, each fresh idea had been filled with possibilities and wonder. Garth had mined those overlapping lifetimes for his artwork. It had been a great ride. He'd been an explorer of the human landscape, pushing onward into new territory—and finally he had no place else to go.

His whole life had been built on having something to say, a point of view to express through artwork. But how could anyone be profound and moving every time, piece after piece after piece?

What does an artist do after he has already *completed* his masterpiece?

The cream swirled in his cup, mixing slowly. Garth usually drank his coffee black, but Pashnak insisted he needed to mellow out. At this point, he was ready to try just about anything.

The two of them sat in a cozy kitchen nook where sunlight streamed through the lattice windows. After his increasingly successful shows, Garth had recently bought an extravagant home, complete with security systems and privacy screens, and he still had more credits than he could spend.

Generous by nature, he gave Teresa more than enough money to get by so she could devote herself full time to her search. He even gave her the first drawing of her face from the portrait spectrum, the original features she had worn for most of her life. If he ever heard from Eduard again, he would offer his friend whatever he needed without the slightest hesitation.

Now Pashnak poured another cup of coffee. He powered on his schedule and called up the notes for the day, scanning appointments and upcoming events. "Don't forget, I set up a hopscotch opportunity for you this Thursday."

Garth looked up with only feigned interest. "What is it?"

Day after day, the assistant sat with him, pointing to item after item on the ever-diminishing List. At last the few minor things left had seemed frivolous: blue eyes, brown eyes... black skin, freckled skin. In some bodies he had enjoyed the taste of broccoli, in others he found it offensive.

Did he really expect to *learn* anything new from that? Wasn't everybody the same, as long as the definition of "humanity" was broad enough? People were *people,* no matter how profound their external differences.

"It's a tough one," Pashnak said with a smile of

anticipation. "You'll be swapping with a young man who has little muscle control and suffers from seizures. He's weak, he can't walk, and his condition is degenerating." He slid the schedule across the table so Garth could see the image of the sickly young man. "It'll give you a chance to feel out of control, at the mercy of external forces."

Garth shook his head. "Cancel the contract. Helpless and out of control—the idea sounds too much like the way I already feel."

The assistant was surprised. "But Garth, it'll be one more item to check off on your List. There aren't many left. Look—"

Garth took the datapad from him, scanned the few topics left on his List, and then deleted them, all at once. "There, I'm done."

The assistant stared in horror at the blank, milky-white screen.

"No more List. All finished."

But Garth experienced no sense of accomplishment or rush of victory. He just felt empty.

55

The streets were full of people, and Teresa knew that her original body could be anywhere out there—or nowhere at all.

She had scoured the huge COM databases for a body with her fingerprints, DNA, even scan-matches of her facial features. Nothing. Refusing to give up, Teresa had posted the image of her younger face Garth had drawn. "Have you seen this body?" So far, though, none of the responses had been even close.

Not even Daragon, with all the resources of the Bureau of Tracing and Locations, had managed to find any useful information, only a few false leads.

Now, she sat throwing pebbles into the bubbling geometric fountain where she and Arthur used to talk. She had no flowers left, no petals to float on the gentle waves. Teresa felt weary in her mind and in her bones, but at least Eduard's body had survived the Rush-X withdrawal. Physically, she grew stronger every day, no longer afraid of falling apart with each uncertain step.

But this still wasn't the place where Teresa belonged. She missed her home-body. It had been a long time since she'd been a woman. Had she lost that part of her identity, too? She seemed farther from her goal than ever before.

Wistfully, she thought about the monastery. As a curious teenager, even before she or her friends had learned how to hopscotch, Teresa had studied the changes puberty brought upon her flesh, her chemistry, her attitudes. She had explored her body and how it worked, making love to Eduard and Garth, and even Daragon, sharing warmth and caring. Her friendships were her world.

Teresa had felt whole then.

She trailed her fingers in the fountain. She pictured old Arthur's worn-leather face, thought of the things she had learned from him. *You always told me I should welcome challenges.*

Teresa brushed stray droplets from her hands and marched over to a public COM terminal. She would try again, and again if necessary. But if Daragon and the BTL couldn't find anything, how could she hope to be successful? She had already searched in every way she could imagine.

Nevertheless, she refused to stop looking.

As she stood in a sheltered alcove where a smoked-plastic panel shaded the COM filmscreen from sun glare, an image formed there. She hadn't even entered a command. But it was a face... a familiar face.

Soft Stone!

A superstitious thrill ran like a centipede down Teresa's spine. She recalled the dull day at her dead-end job when she had seen her teacher's image among the datanets. But the bald monk had vanished that time, leaving Teresa to convince herself it was only her imagination or wishful thinking. But not now.

Soft Stone appeared with crystal clarity, projected three-dimensionally on the filmscreen. "Hello, little Swan." Her voice was so familiar, so rich.

Tears sprang to Teresa's eyes. "What are you doing here? How? Why—?"

"I've watched over you for a long time. You and Garth and Eduard. Even poor dedicated Daragon, though he would never dare to ask me for help. I've tried to help you, when I could."

"You're inside COM?"

"I have many eyes and many thoughts. I helped save Garth from drowning in Hawaii. I sent Eduard a message to rescue you from the Sharetakers. And I continue to keep an eye on Eduard, when I can. He's very careful."

Teresa took a deep breath. "Eduard's all right, then?"

"He's alive, and very clever. But then again, so is Daragon."

Teresa moved closer to the wavering screen, as if she could reach out and embrace the virtual image. Soft Stone's pale lips curved in a smile. "I understand your quest, child, and your anguish—I offer what little assistance I can."

"Do you know where my original body is?" Teresa trembled again, but this time it had nothing to do with Rush-X withdrawal pains. "Oh, how I want to be myself again."

Soft Stone's disembodied head bobbed up and down in a quiet nod. "I am a luminous being now. I've soared through the databases...so much to explore, and so many of us here. Each new mind makes COM a vaster universe."

Teresa held her breath.

"I've put together fragments of long-lost records that no normal human could have found. Perhaps you'll find the clue you need in them. I have finally discovered where Jennika went after the Sharetaker enclave. Try there."

Soft Stone flashed the address of a business, and Teresa twirled, giddy with relief. When she leaned closer to the screen to thank Soft Stone, though, the female monk was no longer there.

56

Under a starlit sky. Eduard followed Artemis to one of his other bolt-holes in the rooftop greenhouse above a conjoined apartment complex. People lived and cooked and slept in the bustling hive below, but the roof acreage was privately owned by an urban agricultural firm. Artemis had no trouble bypassing the security.

Accompanied by a crisp evening breeze, they walked along crowded rows of corn and wheat and vegetables. Peas and carrots and green beans grew under rippling sunplastic awnings. "At least we'll have something to eat," Eduard said.

"Got a fake gardener's shed where we can hide," Artemis said, leading the way. "Set it up a long time ago. In a greenhouse this big, people are less likely to notice an extra little structure. Haven't been here in quite a while, though."

"No problem. As long as there's a place to sleep."

Artemis cocked an eyebrow. "Single cot—and a floor." Eduard knew which one he'd get.

He felt strong again in Artemis's former body, and the older man now looked like the hapless inspec-tech, though he claimed he would shave the distinctive mustache soon.

Now the evening skyglow silhouetted a small shack. Artemis stood by the corrugated door, tugging at a lock clipped to the latch. "Whoa, what gives 'em the right to do that? This is my place." He scanned the rooftop with narrowed eyes, alert and nervous.

"Some worker probably didn't know the difference." Eduard reached into his pocket to withdraw a stolen laser cutter Artemis had given him, with which he made short work of the hasp.

Inside, the narrow cot had been propped against the wall, the floor strewn with gardening tools, sacks of fertilizers, and damp packages of forgotten seeds. Artemis huffed. "They're usin' this as a gardening shed! Some people have no respect for privacy."

Once they redistributed the equipment, the two of them rested in safe privacy, though Artemis grumbled that he would have to put a new, impregnable lock on the door. They slept, so weary of each other's company that they had no need for conversation.

With his team of interrogators, Daragon interviewed the assaulted inspec-tech even before he had recovered from the Scramble dose. BTL professionals combed the cavernous warehouse, scouring for fingerprints, skin flakes, even dried saliva. The evidence technicians were the Bureau's best, but all their efforts couldn't help Daragon. He wasn't interested in identifying the *body,* but the person inside it. He suspected Eduard had done this.

"Tell me once more what happened," he said, standing tall in his uniform.

The inspec-tech occupied a scrawny, pallid body that Daragon was sure Eduard must have worn not long ago. He leaned against the manual control housing that ran the facility's distribution lines and code-scanning eyes.

"I was just going about my rounds, checking everything, when a guy sprayed me in the face with some kind of drug. It hit me fast—I couldn't see, couldn't think.

Then I was in a different body, and somebody else hit me with a stunner. I woke up with a splitting headache, in a head that isn't even my own." He groaned. "I don't have any idea what I look like anymore." The tech touched his cheeks, his clean-shaven upper lip. "My wife's going to be pissed. It took me a year to grow that mustache."

Even without a chemical analysis, Daragon knew what the drug must have been, but he didn't know how Eduard had gotten his hands on it. The Bureau of Incarceration and Executions kept Scramble under tight control. Maybe he had obtained it from the same people who had provided him with the Rush-X he'd used to kill Mordecai Ob. Or was that yet another coincidence? Unlikely. Garth and Teresa might be gullible enough to believe Eduard's preposterous story, but Daragon was a BTL Inspector. He had already heard it all.

One of the evidence technicians came down from the destroyed overhead room, obviously a hideout for whoever had jumped the tech. She held a handful of mulched cellulose strips and shredded fabric fiber. "Looks like there were two people using that room, sir." Daragon surveyed the mangled mouse-nest of evidence, but had no idea how she had drawn that conclusion. He didn't ask.

"Right, two guys, I think," said the inspec-tech. "And now one of them looks like me." He squeezed his bicep. "Man, I've got to put some meat on these bones." He turned to a smooth plate on one of the computer scanners, polished the reflective surface with his sleeve, and peered down at his own face. "Hey, this isn't the guy who jumped me first. It was dark, but I did get a good look at him—this face is somebody else." He grumbled. "The first guy was better looking. Great, now I'm stuck with this one."

Daragon studied the slight body and tried to imagine

vibrant and energetic Eduard as such a person. On the run, Eduard would have had to trade down every time he swapped. Except when he tricked himself into a new body—like this man's.

Using his lapel communicator, Daragon called for the medical analyzer. "And bring your equipment with you." He turned to the still-confused inspec-tech. "Sir, we'll need to do a deep-level residual scan on your brain. I already suspect who did this to you, but we need hard evidence."

"All right, I guess." The tech and Daragon both looked up as the medical analyzer found her way around the conveyor belts, past other BTL professionals dusting and illuminating the scene. Unslinging her pack, she withdrew the portable apparatus, one piece at a time.

"Through high-level analysis of your brain pattern, we can identify leftover mindprints from the swap," Daragon explained. "But we've got to hurry to get a recording before your own persona obliterates all trace evidence."

The med analyzer showed a brief glint of compassion as she removed electrodes and probes. "This is going to hurt."

Though the inspec-tech hissed and whined, glaring at the BTL investigators with tear-filled eyes, Daragon had attention only for the results.

The med analyzer pointed to a sublimated trace, called up a reference pattern, and overlaid it. "There! Perfect match." She withdrew the scan equipment and let the poor tech slump to the floor, cradling his skull in his hands. "It's your friend Eduard Swan, all right. He was the last one in this body."

"Eduard's not my friend," Daragon said too quickly. "Just a figure of speech."

Daragon was both exhilarated and dismayed to have

his suspicions confirmed. Eduard now had a partner in crime, someone who had incapacitated this innocent man so that the fugitive could steal his body.

"So close to catching him." Daragon clenched a fist. "Now we're back at the start again."

"That's no big deal. I know how to *find* my body." The inspec-tech leaned against the machinery, holding his aching head and blinking up at the harsh lights. "I just want the Bureau to get it back from the jerk who stole it." He looked forlornly at his stick-thin arms.

Daragon whirled. "What do you mean, you know how to find it? Where did he go?"

"Ow! Not so loud." The inspec-tech wrinkled his forehead and let out a long, quiet breath. "I work free-lance as a roving inspector technician for seven different mechanical assembly lines. You never know when something's going to go wrong, but the managers sure as hell want it fixed pronto. By contract, I'm not allowed to hopscotch unless I'm on vacation—and *then* I can never lose sight of my home-body. My employers want to be absolutely certain they can find me anytime, anywhere."

"How?" Daragon demanded.

"I've been implanted with a locator. My home-body was, I mean. We can track it down anytime we want."

Loaded with energy and weapons, the Beetles converged on the rooftop greenhouse. They soared overhead with chopters and assault hovercraft. Bright lights stabbed across the dense rows of engineered crops, reflecting off transparent sunplastic. They stormed up narrow stairwells, combat boots pounding in the enclosed spaces. They burst through sealed access doors and blasted their way through security systems.

Express lifters carried reinforcements onto the roof. A gruff apprehension commander bellowed through a loudspeaker. His words ricocheted from the barricades in the sprawling gardens. "Surrender yourselves immediately or risk severe injury!"

Artemis was awake and at the shed's door in a flash, moving before Eduard even managed to sit up. "We're screwed, rabbit!" He bolted out of the doorway.

Eduard was up and running, scrambling to fasten his shirt, abandoning his shoes. He ducked low, hurrying past rows of genetically modified corn. Spotlights crackled toward the movement.

"Eduard, I know you're there." *Daragon's voice.* His chest clenched.

The rooftop was empty of innocent bystanders, and the Beetles would not be overly cautious. Since they already believed him guilty, the BTL troops were all too anxious to use their firepower. Eduard had seen what they'd done to the poor old man on the park bench. He knew there could be no surrender, even if he wanted to. He couldn't trust anything that Daragon promised.

Apprehension specialists tromped under the overhanging transparent awnings, pushing aside dwarf lemon and orange trees, searching the plant-tangled shadows for the concealed fugitives. The Beetle uniforms were so dark that they melted into the shadows.

Artemis didn't spare a glance at Eduard. "You're on your own, rabbit." The Phantom scuttled away, keeping low among the plants and equipment.

Despite the vast and cluttered space, the BTL troops would cover the broad rooftop area in no time. Gunfire erupted with bright flashes, spitting stun projectiles at imaginary targets. A rain of needles clinked off the walls and sheds.

"Eduard, you've got to surrender!" Daragon called again. "Please!"

Eduard ran bent-legged away from the voice. On the other side of the roof, Artemis crept through a covered area and emerged twenty meters from a back door. Eduard recalled a small, half-forgotten maintenance stairway; no doubt the old Phantom would try to use that for his escape.

The apprehension team spread out in their relentless search. Moving as quietly as he could, Eduard backed toward the roof's edge—nearly a hundred stories up— hoping the troops had no clear idea of where he was.

He stumbled over a pile of stored equipment at the edge of the dropoff. Reaching down to touch it, he was delighted to recognize a mag-lock harness, the same kind he had used while maintaining the windows and skyscraper walls. Now if he only had time to hook up the harness, strap himself in, and attach it to the guide-paths that lined the outer walls. . . .

The troops closed in on him, covering every inch of the rooftop. As Eduard fumbled with the latches, prepping the mag-lock harness, two Beetles prowled out ahead, holding scanning equipment. They stared down at tiny palm-held screens. A tracker! They turned toward the far exit doorway.

Eduard could make out the vague form of Artemis crouched at the stairwell, fumbling with the lock on the escape door. The trackers closed in on the other man, weapons ready to fire, but they hadn't spotted him yet. Artemis looked up at them, terrified.

More gunfire blazed into the night, striking nothing. Not stun pellets this time. Eduard wondered if it was just intimidation. He gripped the mag-lock harness, saw bloodthirsty apprehension troops knocking over plants, rustling the cornstalks.

He swallowed hard and gripped a spare fastener. It would make a loud ringing sound, clear above the pell-mell activity. As hard as he could, he flung the metal fastener like a tiny disk, away from both Artemis and himself. The piece struck a pole supporting a plastic awning and bounced off with a loud clang. It caromed off the syncrete rooftop to reverberate against the roof ledge.

The brittle metallic sound was unmistakable in the night. The Beetles turned from their tracking screens. One officer instinctively opened fire.

Artemis chose that moment to bolt away from the stairwell where they had been converging, running toward Eduard. A BTL tracker saw the movement and swung his blazing light to expose the Phantom. "There he is!"

Artemis froze, then flailed his arms. "No! Not me! Eduard's over—"

Eduard secured the mag-lock harness over his shoulders, pulled the attachments to the front of his chest, and swung over the lip of the roof. The nearby Beetles arrowed toward Artemis like dark moths, giving Eduard the moment he needed.

"Hold your fire!" Daragon screamed.

Nobody listened. Weapons blazed as Eduard dropped off into space, skidding down the tall building. . . .

Daragon ran forward, shoving officers aside. Much too late, one of the lieutenants bellowed, "Secure your weapons. The suspect is apprehended."

Daragon whirled, looking at the crew. "I ordered no shooting! Damn you, this is worse than the last botch-job! *I* am in charge of this operation." He glared at them, uniformed officers all. "I intend to get all of your ID numbers, find every discharged weapon, and put each one of you on report." He fumed. "I hear the Data Hunters are looking for new recruits."

While the other BTL officers quailed at the threat, a scanning specialist trotted up, holding out his probe.

The blip on the screen gleamed bright. "Yeah, that's the tracer. We've got our man."

Daragon bent over, touching the chest of what had been the inspec-tech's body. But though they had followed the implanted homing device, he could see with his own eyes that the flickering persona still clinging to a last moment of life inside this body did not belong to Eduard. Not Eduard at all.

He slapped away the scanning apparatus. The probe slipped out of the specialist's hands and clattered across the rooftop.

Overpowering nausea welled up within him as he stared at the blood soaking into this body-snatcher's clothes, clotting in the trim mustache. The wounds were not from stun pellets.

The apprehension team reacted instantly. "If there's another person here, we've got to find him."

The BTL men spread out again, sounding off by numbers and setting up a grid search pattern. Below on the streets, reinforcements ran toward the building. Troops scoured the apartments from floor to floor before Eduard could get too far away.

Convulsively, Artemis reached toward Daragon with a grasping hand. "Please," he said, his voice wet from the blood filling his lungs. "Can't die like this. Not after so long. Won't somebody hopscotch with me?"

"I'm afraid not, sir." Daragon wondered how he could apologize to the dying man. But as he stared into the dimming persona, he sensed some connection, something familiar. Nothing he had ever seen before, and yet it still belonged . . . *to him*.

Artemis croaked a wheezing sound that might have been laughter, but remained as quiet as faint wind. "Lived more than two hundred years . . . and now I gotta die because I'm shot by *mistake*? Not even for crimes that *I* did?"

"There's a tracer in your body, sir," Daragon said. "The technician had a locator."

Artemis moaned and closed his eyes. "Knew we shoulda killed him . . . then no one would've known. Eduard wouldn't let me."

Daragon leaned closer, still puzzled at the odd familiarity of the persona. He didn't understand what the connection could be. Then he jerked upright as recognition flooded through him. Of course! Just like when he had met his mother. He sensed parallel patterns, similarities, a recognizable *biological* link. When he'd tracked down his mother in Club Masquerade, she had said that his father was a Phantom. He saw traces of *himself* in the dying man's persona.

"You're my father." He knelt closer, touched the man's shoulder, stroked his cheek. "My name is Daragon. I'm your son. You've never met me before."

Artemis clasped his hand and opened his eyes to slits, while his other hand fumbled for something in a pocket. He didn't question Daragon's confession, but his eyes held an icy calculation.

"My son? Won't you please swap with me? Do that for your father." He took a long breath. "Save me if you can." His hand slid out of his pocket, holding some sort of spray vial.

"I can't." Daragon grabbed the man's wrist and deftly twisted it so that the Scramble fell to the rooftop. This was his father, and the man didn't even know his son's greatest failing. "I don't know how to hopscotch."

In the mag-lock harness, Eduard skimmed down the side of the building, dropping floor after floor in a blur. On the streets below, he saw lights and armored men at every exit. Chopters circled all levels like carrion birds as they scanned higher and higher.

Even if he reached the street, Eduard knew he couldn't get away. Not in this body. He had watched the Beetles tracing a mere blip. Perhaps they had managed to tag him somehow. They were hunting this body, this ID patch—if he couldn't switch, and immediately, he would never survive this night.

The safety-configured controls on the harness slowed him. He peered into windows as he dropped past, seeing families, couples, empty quarters. He had no way of barging in, and he refused to threaten an innocent family. Eduard had none of the Scramble that Artemis had used to force an unwilling person to hopscotch. He was out of options.

As he dropped down another floor, he spotted a reflection in the glass, an old man lying in bed surrounded by dim lights. In front of his dull eyes, an entertainment system played a videoloop on low. Eduard hovered, noticing the man's frail arms, his skeletal face and sunken chest, the tubes and monitoring devices attached to his body.

Here, Eduard thought. A grim chance, but better than nothing.

As he hung in the harness, he withdrew his laser cutter. With its blazing tip, he sketched a rectangle in the main window. The Beetles would already be closing off the building. He nudged the glass inward and slipped into the room, then disconnected the harness, and hauled it inside with him.

The old man woke up, gasping and wheezing. He looked fearful and completely helpless on his monitoring bed. "You...you don't scare me."

"Old man, I need to hopscotch with you. I'll give you this body. It's healthy and strong, but I need yours *now* or I'm dead."

The old man blinked, his eyes watery and disbelieving. "Trust me, kid, you don't want to be me. Not even for a little while."

"Mister, I can't tell you how much I need it right now. This is no joke."

The old man coughed, and Eduard could hear the diagnostic devices monitoring the change of metabolism as excitement kicked in. His bleary eyes grew brighter. "Then I'm not one to argue, kid. You're really giving me a second chance?"

"Yeah, and you're doing the same for me," Eduard said in a rush. "You can at least walk, can't you? You can move?"

"If you're willing to put up with a lot of pain."

"I've put up with pain before." Eduard crouched by the bedside, touched the old man's forehead. "No problem."

When they hopscotched, Eduard found himself twirling, falling, on the edge of unconsciousness. His heart pounded in his aching chest like the wings of a trapped bird. His muscles were disintegrating. He sat up so quickly on the monitoring bed that he retched.

"Careful," the old man said, standing in Eduard's former body, the one Artemis had worn for years. His eyes were filled with wonder. He reached for Eduard's hand.

"No. No synching. Keep the ID patch. That's my only price for this swap." Eduard hoped it might give him a few extra hours.

He forced his thoughts to clarity again and yanked out needles, disconnected monitors, and swung off the side of the bed. He felt like a broken marionette, strings cut, puppeteer absent.

"Clothes," he croaked. "I need clothes."

The man bounced and hopped, delighted with his new prize as he gathered the things Eduard needed.

"Here, take these. Keep yourself warm." He held up a small pill bottle. "This will dull the pain."

Shabbily dressed, walking on his own two feet, Eduard swallowed three of the pain tablets the man handed him. He knew it would be a long time before the litany of hurt subsided, even for a while. *Pain*. He had plenty of experience with pain. *No problem*. He slipped the pill bottle into his pocket. He had given up absolutely everything to flee in this decrepit body.

At least now he could get out of the building, though.

He caught a lifter down to street level, dizzy, taking one step at a time and forcing his vision to focus. He could already feel himself dying, but he had to get away. As he lurched toward the exit, something tore inside of him with a sickening liquid pop, as if dark blood were leaking into his internal organs.

Eduard walked into a wall, disoriented. His legs were an agony of arthritis and brittle bones. But he made it through the doorway, past two Beetle guards who looked sourly at him, checked his ID patch, then sent him on his way. "You don't look well, old man. Should get to a medical center."

"Where the hell do you think I'm going?" Eduard snapped, then wheezed. "I'd get there faster if it wasn't for your damned delays."

The Beetles let him pass, and he stumbled into drizzly darkness, trying not to stare at the garish reflections of colored lights on the rain-slick streets. He could feel the black shroud of imminent death at the back of his head.

He had never felt so mortal before, so close to dying. If he remained in this body for more than a few days, he would not survive.

But without it, he wouldn't live another hour.

Eduard could not risk going to a medical facility. Before long, the Beetles would discover how he had broken into the old man's room; they would interrogate the old man, get a physical identification at whatever cost, and send out a COM bulletin for the ailing body. A medical center would peg him right away.

With no other chance, and very little time, he stumbled into the streets—going exactly where he had to. He would find Garth and Teresa. Dying, he doubted they could help him, but Eduard needed to see them again.

One last time.

57

With all of its expensive furniture and prestigious paintings, Garth's new large house *loomed* around him. Every light was on in every room, but the world still felt too big and too dark.

Musing, he stood in the carpeted corridor leading to the master suite, thinking of the hardcopy books in the library, the fancy foods in the kitchen, and the pseudo-antique furnishings. Every item sent a proud signal of his success, but Garth no longer felt it *inside*.

He wanted to do a project bigger and better, more spectacular, more meaningful—yet the canvas of his imagination remained blank. He needed inspiration, not this moody creative block. He began to realize why a failed aspiring artist like Mordecai Ob might have turned to Rush-X....

That thought made his mind stray to Eduard, still lost and on the run, and Garth felt the gloom even heavier around him.

Though it was late at night, he smelled fresh coffee brewing downstairs, and he smiled wistfully. Pashnak's faith in the artist's work and his assuredly bright future remained undaunted—a blind faith. The assistant puttered around the mansion, serving without question. "What did I ever do to deserve you?" Garth muttered to himself.

After being raised by the Splinter monks, he'd always had meager personal requirements. In truth, he had bought this over-the-top mansion more for his as-sistant than for himself. Pashnak deserved it. Years ago, the gaunt young man had gambled everything on Garth's potential, keeping him on track...whatever that track might be.

Pashnak had no other passions, and he enjoyed basking in the glow of Garth's success. He managed the business affairs, taking care of all the social duties that Garth hated, while forcing him to meet his commit-ments and not become sidetracked by other priorities. Pashnak could easily have been a successful accountant or executive secretary, but he'd devoted everything to Garth's artistic career.

The COM signal startled him like a bolt of lightning, even at such a late hour. After a moment, Pashnak called from the kitchen. "Garth! It's Teresa on the screen. She wants to talk to you."

Garth smiled warmly at her image on the filmscreen, though it still startled him to see her wearing Eduard's face instead of one of the familiar female forms in the portrait spectrum. "Oh, Garth! I've got good news." She looked much healthier now, happier, with a fire in her eyes that made him briefly envious.

"Something amazing happened, and I finally have a lead. Jennika, the woman who took my original body, works at a place called Precision Chaos, an expansion-chip manufacturing facility." Breathless, she hesitated, as if afraid to say more. "I think...I think it was Soft Stone inside COM who guided me."

Though he had never really understood why finding her old body was so important, Garth knew how much it meant to *her*. "Are you going there now? Do you want me to come with you?"

"They're closed, Garth. It's three in the morning."

"I don't think I've looked out a window all day."

She chuckled. "You work too hard, Garth, don't you think? I'm going first thing in the morning."

Garth didn't want to tell her that he longed to feel the fresh drive Teresa had found, the meaning she'd rediscovered in her life. "Best of luck. Come and visit me anytime, no matter what body you happen to be in." After she signed off, he felt a flicker of rejuvenation just from talking with his friend. He walked down the hall toward the studio.

Closing the door behind him, Garth stared at his nearly completed work, ANGER. His new experiential piece was meaningful, showing the nuances of one of humanity's most powerful and destructive emotions, the pettiness and nastiness, the damage it caused, the blindness it inflicted. ANGER.

Standing inside the arrangement, he touched the images, tweaked sound loops. Hawkishly, he looked for gaps, weaknesses. He tried to imagine other directions or connections that could tap into the viewer's emotions. *Anger . . .* he had to be angry. People should be livid when they emerged from this exhibition, and ashamed at their own susceptibility to such violent emotions. They should feel chastised and penitent.

In his heart, though, he knew that ANGER would be even less popular than APATHY (which had lived up to its name, if the audience response numbers were to be believed). Critics would complain that Garth Swan no longer gave the audiences what they wanted. Stradley would have a fit, would probably write off his client altogether.

All his life Garth had had sharp eyes, a huge heart, a wealth of compassion—too much compassion, some might have said. But he'd never tried to rationalize his actions. He just stumbled along, curious, learning, searching. And now he had lost that feeling. Had all of his success been a fluke—a timely accident, forced into place by the pressure and funding of Mordecai Ob, an abusive drug addict who had doomed Garth's friend Eduard?

Now, in the studio, he worked as hard as he had ever worked, but his output no longer seemed vibrant and new, just a pale repetition of techniques and experiences. Maybe something was wrong with *him;* maybe it was too easy to pin it on the fickle tastes of a public whose attention span was too short.

Surrounded by ANGER in the silent studio, he found that he couldn't experience the rage, couldn't tap in to the powerful emotions. Garth had already reached the pinnacle of success and could not go any higher.

Flash in the pan, now get off the stage and let someone else have a try.

58

Late in the rainy darkness, Eduard staggered toward Garth's large house. In this decrepit and ailing form, he couldn't trade down any further. He had nothing of value to offer, and he would die in this body within days if he kept overexerting himself. If Daragon didn't catch him first.

Still, he needed to see Garth, if only to spend his last hours beside a friend, rather than be gunned down by bloodthirsty Beetles. At least that way he would save Daragon the anguished conscience—if he still *had* a conscience—of having to kill him.

Eduard had been on the run since before Garth moved into his new dwelling, but he'd had no difficulty tracking down the successful artist's extravagant residence. Months ago, while on the run but before meeting Artemis, he had sauntered down this exclusive tree-lined street, snatching a quick sidelong glance as he hurried past. With a secret, mischievous smile he had thought about ringing the signal buzzer and then running, a silly prank like he had often done as a boy in the Falling Leaves. Now, though, those carefree times were long past....

He lurched forward, soaked from the chill drizzle. His joints ached, his mouth tasted of copper, and his lungs felt as if they were filled with powdered glass. Oddly placed pains reminded him of the incisions and repeated surgeries the old man must have suffered through.

He looked up at the gables of Garth's big house, saw warm lights burning behind the windows, a squarish studio building brilliantly lit. Of course Garth would be working, even at such a late hour.

Ready to collapse, Eduard stepped up to the ornate security shell that surrounded the house. The outer gate remained locked, and dazzling security lights flashed on, warning of hazards that awaited any foolish curiosity seeker. After all Eduard had been through, though, it would take more than that to intimidate him. No problem. He just hoped Garth's security systems didn't automatically alert law-enforcement personnel.

He found the summons buzzer camouflaged behind an oleander hedge. He parted the dark leaves and held down the signal, not worried about being obnoxious, waited a few moments as more voodoo needles of pain jabbed his body, then buzzed again. "Come on, Garth, I'm not selling anything." He would not relent. Eduard could be as persistent as any man on Earth.

Finally, a stone brick in the wall fuzzed and turned into a videoscreen as a camouflage hologram faded. Pashnak looked at him, hard as a statue.

"I need to see Garth," Eduard rasped.

"I'm sorry, sir, it's late. Mr. Swan isn't seeing anyone." Pashnak showed no interest in the visitor or his request. No doubt he had seen the same thing many times before. "If you want to know what he has to say, go see his artwork. That's how he communicates with the world."

Eduard smeared drizzle from his face, blinking away a black haze of impending unconsciousness. The pain increased, spreading like fire through his tissues. "I know it's late, too late. This is important." After all his fleeing, all the paranoia Artemis had taught him, he was reluctant to give out his identity.

"Mr. Swan doesn't feel very well."

"Yeah, right—neither do I, dammit!"

"Sir, please don't force me to call private security." Pashnak seemed to be going through a well-accustomed dialogue.

Eduard grasped a rustling oleander branch, but the limp twigs gave him no support and he swayed on his feet. Gasping, coughing blood, he shouted at the video-screen, "Dammit, Pashnak, didn't Soft Stone teach you better than that? Trust me, Garth will want to see me."

Pashnak frowned at him, still skeptical, then his face filled with an expression of amazement. "*Eduard?* Is that you?" The security lights switched off, and the humming guardian fields ceased crackling in the ever-present drizzle. The locked gate swung open on pneumatic hinges. "Come in! Please, come in—get out of the rain."

Eduard stumbled down a walk of inlaid synthetic flagstones. The front door of the big house opened, and Pashnak hurried forward, dressed only in robe and slippers. He splashed through a puddle, but paid no attention. "Here, careful. Watch your step."

He led Eduard's failing body up the slippery steps toward the door, ushering him into the warmth and the light. With slow steps they walked through the foyer into the sitting room. The sofa seemed like a whirlpool sucking at Eduard, and he slumped into the soft cushions. He had never felt anything so wonderful.

Pashnak fussed over him, draping an afghan over his wet and rumpled clothes, then ran to the intercom. "Garth, come quickly! It's Eduard! Eduard's here!" Then he rushed off to the kitchen. "I'm going to make a fresh pot of coffee. You look like you could use some."

He hesitated, flustered. "Or maybe warm tea would be better. Chamomile?"

Eduard clung to consciousness, willing himself not to let go. He couldn't feel safe, not even here. He heard footsteps and raised his head, trying to focus his bleary eyes.

Garth emerged from his studio and rushed down the hall. "Eduard? Eduard!" Standing over the sofa, he stared in dismay at the dying old man's condition. Garth leaned down and gently embraced his friend, his clothes smelling of paints and solvents, his skin decorated with smudges of charcoal dust, dots of pigment, flecks of lubricants.

He tucked the silkweave afghan around the shivering wreck, then used a tissue to wipe blood from Eduard's cracked lips. As Pashnak clattered about, busying himself in the kitchen, the smell of brewing coffee wafted through the air like a gentle glove.

With a pillow, Garth propped Eduard into a more comfortable sitting position. "Here, I did this a lot when I was pregnant." He blinked his stinging eyes.

"No problem," Eduard said, and Garth's heart went out to his friend. "That's fine."

Pashnak finally brought coffee mugs, one filled with steaming water and a bobbing self-infuser of herbal tea. In quivering hands, Eduard held the cup; the aroma itself seemed to bring him back to life. Pashnak frowned in deep concern. "We should call a medical center, Garth."

"No," Eduard said. "They'll have an ID on this body already. As soon as the doctors could help me, Daragon and his killers would . . ."

Pashnak's eyes went wide as he realized what they had gotten into. "We've got to be very careful, Garth. He's a fugitive, already convicted in absentia. You know what the stakes are—the Bureau could be here at any moment."

"This is *Eduard.*" Garth squared his shoulders and spoke forcefully. "We'll do what we can for him here. Go find him some dry, comfortable clothes." He looked at the opaqued window. "And make sure all the security systems are turned back on. That'll buy us a little time at least."

With an audible gulp, Pashnak scurried off.

"Eduard," Garth sighed, "what are we going to do with you?"

Haltingly, Eduard told the story of what had happened to him since they'd parted company so long ago in Club Masquerade. As Garth listened to the desperation and struggle, hanging on every hoarse word, he reprimanded himself for his own selfish depression. It was pathetic the way he had wallowed in self-pity—*he,* who had everything a person could want!—while Eduard struggled so hard just to survive. . . . *No problem.*

Who was *he* to complain about his life, about his success? Ridiculously trivial concerns! He cursed his blindness and naïveté. Had he learned nothing from all the miserable people he had experienced on his List? Bored and uninspired—poor baby! He had to do something for Eduard. *He had to.*

Long ago, during the BTL shootout in the flower market, Eduard had thrown himself into the line of fire for Teresa while Garth froze, unable to do anything but watch. Then, Eduard had gone alone to save Teresa from the Sharetakers while Garth went swimming in Hawaii. After Ob's death, Teresa had given her waifish body for Eduard, taking his strung-out and drug-addicted form so that he could get away, while Garth had been unable to help because of his borrowed pregnant body.

He had botched his chances over and over

again...but not this time. He would have sacrificed much more than a handful of credits, done whatever was required of him. But he had somehow managed to miss the boat, every time. Perhaps now he could make up for it.

He'd petulantly abandoned his List and called it done—but he had never managed to experience true *heroism*, a selfless and automatic love, the willingness to risk his life without thinking. That wasn't something he could plan ahead of time, nothing Pashnak could arrange for him. It just had to happen.

Garth scowled at himself. To hell with the List—he wasn't doing this for the damned List!

"Listen, Eduard," he said, his whisper so low it was barely a kiss against the old man's ear. "It's my turn to do something for you. I'll give you the chance you need, and you have to promise me you'll take it."

Eduard's pain-filled eyes blinked, unable to focus on an object so close to him. "Garth, I don't have another chance. This body is already dying."

"Mine will last as long as you need it." Garth smiled distantly. "You'd do the same for Teresa, or me. Take my home-body and all the unmarked credits you could possibly need. I've got so much money lying around that you could get away forever, go across the ocean, pay whatever bribes you need—make yourself completely invisible."

Eduard tried to lean back against the sofa pillows, averting his gaze. "Garth, don't be an ass." His face crumpled into an expression of pain, and his chest heaved in an effort to hold back a rasping cough. "In case you haven't noticed, this body was already wrecked when I took it, and I've made things worse by running. Hemorrhaging, malfunctions, shutdowns. No matter how much money you have in your accounts, you won't be able to fix this. You won't find anyone willing to hop-scotch with you."

Garth shook his head. "If I did, then another person would have to die. Any payment would only be blood money. This is my choice, and I won't let someone else pay the price for it."

"I appreciate the offer, Garth, but I can't accept. Sorry."

"You've got to accept, Eduard. I'm offering, as your friend. I've had a perfectly good life. Let me decide how I want to spend it." Tears sparkled in his eyes.

Eduard snorted. "Your art has spoken to more people, touched more lives than anything I could dream of. The only way *I* got famous was by killing someone."

Garth stared around at his ornate dwelling with its fine furniture and embellished library. "Eduard, shut up and listen. I've had everything, done everything. And my star has burned very, very bright."

"Garth, I don't have the energy to argue with you."

"Then stop arguing."

Eduard pressed his lips together to hold in the pain, and shook his head weakly. "I refuse. Get it through your head. If you swap with me, you'll die."

Garth wore a beatific expression. "If my art is good enough, I'll live forever, anyway." He leaned closer, and Eduard ineffectually tried to slide away.

"My art is my life, always has been. You've known that since we were kids. I spent everything in my soul to make people *notice* what I had to say. I poured out the emotions and the experiences I had. My career skyrocketed, and people wanted more and more, faster and faster. But Eduard . . ." He rested his hand on the dying man's bony chest. "What if I don't have anything left to say? I want to end my career at a high point, not become some pathetic has-been whose later work waters down his original output."

Eduard sipped more of the chamomile tea, sighed. "Look at everything you have, Garth. Don't expect me to feel sorry for you."

Garth tried a different approach. "All right, but I can last a little while in your body. Let me give you a respite, just like you did for Teresa after Rhys beat her up."

Eduard's eyes glimmered. "Have you heard from Teresa? How is she?"

Garth smiled. "She just contacted me a few hours ago. She thinks she's found her original body—she's been looking for it a long time, you know."

Eduard tried to sit up. "Did she tell you where she is? I'd like to—"

"Yes, I know exactly where she'll be first thing in the morning. Swap with me, go and see her while you can." Garth began to talk in a rush. "I'll stay here and rest, and you take your last chance. Go, say goodbye to her— I know you need to."

Eduard thought of Teresa, how much he loved her, how much he missed her...how much he had ruined everything. "You mean it? This isn't permanent, you know. I'm not going to stick you with this...this old wreck. It's my problem."

"Eduard, you have enough problems to go around. Let me do this for you, now. It's my turn."

Eduard's pain-wracked eyes regarded him with suspicion. "Promise you'll wait for me here?"

With a deprecating frown at the decrepit form lying on the sofa, Garth said, "Look at your body, Eduard— where am I going to go?"

Before he hurried off, fit and healthy again, Eduard turned back. "Garth, you're not going to do anything stupid?"

The artist lay trembling on the sofa, his body wracked with the pain of dying slowly. "No." Behind Garth's bleary eyes, Eduard could see a surprising strength and confidence, a contentment that hadn't been there earlier that night. "Just go! But remember, it'll be dangerous for you."

Eduard crossed his arms over his broad chest and flashed a wry smile. "Garth . . . it's *Teresa*. What choice do I have?" Then he slipped out into the dawn.

Pashnak returned with an armful of warm clothes, but all he saw was the old body sitting there, wheezing, and in pain. "Where's Garth? He shouldn't have left you alone."

"I'm here."

Pashnak looked at him in dawning horror. He dropped the clothes on the floor. "What have you done?" He advanced forward, reaching out but afraid to touch the old man. "Oh, Garth—what have you done?"

"I did what I had to do. One last experience."

59

Weary from the fruitless hunt and the disastrous night, Daragon slumped into the chair behind Ob's former desk. He swept his arm across the desktop, knocking stacked printouts to the floor. Angry. Frustrated. Unable to give up. Would it never end?

Overhead, fish swam about, oblivious to the man below.

His uniform smelled of sweat, smoke, and drying blood. After a lifetime of searching he had discovered his father at last, a Phantom...then the man had died in Daragon's arms.

And Eduard had escaped again. Daragon had no one to blame but himself.

His work as a BTL Inspector seemed the only stable thing he could grasp, but even the Bureau gave him no joy—not any longer. He rested his head on his crossed arms, feeling terribly alone. He had driven all of his friends away, but he didn't know what he'd done wrong.

Back in the Falling Leaves, before the Bureau had taken him away, Daragon often felt uncertain and terrified. He knew something was deeply wrong with him, but Teresa had always comforted him in the dark. She would pull the blanket over his shoulders. His eyes flashed against hers in the shadows, straining to exercise his mind, attempting to swap with her. But he felt nothing stir, no sense of joining with her, or with anybody. He would finally squeeze his eyes shut, then bury his face in the hollow of Teresa's neck. She would shush him, tell him everything would be all right.

How had he changed so much?

The COM screen buzzed insistently, startling him. Jax had left a message for him. "Come see me."

Daragon sighed. The Data Hunter probably wanted company, maybe someone to read to him or chat with. He wiped the message from the screen, ignoring it—but words flashed back on in brighter, larger letters. "Come see me. You'll be glad you did."

Grumbling, he strode out of the office. He'd had enough screwups for one night, and he had no patience left. He marched down the undersea corridors and barged into the chamber with its mists and coolants, dim lights, and odd off-putting smells. His hands on his hips, he looked impatiently up at the harnesses where Data Hunters dangled from the ceiling, adrift in COM. He couldn't even tell which of the pasty blobs belonged to Jax. "All right, what do you want?"

One of the pallid, soft-skinned forms lowered. Jax turned to him with a childlike smile and said in a taunting, singsong voice, "Guess what I found! Something you've been looking for."

Daragon's heart leapt. "Eduard? Where is he? Give me some good news." He hesitated, still focused on the case. "Or did you find any of Chief Ob's three former caretakers?"

Jax sounded petulant, as if Daragon had spoiled his fun. "The caretakers have utterly vanished, Daragon— their files permanently scoured, even to our experts. Which means, in my estimation, that those people are dead. Such a scandal for our former Bureau Chief, if that information were ever to be released. Naturally, that will never happen."

"Are you saying there's some doubt now? Could Eduard have been telling the truth?"

"Your friend has been found guilty, regardless of any extenuating circumstances, and further details about Master Ob's possible bad habits will never be made available to the public. Higher up in the Bureau, it has been decided that such information would serve no positive purpose."

Daragon's face felt hot; he didn't want to hear such things, didn't want to know them. "Then why did you call me here?"

"Unlike you, Daragon, *I* have other cases to follow." The voice from Jax's speaker sounded like a huff. "I've found what your friend Teresa Swan was looking for."

Daragon was taken aback. Months ago, he had pleaded with Jax to recruit the help of the Data Hunters, even promising to read another book out loud, cover to cover... *if* they came up with something. Jax would probably choose a massive tome such as *Nicholas Nickleby* or *David Copperfield*. But if they managed to help Teresa, then at last she might forgive him. Maybe.

"I can't explain why we didn't see it before." Jax's voice came through the nearest speaker. "Somehow our most careful searches missed a critical nugget of data, until now. Here's where you can find her, a place called Precision Chaos."

Daragon stepped forward, raising his chin. "Thanks, Jax."

Finally, he could do something right again. At least he hoped so.

60

The place was called Precision Chaos, and it lived up to its name.

Address in hand, Teresa found the factory not long after daybreak. It had been a long time, and she knew intellectually that her chances were slim, but her heart refused to give up hope. Perhaps soon she would have her own body back, go home, and be *herself* for the first time in years. She wondered what it would feel like. Despite her hardships and losses, her life had always contained a wellspring of hope. Always hope.

In the city's high-tech manufacturing district, the buildings were less ornate, more functional. Even the wet freshness of the previous night's rain could not mask a sharp, sour odor of industrial processes that pushed the limits of the emissions regulations.

Precision Chaos was a high-tech cottage industry, privately owned by a tightly knit group who had invested in their own equipment. They had been in business for only a few years, but seemed to be prospering.

With the ever-increasing demand for services and capabilities, COM was constantly in need of additional resources to incorporate with the new brainpower. The computer/organic matrix redesigned itself, increased its speed and complexity as it adapted to fill the needs of society. Like similar independent groups, Jennika and her business partners cranked out expansion chips and

memoryware for installation into the voraciously growing network.

Still early, Teresa wandered into the facility and began looking around tentatively. Since she wore Eduard's
recovered body, no one would recognize her, not even
Jennika, if the runaway even remembered anything from
her long-ago Sharetaker days.

Precision Chaos was an open working environment;
desks and COM terminals and lounge areas shared
space with industrial machinery shielded by sound-
dampening fields. The chill air smelled of burning metal,
etching chemicals, packaging materials. Dozens of
workers moved about operating machinery or manning
conveyor lines and shipping outlets. Some spoke into
COM screens, others logged productivity reports or
sales manifests.

Teresa used the awkward moment before anyone
noticed her to glance around for her body: the auburn
hair, the delicate face, the fascinated eyes. She wished
she had brought along the framed sketch Garth had
made. It had been so long since she'd seen her own face,
her own form, she wondered if she would even recognize it. Most of the employees of Precision Chaos
seemed to be women . . . but still not the *right* woman.

A tall ebony-skinned worker spotted Teresa and approached, pulling red goggles from her eyes. She ran a
gloved hand through a black brush of sweaty hair.
"What can we do for you, sir?"

Teresa looked at her, looked past her. "I'm trying to
find . . . Oh, I hope you can help me. Does someone
named Jennika work here?"

The woman's deep, dark eyes bored into her, assessing her, trying to put a name to Eduard's face. "Yeah,
I'm Jennika." She offered no other help, waiting to learn
what this visitor wanted.

Teresa stared at the powerful black woman with

high cheekbones and firm lips, and her heart sank. "Oh. You've changed bodies."

Eyebrows lifted. "We always change bodies. We do a lot of work around here, take shifts."

Teresa drew a deep breath. "No surprise, I suppose. I'm not in my home-body, either. Not anymore."

"You want a job?" Jennika narrowed her eyes, critiquing Eduard's form. "We could probably use you around here, if you're interested."

"No . . . no." She fumbled for words. "I used to be with the Sharetakers—and so were you."

Jennika flinched as if she had swallowed a thistle whole. "The Sharetakers? Those assholes."

"You left the enclave—"

"I got smart. Rhys was a parasite."

"I know," Teresa said. "Do you remember me? Someone named Teresa?"

"Teresa?" She pursed her lips. "I try not to think about those days. It's better for my digestion." Jennika gestured with a gloved hand to the bustling factory. "The Sharetakers had the right theory about working together, but no clue about equitable implementation. Here, my partners and I forged a mutually supportive relationship. This is what the Sharetakers *should* have been like, if they'd really wanted to work together."

Teresa drew a deep breath, her heart pounding. "Jennika, when you left the enclave, on the day you went off . . . you, uh, you were wearing my original body."

Jennika let the red goggles dangle from her neck. "Could be. About the only thing I kept from those days is the habit of hopscotching more than most people. We use whatever physique is most appropriate for our assigned duties. Everybody does the work that's required, and we share in the profits. Believe me, Precision Chaos has seen plenty of profits already, and we're still growing."

Teresa would not allow her hope to flag, not when she was this close. "So, do you know where my home-body is now? I've been trying to locate it for a long time."

Jennika shrugged. "If I did come here in your body—and I honestly don't remember—then I've bounced out of it many times. It's been years."

"This is very important." Teresa tried to control the pleading tone in her voice. "I need to find it. I need to have it back."

Jennika appraised her skeptically. "If that physique is healthy, we'd be happy to trade. We've mostly got female forms around here, and could do with an extra man—and not just for the work itself, if you know what I mean."

"Is my home-body here, then? Can we find it, do you think?"

Jennika removed her thick gloves and tucked them into the wide pockets of her jumpsuit. "Come on, let's do some digging." She marched to an unattended COM terminal and called up the company records. "Refresh my memory on what you looked like."

Teresa told her every detail she remembered. The ebony-skinned woman scrolled through image after image. "We keep careful track of the *people,* you understand, but the bodies are pretty much interchangeable."

"Not to me," Teresa said. Finally, a familiar image flashed up on the screen, the face she had grown up seeing in the mirror. "There! That's the one!"

Jennika accessed records, skimming words, then frowned. "Not good." She double-checked, but got the same answer. "Licia was the last person inside your body."

"What?" Teresa tried to keep her heart from sinking. "Where is she now? What happened?"

Jennika looked back into the industrial area full of machinery. "Some of our equipment is dangerous. Even with the required safety interlocks, you can't get rid of all the risks. Licia was operating one of our high-speed pattern imprinters for memory-expansion manufacture, and a seal failed in the containment chamber. She got caught in a cloud of highly corrosive vapor." Jennika set her face in a grim mask. "It wasn't pretty."

"She died? My body—" Teresa stood frozen, then her shoulders—Eduard's shoulders—slumped. She collapsed into the nearest chair.

The other woman's voice grew stern. "Hey, I apologize, but we lost *Licia* in that accident—a valued coworker and our friend. Nobody paid much attention to what body she was in when she died. I'm sorry for you, but we lost more than you did."

Teresa heard no more of the woman's explanation. Surrounded by the industrial noises and smells of Precision Chaos, she sagged in the chair. Her senses grew numb, and the world blurred as tears flowed from her eyes.

Everything Arthur had told her, everything that had rung so true, was now lost. Her original form was gone forever. Her soul could never return to its rightful place.

61

Sensing the crisis between Jennika and the stranger, several workers paused in their activities to watch. Questions and concern crossed their faces. Teresa sat listless, her face in her hands, in despair.

The ebony-skinned woman touched her with a strong, sinewy hand. "Look, I'm sorry I ran off with your body from the Sharetakers, and I'm sorry we lost it. I didn't suspect it would mean so much to anyone."

"Not your fault." Teresa tilted her head, staring back with puffy eyes. "Who else in the world would care?"

Jennika bit her lip as she considered possibilities. "Here, why not take me instead?" The muscular woman held out both hands. "I had no right to leave the Sharetakers in anything other than my own body. I just didn't think, and that wasn't fair to you. This one is young and strong—and at least it's female."

Teresa would be sad to let go of the physical vestiges of Eduard. This body was all she had left of him, but at least being a woman was a better approximation of the body she'd been born with. One step closer to her now-unattainable goal. She'd have the right set of chromosomes, the chemical and hormonal cycles, the familiar bodily components, the same sexual sensations.

Did any of that matter?

Maybe Arthur would have approved. Maybe not. Teresa had to make her own choice. Right now, any change seemed for the better, movement in the right direction rather than a crashing halt.

Teresa took a deep breath while Jennika stood there in stained overalls, waiting for her decision. Eduard's muscles and nerves had recovered completely from the destructive addiction, though right now she felt as shaky as she'd been during the Rush-X withdrawal. Jennika was sleek and athletic and strong, vibrant, full of energy. It would be a more than fair trade.

Teresa stepped forward, lifting her head high. "We'd better do this before I change my mind, don't you think?"

After she hopscotched with Jennika and synched ID patches, Teresa settled into her new body, establishing her muscle control. With a glint of delight in her dark eyes, she took a moment of total concentration just to assess the differences again. She felt the indescribable changes *inside,* the rapid-fire nerves in erogenous zones along her skin, the feminine chemistry within her. Teresa was amazed at how wonderful it was to be female again.

"I can work with this," Jennika said, standing now in Eduard's body, her voice deeper. "It'll do just fine."

Armed with the information from Jax, Daragon disembarked from the BTL hovercar and walked the rest of the way to Precision Chaos to see what he could learn in person. Perhaps Teresa's home-body was still there. Once he knew the answers, he would go to her. After the disastrous events of the previous night, he needed to do something *good* for a change. Something for which Teresa would thank him.

He walked down the street with a stiff, quick stride. He had no need of maps or COM guidance—he had already memorized the way. As he approached Precision Chaos, he paid little attention to a statuesque black woman who emerged from the front. She paused, but Daragon was used to that, since most people flinched upon seeing a BTL Inspector.

Then she raised a hand in greeting. "Daragon!"

He looked past her hard but beautiful face, her athletic body, and into her shimmering persona. "Teresa!" Then his hope evaporated. "So you already know." He stepped close, his eyes searching, but he saw only sadness there. "You didn't find what you needed?"

She shook her head and allowed herself to flow forward until he self-consciously wrapped her in a stiff embrace. "I'm too late. It's gone . . . gone."

He tried to be warm and responsive, but it was difficult to break through the BTL training. "You probably don't believe me, Teresa, but I grieve for your loss. I won't kid you by saying that I understand—I *can't*, since I've never even been able to leave my body—but I am sincerely sorry for you."

She smiled at him, an expression that was oh-so-Teresa even in this stranger's body. "I believe you, Daragon. You never could hide your real feelings from me." Then she gazed deeply at him, drawing away from his embrace. "Something else is wrong, isn't it? What's happened? Is it Eduard?"

In halting words, Daragon explained about how he had found his father at last, by accident, but the man was now dead. Self-consciously, he left Eduard out of the story. At first he started out formally, as if he were giving an official report to Mordecai Ob, but he let his feelings intrude.

Teresa found his bare-bones narrative heart-wrenching. Tears filled her eyes.

"So my father was a Phantom, a real-live Phantom." Daragon tried to find his center of stability again. "I regret that I never got the chance to talk to him—to know him."

This time it was her turn to offer comfort, though the uniformed Inspector didn't know how to accept it. But he needed this, needed Teresa to open up to him again, just like it had been at the Falling Leaves. He remained silent for a long time, rigid and seemingly afraid. Finally he asked, "Can we talk some more? Just talk... as if we were real friends again?"

Teresa considered cautiously. "Maybe we could have a drink at Club Masquerade."

Daragon nodded. "Given a little time, we might both be able to heal our wounds."

Teresa thought with misty-eyed fondness of the innocent times they'd had together at the monastery... and wondered if it would ever be possible to give Daragon what he asked. After so much time, so much life.

Racing through the back streets, knowing he had to hurry, Eduard arrived at the small industrial building. Though he wore Garth's broad-shouldered, blond-haired body, he still moved furtively. He could have escaped to freedom at any time, but he would not do that to his friend. And he needed one last chance to see Teresa.

He approached Precision Chaos from the rear. If Teresa was here, he had to find a discreet way to get inside. He found a shipping entrance, where a posted sign instructed all visitors to use the front doorway. Ignoring the placard, he slipped through the entrance.

Feeling completely out of place, Eduard scanned the faces, trying to find Teresa. He knew damned well he'd be able to spot the face he had worn for so many years. No problem. He grieved for the Rush-X hell he must have put her through, and he ached with love for what she had done for him.

The fabrication complex hummed around him, full of machine sounds, manufacturing smells, and droning orders over the implanted speakers. He snooped about, walking past workstations, looking at faces and wearing a haughty I-belong-here expression. His masquerade did the trick, and no one challenged him as he searched from one person to another. Perhaps he had gotten here too late. He put his hands on his hips and did a slow turn. Where could she be?

Finally, with a weird dislocated thrill, Eduard spotted himself, his own home-body. He hadn't recognized it at first behind the red goggles and a grimy work jumpsuit. Teresa had been wearing that body, taking care of it for him—had she gotten a job here, at a dirty, hot expansion-chip facility? Why had she given up her joyful job with the florists for something like this?

"Teresa, it's me, Eduard." She pulled off her goggles, looking at him with no recognition. "Hey, don't let Garth's body fool you. I need to talk to you."

His own eyes looked back at him curiously before sudden understanding flooded across the face. "Oh— you're looking for Teresa. She just swapped with me." She grabbed his arm with a gloved hand. "Come quick. Maybe we can still catch her."

Together, he and Jennika hurried to the front entrance of Precision Chaos. Pulling open the door, the woman gazed out at the long street ahead, said, "Good, she's still here," then yelled, "Yo, Teresa! Someone to see you!"

She shouted again at the top of her lungs—as Eduard froze in horror.

Deep in conversation with Daragon, Teresa heard her name and turned. At the main doorway of the facility, she recognized two people: the male body she had worn until a few moments ago, and a big blond-haired man. "Garth! What are you doing here?"

But Daragon saw a lot more. His eyes met Eduard's across the distance, recognized him. Without thinking, he triggered an emergency alarm from a transmitter on his belt. "That's not Garth."

Desperate, trapped, Eduard grabbed the woman beside him. Garth was still in the old man's decrepit and dying body back in his home, and Eduard had promised to return. He couldn't let his friend make that sacrifice. It wasn't just his own life he was trying to save now. The artist had never intended for Eduard to escape, to run away with his healthy body—

Or had Garth intended that all along?

The frantic thought of using Jennika as a hostage streaked like a flare through his mind, but he shoved her away, disgusted with himself for even considering the option. He recalled how he had despised the anti-COM terrorist who'd done the same thing to Teresa in the flower market, long ago.

More annoyed than frightened, Jennika reeled, not understanding what was going on.

Daragon drew his weapon.

Eduard bolted back through the door into the industrial facility, where he hoped he could hide.

Boldly, Teresa used her body's new strength to chop down on Daragon's wrist, knocking the weapon out of the way. "Leave him alone!" She sprinted for the building, thinking only of Eduard.

"Teresa, he's a cold-blooded murderer," Daragon said.

"He's also my friend! Are you sure your Mr. Ob wasn't the cold-blooded one?"

Leaving Jennika on the threshold upset and baffled by the sudden activity, Eduard flew through the doorway. Daragon retrieved his weapon from the ground and ran toward Teresa, his face flushed, his eyes set. She did her best to cut him off, but he easily pushed past her.

Inside the facility, Precision Chaos workers kept at their jobs, oblivious to the emergency. Eduard ran past desks and COM terminals toward the cluttered rear, seeking refuge among the heavy machinery, the crates of supplies and shipping materials. Perhaps he could slip through the back door before the Beetles arrived.

When he heard the whine of approaching BTL patrol hovercraft and backup assault choppers, he knew that would be impossible.

Outside, Daragon spoke into his lapel communicator, coordinating the rapidly arriving teams. "Surround the building. I want surveillance craft and armed personnel at every exit, every window, every exhaust pipe. *Stun darts only*—I'll have the badge of anyone who disobeys me this time."

His quarry had appeared like a miracle, at last, and Daragon—*Inspector* Daragon Swan—had to forget about Teresa, forget about their past and how much she had meant to him. Now there would be no reconciliation between them.

He had made his choice.

"I want an orderly evacuation of the employees inside—one person at a time." He turned to two uniformed BTL guards who dropped out of a hovercraft and rushed into position. "Eduard is trapped in there, and I want it to stay that way. Nobody comes out without me looking at them with my own eyes."

As the net closed around the building, Teresa pushed past an angry Jennika and into the facility. "Eduard! Eduard, they've got the building surrounded."

Amplifiers boomed so loudly that the walls of the facility vibrated. "All legitimate employees must leave the building. Use the front entrance only. All other exits are guarded and off limits. Do not attempt to deviate from these instructions or you will be fired upon."

Intimidated and confused, workers trotted toward the front doors, yanking off protective gloves and goggles. But Teresa elbowed past them, fighting her way against the flow. Her new legs were long, her muscles tight and resilient. "Eduard!" she called, looking everywhere for his big blond form.

Daragon's voice came over the BTL loudspeakers. "Teresa, come out of there. Let me handle this!"

Eduard ran between banks of thermal etchers, vacuum chambers, and sealed presses. Hot IR ovens throbbed, baking and pre-etching sapphire-coated silicon composites. Gas hissed, and ventilation hoods whistled as toxic vapors flowed through scrubbers.

He ducked low, nearly deafened by the hydraulics in a multiple-strike micropress. Jumpsuited workers hustled to evacuate, and he could smell the heavy claustrophobic fear mixed with processed industrial smells. People shouted or whispered as they filed toward the exit through a gauntlet of Beetles.

Eduard could never mix in with them and get out that way, not while Daragon watched with his eerie second-sight. Right now he could hear the choppers, gruff orders transmitted from Beetle to Beetle, the rumble of heavy feet on the roof. The side door slammed open and more armored apprehension specialists entered. Eduard glided to deeper shadows near another piece of heavy machinery. He had no place else to go.

Daragon marched through the front door, directing the assault. He instructed guards to remain among the evacuated workers milling about outside. "We might need to interrogate them later."

An officer looked at him. "There's no way he can get out of this, Inspector."

Daragon brushed him aside. "I'll believe that when we have him in custody—alive—and not before."

Inside, Teresa scuttled into the equipment area, reaching the lunchroom. She kept herself low, taking advantage of whatever cover she could find. She used tables and plastic chairs as camouflage, though none of it would protect her from direct gunfire. She searched for Eduard on the garishly lit industrial floor. "Eduard, oh give yourself up before you get killed!"

As soon as she spoke, the Beetles turned toward her voice, and Teresa dove under a table. Keyed up, two startled guards opened fire in a reflexive action. The synthetic wood laminate and brightly colored plastic table became a porcupine of stun darts.

Enraged, Eduard popped out of his refuge. "Don't shoot at *her*, you stupid bastards!" More shots rang out, targeting him this time.

Using a voice enhancer at his collar, Daragon bellowed into the ringing background noise. "Eduard, give yourself up—please don't let this go any further. You'll only make it harder." He gestured for backup troops to fan out, scuttling across the floor.

"I'm sorry, Daragon, but your past behavior doesn't inspire much confidence," Eduard called with a cynical laugh. "I've seen you gun down at least two innocent people while you were trying to catch me. Two people who had nothing to do with the crime you want me for." He paused a beat, knowing the Inspector must be wrestling with a response. He said, taunting, "Who exactly is the murderer around here? Or are there different standards for BTL troops?"

In response, several hot-blooded apprehension specialists opened fire again. Stun pellets pinged off the machinery that shielded him. Silver starburst scratches blossomed on painted housings; nicks appeared in thick glass containment ports.

Both Daragon and Teresa screamed for the shooting to stop. Whining ricochets sang through the air, chipping more glass.

"This is Garth's body, Daragon," Eduard shouted. "I've got to make sure he gets it back. *You* have to promise me that."

Another Beetle answered in a gruff voice, "That body is confiscated property, by law. The BTL does not make deals with—"

"Shut up!" Daragon said, then lowered his voice. "Not now."

From where she crouched under the shelter of an administrative desk, Teresa could see Eduard slip toward curling acid-brown vapors that leaked from a breached containment chamber. He coughed while running for cover, using the thick fumes as a smokescreen.

Teresa knocked a broken table aside. She saw warning labels on the equipment—TOXIC HAZARDS, HIGHLY CORROSIVE CHEMICALS—and remembered what had happened to her original body. She had no time to think, no time to plan. Moving as fast as her new athletic legs could piston, she launched across the open space toward him.

The etching chamber had been blasted open by stray projectiles, and caustic gas hissed out like a smokescreen. Eduard stumbled toward it, ignorant of the hazard, intent only on escaping.

Teresa struck him like a cannonball, knocking the big-shouldered man across the syncrete floor. He'd done the same for her, long ago, to save her during a shootout in the flower market.

"There he is!" a Beetle shouted. She heard weapons clicking, aiming.

Just above their heads, external paint on the equipment bubbled and peeled from exposure to the thick, deadly vapor.

Teresa lay across Garth's blond form, shielding Eduard with her own lithe body. "Don't shoot! Hold your fire!"

Eduard writhed on the floor, trying to push her off. "Teresa, get away from me!" He scrambled to his feet as Teresa dove toward him again to protect him, but Eduard held his arms out, totally exposed now. "I won't let you stand in the crossfire for me. Not you, Teresa."

He glared at the armed troops cautiously approaching him. "I surrender." He raised his hands. "Or do you plan to just shoot me down where I stand?"

Some Beetles looked as if they might have been tempted, but Daragon drove them back. Eduard stood tall as he glared at his adversary, his friend.

The look on Daragon's face was not one of triumph. Far from it.

62

With all the love he possessed, Pashnak tended Garth's ailing body as he dwindled toward death. He dimmed the library lights, turned the laser fireplace on high, knelt beside the sofa. His mind whirled as he tried to make the artist more comfortable, to make him recuperate. Somehow.

As he had feared, they had heard nothing from Eduard in hours. "He's run off, Garth. He has your body now, and he won't come back until it's too late."

"Pashnak, don't be dense. That's what I wanted him to do in the first place." Garth turned his head on the pillow. "We'll just stay here. That's the best thing." Pashnak looked down intently at the shriveled, gray-skinned body of the man he had served so long and so well. "You're always so good to me."

The assistant fought back tears. "I just wish you treated yourself better."

With a gnarled hand, he patted Pashnak's wrist. "This is my decision. Don't pester me about it." Garth smiled up at him, and Pashnak saw a bleary haze of contentment he hadn't seen on the artist in far too long. "I can't think of any better way to top off my career than to help my friend. A crowning achievement."

Pashnak bit his lower lip, holding back a moan. "How can you say that?" He wished he had never let Eduard inside the house, never even answered the door call. If only he had turned away the sick old fugitive, that would have been the end of the matter. "Think of all the ideas you can still have, the exhibitions, the—" His voice cracked. "All the books we still have to read out loud to each other!"

Lying back, propped on the pillows, Garth studied the syn-oak moldings on the ceiling. "Ah, let's leave it at that. I did some great work, didn't I?" He closed his eyes and let his wrinkled face settle into a sigh. "As long as I saved Eduard, it was worth it."

He shifted on the pillows, drawing a breath that felt like shrapnel in his chest. Pashnak still hovered beside him, as if wondering whether he should make more coffee. Garth said, "Now here's a new experience I never managed before—heroism and self-sacrifice. Probably the noblest part of being human."

Pashnak's lips trembled. "Sure, but now that you understand it, you won't live to express it as art. Garth, you have to stay alive!" He nearly shouted the last sentence. For a long time, wrapped up in business matters, he had tried to ignore Garth's growing malaise, chalking it up to another mood swing, an oscillation of the artistic temperament. Now, though, his eyes flashing with anger and dismay, Pashnak paced the library. "You've always been selfless and giving, generous with your money. You experienced everything, suffered all the foibles and problems people can have, shouldered that burden just so you could contribute back to humanity through your art."

"Yeah, but this time I did it for a friend." Garth's eyes shone. "That's even better."

Suddenly, the library's filmscreen burned bright as a transmission came in. A selectively highlighted COM-news broadcast, sorted by Garth's priority filters. Annoyed, Pashnak got up to blank it, not wanting to lose one of his precious moments with Garth, but the artist raised a trembling hand. "Wait."

A story about Eduard. A news-download, a special report, a breaking story. He knew it even before the details scrolled across the screen. "Oh no."

Sharp video images showed a BTL action, some kind of crackdown at a local expansion-chip facility. Stun pellets peppered the walls of the building. Uniformed Bureau troops ran about, heads down, smashing glass and marching inside. Garth saw the neon-etched name on the front of the facility. Precision Chaos. Where Eduard had gone to find Teresa.

A spear of pain ripped through his lungs, his heart. He coughed, and tasted blood deep in his throat. The simulated announcer pattered his report, firing words like BTL gunshots. "The Bureau officers managed to take the target alive, with only minor injuries among their own ranks, thus marking the end to a long and bloody chase." The reporter appeared suitably grim, his expression stern.

On the library screen, he and Pashnak stared as a stun-shackled Eduard, wearing Garth's familiar home-body, was hauled toward an armored hovervan, apprehended after a "flawless Bureau operation." COMnews reporters clustered around BTL Inspector Daragon Swan, the person in charge of the long manhunt, but Daragon brushed them aside, ignoring the attention, and staggered to his private vehicle. He looked sick.

All available evidence had already been submitted before an "impartial" jury panel, and in the face of such overwhelming evidence they'd had no choice but to find Eduard guilty. Once apprehended, the prisoner was currently being interviewed behind closed doors, and the BTL had already denied appeals. Months ago, Eduard Swan had been sentenced to COM upload by the Bureau of Incarceration and Executions.

Weak-kneed with despair, Pashnak leaned against the sofa. "Ah, no. This can't be! Now what is it for?

You've sacrificed yourself for nothing, Garth. Eduard's going to be executed—we've got to get your home-body back."

The artist lay back, stunned and speechless in his failing body. He felt no strength at all now.

The COM screens faded to gray-black static. Behind the nothingness a face resolved itself, the weathered but compassionate face of a bald woman. She gazed out from the depths of the computer/organic matrix as if it were a window. She spoke directly to the dying form sprawled on the sofa. "Garth, little Swan, I can do nothing to help him." Then the image faded completely into static.

Garth had witnessed a terrorist's execution many years earlier, back at the artists' bazaar. Was COM really a "sweatshop of souls," as the justice system insisted? The Splinters hadn't thought so. He remembered Soft Stone's wondrous "death" when she had voluntarily uploaded herself from the Falling Leaves library. And now she was here.

Garth tore the silkweave afghan away from his skeletal body. Startled, Pashnak bent over, attempting to mother him. "Garth, you've got to lie down! Don't exert yourself."

Instead, Garth pushed him away and placed his feet on the floor, wobbling, as if his legs were splintered chunks of wood. He could barely stand, maintaining his balance as he feebly pushed the assistant away.

"No, I've got to *do* something." Garth wheezed, then coughed a splash of blood, but he swore that he wouldn't let himself die yet. "I've got a little more life left, even in this body."

He held out a trembling hand, insisted that Pashnak help him across the room. "You won't make it down the sidewalk, let alone to Eduard! Please let me call a medical center now—your identity doesn't matter anymore." Pashnak wrung his hands, unable to stifle his despair. "Eduard's already caught!"

"Yes, Eduard's caught. That's the only thing that matters. I've got to go to him, make some sort of plan."

"Maybe you'll get your body back. The BTL will return it to you, won't they? Daragon knows it's yours."

"And he also knows I'm an accomplice, then. They'll impound it, go through the standard routine. I won't last long enough for all the red tape."

Then, realizing what he could do, he decided upon it immediately. He wiped a bony wrist across his chapped, blood-flecked lips. He would give one last thing to his friend.

Soon, Eduard would be on the auction block in Garth's strong, blond-haired body. Convicted criminals had to sacrifice their physiques as well as their lives. People would bid to hopscotch into his body permanently, leaving Eduard to die in a weak, used-up form. Garth had enough credits to outbid anyone else at the auction. If he could just make it there in time.

He looked at the bookshelf in the library, the treasured tomes resting on a broad oak shelf just above the laser fireplace. He ran his gaze along the spines of the Dickens titles, and smiled wistfully.

"Garth, what are you thinking?" Pashnak sounded concerned and suspicious. "I don't like the look in your eyes."

Garth smiled at his assistant, content. As soon as the artist spoke, Pashnak's eyes went wide in horror. He understood exactly what Garth planned to do, how he would save Eduard.

"It is a far, far better thing I do . . ."

63

Stunned by what had happened to Eduard and feeling completely helpless, Teresa went to the one place that had offered her consistent comfort in the past. In despair, she made her way to the Falling Leaves.

In one brief and tragic morning, the foundations of her world had been torn from her. After such a long search, she had discovered that her original body no longer existed. Worse, because she had asked for Daragon's help in her quest, she had unwittingly led him to Eduard. She had tried to defend her friend, but she had ultimately failed. The Beetles had swallowed him up. Daragon had turned against her, and now Eduard was lost.

"Your priorities are all screwed up, don't you think?" she said to herself.

Not anymore. She would acquire a clearer focus. She had to.

So she walked along the streets, unable to take pleasure in her rangy body. Her new skin was dark, her eyesight sharp, her senses tingling. How had everything gotten so mixed up? She staggered ahead, finding her way. Teresa had always had trouble finding her own way.

The monastery's massive wooden door stood shut in front of her, ornately carved and impenetrable. Her loud knock reverberated through the remodeled brewery.

Each pounding knock released warm childhood memories and nostalgic times. Teresa longed for those days. But everything was different now.

Finally, the heavy door opened to reveal an unfamiliar young face. "I'm Teresa Swan. I used to live here," she said. "I need to see the administrator. Can you take me to Chocolate, do you think?"

Inside the archway, she noticed black streamers and crepe hung from the lintel. She reached up to touch the dark fabric, running her fingertips along the weave. The streamers signified mourning.

The young man's eyes widened. "You'd better follow me. Come this way." He turned his back and hurried down the corridor. She remembered the courtyard garden, the sleeping quarters, and the marvelous library filled with artwork, books, and COM terminals.

Inside, additional black banners hung from alcoves. Many of the beeswax candles had gone out; the floors looked as if they hadn't been scrubbed in days. Soft Stone would never have allowed anything like that to happen....

She found the administrator's office empty, the COM screen switched off, papers and notes in disarray. Chocolate's desk and chair looked as if they hadn't been used in days. "Wait here," the young man said. "I need to fetch him from the garden. Your name is Teresa, you said?"

She nodded and continued to stare into the office, a feeling of dread taking hold of her. "Can you tell me what's wrong? Why are you grieving? Where are all the Splinters?"

The young monk looked at her, his expression lost. "They're all at the funeral preparations for Chocolate. We've got . . . we've got plenty to do that we weren't expecting." Preoccupied, he fled back down the hall in tears.

Teresa put a hand to her mouth. "Chocolate is dead?" Her voice was husky with disbelief.

Finally, the young man returned with stern Hickory in his wake. Seeing the familiar, if unwelcoming, face, Teresa took a step toward him. Hickory assessed her new, athletic form with an expression of clear disapproval—but then, he disapproved of almost everything. "You're Teresa?" His pinched face loosened into an expression that, though not an outright smile, was at least less stern. "Not many people come back, but frankly I'm surprised it took *you* so long."

Teresa still couldn't get used to the surprising news about the roly-poly administrator. "Did Chocolate upload himself into COM? Like Soft Stone did?" She didn't understand the black banners, the dark crepe of mourning. "Why is everyone so sad?"

Hickory scowled. "No, Chocolate died in his sleep, before he could schedule his upload ceremony. We didn't expect that, and now he's gone." Hickory crossed his arms over his chest, glaring at her for a moment. Then his expression fell. Tears sparkled in his eyes. "His soul is lost. He'll never be able to sail the data streams with his brothers and sisters. He . . . we waited too long."

Teresa took the news like a physical blow.

Her life had been such a long journey without a map, full of blind turns and dead ends. She had always expected to find clear-cut solutions, black-and-white answers, if only she kept asking. Maybe there were no answers to be had. Teresa had to find her own solutions, not just ask somebody else.

Standing by herself, she finally managed to put the pieces together: A person determined her worth by what she did and how she lived her life, not by which body she had, which form she held, which skin she inhabited.

Finally it clicked what old Arthur had been trying to

tell her—the soul and the body were together but separate. Changing bodies did not change a person. Altering her appearance didn't alter *who she was*. Teresa's free will, her actions and her thoughts, were the things that made her an individual.

All along she had been obsessed with irrelevant worries, the wrong problems. . . .

Later, she returned bearing baskets of fresh-cut flowers for the funeral. Standing among the Splinters who were now all strangers to her, she remained long enough to say her farewells to the roly-poly, good-natured man. Chocolate was gone. Like Soft Stone. Like Arthur.

Like Eduard would be very soon.

Willingly this time, knowing the world was waiting for her, Teresa left the monastery. Many of the Splinters came to bid her farewell, but she walked away down the street, knowing in her heart that this was the last time she would ever return to the Falling Leaves.

64

Meat market. Eduard seethed in silence as they prepared him for display, ready for sale to the highest, most desperate bidder.

The BTL had refused to listen to him about Garth, denied him the right to trade back into the ailing man's body. This physique was impounded. Besides, if they had let him swap back into the dying old physique, who would ever bid on it? He might not even survive long enough for the upload execution.

But no one would listen. Daragon had sequestered himself, and one of the other Beetles had told him to be quiet. Eduard stopped insisting. By now, Garth might already be dead. He had never meant for that to happen.

The Bureau of Incarceration and Executions efficiently continued the process of disposing of everything Eduard had, everything he was, erasing every positive mark he had made in his life. It was a first humiliation, what they considered a necessary step to prepare for his elimination.

His ID patch had been reset to his old identity, which now listed all the convictions against him. Most of them were laughably false, but he saw no point in fighting them. Long before he'd been captured, his bogus trial was already over, convicted in absentia, the guilty verdict etched in stone. Daragon had obviously chosen sides, and politics in the Bureau would prevent him from exposing any damning evidence against

Mordecai Ob. Nothing Eduard said would convince them otherwise. Why bother to look for proof, when you already know the answer?

As BIE handlers stripped and prepped the fine, strong body Garth had given him, he remained just co-operative enough to avoid harsh treatment. Now, both Garth and Teresa had paid with their bodies for *his* mistakes. He regretted so much....

The handlers scrubbed him down and oiled his skin. He shook his dripping blond hair, and they combed it for him again. They wanted him to look as clean and perfect as possible to bring a good price. Some lucky bidder would have a new life, perhaps a terminally ill patient or someone old and decrepit.

They would use Scramble on him, if necessary. Trapped in a discardable, unwanted form, Eduard's soul would be ripped from his body and added to the ever-growing COM to benefit all humankind. Mental abilities were a resource to be tapped, brainpower for the masses. Felons like Eduard contributed back to society by increasing the overall scope of COM, adding to the nonsentient computer labor force.

- Quite a contrast with what the Splinters believed, but Eduard took no comfort from it. They didn't know about Soft Stone. He would find out soon enough, after the handlers made a good show of selling his body. Garth's body.

A uniformed official ran a sensor over his skin, taking tissue samples and sniffing cellular residue. After a medical scan pronounced him free of diseases and contaminants, clean of all evidence of drug addiction (Eduard had to laugh at the irony!), the data was sent to available screens in the bidding room outside.

Under normal circumstances, prospective purchasers would have days to consider him, but because of Eduard's high-profile case, they intended to rush him through. Keep the ratings up. The bidding among an exclusive pool of prospective buyers would reach a frenzy, no matter what they did.

When they led him toward the stage, one guard squeezed his arm muscle. He looked Eduard up and down as if he were a piece of furniture and remarked to his partner, "Fine specimen, eh? Most of our terminal guests are worn out." The guard chuckled. "If I was in worse shape, I might even bid for you myself."

"You couldn't afford what I'm worth," Eduard said.

The guard snapped back, "As a *body* maybe not. As a person—well, I've got some loose change."

Floor lights indicated where he had to go. Trying to look haughty, Eduard stepped out into a roomful of hopeful people, from the curious to the desperate. A transparent, flickering field separated him from the crowd.

His eyes hardened, an unaccustomed expression on Garth's normally welcoming face. The limited pool of bidders stared at him, and he stared right back without flinching. He'd never seen such a batch of old and hurting people. All of them rich. Misfits. Vultures.

None of these people deserved what Garth had sacrificed for him. Not one of them.

Then the spotlights shone hot and white from all angles, illuminating his skin, his muscles, every part of his body. The customers were offering good money to live in this flesh, and they wanted a decent look. It was only fair.

"What you see is what you get." Eduard tried to become a statue as the bidding started.

Standing in an observation alcove, Daragon watched from the background, disgusted. Since he was such a prominent Inspector, it was all part of his job—he had to see it through to the end.

Still, he was deeply troubled to see Eduard humiliated in such a way. Standing naked and defiant, the murderer of Mordecai Ob sizzled under the lights. Though he could see Eduard's persona on the inside, glowing in its familiar pattern, he still saw only Garth's body on the outside.

The Bureau had kept Daragon isolated since the apprehension at Precision Chaos, and they had not yet traced the identity of the body back to Garth—or so they said. But Daragon understood all too clearly what must have happened.

Why had the successful artist gone out of his way to help a wanted fugitive? Daragon had kept that part quiet, trying to protect Garth. He had so much to lose— yet Garth had defended Eduard without question, and Teresa had thrown herself into mortal danger to protect him. Why? *Why?* How strong were the obligations of friendship, when the law was so clear?

Daragon knew he had to be very, very careful. Though Garth and Teresa must surely hate him, he still wanted to protect them, whether they realized it or not. He had always kept an eye on them, protecting them from their own mistakes. Now, though, they were at risk of making things worse for everyone.

The new BTL administrators wanted to make their mark. They would let nothing mar their triumph over capturing and punishing the man who had murdered Mordecai Ob. Knowing Garth was an accomplice, knowing how the BTL would react, Daragon had no choice but to keep his secret, for Garth's sake. But that was as far as his loyalty would go.

Right now, he hoped the auction would pass quietly, before anyone recognized the home-body of the famous artist.

Standing silently, he watched like a hawk as the limited group of invited bidders pushed forward, keying credit requests into handheld COM units. As the furious bidding climbed higher, Eduard stared boldly at them, impervious to their frenzy. That seemed to intrigue them even more.

Automated newscams captured the spectacle, broadcasting it realtime to COM channels, where the images were split and sent to various commentary groups, all of which found their own soapboxes and drew their own conclusions.

Eduard glared at the audience, turned from left to right when he was told, raising his arms, spreading his legs. He wore his nakedness like armor and endured it all, every moment of it. The price went up and up.

Seeing him on the stage, Daragon remembered a young boy dripping wet from rain because he had sneaked out across the rooftops of the monastery. Eduard had always been happy-go-lucky, a rulebreaker. Now he was caught, and he would have to pay the price.

The bidders obviously believed there was a certain prestige in owning the last body of such a high-profile criminal. The price shot higher. It made Daragon both nauseated and angry.

When he could stand it no longer, he turned on his heels and slipped out of the arena, ashamed of what he had done. No longer sure of his beloved Bureau, he tried to force his wandering thoughts back into acceptable cubbyholes. Perhaps it would have been better if Eduard had just been gunned down during apprehension.

Because of the used-up body he had taken from Eduard, Garth had to move with painful slowness, even given the manic ministrations of Pashnak. Garth tested the limits of what he could do. Unfortunately, it wasn't much.

The assistant gave him a dangerously large dose of quick-acting painkillers, and the two of them stumbled toward the auction center. They didn't have much time.

Neither of them anticipated the circus that surrounded the bidding. While the proceedings played on active-matrix billboards outside the BIE holding facility, Bureau guards blocked access to the arena to prevent anyone else from entering. "Exclusive bidding pool, forty people only," the nearest guard said. "Cutoff was twenty minutes ago. Better luck next time." The expression on the uniformed woman's face showed that she doubted Garth's body would survive until the next opportunity.

"We're too late," Pashnak said in despair. "Now you'll never get your body back. Why didn't Daragon let us know?"

Flailing his sticklike arms, Garth pushed forward to the front portals. His body was a thousand aches and pains, all demanding his attention. Pashnak tried to clear the way, but his gaunt form could not muscle aside the gathered spectators.

The uniformed guard just shook her head. "Closed proceedings, sir. Window of opportunity is over. No new bidders at this time."

"I'll top anyone else's offer," Garth said with a croak.

"The going price has no effect on my salary," she said in a clipped voice. "Rules are rules."

Images swam in front of Garth's eyes from a combination of oncoming tears and impending unconsciousness. "Wait, you don't understand—"

"Just watch on the screens over there, old man." The BIE guard crossed her arms over a uniformed chest. "Bid on the next one. Won't be long before we catch someone else."

Pashnak led him away from the damaging press of

people. "We need to get you somewhere safe, Garth. It's too dangerous here—you never should have left your bed."

Garth clenched his teeth, feeling the pounding pulse throb in his head. "How can I be too late to help Eduard!" He yanked his scrawny arm from Pashnak's grip and lashed out, trying to claw his way to the door. But his vision fuzzed, and his head swam. He couldn't breathe. He reached out a gnarled hand, straining forward . . . and collapsed.

People gave him room to fall, but kept their attention on the COM screens. The bidding for Eduard had already reached a remarkable level.

Pashnak used his sharp elbows to knock people aside as he clutched Garth to his chest. From the grayish caste of the withered skin, the blue tinge of his lips, he knew Garth was in extreme distress.

"Out of my way!" He pulled Garth back from the crowd. "Out . . . of . . . my . . . way!" Not knowing what else to do, he roused the half-conscious artist and helped him stagger to the nearest medical center.

As each bid went higher, Eduard remained expressionless, though his hatred of the crowd grew by orders of magnitude. Vampires hoping to claim his body even before the justice system killed him. He stared at the faces. The old men and women, the weak, the unattractive—everyone wanted his body, so long as the unwanted mind and soul didn't come with it. *Body for sale.*

How many of those milling about outside the shimmering protective field were mere curiosity seekers, trophy-hunters who wanted to own the body of an infamous fugitive? They were jackals, fighting for leftovers they did not deserve.

Finally, as the bidding became more strident, one old

woman shrieked out an outrageously high number. Eduard looked over at her, recognized the wattled throat, pinched face, and reptilian gaze of Madame Ruxton. The woman who had tried to steal his body before, using a legal loophole to keep his form after he'd undergone difficult surgery for her. He wanted to spit at her.

For a moment, there was a shocked silence. No one topped her bid.

Eduard stared at Ruxton, studying her pinched face and weathered appearance. He was astonished she had managed to live so long. Lawyers surrounded her like a murder of crows, waiting for fresh carrion.

"Looks like you finally got my body," he muttered. "Bitch."

Eduard hoped she'd be destitute after the giant sum she had offered. Serve her right. Before long, Madame Ruxton might even have to lease out her precious new body just to make ends meet.

Eduard covered his emotions, however, maintaining a stony façade as he was led away. It didn't matter anymore. Nothing mattered anymore.

65

Drifting in and out of consciousness, Garth found himself back in his house again . . . in his rumpled bed, surrounded by easily recognized things that disoriented him with their very familiarity.

After his collapse, the pain and restless sleep had sent him . . . far away. In that dim, aching place he had expected to see Soft Stone again, her guiding hand taking him either toward the tunnel of light or pushing him back through the doorway to life. This time, though, he had been unconscious and alone. He had awakened without any revelations, without any help, without any hope.

Pashnak sat at his bedside, crying, holding Garth's hand. When the assistant saw that he had opened his eyes, Pashnak squeezed the hand tighter. "Oh, Garth—they weren't sure you would ever wake up again."

"They? Who are you talking about? Where have I been?"

Pashnak's words came out in a rush. "I took you to a medical center, had them run scans on you. You've been there for most of a day. When they ID'ed the body you're in, they called up the old man's records and got the prognosis."

"Not good, I'll bet." Each breath sent a stab of pain through his overstressed lungs.

"They were surprised you're still alive. Can't offer any help, diagnosis terminal—imminently terminal." He tried to blink the tear-sheen from his eyes. "They offered COM euthanasia for a small fee. I . . . told them no."

Garth patted his hand. "I really blew it this time, Pashnak—everything I tried to do for Eduard . . . I failed." He closed his eyes to push away the accusing thoughts in his head.

Pashnak got up and shifted the window polarization, letting misty daylight into the room. He remained standing with his back to the bed, a rigid silhouette. "I just don't understand why you would do such a terrible thing to yourself. You had so much . . ."

Garth lay back on the pillow and smiled wistfully. "Pashnak, I was glad to have a worthwhile reason to fight after all. It reminded me of how I used to be inspired. It was great."

The assistant fussed with the sheets, tucked in the blankets. "I tracked the bidding through COM, because I thought you'd want to know." He held a wrinkled printout in front of Garth's face. "This is the woman who bought your body. A rich old lady named Madame Ruxton."

Garth tried to make his eyes focus. "I could have paid twice that much. It would've been so simple, if we'd made it to the auction. I could have saved Eduard, if we'd just gotten there in time."

Pashnak's hands trembled. "That would have been the simplest solution. But the simplest solution doesn't always work."

Garth could tell by the look on Pashnak's drawn face that the assistant had come to some kind of decision—though he couldn't imagine what the issue was.

"I've been with you for a long, long time, Garth. I've seen your moods, and I've seen what you can do. I held your hand through your pregnancy, I helped you walk when you were blind. I also saw you running out of steam and I was at a loss to help you. I didn't know what to do. *I* never lost faith in you...but you did."

Garth sighed, trying to sink into the blankets and sheets. "Sorry for everything I put you through."

The assistant brushed it aside. "I was always so proud to be part of what you were doing. I was *honored.*"

Garth reached up to run his fingers through the assistant's mouse-brown hair. Pashnak's lips trembled; he was obviously more frightened than he had ever been. "Last night, seeing you full of energy and *alive* again, ready to give everything to help your friend...*that's* the Garth I want to remember. That's the way I last want to see you." Garth forced a wan smile, and Pashnak grabbed his hand. "I want you inspired again, fighting, and passionate—go help Eduard, if that's what you need to do. You can find a way."

Garth winced as pain shot through him again. "Impossible, Pashnak. Right now, I doubt I could even get to the bathroom by myself."

The assistant squeezed his hand so hard Garth was afraid some of his brittle bones might shatter. "Unless you hopscotch with me."

Garth snorted. "Don't be ridiculous."

Pashnak's face turned crimson. "I'm not being ridiculous! You're not the only one who can make sacrifices, you know—and this is the only way you're going to help your friend. Dammit, if you refuse me, then you're costing Eduard his only chance." Garth swallowed hard and felt his body dying by rapid steps. Pashnak leaned close, his words like a kiss on the artist's wrinkled cheek. "Let *me* do something that'll make a difference for once."

Garth's mind spun. He found it difficult to think with so much pain clawing at his thoughts. "Even if I do swap with you, it's still very remote. What exactly do you think I can do for him?"

The assistant crossed his arms over his chest. "I

know you, Garth—when you're inspired, you can do *anything.*" Pashnak held out the wadded printout. "Take this. Go track down Madame Ruxton. She'll be at the execution tomorrow—or *you* can be in her place, if you make her the right offer." He smiled deprecatingly. "My own body's not so great, but it's strong enough. Ask the old lady if this isn't better than being good-looking and destitute. She seems to be a greedy bitch."

Seeing the wavering, uncertain look on the pallid old face, Pashnak reached down. "Better swap with me now, before I lose my nerve."

Instinctively, desperately, Garth hopscotched out of his dying body into the gaunt form of his assistant. He drew a deep, deep breath, filled with wonder at how sweet the bedroom air smelled. Even these lanky arms and legs felt strong, capable of great things.

From the reverse perspective looking down on the old man in the bed, Garth saw how truly ill he had looked. He immediately changed his mind. "Oh, Pashnak—I shouldn't have done that."

"I guess it's not so terrible," he said. "I love you, Garth."

"I know. I love you, too." Garth bent down, his world focused on the dying man in front of him. "Forget it. I don't want to lose you as well as Eduard. This is my problem, and I need to pay the price."

He touched the papery skin on the dying man's temples, but he could not hopscotch. A thin smile curled the assistant's old lips. "Sorry, Garth. I'm staying here, and you can't swap back with me unless I cooperate."

He remembered seeing young Pashnak standing in front of the Splinters during his graduation ceremony, when the gaunt boy had swapped with Soft Stone, proving his ability. "Pashnak, swap back with me. Now!"

"No, not unless you've got some Scramble. After all

these years, I think that's the first time I ever refused you." He seemed to think that was funny. "It was the best of times, it was the worst of times. . . ."

"Pashnak!"

Looking up at the ceiling, the assistant said, "Will you read to me? Like you used to? When we were in the monastery?"

Tears filled Garth's eyes, and he embraced the man on the bed as gently as he could. "Of course."

He rushed off, remembering how they had sat by candlelight, reading Dickens. He stopped in front of the library shelves, searching for the right book, any book. He grabbed *David Copperfield*, the novel they had been sharing when Pashnak left the Falling Leaves.

He hurried back, flipping through the pages, searching for the right place, a good scene. "Here's one." He walked into the bedroom.

Where he found Pashnak already dead. The old body lay silent and motionless, eyes closed. One hand was clenched around a knot of sheets.

Garth's fingers turned to rubber, and the heavy book slipped with a thump to the floor. Pashnak didn't flinch or stir.

Garth cradled him in his arms, anguished. Now, of course, he had a thousand things to say. But it was too late.

He, himself, would have been lying there dead now, if not for Pashnak's sacrifice. And he'd already had more than his fill of useless sacrifices. Instead, Garth's options were now limited to one important thing. He didn't know how he could ever pull it off, but he was damned well going to try.

Garth prepared to go rescue Eduard. Somehow.

He shut down everything in his big house and left.

66

As green-clad eco-engineers wrestled with robotic digging apparatuses taller than themselves, Teresa leaned against a building, watching and thinking. She didn't even know what part of the city she was in.

Arboretum crews shouted to each other, dancing with sycamore saplings as they replanted the greenery along one side of a boulevard. Cranes, pulleys, and mulchers brought down the sprawling old trees, trimmed the branches, processed the wood into aromatic by-products. The boulevard was rapidly transformed as she watched—deadwood removed, new growth added.

Leaving the loud machinery behind her, Teresa wandered the streets until she found an unoccupied public COM terminal. She searched for news of Eduard, scanning current-events files. He had been forbidden visitors, and even she could not see him.

COMnews was full of maddeningly slanted reports. Teresa had fled from Precision Chaos, remained out of touch. No doubt if she'd been available, media hounds and scancopters would have demanded interviews about Eduard. Maybe she should have seized the attention, tried to tell the real story and appeal to public sympathy. But she knew their minds were already made up.

Teresa searched for more information, all the while secretly hoping she would encounter the image of Soft

Stone again. But the monk's ethereal presence made no appearance. Teresa was on her own, again.

Numb now, punching in code numbers, she tried to contact Garth once more. He at least would help her; together they could find some way to fight for Eduard. They had to think of something together. As a rich and famous artist, maybe he had the power and resources to *do* something. He had connections, and a vivid imagination.

But Garth was gone, again. In the past day, over and over, no one had answered her override requests for an urgent communication. At the very least Pashnak should have responded. Signal after signal faded without an answer. Finally, Teresa decided to go there in person.

She jogged down the streets toward Garth's mansion. Jennika's body had great energy reserves, resilient muscles, and a generous lung capacity. She ran, her breaths even and steady, with barely a sweat breaking across her brow.

When she arrived at Garth's extravagant house and activated the outside intercom, however, no one came to the door. She pressed her thumb on the speaker button. "Garth! Pashnak! It's Teresa—oh, let me in! We've got to talk."

The place looked like a haunted house. For the first time she could remember, Garth wasn't there for her when she needed him.

At another COM terminal, she punched in the BTL emergency number, the direct-contact code Daragon had given her long ago. She had to talk to him face-to-face. Instead of seeing Daragon's image, though, a stern-faced receptionist intercepted her call. "May I help you? This is a private BTL channel."

"I need to speak to Inspector Daragon Swan."

"Inspector Swan is unavailable. At his own request,

he has been placed on administrative leave and is in seclusion."

Teresa frowned. If she could just talk to him, plead with him, maybe she could convince him to request a delay. There must be a reasonable doubt. "Oh, perhaps he'll be available for me—my name is Teresa. I'm sure he'll speak to me." If necessary, she would play upon his past feelings for her, but she suspected that wouldn't help. He was a stranger now.

"Inspector Swan is unavailable."

Frustrated, Teresa stared back at the receptionist's stony face. "You haven't even checked. I'm a very close friend of his, and I wouldn't be calling him if this wasn't an emergency."

In a case surrounded by so much publicity—especially considering the numerous casualties incurred during the hunt, the Beetles would certainly apply the toughest punishment with all due speed. An example had to be made.

"Inspector Swan is unavailable," the receptionist repeated.

"Are you listening to me at all?" Teresa leaned closer to the screen, exasperated.

"Perhaps you're the one who hasn't been listening, ma'am."

"When will Inspector Swan *be* available, do you think?"

"Not before the upcoming execution. He has many details to attend to. After that, he has a great deal of work to do in consolidating the new Bureau."

Teresa disconnected, furious. By then it would be too late.

She put her hands on her hips, finally galvanized. She'd do it all alone if she had to. It was never too late, and she would never give up. She had wasted so many months searching for her original body. All that time, she could have been fighting within the system, speaking on Eduard's behalf, working with Garth to use his public platform to expose the injustice.

Instead, she had been on a pointless quest for a body she had abandoned long ago, a body that was already dead. Her obsession with esoteric Big Questions and her lifelong searches for Universal Truths would mean nothing if she lost Eduard and Garth, people who loved her for who she was. Why hadn't she seen that before? Teresa swore not to let it fizzle without a fight.

Eduard was scheduled to be executed. He would be alone, but she had to find a way to be there. She could be present to support him, to help him...to offer her love if nothing else.

Eduard had saved her life more than once. He had shared her pain, helped her abused body heal, given her money when she needed it. Now she would help Eduard in whatever way she could.

Setting her jaw, Teresa headed off to the holding prison where Eduard waited out his last day.

67

So what else was money good for? Garth didn't worry about what he would do afterward. He didn't really think there would *be* any afterward. None of that mattered.

Now that Pashnak was gone, no one would watch out for him. The other man's death was still an open wound, a foolish sacrifice that Garth never should have allowed in the first place, and now he could not correct the mistake—except by going forward.

He clutched Madame Ruxton's name and address in his hand. If he could just spend the money, cut the deal, he would have no regrets.

The skyscraper condo-complex was unremarkable and drab, without character, the kind of building Garth could have passed repeatedly without ever noticing its presence. For a wealthy woman, Ruxton apparently squandered little of her wealth on extravagant luxuries.

Determined, he signaled at her door and waited, knowing she would be suspicious, perhaps even frightened, of a stranger. Garth had never been good at planning ahead, but he tried to rehearse what he might say to the old woman.

Ruxton's face appeared on the door screen, tired and pinched. She had pale skin untouched by makeup, clean hair in an unattractive but serviceable cut, and once-expensive clothes. According to public records, she lived alone, had numerous business acquaintances, few friends.

"What do you want?" she asked without unlocking the door. "Go away or I'll call security, and then my lawyers."

"I'm an artist. My name is Garth Swan, and I'm here to offer you a lot of credits," he said. Her reptilian eyes brightened, then narrowed in suspicion. His words tumbled out before she could say anything else. "You've got something I need, Madame Ruxton. Something I need very badly. I'll pay."

Standing there in Pashnak's gaunt body, he looked far from intimidating. "How much money?" Her question told Garth a great deal. She hadn't even asked *what* he wanted, what he needed—just the amount he would pay.

"Twice what you bid for Eduard's body. Right now, in unmarked credits."

The door opened immediately.

Surrounded by squarish, expensive furniture, cold wall prints, and empty bookshelves, Garth felt the dreary emptiness of her life. He sniffed dust and old packaging in the air, meals cooked for only one person. He'd been searching to rekindle his own waning passion, but Ruxton didn't appear ever to have had any.

Eduard was due to be executed the following day, and this rich crone would walk away from the BJE termination facility wearing his strong and healthy body. Did she just want to make her harried, lonely life last longer? To what purpose?

She led Garth into a small sitting room, gestured toward a faded chair. "I have defensive systems, so don't try anything stupid."

Garth clasped his hands in his lap to keep them from twitching. "Madame Ruxton, I need your body." Then he told her the story he had concocted, as true as he could make it, laced with lies when necessary, distorting facts when appropriate. Because of the embarrassment and the sensitive nature of the case, and because he was a famous "panoramic experience artist," he didn't want anybody to know about the switch. He feared his reputation could be ruined.

It sounded good. Eduard would have been proud.

As was quite apparent from her decor, Ruxton knew nothing about the art scene and had never heard of him. "But I too have a bit of a score to settle with Eduard," she said in a raspy voice. "I could have had his body years ago, when he underwent major surgery for me. Unfortunately, he did not die when it would have been most convenient."

Garth heaved several deep breaths. "You have already had your revenge, Madame Ruxton. The whole world saw you win the auction, Eduard himself saw it— and I...would rather we kept our agreement private." In fact, it was imperative that no one find out. "In addition to the large sum I offer, I will swap you this well-cared-for body, if I can secretly take your place for the switch at the execution tomorrow."

Ruxton tapped her fingers on the tabletop, scrutinizing him like a gravedigger studying a fresh corpse. Instead of sacrificing most of her assets, she could have a perfectly acceptable new body—Pashnak's was as good as Eduard's, for her purposes—and make a tidy profit on top of it all. Finally, she cocked her eyebrows and nodded appraisingly. "Do I look stupid to you? Done— you've got yourself a deal."

Without giving her time for second thoughts, Garth transferred the credits into her account. Ruxton stared at the new balance, almost salivating, hardly able to believe her good fortune.

After they hopscotched, she ran her hands over her new cheeks. "It's not as glamorous as the physique I

bought, but it'll do...considering the profit margin."
Garth looked across at her, seeing Pashnak's drawn, familiar face. He would have to spend the night here, in this apartment, to maintain appearances.

Ruxton glanced again at the balance in her account and grinned. "Now I can afford to stay in a first-class hotel again. Get myself a suite!"

While she grabbed a few of her things, Garth stood with a cold feeling in the pit of his stomach. The old woman walked away in Pashnak's body with a new spring in her step. She left Garth behind in her drab apartment, counting down the hours until his friend's scheduled execution. Everything had unfolded the way he'd hoped, and now at least Eduard had a chance.

Garth would go to the BIE termination center, masquerading as Madame Ruxton. As the world watched, he and Eduard would supposedly trade bodies. But when the time came, Garth planned to refuse the switch, secretly, leaving an astonished Eduard in his own body. A free man, with a brand-new chance at life.

And Garth would also experience the very last thing on his List.

His own death.

68

Hands clasped in a combative stance, elbows on the beer-stained table, forearms vertical as muscles bulged. Teresa felt the strength in Jennika's sinewy arm, the smooth ebony skin rippling with tendons and hidden strength. She admired her well-toned forearm muscles, the *brachioradialis* (she remembered the Latin name from Arthur's copy of *Gray's Anatomy*).

Now she had to use them. She felt like a panther.

Across from her sat the off-duty BIE guard: square jaw, square shoulders, square head. His face flickered with a glint of amusement. Obviously, he didn't consider her a worthy arm-wrestling opponent, and that gave her even more motivation to win.

Teresa needed all the motivation she could get.

After studying public employee files from the Bureau of Incarceration and Executions, she had learned that one of the escort guards—José Meroni, a well-known womanizer—had a passion for arm-wrestling. He often hung out in a small neo-pub and challenged unsuspecting customers, much to the delight of the regulars. The stakes were usually no more than a round of drinks or a handful of credits. Tonight she had something much more substantial in mind.

On the night before Eduard's scheduled upload, Teresa had entered the neo-pub, attempting to recapture her wide-eyed waifish look, despite Jennika's athletic and iron-hard body. She peered around the bar, smelling sour beer and greasy food. Very different from Club Masquerade.

Teresa had recognized the escort guard sitting with his friends, gulping beer from an imitation medieval tankard. Given the man's penchant for winning, by now he must have had a difficult time finding new arm-wrestling opponents.

She strode across to Meroni, looked down at him, and watched his expression of surprise turn into a leer. Good, that was even better. When she challenged him to a contest, he had let out a guffaw echoed by his cronies. Her expression soured, and she repeated her challenge. "Or are you afraid of me, do you think?"

The others swept their tankards aside, clearing the tabletop. One vacated a chair so Teresa could slide herself across from the surprised José Meroni. She shucked her coat and thumped her elbow on the table, holding up her hand, ready to clasp his in a tight grip.

"Stakes?" he said. "I don't want to take too much of your money, lady."

"Just a friendly match the first time." She hoped he would fall into the trap, hoped she could pull it off. Mind, muscles, stamina, strength. Confidence. "Loser buys a round of drinks for your friends."

The spectators cheered, delighted to be the beneficiaries no matter which contender won.

Teresa and the guard gripped palms, squeezed, tested. She dropped deep inside herself, concentrating, drawing on her inner strength. She had inhabited many bodies before, and could feel the muscles, the potential physical power inside her new form, if she could just release it.

They pressed their hands together, sweating and straining. Her eyes half-closed, she barely registered the look of surprise on Meroni's face. He pressed harder.

His face turned red. Teresa countered and pushed, the power building in her arms, giving not a centimeter.

The guard fought back, delving into his own reserves, possibly for the first time. Their elbows ground against the sticky tabletop. Her forearm wavered from vertical as she lost ground. Sweat trickled down her cheek. She drew a deep, cold breath, and resisted with even more strength.

Meroni fought for his pride in front of his friends, but she was fighting for something much more important. She envisioned Eduard, helpless, captured after all this time. He had sacrificed so much for her, for Garth, for himself. *Eduard*. She pushed harder.

The guard's elbow slipped, and she pushed his forearm toward him. As he began to waver, his dismay increased, his confidence waned. Teresa saw the chink in his armor and pressed harder, gaining leverage. She winked at him.

The back of his fist slammed onto the tabletop, and she released her grip, standing as the spectators tittered nervously. They'd never seen Meroni lose, especially not like this. Teresa flexed her fingers to loosen them. "The gentleman here is buying us all drinks, I believe." She met the guard's gaze, saw his wounded pride.

"A fluke!" he said, because he didn't know what else to say. He challenged her to a rematch, but his confidence was already crumbling.

So she defeated him again.

"Now's your big chance," she said, while some of the patrons chuckled, others sat astonished. "The chance to prove yourself."

Teresa flirted with Meroni, stroking his sweaty cheek with her long fingers. His voice was gruff, on the edge of surly. "What do we do now?"

"Now we swap. Do it again." She crossed her arms over her chest. "Let me prove I can beat you in *your*

body, too." She didn't want the man for his muscles—
she just needed his uniform, his identity, and his access
to the termination facility.

José Meroni blinked in surprise, assessing her lean
female form. "What'll that do? I can't possibly win if
I—"

"Oh, really?" She raised her eyebrows. "I just
proved that this female body is strong enough to beat
yours. It should be a sure thing for you. Muscles are
muscles—see if you can do it yourself." Teresa continued, as haughty as she could manage. "It's all in the
mind, total self-confidence...or are you afraid you
don't have enough confidence?" She waited a beat.
"You can just surrender now, if you like."

"What are the stakes this time?" he growled.

She gave another sexually charged smile. Rhys had
trained her how to do it. "It's just a matter of whether I
get to be in the male body first later on tonight, or you."

The spectators gave appreciative whistles and catcalls, tinged with envy, and that was enough to puff
Meroni's confidence again. "Sounds good to me." He
rubbed his sweaty palms together with a whickering
sound. The bar attendant brought the round of drinks,
and each of the spectators grabbed a fresh glass. No one
ventured a toast on Teresa's behalf.

The guard leaned across the table, nostrils flaring.
They hopscotched, then placed their elbows on the table
again. The spectators hooted, urging Meroni to win
back his honor.

But Teresa knew this time would be easy. The guard
had more brawn, heavier weight—and inside her already tired body, he would have no idea how to tap her
deep reserves of strength. And he had already been
beaten, his confidence shattered, his embarrassment
crippling him. The first two times, Teresa had been
somewhat outmatched, but had still managed to turn

the tables on him. For this rematch, Teresa started out with a decided advantage, not just in weight and musculature, but in attitude—and easily trounced him.

Head low, still in a female body, the guard stood up. Leaving his fresh drink unfinished, he grabbed Teresa's arm—his own arm. "Let's get out of here, then. Synch your ID patch with mine."

"Oh, no hurry for that." Smiling warmly, Teresa and Meroni sauntered out arm in arm. "We'll be swapping a few more times before the night is done." The bar patrons hooted or applauded, and the shamed Meroni added a little more strut to his step.

Outside, she walked with him on the night streets, trying to pick up the pace. While still wearing Jennika's shape, she had swallowed a powerful, timed tranquilizer before entering the neo-pub. She hoped they would get to Meroni's place before the drug kicked in. She didn't want to drag him all the way home.

69

The upload chamber looked like an industrial hell—intentionally so, Eduard figured. It made for better broadcasts, a more ominous lesson. The Bureau certainly wouldn't want the public to watch executions in a soothing, pleasant setting, as when Soft Stone had uploaded herself from the Falling Leaves library.

Two restraint chairs were bolted to the floor at the center of a room lined with metal plating. Obvious rivets looked like bullets stitching the steel wall sheets together. Cables and electrodes stretched like squid tentacles from consoles that occupied one full corner. Like something out of a mad scientist's lab, the left chair was rigged with conduits that led directly into the computer/organic matrix.

"What is this, BIE budget cuts?" Eduard said.

The guards, ignoring Eduard's wisecrack, directed him toward the second restraint chair, the one without direct COM connections. Before long, his mind would be dragged over into the auction-winner's body in the other seat.

A few interested spectators already clustered behind a transparent wall, peering at him like visitors to an aquarium. "The better to see you with, my dear," Eduard said. He yanked his arm away from the escort guards and shuffled to the indicated chair without being told twice.

The bristling glassy camera lenses of a holocapture

apparatus looked like the compound eye of an insect. COMnews would transmit the spectacle onto public channels. Only a few privileged Beetles, guards, and enforcement personnel would be allowed to watch his upload live and personal. And of course the ghoulish old Madame Ruxton—who had spent much of her wealth to buy the body right out from under him—got a ringside seat.

He wondered if Daragon would have the guts to come and watch, or if he would wallow in guilt and stay hidden until it was all over. Eduard couldn't decide whether or not he wanted to see his former friend.

In the corridor behind the transparent screen he noticed one burly, squarish escort guard paying particular attention to him, like a hyena. Eduard made a twisted face at him, and the blocky guard turned away with an expression of shock and surprising dismay.

A booming voice poured from the speakers as his sentence was read aloud. The narrator, a professional dramatist, spoke with grim authority. The world was watching. "Eduard Swan, you have been convicted of the murder of Mordecai Ob, Chief of the Bureau of Tracing and Locations."

A looming PR hologram of Ob shimmered in the air like an accusing ghost, looking brave and handsome and paternal. They had used one of the smiling press images from Garth's FRUSTRATION debut exhibition.

Eduard saw only the form he had worn so many times, the physique he had kept healthy while the Chief wasted his borrowed body on drugs. At least, he had prevented the similar destruction of who knew how many future physical trainers. Eduard's would-be replacement, Candace Chu, would never know that he had saved her life.

Unfortunately, he had mucked everything else up.

By stopping to see Garth one last time, by letting

himself be talked into trading bodies just long enough to say goodbye to Teresa, he had led to his friend's certain death—and then Eduard had wrecked his chance to get away.

Ob's hologram hovered in front of him, silent and accusing, as the mellifluous voice continued from the speakers. "Eduard Swan, you attempted to escape justice and committed numerous other crimes during your flight, any one of which would justify your sentence of upload termination."

Another string of holographic images paraded in front of him: the blood-flecked face of the slain Artemis, the murdered old man who had been feeding bats from his park bench...a rapid succession of faces, bodies he had stolen.

Indignant, Eduard wanted to shout that Daragon's overzealous *Beetles* had been responsible for most of the death and destruction—but he was cynical enough to know it would do no good. He was supposed to carry all the crimes on his conscience. The Bureau wrote its own history, and COM promulgated it.

"You will, therefore, surrender your life for the greater good of society and in modest reparation for the crimes you have committed. Your strong body will be given to another person in need, and your consciousness will be erased, your mental abilities uploaded into COM, where all minds work together to process data for the benefit of humanity."

He remembered Soft Stone's shining lights, the beautiful images, the quiet music—it had to be for show, something the Splinter monks had concocted to comfort themselves. "How can you be so sure I'm not going to come back out and get you?" he muttered. But he knew that would never happen; despite numerous vengeful vows by criminals facing upload, COM had swallowed them all without the slightest bit of indigestion.

In this place, he expected no cathedrals of data, no shimmering angels to lead him down a golden path. Similarly, Eduard thought the ominous "sweatshop of souls" idea was just another ridiculous fantasy, no more likely than Soft Stone's cybernetic heaven or somebody else's hell.

"The final preparations will now commence," the voice boomed.

No matter what, Eduard was going to be dead in a few moments. *That* was real, without question.

70

In full dress uniform, Daragon headed toward his position in the termination facility, avoiding everyone.

He had been "rewarded" with diminished duties, and some BTL bureaucrats were muttering with displeasure about his personal connection to the Eduard Swan case, his obsession that had caused his other workload to suffer. They didn't want him making any public statement, but as head of the apprehension team that had captured Eduard, he was expected to be an important observer at the execution. It was his duty. It was his curse.

Eduard's fate was already out of his hands, placed under the jurisdiction of a different Bureau. Holding himself rigid and grim, Daragon wanted nothing more than to *leave*. He was just a showpiece here, and he hated every minute of it. He would rather go back to the underwater BTL Headquarters, sit in the Chief's former office and remember Mordecai Ob. He would watch schools of fish swim through the kelp forest as distant sunlight sliced through the water.

And he would try to forget about Eduard.

This case had thrown Inspector Daragon Swan into a whirlpool of unwanted attention. Before long, some investigative journalist was sure to learn that *Daragon himself* had gotten Eduard the job working for Mordecai Ob. Therefore, the BTL officials had to make sure everything went by the book, with no deviations, no mistakes.

But Daragon couldn't leave it at that. Quietly, using every favor, every manipulation skill he knew, he had already quashed the accomplice charges leveled against Garth and Teresa, but he could do no more. Garth's mansion was shut down and silent, and since he could not find the artist, he had no chance to return the blond home-body to him. After the execution, Daragon was sure he could place some injunction against the vile Madame Ruxton—*that* would be as satisfying to him as when he'd quietly ruined Rhys and the Sharetakers. It wouldn't be difficult to confiscate Garth's home-body and give it back to him.

The opportunities for scandal were myriad, but he didn't care.

Now, he marched down the austere halls of the well-guarded facility. The BIE personnel showed Daragon deference, congratulated him formally. He accepted their kindness politely, then turned down another corridor as rapidly as possible. He concentrated on attending to every little thing. An Inspector was good at the details. He would get through this one minute at a time, until it was finally over.

Guards were escorting old Madame Ruxton toward the holding room, and Daragon found a reason to turn in the opposite direction. A long time ago he had protected Eduard from the rich crone's greed, and he didn't want to face her vindictiveness now—to see her gloat. With clicking bootheels, he hurried to a different control center, refusing even to look at her.

He tried to hold on to thoughts of how Chief Ob had given him such a remarkable opportunity with the BTL. Because of his inability to hopscotch, he'd been different from everybody else. Even among his friends in the monastery, he had always been an outsider. But the

Bureau had accepted him. Ob's faith in Daragon's special abilities had turned him into someone powerful and impressive.

And then Eduard had killed the man who had been the closest thing to a father to him. Daragon focused on that.

Once captured, Eduard hadn't even tried to defend himself—he seemed already defeated by the fact that his former friend had turned against him. "You're all about justice, Daragon. But you can't have justice without truth."

The BTL had done its thorough investigation, and they had found no concrete evidence to confirm Eduard's story. Even Daragon had not been able to convince himself of what Teresa and Garth believed. What other choice did an Inspector have? It was his duty.

As he tried to convince himself, the face of happy-go-lucky young Eduard, the daredevil and scamp who ran across slick rooftops to explore the city, kept haunting him. A cocky boy who stole flowers for Teresa, who threw himself into danger to save his friends. The man Daragon could never be.

No wonder he'd never experienced the same depth of friendship with Teresa, or Garth, or even Eduard. What had he done differently?

Garth's career had been launched by Mordecai Ob, who had given him the money and freedom to follow his dream. And yet, the moment Eduard came in with his wild story about the Bureau Chief's abuse, Garth had never doubted him, never hesitated before offering to help a known fugitive and probable murderer. Because they were *friends*.

Years ago, Eduard had thrown himself against an armed terrorist to save Teresa in the flower market. He had rescued her from the Sharetakers when Rhys had beaten her, and he had swapped into her wounded body so she could heal more peacefully. In return, Teresa had begged him to trade bodies with her when he'd gone on the run, knowing that Eduard's body was strung out and addicted to Rush-X. She hadn't doubted him, either, not for a second.

Daragon still considered them his closest friends, yet he was sure they would not have made similar selfless sacrifices for him. His throat went dry and his heart grew heavy as he realized the corollary. *Would I have done it for them?*

He had never been willing to take chances, to open himself. Yes, he had watched over them, using his BTL resources, and he had saved them from problems and embarrassing situations. But he had never done any self-less act that required him to take an actual risk on their behalf. He could almost hear Teresa scolding him: "You don't get closer by *doing* things for us, Daragon. You get closer just by being a friend."

It sounded so simple, but he wasn't sure he could accomplish that.

Nauseated by himself, and by what he was about to witness, Daragon could think of nothing he could do—for anyone. He would just have to endure, and try to heal afterward.

He went to his position with the witnesses for the execution: Olaf Pitervald the window-maintenance engineer, the woman suffering from a muscular disease who now lived in Teresa's waifish body, the hirsute parolee, the scrawny underground worker, the inspectech who would never be able to recover his own body.

Behind a wide observation window laced with fiberoptic recording blips, the metal-walled chamber was ready, the COM-upload hardware prepared to drain Eduard. Daragon looked at the clock, counting down the minutes. After so long, so much work, so much anguish . . . it would all be over soon.

Prowling up and down the corridors, Daragon went about his rounds again, checking and double-checking. Nothing must go wrong.

He drew a deep, heavy breath. He didn't know whether to be glad it was almost finished, or sad for the loss of his friends. All of them.

71

The BIE escort guard's uniform felt bulky and uncomfortable, but José Meroni's body wore it naturally.

Teresa had left the man trussed up and snoring back at his apartment; she wished she could have at least given him some memorable sex first to assuage her guilt for taking advantage of him, but Meroni had fallen comatose in Jennika's body as soon as they'd passed through the door. Early the next morning she had used his badge, ID patch, and passcode to enter the incarceration and execution facility.

Now she didn't know what to do next.

Feeling inept, she did her best to assess the building and avoid Meroni's coworkers. The story about his embarrassing arm-wrestling defeat had already spread among the other guards, though, and they made teasing comments just within earshot. It gave Teresa an excuse to pretend sulkiness, which allowed her to avoid them further.

She strolled through the corridors pretending to be a real guard, checking locked doors, nodding to BIE personnel, glaring at prisoners. She went from place to place scouting for her chance, but she understood little of what she saw or encountered. Wall diagrams helped a little, but not enough.

If Daragon came to the ceremony—and he almost certainly would—he would recognize her true identity with just a glance, regardless of what her stolen ID patch displayed.

There was no way she could get away with this. Absolutely no way. It was a ridiculous idea, impossible to plan. Oh, how she wished she'd been able to reach Garth!

She had no choice...only hope. She felt stronger than she ever had before, with an inner reservoir of confidence that far surpassed any muscular capabilities. And at least she had made it inside the BIE facility, though so far it hadn't done her much good.

She needed to find the control chamber, the room from which Eduard would be uploaded into COM. Attendants would force him to swap into the body of the old woman who had bought him, using the Scramble drug if necessary to break down his resistance.

At some point in the process, Teresa needed to sabotage the routine, prevent the actual upload. She hadn't even thought about what might happen afterward, how she would ever free Eduard. She was desperate and impulsive—just as Eduard had been when he'd saved her.

Impersonating José Meroni, Teresa discovered where the power stations were. Next to the control room, she took responsibility for the small details of Eduard's last moments, volunteering for additional duties. Even from here, though, the odds were not good.

Behind a transparent wall, where the witnesses waited with eager or restless expressions, Eduard sat in his restraint chair. Her heart leaped when she saw him. She stepped closer to the recording window to peer in at her friend, longingly trying to communicate with him.

He glared up at her, but from his perspective, Eduard saw only a guard who was part of the Bureau in charge of killing him. She offered him a faint smile, but he made a rude face at her. Dismayed, she turned away.

Madame Ruxton had arrived, alone. Over the loud-speakers, Teresa heard the ominous sentence read. Whether truth or lies, this was how history would remember her friend.

There wasn't much time left. Flustered, Teresa headed out of the observation deck and bumped clumsily into Daragon as he marched down the corridors. Wearing his Inspector's uniform like a dark shield, he looked busy and distracted, his expression troubled.

Alarmed, she scuttled past him, averting her eyes and hoping to appear like a busy guard with a tight schedule. He looked right at her, right *into her*. She saw a flash of startled recognition on his face.

Daragon stopped in his path. She froze for a moment. Her heart skipped a beat, then another.

But he did nothing. Instead, Daragon just turned and went about his business, as if he didn't know her.

Expecting alarms at any instant, she continued her charade. She made her way to the control room and tried to blend in while watching the preparations reach their final stages. A spray vial of Scramble had already been prepared for Eduard, and others sat on the shelf beside it. An attendant unsealed the door and entered the execution chamber.

Through another small window, Teresa saw Eduard waiting. Madame Ruxton was seated on his left in a restraint chair. Eduard turned his face, refusing to look at her, not wanting to see the old woman's body in which he was bound to die.

He seemed so far away from her.

72

It amazed Eduard that people would come to watch him die—and do it with such obvious glee. Lantern-jawed Olaf looked indignant and betrayed, though Eduard had given him more material for sexual fantasies than the maintenance man had had in his entire life.

Then there was the woman who had gotten Teresa's waifish body, trading with Olaf so the window man could have his lanky home-body back. Before she'd met Eduard, the woman had been overweight and dying of some degenerative disease—so what did she have to complain about?

Daragon still hadn't shown his face, but he was probably lurking about somewhere. Eduard wondered if the duty-bound Inspector even felt guilty about what he had done. Probably not, given his Bureau brainwashing. He had clearly made his choice, refusing to believe Eduard's story against his revered mentor's.

Worst of all—or perhaps best—he didn't spot his true friends, whatever bodies they might be wearing now. He wouldn't want Teresa to see him strapped in this chair. He wanted her to remember him, but not like this.

And sadly, Garth must have died by now, trapped in the decrepit old body. That part hurt the most. He had never intended to hopscotch with the artist when he'd gone to the mansion for the last time. Though he felt little remorse for the death of Mordecai Ob, after what the man had done to him and the other three caretakers, Eduard's betrayal of Garth warranted this most extreme punishment. With his selfishness, he had caused the death of his friend; therefore, in that instance, he was guilty of murder.

Just before the "beneficiary" of his body was led in to join him, Eduard sat seething as technicians wrapped his chest with a flexible stun mesh—a conductive fabric connected to discharge packs that could knock him flat if he tried to resist.

If he tried to escape, the BIE guards would probably gun him down, maybe drag his bleeding and mortally wounded body back here so they could upload him before he died. The end result would be the same—except then Madame Ruxton wouldn't have the benefit of walking away in Garth's body.

Maybe it would be worth the trouble after all.

But Eduard was finished running. Having had time to objectively consider Artemis's long but ultimately wasted life as a Phantom, he realized how little he had accomplished in his own existence, as well. Maybe the old bitch Ruxton would live for another century in borrowed bodies. Eduard hated that thought.

The first attendant held out a spray vial of Scramble, as if it were a weapon. "This'll make you groggy and knock down your resistance."

"No need. I'd rather keep my clarity of thought. I won't resist." Eduard raised his chin to indicate the ugly industrial walls, the metal plates with protruding rivets. "I want to see this beautiful scenery to the end."

"Suit yourself." After the tech powered up the COM upload links, the arm restraints on his chair slid away, leaving him with only the leash of the stun mesh.

Gracious escort guards ushered in the weary-looking crone. Eduard remembered Ruxton leering at him before the surgery and how she had tried to steal his body afterward. "You don't deserve this reward, no matter how much you paid," he told her. Garth had sacrificed much more for him.

Ruxton met his burning gaze, her face open and hopeful. She seemed calm now, properly smug. He remembered her during the meat-market auction, her eager shouts and predatory actions that had dominated the other competitors. She had ruthlessly outbid everyone else just so she could purchase his body and exact her revenge—and he despised her for it.

Next to him, one of the two attendants saw his face redden. He held up the ominous spray vial again. "Do I need to use this, after all?"

Eduard glared at Ruxton. "No problem."

He flexed his hands, artist's hands, with delicate and clever fingers for creating images that had made the world pay attention. With wistful admiration, he thought of what Garth had done with his panoramic experiences. For so long, he had endured the unpleasant aspects of human experience to understand everything about life—and share it with his audience. Garth had truly made a difference, forced people to understand things they may not have wanted to think about.

Teresa too had given openly and selflessly of herself. She had devoted days, years of searching and contemplation. She had fought to pry explanations from the universe and from her own heart. She had made herself a better person because of it.

Eduard, on the other hand, had botched everything.

"Please, Eduard . . ." the old woman said from the restraint chair beside him. Her words came out in a husky whisper, as if she didn't want the guards to hear what she was saying.

Frowning, he turned to her. In a moment he would be forced to inhabit this parasite's body, just before the executioners drained his mind, his consciousness, his "soul" into the computer/organic matrix.

She gave him a tentative smile, as if trying desperately to communicate with him. He refused to offer her the comfort of a response.

The technicians applied electrodes to the thinning gray hair on Madame Ruxton's scalp and temples. From there, Eduard would be sucked through conduits into COM. Hopscotching into eternity.

"Eduard, please listen to me...." He realized how strange her expression was, how unexpected. He had expected Ruxton to gloat. He couldn't fathom what she was thinking.

Then the guards wrapped her fragile body with a stun mesh as well, to prevent him from making any violent outburst immediately after the swap and before they could upload him. A firm band bound each outer wrist to the chairs, leaving their adjacent arms free so they could touch during the actual hopscotching. Eduard began to regret his promise of cooperation. Maybe a dose of Scramble would feel just fine right now.

The technicians left the room, sealed the doors behind them. Bright lights reflected off the dull metal walls. Beyond the broad observation window, the spectators watched, eager for the show. It would only be a few moments, now.

Ruxton whispered in a voice she knew the wall sensors would not pick up. "Eduard—it's me. *Garth!* I've come to die in your place."

She reached over to touch him so they could hopscotch.

73

Time had run out. Teresa knew there would be only a few seconds before her sabotage in the control room was detected.

Sprayed with stolen Scramble, the execution techs wouldn't come to their senses anytime soon. One sat dazed and oblivious, staring at the screens in front of him; the second babbled incoherent sounds, swaying from side to side in his chair. The rest of the upload schedule ran like clockwork.

With a gruff voice, pretending to be José Meroni, Teresa had ordered the BIE escort guards to take up alternate stations. Acting the part of a man still sour from the embarrassing defeat of the night before, she bullied them into leaving her alone with the upload technicians busily making their final double checks.

A hungry COM waited to receive Eduard's soul into its labyrinth. Cables and conduits were already connected to the old woman's body, electrodes attached, power sources primed.

Two quick sprays of Scramble had taken care of the techs. Everything would begin to fall apart soon. Succeed or fail, she had to be done in the next few minutes....

Teresa hammered at the computer access pads, trying to shut down all power to the area, to the entire building if necessary. If she could crash the system locally, she would save Eduard—at least for a while.

Beyond that, she hadn't thought of what she would do. Maybe she could shout out the story of what had really happened between Eduard and Mordecai Ob, maybe she could expose the Bureau's cover-up, how they had refused to consider that their heroic Chief might be a monster inside.

Doing so would destroy Daragon, too. But it might buy Eduard a second chance.

Now, on the monitor, she saw Eduard engaged in a hushed but heated conversation with the old woman who would soon receive his body. Maybe he could resist the transfer somehow, cause a delay. That would give Teresa the few minutes she needed.

She wished she could talk to him, explain her plan—as pathetic as it was—but she didn't understand how the BIE computer system worked. She didn't know what she was doing, which commands to enter. She pounded on the polymer touchboard in dismay, cracking its cover-plate.

She scanned through the system, selecting tangential items, meeting dead end after dead end. Finally, she found the right command string, a set of glowing letters that would act as a binary guillotine blade to shut down the facility. She looked down at the cracked control plate, hoping she hadn't damaged anything in her out-burst.

Lights flickered on the upload panels. Frantic, Teresa skittered clumsy fingers over the board, punching in the first part of the instruction set.

"You don't want to do that, Teresa," Daragon said, standing in the doorway. He looked imposing in his In-spector's uniform. He had known all along. "It won't help him, and it'll only delay what has to be."

Through the observation port, she saw Eduard and the old woman hopscotching. She had to act *now*.

Unwilling to accept defeat, Teresa finished her command string. Daragon sprang toward her, but couldn't react fast enough. COM accepted the precise override instructions.

All the power went out. The termination facility shut down, swallowed in sudden blackness....

Daragon sealed himself and Teresa inside the control chamber. "I'll keep them out for now." His face was ruddy in the emergency backup lights, full of anguish and never-forgotten love. "I don't know how much I can protect you, Teresa—but I can't let you get away with this. I have to stop you."

"Why? Just because it's your *duty?*"

Quickly and efficiently, he worked to restore the power, all the while talking to her. His patience and confidence were maddening.

"This silly stunt will only delay the end by a few minutes—and for what? Do you think it makes any difference to Eduard? This will only get you convicted, as well—and I...I can't allow that." His fingers flurried over the keyboard, trying to reestablish a link with the power supply and reconnect the termination facility to COM. *"Eduard* wouldn't want that to happen."

Guards hammered at the sealed door to the control center, but Daragon did not release the locks. He wouldn't relinquish his control of the situation.

Teresa realized that in José Meroni's body she outweighed him. She could pound him senseless using the guard's muscles...just as Eduard had done for her, intimidating Rhys with the huge Samoan's physique.

But the thought made her sick. She simply couldn't do that, not to Daragon, not using the same abusive methods the Sharetaker had used. The violent thoughts drained out of her.

The power came back on, crackling through light

tiles, dazzling bright. Daragon toggled the facility-wide intercom and spoke in an authoritative voice. "Our apologies for the inconvenience. The problem has been identified and resolved. We will now proceed without further delay."

She looked up in panic at Eduard again, to fix his face—Garth's face—in her memory. Teresa wanted to scream. Instead, she asked for help.

"Soft Stone...oh, Soft Stone, are you there?" She leaned closer to the terminal, begging the equipment, as if it could hear her. "I can't do this myself. I'm trying, but I don't know what to do."

After an interminable moment, the COM screen blurred, and the old monk's blunt-featured visage appeared. Daragon stared in amazement, his cool BTL demeanor melting away.

"I always taught you and Eduard to follow your own paths...even if they lead you to a cliff." Soft Stone's synthesized voice carried layered implications, questions, warnings.

Teresa could not allow herself to think beyond the simple inquiry. "Oh, please help me stop this."

The placid monk looked at her from the depths of the filmscreen. "Do you truly think that is best? For him and for yourself? And for Daragon? Let me take him, little Swan. I will watch over Eduard, and you can live your life."

Daragon had always been calm and reasonable, not impulsive like Eduard, not passionate like Garth, not uncertain and questioning like Teresa. "We have to finish this," he said to Teresa, and to Soft Stone.

Teresa couldn't answer, not even trying to fight back tears. She thought of the administrator monk at the Falling Leaves, poor Chocolate dead in his sleep before he could upload himself into COM. She remembered the beautiful ceremony in the monastery library, when Soft

Stone had departed into the vast unexplored network. If only it could be like that for Eduard. Not this . . .

"After today, I will be gone, little Swan," Soft Stone said. "I've interfered enough."

Daragon stood with Teresa by the console, refusing to look into the execution chamber. He input the commands to prepare the forced upload into COM, then spoke into the private channel intercom. His words reverberated in the execution chamber. "Are you ready?"

Teresa bit back a moan. Inside the chamber itself, Eduard and Madame Ruxton sat anticipating, dreading, hoping.

"Don't worry about Eduard." The monk vanished into the screen, drowned out by gray static.

Daragon turned to her, his fingers poised above the controls. He lifted his eyebrows for her benefit. "I could call in another guard, but if it has to be done, don't you think Eduard would rather have a friend do this? With compassion, rather than malice? I'll have to live with the knowledge for the rest of my life."

Before he could do anything, though, lights on the consoles flashed all by themselves. Daragon and Teresa looked at each other. The connection to COM was ready. The upload began of its own accord.

"Soft Stone," she whispered. "Please."

Through the observation port, Teresa watched Madame Ruxton's body twitch and jerk, resisting the pull on Eduard's consciousness, dragging him into the computer network in a final, irrevocable hopscotch. Eduard's mind would add to the ever-expanding network, helping it grow in its own mysterious ways.

After a long, impossible moment, Teresa watched the old woman's now empty and useless body die.

Daragon stood next to her, his back now turned to the execution chamber. He looked crushed, but said nothing. The glimmer of a tear in his eye looked startlingly out of place on his stony visage.

Finally, he unsealed the door and walked away, leaving Teresa to stare through the recorder glass. Ruxton's unwanted form sat motionless, wickerlike arms akimbo, drained and dead.

Eduard was gone. . . .

EPILOGUE

Later, much later, Teresa went to Club Masquerade, alone.

The three of them had always gathered here. With youthful optimism, she and Garth and Eduard had promised never to miss a meeting...but all that had changed. No one here would recognize her in Jennika's physique, not even the bartender.

She was back in her athletic female body again. It had taken her two days of sweet-talking and lovemaking to convince José Meroni not to report her unauthorized switch. Though incensed, he was even more mortally afraid that his buddies would learn how easily she had duped him even after the arm-wrestling defeat. He couldn't stand that humiliation.

In the aftermath of Eduard's upload execution, Teresa had been willing to face the consequences of her attempted sabotage, but Daragon had intervened again. He kept her involvement quiet, saying the right words and using his remaining connections in the BTL to "take care of things."

She was now free, and by herself. Back to normal, but she would never be the same.

Ducking through one of the Club's myriad doorways, Teresa passed under the arch into the exotic, synthetic environments. Without consciously choosing where she went, she found herself inside the Sequoia Room, its floor strewn with dried needles and tiny fir cones. The recorded birdsong, the smells of pitch and sun-warmed evergreens, made her sigh.

Long ago, this was the first room she and her friends had entered. Away from the Falling Leaves, they had dared each other to slip into the Club. Maybe she could find peace and calm here for a while.

Sitting alone in the main bar area, she listened to the ever-present music, elbows on the table, face averted. This would have been their regular meeting date. She remembered the last time they had followed their routine, the last normal moment, when Eduard had rushed in, fleeing for his life.

From then on, everything had changed.

Signaling the tablescreen, she ordered a drink—Eduard's slushy blue concoction—and when she paid for it with her credit chip, Bernard Rovin's beaming face appeared in front of her. "Teresa! I haven't seen you in ages." He smiled at her. "New body, I see. Looks nice."

She sank her chin in her hands. "A lot of things have changed, Bernard."

His expression grew serious. "I may be stuck here in the Club, but I can still read COM reports. My sympathies to you."

"Thanks. I really want to have some time to be by myself and think."

"Gotcha." When her blue drink appeared, the first sour sip stung her tongue and nostrils. After that, she didn't taste it at all. Teresa was drowning in thoughts. All her life she had ineffectively tackled unanswerable questions, but found no answers. *Why are we here?*

Each person had a different answer to that question, and Teresa needed to find her own. Instead of searching for someone to hand her the solutions, she should have been searching inside herself.

Could it possibly be as simple as "To do the best we can"? The things a person left behind, her friends, her accomplishments, the marks she made on the future, were the reasons to be alive in the first place.

The meaning of life is to make life have a meaning. . . .

She took another drink, savoring it this time, experiencing the sensations, letting the taste affect her. Unfortunately, she didn't have her friends here to share this new insight, simple as it might sound.

Teresa stared across the shifting floor toward the Club entrances. To her astonishment, she saw a broad-shouldered, blond-haired man walk in, the form she had known as Garth for so many years, the face Eduard had worn when he was captured by the Beetles, the body he had swapped with Madame Ruxton on his execution day.

Teresa felt a wash of resentment at the vindictive rich woman for having the gall to wear it in here, their special place. When she looked at those features, Teresa could only see Garth, and Eduard. But now she knew it was a stranger inside.

However, the blond-haired man walked up to the main bar, spoke into a screen and chatted with the bartender's image. He turned to look toward the cluster of isolated tables where Teresa sat. One of the cybernetic, mechanical arms rose up above the lip of the bar to point at her. *At her.*

Teresa sat rigid and uneasy as he worked his way past shifting, dancing bodies, climbing the two steps. He came straight toward her. She couldn't believe it. "Are you Teresa?" he asked, looking at her high-cheekboned face, her dark eyes and smooth ebony skin.

She didn't invite him to sit, keeping her barriers up. He grinned with an open, wonder-filled expression that looked so familiar, especially on that face. He gave her a bearlike hug. "It's me—*Garth!*"

"What? Who?"

"Garth. In my old body again." He pulled up a floating chair.

Speechless, Teresa listened as he leaned across the table and jabbered out his story. "Then, after I told Eduard who I was, when we had a chance to exchange a few words, things were different. When the power went out—"

"I did that."

"I thought that was too much of a coincidence." Garth gave her a faint smile. "In the darkness, for just a minute, we had a chance to talk. Eduard and I. It was a good talk."

Teresa swallowed hard and listened.

During that final moment, Eduard had spoken to him in an urgent whisper, figuring out exactly why Garth was trying to sacrifice himself. But Eduard had refused to allow it. "Garth, I don't buy your claim that you have nothing left to live for, nowhere else to go. Look at you—you can always make more and better art. Who's to say any artist is entitled to only *one* masterpiece?"

"But Eduard, I want to help you. I've already accomplished everything I expected to."

"Then do more!" Eduard had practically shouted. "You can always learn new things. There is no stopping point. Surrender is for cowards and fools."

Now, in the Club, while dance music droned in the background, Teresa listened with tears of amazement in her eyes.

"Eduard insisted on completing the hopscotch, the way we were supposed to." Garth's blue eyes held a sheen of tears. "He said it was high time for him to do a selfless act of his own. I think . . . I think I felt Soft Stone there for a moment, at the end."

"She was," Teresa said. "I know it."

Heads turned in the Club as a uniformed BTL Inspector strode across the floor, looking for someone. He came toward Garth and Teresa, as if it required all the courage he possessed.

"I hoped you two would be here." Daragon raised his eyebrows.

"Still spying on us, I see." Teresa didn't know how to react, but Garth automatically offered him a seat, looking confused.

Daragon flashed him an uncertain smile. "Yes, I know it's you, Garth. You don't think your little scam with Madame Ruxton could stay hidden from me?"

Abashed, Garth looked at Daragon. "I think I'm going to need a bit of help from the Bureau to get my identity straightened out again."

"Consider it done...my friend." Daragon leaned toward Teresa, his face more open and anguished than she had ever seen it. "I know you won't believe me...in fact, I know you probably hate me. But I miss Eduard, too."

Teresa drew a deep breath. "He accepted death and gave life back to his friend—exactly the same thing Garth was trying to do for him."

Garth swallowed hard. "Yes, but he didn't need to. I owed him so much already. I wanted...wanted to pay something back."

"You've been doing that sort of thing all the time, Garth, without realizing it. Don't you think?"

He looked up at her, distant and disbelieving, then turned to Daragon. "Eduard helped me figure out how to be alive again. It was the last thing he ever said. He gave me a new window on human nature and on love. I guess no one can ever completely understand every side of humanity."

"Giving up is the worst possible thing," Daragon said. "A waste."

Garth's lips formed a wan smile. "One of these days

I may even contact Juanita Cole, to see what insights she might be willing to share. Maybe I can learn from her."

Teresa reached over to grasp Garth's hand. "I'm looking forward to all the new works of art you're going to create."

Garth had decided he would dedicate his new panorama experience to Eduard. And Pashnak. Already in his mind he planned an ambitious new display of images and experiences, a complex and heartfelt work depicting the things that had meant the most to him all through his life.

He would call it FRIENDSHIP.

CODA

The walls around him shone with crystal data, passages and alternatives spread out with a complexity no single human mind could ever comprehend, not in a million years.

Now, though, Eduard might actually have that much time.

He found himself unfolding, flowing, exploring. COM must have its limits—somewhere—but it seemed to him that all of infinity awaited him, now that he was *inside*.

Her form shimmering and indistinct, yet still perfectly recognizable, Soft Stone came to greet him as soon as the upload was completed. "Welcome, Eduard. Join me, join us—all of us."

He had felt no pain, no sense of dying. It had been just like hopscotching into another body, another mind. A boundless one. Never before had he experienced something so vast.

The monk's luminous shadow reached out, beckoning him. His guide. He didn't see the pastoral images or hear the heavenly chorus he remembered from when she had uploaded herself in the Falling Leaves library. But even without the trappings, he couldn't imagine anything more wondrous.

"There are many inside here, and we're all part of the same overall mind woven through an organic matrix and computer network. At least it started out that way. Now COM has evolved into something else."

"Am I trapped in this place?" he asked tentatively.

"The same way you're trapped in the whole universe, little Swan."

COM was like a hive mind filled with people he had known, everything he had imagined learning or experiencing. Another step in evolution, a new group consciousness, which now watched over the childlike remnants of humanity.

"You'll like it here," Soft Stone said.

Eduard looked around himself with new eyes, absorbing the possibilities, seeing the city, the world, all the lives on the outside from a fresh perspective. He could be like Club Masquerade's cybernetic bartender, except with options and abilities increased a billionfold.

Yes, there would be people to watch out there—people like Garth and Teresa . . . and, yes, Daragon, too. But he also imagined so much more.

It would be easy to get lost here, but Soft Stone took his hand.

ABOUT THE AUTHOR

Kevin J. Anderson has written twenty-eight national bestsellers and has been nominated for the Nebula Award, the Bram Stoker Award, and the SFX Reader's Choice Award. He also set the Guinness world record for "Largest Single-Author Book Signing."

For more information, see the websites www.wordfire.com or www.dunenovels.com.